the pearl jacket
and other stories

the pearl jacket
and other stories
FLASH FICTION
from Contemporary China

edited and translated by
Shouhua Qi

Stone Bridge Press • Berkeley, California

Published by
Stone Bridge Press
P.O. Box 8208
Berkeley, CA 94707
tel 510-524-8732 • sbp@stonebridge.com • www.stonebridge.com

The publisher wishes to acknowledge the cooperation of Shanghai Foreign Language Education Press in the publication of this book.

Compilation and translation copyright ©2008 Shouhua Qi.

Printed in the United States of America.

LIBRARY OF CONGRESS CATALOGING-IN-PUBLICATION DATA

The pearl jacket and other stories : contemporary Chinese flash fiction / translation and preface by Shouhua Qi.
    p. cm.
    ISBN 978-1-933330-62-4
    1. Short stories, Chinese—21st century—Translations into English. 2. Chinese fiction—21st century—Translations into English. I. Qi, Shouhua.

PL2658.E8P43 2008
895.1'30108052—dc22
                        2007051844

contents

family 65

portraits 97

society 163

truth and art 227

existential moments 251

the strange and extraordinary 287

preface

Flash fiction, or *wei xing xiao shuo* 微型小说, as it is known in Chinese literature, also goes by the name of Minute Story (*yi fen zhong xiao shuo*) 一分钟小说 (most likely for the amount of time required to read one); Pocket-Size Story (*xiu zhen xiao shuo*) 袖珍小说 or Palm-Size Story (*zhang pian xiao shuo*) 掌篇小说 (alluding to its small size); and, perhaps most evocatively, a Smoke-Long Story (*yi dai yan xiao shuo*) 一袋烟小说, where one can imagine the reader taking a drag from a delicious cigarette in some smoky salon, while relishing a few lines from some make-believe world.

In the West, flash fiction can be found in the story of the boy who cried "Wolf!" on that Grecian isle over 2,600 years ago, as well as in other Aesop fables and parables. The earliest examples of Chinese flash fiction are in the remarkably "grand" creation myths of Nuwa (ca. 350 BC), Fuxi, and Pangu. The story of Pangu, for example, which first appeared in written form during the Warring States period (AD 220–63), has a word count of 350 Chinese characters.

The stories in this anthology represent the achievements in flash fiction in modern to contemporary China, that is, early 20th century to the present day. Taking root in China's fertile native cultural soil and drawing nourishment from influences inside and outside China, flash fiction has matured as a literary form. The birth of the Microfiction Association of China in 1992, and the popularity of literary journals devoted to such fiction exclusively, e.g., *Journal of Microfiction*, *Journal of Short-Short Story*, etc., attest to the popularity of flash fiction in China in recent years. New technologies such as text messaging and blogging and extensive (though still tightly controlled) use of the internet in China make it possible for millions of people to dally with writing their own stories and "publishing" them to family, friends, and, often, complete strangers. There is instant satisfaction when the desire to be heard, and to be known, is met ("Sir, I exist!"). Imagine a nation of tens of millions of story-tellers! The future of flash fiction, it seems, is as bright and hopeful as enthusiasm (and technology) can carry it.

If writing flash fiction is exciting, translating such stories is just as so, if not more. Each of the stories in this book comes from a distinctive time and place; each has a distinctive beginning, middle, and end; each speaks with a distinctive cadence of voice; each showcases a distinctive style, whether simple, minimalist, folksy, erudite, ornate, or elegant. No two stories are alike. Therefore, instead of trying to conquer a 130,000-meter tall mountain (the approximate word count of the original stories in Chinese), I instead had to climb 130 1,000-meter high hills; each time I barely had time to utter "I came, I saw, I translated" before I had to plunge ahead again and start climbing the next hill, which, more often than not, revealed quite different topography altogether.

Among these stories are a few not so contemporary ones by the great masters of modern fiction such as Lu Xun, Lao She, Guo Morou, and Yu Dafu, all of which are exemplary in freshness of idea, depth of meaning, and intensity of feeling, as well as in execution (flow of story, character development, use of language). Other writers, such as Shen Congwen, known for his vernacular style of writing that blends the strong influence of both classical Chinese and Western literature, and Wang Meng (1934–), the writer and essayist and one of the first to experiment with the stream of consciousness technique in Chinese fiction, serve as the anchoring point for works to be written generations later. The absence of stories since the great masters (until around 1980) can be attributed to China's turbulent history: The Great Proletariat Cultural Revolution of 1966–76 nearly wiped Chinese literature off the map. Then, in the 1980s, flash fiction re-emerged on China's literary scene with a vengeance. Among my favorite of the stories produced since the 1980s are: "A Hawk in the Sky," "A Serious Speech to Promote *Mark Twain's Humorous Speeches*," "White Gem," "To Kill the Sister-in-Law," "Precious Stone," "Immortality," "Straw Ring," "Merchant of Wills," "Concerned Departments," "Floral Shorts," "Mosquito Nets," "'Oh, Isn't This General Manager Gao?'" "The Same River Twice?" "A Caterpillar on Your Shoulder!" and "The Outside World." Some of these stories are traditional in their narrative mode and appear to be politically innocuous enough, but embedded in them are critical barbs no reader familiar with Chinese irony and satire will miss. In Ling Dingnian's "Cat and Mouse Play" (2004), the historical lesson the General taught his Second-in-Command may, ostensibly, have to do with China's distant imperial past, but the story's political subtext, its pungent satire directed at the political life of modern China, especially what Mao Zedong did to his Long March comrades-in-arms during the Cultural Revolution, becomes apparent when one considers the fact that "Using Ancient History to Satirize the Here and Now" has been a favorite trope among Chinese writers (and dissident intellectuals) since time immemorial.

Some of the stories treat their historical source material rather playfully and give well-known, classic stories a postmodern twist with delightful, refreshing effect. Such is the case of "To Kill the Sister-in-Law" by Jia Pingwa, a writer known in the West for his *Turbulence* (2003), *Fei Du* (*Defunct Capital*, which was banned in China when first published in 1993), and other fictional works. Jia draws from the classic Chinese novel *Water Margin* (*Shuihuzhuang*): the story of Wu Song—the tall, handsome hero famed for having killed a fierce tiger with his bare hands—avenging the death of his ugly, midget brother poisoned by his sister-in-law Pan Jinlian (the infamous Golden Lotus) and her rakehell lover Ximen Qing. The heroic and righteous Wu Song, who had earlier rebuffed the adulterous advances of the ravishingly beautiful sister-in-law, never wavers for a second in meting out justice. Here, Jia adds a playful revisionist twist.

Whether drawing from the here and now of contemporary China or from the nation's collective memory of its long and distant past, whether traditional, experimental, or avant-garde in their narrative modes, these and many other stories resonated with me intellectually and emotionally while I was trying to render them into English. They not only capture the pulse of life of a given time and place but also have something profound to say about the human condition, which transcends the bounds of time and place.

Of the stories featured in this book, nineteen (some of which are undated in the anthology) are from Taiwan, Hong Kong, and Macau. These stories enrich the thematic, emotional, and stylistic tapestry of the anthology in no small ways. If I feel the "yang" force pulsing restlessly in stories from mainland China, I find myself drawn to the quiet "yin" force in these stories, pleased by their well-tuned sensitivity, ease of flow, and the satisfying yet disquieting sensation that lingers long after the reading. Stories such as "My Bride," "Wrong Number," "Feelings," and "Time" read like prose poems, too. "Parrot," the last story in this book, is fable, myth, and nightmare all in one.

The stories in this anthology tell the truth; a tall order indeed. Truth, big or small, emotional as well as intellectual, gives each story life and makes the minutes (the time it takes to finish a smoke, for example) spent by the reader a fascinating and rewarding experience.

Finally, I want to say that as a translator of these stories I have invested enough time, effort, and emotions in them to feel they have become my stories, too. Therefore, any imperfections readers may find are as much mine as the original authors'.

relationships

Door Forever

Shao Baojian

An old town in the South. A small compound with an old well. Inside the compound live eight or nine ordinary families. The same old-styled one-story houses, the same configurations for many years, despite the addition of modern gadgets inside the houses recently.

Among the eight or nine households, two of them have only one resident each: old bachelor Zheng Ruokui and old maid Pan Xue'er.

Zheng lives right next door to Pan.

"Morning," he greets her.

"Leaving?" She replies and passes him, not slowing one step.

How many times have the neighbors seen the two passing each other in the compound but heard only those two words? They are disheartened by the simple, emotionless repetition.

Pan is a bit over 40. Slim, oval face, pale skin, dressed simply but tastefully. She can still be considered charming. She works at the florist down West Street. The neighbors have no idea why such a charming woman would want to remain single. They only know that she is entitled to love yet has never married.

Zheng moved into the compound five years ago right after Pan did. He is an art worker for a movie theater, a painter more conscientious and careful than talented, it is said. He looks much older than his age of 45 or 46. His hair, dry, messy, faded, shows no benefit of being combed often. His back humps visibly. Thin face. Thin and narrow shoulders. Thin hands. Only that pair of large eyes always glint with light of youth, and of dreams.

When he returns home, he often carries a bunch of fresh flowers, roses, crabapple, wintersweet, and so on, in all four seasons, and places the fresh flowers in a tall and translucent blue vase.

He isn't in the habit of visiting the neighbors. Once home, he stays inside. Sometimes he comes out to wash clothes, dishes, and that tall, translucent blue vase. He then fills the vase with clear well water and carries it home with extreme care, his mouth pouting.

A thick wall stands between his bedroom and that of Pan's.

Next to his bed is an old bamboo bookshelf, the height of an adult, set against the wall. Atop the bookshelf on the right is the permanent place for this blue vase.

Besides this are some paintings, hanging here and there, some Chinese, some foreign, some by others, some by himself.

It would be apparent from the configuration of furniture and the film of dust that has gathered, that this household misses the presence of a woman, the aura of warmth only a woman can create.

Yet the vase is always cleaned spotless, the water inside always crystal clear, and the flowers always fresh and in full bloom.

The neighbors have once cherished a fond hope that the flowers he carries home would one day appear inside the house of his next-door neighbor, Pan Xue'er. Yet this miracle never happened. Naturally they began to develop a sweet and gentle feeling of sympathy for Zheng.

It drizzled one early morning in fall.

Zheng, holding an umbrella, greeted Pan as usual: "Morning."

Pan, also holding an umbrella, replied as ever before: "Leaving?"

The rain stopped in the evening. She returned home from work, but he didn't.

Word came that Zheng, while painting in the studio of the movie theatre, had a heart attack and fallen to the ground. He died upon arriving at the hospital.

Some in this ordinary compound sobbed.

But Pan did not cry, though her eyes were red.

Wreathes were brought in, one after another. That big one decorated with all kinds of fresh flowers but without an elegy band, was from her in memory of him.

In this ordinary compound the sudden absence of an ordinary man, an old bachelor who had not been favored by love, was felt keenly and with regret.

A few days later Pan Xue'er moved away. Sudden and unexpected.

While packing up Zheng's things one day, the neighbors couldn't help being amazed: That blue vase looked like it had been cleaned recently; the white chrysanthemum in it had not faded.

Everyone's eyes popped when they moved the old bamboo bookshelf.

A Door! On the wall was a finely crafted purple-red door with a brass handle!

Their hearts were tossed into turmoil: So *that's* what was going on!

The neighbors grunted and sneered. The sorrow and respect they had felt for this old bachelor only a few days ago was gone, replaced by an anger that could not be described or uttered.

Then, someone reached to pull the door open, but cried out—the brass handle was flat, and the door and its frame were as smooth as the wall.

A door painted on the wall!

(1986)

The Moonlit Window

Deng Kaishang[1]

The moon, pale as jade, peeked from behind translucent clouds, drifted in through the delicate window, and fell onto the small writing desk in the room. The tenant's exquisite writing brush, breathing in the fragrance of fresh ink, rested on a small, finely-carved wood stand.

Five water chestnuts. No, four and a half, to be more exact: one of them having been bitten in half by the tenant. The remaining half, its stem still intact, lay upright on the small desk. Basking in the pale, pure moonlight, it looked like a miniature pyramid.

A small piece of square-shaped marble, exquisite, pure as a beam of frozen moonlight. Underneath the rock was a stack of manuscript paper, words written in graceful penmanship, its title: "Revision Suggestions for *On Spring Vistas in Mountainous Villages* (Three Volumes)."

Underneath the stack of manuscript paper was a family letter, which cracked visibly somewhere along the lines where it had been folded; the V-shaped rupture rippled with moonlight, shiny like a dagger. The visible portion of the letter showed words written with both resolve and feminine sensitivity:

Full moon beaming in the sky, stars sailing to the west, but woe welling up in my heart: A full moon is not as good as a full family! 'Once a couple, forever a couple,' and we had that 'once' for 12 years! My conscience, a woman's conscience, tortures my soul to this very day that we have been washed apart by the currents of life. My soul cries in pain; my soul is bleeding. Oh, let's get married again! I beseech you. The only thing I will ask of you is to quit this editor's job. What did you get in return for 'making bridal dresses' for others half of your life? Ten years of cold wind and rain, a head of frosty hair. So listen to me this time!

The letter closed with: "I beg you to quit smoking." In a corner of the letter were two red, bean-sized marks: two drops of blood having soaked deep into the paper. Next to them was a line from the tenant after reading the letter: "Endless will flow this feeling of love!" It was taken from Bai Juyi's poem "Endless Sorrow;" only that the tenant had replaced "sorrow" with "love."

A gentle breeze murmured a serenade. It drifted into the moonlit window, caressed a sheet of manuscript paper, the ink on which was still fresh, and dropped on it a strand of frosty hair. The page number read: 109.

(1981)

Nest of Oat Stalks

Cao Naiqian

All is quiet under the sky. The bright Moon Granny shone on the threshing ground. On the side of the oat stalks stack facing Moon Granny he made a nest for her and himself.

"After you."

"After you."

"Then let's get in together."

Together he and she crawled in. The nest collapsed. The collapsed stalks fell over their heads.

He raised his arms to hold the stalks. "Forget about them. It's not bad." She nestled in his arms and said: "Ugly Brother must hate me so."

"No, I don't. Darkie Kiln is richer than I am."

"Who cares about his money? All I want is to save money so Ugly Brother can marry a woman."

"I don't want your money."

"But I want to save for you."

"I don't want it."

"You have to want it."

He could hear she was on the verge of crying and didn't say another word.

"Ugly Brother," she said a while later.

"Yes?"

"Ugly Brother, give me a smooch."

"Don't do this to me."

"I want to."

"I'm not in the mood."

"I want to."

He could hear she was on the verge of crying again and bent to kiss her cheek. Silky, soft.

"Wrong place. Here!" she pouted. He bent and kissed her lips this time. Cool, moist.

"What does it taste like?"

"Oat cake."

"Wrong, wrong. Why don't you try again." She pulled his head low.

"Still like an oat cake," he considered and said again.

"Nonsense. I've just had candy. Try again!" She pulled his head low again.

"Candy! Candy!" He exclaimed right away.

Neither said anything for a long while.

"Ugly Brother."

"Yes?"

"How about . . . how about me doing *that* with you today."

"No, no. Moon Granny is watching outside. That won't be right. Our Weng Kilnville girls never do that."

"Okay, we'll wait then. Wait till I'm back."

"Okay."

Neither said anything for a long while. All was quiet except for the footsteps and sighs of Moon Granny outside.

"Ugly Brother."

"Yes?"

"It's kismet."

"Kismet."

"Our kismet is not good."

"Mine is not good. Yours, good."

"Not good."

"Good."

"Not good."

"Good."

"Not good at all!"

He heard tears in her voice this time. Tears rolled out of his eyes, strings of big warm teardrops, and fell on her cheeks.

(1989)

July 28, 1976

Yuan Bingfa

"You are something!" My wife muttered angrily when I came back home after a day's work. "Jazzing up your life with a little romance . . . an affair with this Yan woman from Tangshan!"

I was puzzled and said with a smile on my face: "Thank you for trying to flatter me, but I would never have such guts. When you and I were dating, it was you who made the first move, remember?"

My wife wasn't pacified by my lame joke: "Don't pretend to be an innocent lamb. When men are bad, they have more guts than a stag in heat!"

I knew it was more serious and asked: "What on earth has happened?"

She tossed me a slip of paper, which I opened right away. It read:

My Dear:

Perhaps it was destiny that you and I met during that long, lonesome trip. You gave me not only company but also so much precious comfort which I can never forget. If you desire to keep in touch with me, please write me at the address below:

Four-Horse Street
Building 2, Apartment 201
Nankai District
City of Tangshan, Hebei Province

Love,
Yan

I didn't know if I should laugh or cry when I finished reading the note. "From what trash can did you find this?" I asked my wife.

"Trash can? I wouldn't have bothered you if I had picked it up from a trash can. It's from inside one of your books, of all the places in the world!"

"Inside a book? Which book?"

"That novel, *Extramarital Affairs*, by a Taiwan author, Li."

"How can that be?"

"I was puzzled, too. How could my honest, beloved husband have done something like this? Yet how can I argue with this solid evidence in front of my eyes? Do you have a good explanation, Mister?"

"No, I don't."

After a pause I said: "Although I can't explain, I am willing to swear to Heaven that if I am having an affair I would be a dog, a chicken, a duck, a buffalo, a horse, a poop, a pee, a nothing, or an anything but a human being!"

At this my wife laughed, bitterly: "I don't care what you are. All I care is to find out about that Yan woman in Tangshan!"

I was speechless.

She then said: "I'll go to Tangshan tomorrow to look for the Yan woman at the address in the letter." I thought she was being carried away by her anger at the moment and didn't take her seriously. So I went to work as usual the next day. When I came back from work in the afternoon, I saw a note from my wife on the writing desk saying that she was indeed on her way to Tangshan.

At this I was furious. Woman! Impossible woman!

Then, I thought, this trip might do her some good. If she could really find that Yan woman in Tangshan, the cloud of suspicion would be cleared.

Unfortunately, the next morning, I was dumbfounded to hear this news from the radio: "At 3:40 this morning, a severe earthquake occurred in the eastern part of Hebei Province. According to the National Earthquake Information Center, the magnitude of this earthquake was 7.8 on the Richter Scale, as powerful as 400 nuclear bombs the size of the one dropped on Hiroshima, all exploding at the same time about 16 kilometers deep inside the earth."

I was drenched in sweat. I knew that the worst might have happened to my beautiful and beloved wife. Based on time nd distance, my wife must have arrived at Tangshan the very night right before the earthquake happened.

That day, with a heavy heart, I went to ask for leave so I could go to Tangshan. There I saw the eyes of one of my colleagues, Young Zhang, red and tear-streaked, too.

I asked: "So, you've heard about Tangshan?"

Young Zhang nodded: "A woman I love lives in the city that has been leveled by the earthquake."

I blurted out: "Is her name Yan?"

Young Zhang's eyes brightened up at the mention of the name: "Yes! You. . . . "

"Did she write you a letter?"

"Yes!"

"Goddamn it! How did that note get into one of my books?" I asked angrily.

"Oh!" Young Zhang slapped himself on the thigh. "I borrowed books from you."

Now everything was clear. I gripped Young Zhang's collar and hollered: "You turtle's son, give me back my wife!"

My wife never returned. It was later officially confirmed that she became one of the 242,419 that perished in the Tangshan earthquake.

The date of my wife's death is July 28, 1976.

(1996)

The Girl in the Red Skirt

Yue Yong

Early this year I started to work as editor of a magazine in Guangzhou. Since there is quite a bit of distance between my apartment and my office, I pedaled my bike to work every morning.

One morning my alarm clock didn't go off and I overslept for 15 minutes. The minute I had washed my face I jumped on the bike and pedaled like mad to the office.

I was flying toward an intersection when the red light came on suddenly.

I applied the brakes hard but still managed to bump into the back of the bike ahead of me. "Sorry! Terribly sorry!" I apologized as I wiped away the sweat on my forehead. On the bike was a girl in a red skirt. She turned, smiled, and shook her head, meaning she wasn't hurt. On her pretty face were two cute dimples. What a beautiful girl! I murmured to myself. Just then, the green light was on. The girl in the red skirt stepped on her bike again, made a left turn at the intersection, and vanished.

Strangely enough, almost every day after that accident I'd see the girl in the red skirt on my way to work. She would ride alongside me for a while before turning left at the intersection.

When we met every morning we would greet each other with a "Hi," a nod of the head, or a simple smile, like two old friends.

One beautiful sunny morning we were both stopped again by the red light at the intersection. She nodded to me, somewhat awkwardly. Right before the green light came back, she stuffed an envelope into the basket in the front of my bike, stepped back on her bike, and disappeared like the wind.

Confused and curious I opened the letter:

Hi, Yue Yong:

How are you? I've seen your picture and work in many magazines and like your writing a lot. Can we be friends? If you are interested, please drop your reply in the basket in the front of my bike.

I was elated, and wrote a reply that very evening—"Yes, I am very interested!"—and dropped it in her basket the next morning.

On the morning after that, she dropped another letter in my basket. After that I wrote her another reply. . . .

We went back and forth like this for a while until we became very good friends between whom there wasn't anything we couldn't "talk" about.

It turned out that she was very interested in literature. Sometimes she would give me an envelope containing her submissions. She had a unique style in writing, reflective and exquisite. I published them all.

One morning three months later, she asked in a letter, out of the blue: Do you have a girlfriend?

My reply: No.

The letter she gave me the following day had only one line: Can I be your girlfriend?

I almost jumped for joy! This was what I had been dreaming of for quite some time.

The day after that I asked for a half-day leave so I could go and buy a bunch of blooming red roses. However, I never gathered enough courage to present the roses to the girl in the red skirt at the intersection, and cursed myself when I watched her turn left and continue on her way.

Not ready to give up, I turned left, too, and followed her so I could present the flowers to her when she stopped at her destination.

Not knowing she was being followed, the girl in the red skirt turned into a large gate of what appeared to be a school.

I pedaled harder toward the gate and was about to make a desperate dash when I stopped suddenly, stunned by what I saw on the nameplate above the gate:

LOVING HEART SCHOOL FOR THE DEAF-MUTE

So *this* was the reason why I had known the girl in the red skirt for so long yet she had never spoken a word to me. . . .

All that passion inside me was gone instantly. The flowers slipped out of my hand, too.

After that I would go to work via a detour and I never saw that girl in the red skirt on my way to work again.

It was about half a year later when I saw her on a live Loving Heart Charity Fundraising TV show. She looked stunningly beautiful under the limelight in that same red skirt, and her song "Love's Labor" brought everyone in the audience to tears.

She was introduced as an outstanding sign language teacher at this deaf-mute school.

(2001)

Odd Day, Even Day
Ling Rongzhi

Xiao Ju became a mistress at a very young age. Pretty and bright, Xiao Ju never thought she would be a mistress one day, but many things happen not because we want them to happen, but because they are destined to. Xiao Ju's family was poor. She passed the college entrance exams, but didn't have the money to pay tuition and fees. She got acquainted with a fat cat who paid for her college. Before a year was over, she became his "beauty hidden in a gold house."

Xiao Ju didn't want it to be like this at first, but one time she had a glass of wine, which went to her head, and she consented. Once he had got what he wanted, he was worried that she might be lured away while in college. So he bought this house for her to live in.

Xiao Ju wasn't quite settled emotionally, though, because in her heart was someone else, her high school sweetheart, Ah Fu. Ah Fu was poor, but he was honest and was as nice to her as she was to him. But Au Fu had no money to pay for her college, let alone to support her. The fat cat, however, could not only support her, but support her extravagantly and toss her lots of money for her to spend, too.

So Xiao Ju was sheltered in this villa, and everything seemed good: good food, good clothing, yet one thing wasn't good: boredom. The fat cat was still married with a son and a daughter. His wife was quite sharp and watched him closely. Every time he came, it was on an odd day. He would sneak here from work. He would spend two hours here at the most. When he finished he would toss some money and leave no matter how badly Xiao Ju asked him to stay.

Every day Xiao Ju had nothing to do but take care of the flowers and plants in the garden and her cat and her dog to kill time. Xiao Ju had endless amounts of money to spend. Her cat and dog ate better food than most average people. She played with her dog often, which she named Ah Fu, because the young man was still in her heart.

One day the dog fell into a ditch and couldn't climb back out. Desperate, Xiao Ju called aloud: "Ah Fu! Ah Fu!"

Ah Fu, the young man, happened to pass by on his way home from work. When he saw who it was calling his name, he almost jumped for joy. "Xiao Ju, is that you? Why are you here?"

"Ah Fu?" Xiao Ju held Ah Fu's hands and wouldn't let go. "Why are you here, indeed?"

"Work, of course! I'm a worker at a factory not far from here." Ah Fu pointed. "What about you? Aren't you a college student?"

"Come in so we can talk," Xiao Ju led Ah Fu into her home.

"This is your home? Oh, so big and beautiful!" Ah Fu couldn't stop looking around, his eyes wide-open. "Where did you get the money to buy such a big house?"

With tears in her eyes Xiao Ju told her story. When it was over, she held him in her arms. "Do you hate me? Can you forgive me?"

His head low, Ah Fu said: "No use talking about hate or no hate. It's all because I'm poor and have no knack for anything. I don't understand why this world is becoming so practical and cruel."

Wiping away her tears, Xiao Ju looked up and said: "Ah Fu, don't go and work at that factory any more. I'll support you."

Ah Fu almost laughed aloud: "You want to support me? You?"

Xiao Ju nodded: "Yes, I will support you. He gives me lots and lots of money anyway, enough to support me, and you, too."

Ah Fu wanted to say something, but Xiao Ju put her hand to his mouth.

Afterward, Xiao Ju kissed Ah Fu and said, breathlessly, "Ah Fu, you know in this whole world I only love you. Be sure to come often."

Ah Fu asked: "What if I run into him, if I come often? Then we'll be finished!"

Xiao Ju gave Ah Fu another kiss and said: "Blockhead! Come often doesn't mean come every day. He comes only on odd days, not on even days. So, why don't you come on even days, to be safe."

Ah Fu said: "Okay, I'll come on even days."

So from then on Ah Fu came over every even day. Once he was here they'd talk some sweet nonsense first. Before long Xiao Ju would make the first move. When it was over, Xiao Ju would give Ah Fu a big sum of money. At first Ah Fu didn't feel comfortable taking the money. Xiao Ju said: This money is free, free of charge or anything. Take it and put it aside. It'll come in handy. At this, Ah Fu took the money.

From then on Xiao Ju was not bored any more. On odd days the fat cat came while Ah Fu came on even days. Everyday someone came to be with her. Odd days she would harvest lots of money; even days, she would harvest lots of "love."

Ah Fu was not the same poor Ah Fu any more. Now he had a cell phone, a motorcycle, and everything he needed. On even days he would harvest lots of money, too.

Ah Fu would hold Xiao Ju in his arms and say: "We can't go on sneaking around forever."

Xiao Ju nodded: "I know. How about this: give me two years so that we can save up enough money for the rest of our lives. Then we'll go back to our home village to have kids and enjoy life."

Ah Fu said: "Okay, two more years."

One day Xiao Ju was taking a stroll in the street when she saw an affectionate couple walking ahead of her, the man looking quite familiar. So she followed them out of curiosity.

The woman said: "Why do you come to be with me only every other day?"

The man said: "On even days I have to go to work. Why, I am with you on all odd days. Not enough?"

The woman said: "We can't go on sneaking around like this for the rest of our lives! When can we be together like a real couple?"

The man said: "Soon, in about two years. By the end of the two years I will have made enough money to support us for the rest of our lives. We can build our home and have kids."

Heavens! That man was none other than Ah Fu! Xiao Ju fainted before she could cry "Foul!"

(2002)

You Are My Only One

Wei Jinshu

Both Honghong and Qingqing are very good girls. Honghong is outgoing while Qingqing is quiet, each charming in her own way. That makes it so difficult for me to choose. Even though nowadays it's really no big deal for a man like me to be going out with two girls at the same time, I still don't want them to know.

In matters of love women are more devoted than men. They are most dead serious about their feelings and least tolerant of their men hot in love with one in the morning and chasing after another in the evening. I have to juggle between the two girls with extreme care.

If I have to choose between Honghong and Qingqing, then, I'm more inclined toward Honghong because she seems to have a lot more going for her. Yet what I am not happy with is Honghong has been ambiguous with me. We've been going out for months and she won't even let me kiss her. Qingqing is quite different. She is so devoted and soft like water and we have been thick and cozy together. If I have to break up with her, I would find it hard to tear myself away. Since my relationship with Honghong is yet to be secured, under the circumstances, Qingqing isn't a bad backup, or runner-up.

In order to win Honghong's heart, I decided to write her a love letter. I've been in love ever since I was 14 and writing love letters is my specialty. Despite my knack and expertise in love letters, I still went all out in drafting this particular one. I pondered over each word and sentence long and hard and polished things left and right so the whole thing flowed lyrically, sounded smart, and throbbed with passion. Even I myself was touched by it when I read it over one more time. I gave this letter a title: "You Are My Only One!"

In the letter I recalled every single beautiful moment we shared together, retraced the steps of our emotional journey, and projected how beautiful our life together would be. I emphasized over and again that she was my one and only love, which I would cherish in my heart forever and ever. I thought that upon reading this letter, Honghong had to be touched profoundly. About this I was one hundred percent positive.

Having finished the letter I sighed with relief. Then, it suddenly occurred to me that I hadn't mailed the letter for Qingqing that I had written a few days ago. So I took it out and intended to take it to the post office together with this new letter.

As I was putting the letters into the envelopes I thought: I should mail the one for Honghong first and see how she will respond? If my letter really moves her and wins her heart, Qingqing won't be that important any more. And that touchy-feely letter for Qingqing, well, there will be no need to send it anymore. If, I mean *if*, Honghong remains unresponsive, it won't be too late to mail Qingqing's letter. Only a few days' difference.

Yes, that's the way to do it. Once I made up my mind, I sealed the letter for Honghong resolutely, hurried to the post office, and tossed the letter into the mail box.

Once home I held the letter for Qingqing in my hand and, since I didn't have much else to do, I pulled the letter out of the envelope. Just one glance and I jumped up in shock. Right in front of me on the very top were these words: "You Are My Only One!"

Damn! This was the letter intended for Honghong. Which meant I had put the letter for Qingqing into Honghong's envelope.

I bolted up and went flying to the post office hoping that I could take back the wrong letter. I got there in time to see the green postal truck disappearing around the corner, leaving behind a dusty cloud. I almost fainted.

It's all over. It's all in Heaven's hands now. I hated myself so!

The following day the most feared thing happened: Honghong's reply letter arrived. At this time, somehow, I became calm, resigned to my fate.

I opened the envelope and pulled out that familiar color paper. In front of me was Honghong's neat and graceful handwriting:

Ah Ming:

How are you? Oh, how I miss you!

I am so touched by your deep, heartfelt feelings for me and so grateful. Do you know that my feelings for you are just as deep and heartfelt? Oh, I will never forget for the rest of my life the beautiful time we have spent together ever since I got to know you. Yes, Ah Ming, thanks to you, I feel life is so beautiful, so rich and colorful, and, Ah Ming, I feel so happy and happy!

Please remember, Ah Ming: You are mine and I will love you forever: You are my one and only love. . . .

With loving kiss,
Yours,
Honghong

I couldn't help but smile and then shake my head. I took out the cigarette lighter, lit up the beautiful letter, and watched it wither into a black roll as those tender words evaporated in dreamy whitish smoke.

My name is not Ah Ming. My name is Ah Qiang.

(2003)

A "Lovebird" for You

Xing Qingjie

The day the girl's flower shop opened, there was not much business. Only one young man came and strolled around with a bored look on his face. Then, almost whimsically, he bought three red roses, and asked the girl to deliver the flowers for him. Since she ran the shop all by herself, she asked the young man to take care of the shop for her before she returned. The young man said yes readily. When the girl had wrapped up the flowers, she picked a green flower from the bucket, inserted it into the red roses, and said:

"You are my very first client. So here is a bonus 'lovebird' for you!" Seeing the confused look in the young man's face, she said, "Oh, it's a flower from the south. 'Lovebird' is its name."

The girl delivered the flowers to the address the young man had given her and saw the girl by the name of Quan. When Quan took the flowers and checked the name on the card, she murmured "thanks," put the flowers aside, and went on doing whatever she was doing.

The girl felt sorry for the young man. Yet when she returned to the flower shop and met his warm eyes, she told him, against her own instincts: Quan was thrilled with the flowers and asked me to say thank you. The young man's face blossomed with joy.

From then on at around the same time each weekend, the young man would come to the flower shop, buy three roses, and ask the girl to deliver the flowers to Quan. Every time Quan took the flowers from her, there was no look of joy in her face. Sometimes she even looked annoyed. So the girl felt she had to tell the young man the truth so that he would not waste any more time and money on Quan. Yet how could she bring it up to him? The girl thought: Perhaps with time Quan will be touched by the young man and he will win her heart. Gradually the girl became convinced of this possibility and didn't think much of it any more.

Thus about half a year passed. One weekend morning the young man came to the flower shop quite early. He said to the girl: "Please deliver flowers for me one last time. Today Quan will be engaged." The girl was surprised by this unhappy ending and even more so by the young man's calm acceptance of the inevitable.

Once again, when she wrapped up three roses, she inserted a "love-bird" right in the middle: a perfect fusion of brilliant red and tender, dewy green. The girl said: "For last time's sake, here is another 'lovebird' for you, on the house."

When she was about to leave, it began to rain heavily. The young man was concerned, but the girl said: "Don't worry. I'll take a taxi."

When the girl returned it was still pouring like crazy. Once out of the taxi the girl dashed to the flower shop, but was still drenched from head to toe. The young man didn't turn to leave as usual, though. He said to the girl: "I . . . I want three more red . . . red roses." The girl looked at him, puzzled. She wrapped up three flowers and, once again, inserted a "lovebird" in their midst. The young man took over the flowers, bent to smell them, and then presented them to her with both hands: "This is for you!"

Stunned, the girl lowered her head, her face reddening. Then she looked up and said; "Your feelings for Quan are so deep. How can you start to court someone else so fast?"

The young man said mysteriously: "It is time I tell you this secret: Quan is my sister."

"What? You sent flowers to your own sister?" The girl couldn't believe her ears.

The young man looked into the girl's eyes and said: "Otherwise, what excuse do I have to come and see you?"

The girl smiled, her face blossoming like a flower.

(2003)

Mosquito Nets

Wu Shouchun

Qun succeeded his father and became a worker at the chemical fertilizer factory.

The factory's living quarters for its workers were very cramped. As it happened, one of the workers in the men's living quarters, who had been married for two years, was finally issued the key to a one-room unit. The "freed up" berth was assigned to Qun.

It was right in the middle of a cold winter. Yet the other three beds all had their mosquito nets up. Only his bed was bare like a pared-down chicken. Mosquito nets are for protection from mosquitoes. What's the use of having mosquito nets up in winter when there are no mosquitoes? Isn't this trading energy for inconvenience? When Qun strolled down the hallway, he noticed that the beds in all the rooms, men and women alike, had their mosquito nets up. Qun was even more puzzled.

The room was small and didn't have even a stool. In leisure time when buddies gathered here, everyone and his brother sat his butt along Qun's bedside because his bed was the only one that didn't have a mosquito net hanging massively all around it. The bed groaned with so many people sitting on it; his quilt and clothes were pushed aside in a messy pile. Qun figured out the answer to the puzzle and followed suit right away. At first, being inside the mosquito net felt so stuffy, as if a wok was hanging over his head. Gradually, though, he became used to its presence.

One day he was changing shifts and was supposed to go home, but failed to catch the bus. So he came back to the dorm and crawled into the mosquito-netted bed, following the folksy wisdom of "Early to bed, late to rise/the Sun warms you in daylight/Saves you firewood and rice." Soon he fell asleep. In the middle of the night he was woken up by some squeaky noises. It reminded him of a scary movie he had seen. He became alarmed. Of the three roommates, one was on sick leave, and the other two had gone home. Where did the strange noise come from? Had a burglar broken in? Qun was too terrified to make any noise or move himself. He listened hard. The noise came from Master Zhang's bed diagonally across from his own. Mixed in it was a moaning sound. Qun sensed what was going on. Damn! When did Master Zhang return to the factory with his new bride? Must be because of the mosquito net, he thinks I have gone home and the coast is clear. That night Qun didn't dare get out of bed despite the pressure mounting in his bladder. Not until Master Zhang and his bride had quieted down did Qun dare to tiptoe out and run to another room down the hallway to seek shelter, much like a lost monk.

The next morning when Master Zhang saw Qun, he asked: "I knew your schedule. Why did you return after only one night at home?" Qun caught a glimpse of Zhang's bride and blushed as if he had done something really shameful. He mumbled some excuse and let it be.

That evening Qun sought a place in another room so as not to be in the way.

The next day Qun worked the second shift. Master Zhang said to him, "Don't act like a guerilla when you come back from work at night. Just go to bed and you'll be fine. Me and my wife are not shy first-timers any more and couldn't care less. If you try to mess around and cause trouble, though, my wife will beat you up until you cry uncle. So when Qun came back from the shift, he crawled into the mosquito net. He was amazed that besides protection from mosquitoes, the mosquito net had other unintended functions.

Qing, his girlfriend, came to the factory to visit Qun.

Puzzled by the mosquito net, she rolled and strung it together and asked: Why use a mosquito net in winter? Qun smiled meaningfully and said: You'll understand shortly.

Before leaving, Master Zhang and the other two roommates said: Settle down and have a good time. Don't worry about us.

So the two settled down in their own territory and space: inside the mosquito net.

Qun tried to kiss Qing. Qing dodged and warned him with a half-hearted punch.

Qun said: Nobody else is in here. They are either on the night shift or in beds in other rooms. Don't worry.

Qing was still worried.

When Qun made his move again, Qing struggled, freed one hand, and pulled off a movie actress picture pinned inside the net and said: Isn't she watching?

Qing would come more often. Before long, with "the rice already being cooked," they got married.

From then on, when Qing came again, Master Zhang and the others didn't need to leave any more.

The good thing was every bed had a mosquito net on.

When Qun was assigned a one-room unit, he still had the mosquito net on, summer or winter.

Later his factory went bankrupt. Qun and Qing began to do business. They made money and bought an apartment in a garden-like residential compound.

The entrance door and all the windows of their new home had insect screens. They had all the furniture they needed. Yet occupying the middle of the bedroom was the same old canopy bed.

At the sight of this bed in the bedroom, which seemed so out of place, visitors would always ask: You've spent tons of money for the new home and everything else, why not go all the way with just a bit more? Qun said: The canopy bed is convenient for hanging the mosquito net. The visitors would say: Don't you have all the insect screens? Look around and see what age we are living in. Sleeping inside a mosquito net in the bedroom, isn't it suffocating?! Qun mumbled: "Double-safety feature, you know."

So Qun discussed this with Qing: Why don't we buy a new mattress to replace the ugly canopy bed. That'll shut people up.

They spent 2,000 *yuan* on a nice new bed.

However, somehow they didn't feel comfortable in it. The worst was when they got into the mood, they just couldn't follow through.

Qun turned their wedding photo on the wall to its back and said: No need to be afraid now 'cause nobody is looking any more. Qing said: It's so empty and open all around. Don't feel safe.

One day Master Zhang came to visit. When he saw the mosquito net hanging around the new mattress bed, he couldn't help laughing.

Qun asked, "What's so funny?"

Master Zhang said: "So you still have the mosquito net on too. . . . "

(2003)

A Caterpillar on Your Shoulder!

Liu Weiping

Many years ago a girl lived in an out-of-the-way mountain village. There the girl had her first love. At the time the girl was still quite young, but she was already budding with pubescent feelings. She had a crush on a boy from the same village. And the boy had a crush on her, too. This she could sense from the fire in the eyes of the boy when he happened to look at her.

Yes, when it started, all that happened between the boy and the girl was exchange of tender glances. The girl saw in the eyes of the boy a ball of glowing fire. The boy saw in the eyes of the girl a spring of tender longings.

Then the boy and the girl began to see each other. Most of the time they met in the woods. This was how they sent signals to each other. When the girl wanted to go pick wild fruits somewhere, she would say nonchalantly in front of others: "I'm going to the hill to pick wild fruits." When the girl came to the hill with a basket on her back, she could be certain that the boy would be there gathering firewood. Sometimes the boy would nonchalantly give away the place where he would go gather firewood. When he had gathered half a bundle of firewood, the girl would surely appear nearby, humming folk songs.

That's how the boy and the girl saw each other in the woods. Deep and quiet, the woods were an ideal place for such encounters. You can imagine the many intimate moments of passion and tenderness when they were together in such a locale.

Yet, here is the surprise. During those days in that mountain village, people were quite conservative in such matters. All the boy and the girl did when they were together was to look into each other's eyes and chitchat some mundane nonsense. The most intimate moment between them would be sitting shoulder to shoulder on the grass.

The biggest desire the boy cherished would be to hold the girl in his arms. The girl, on her part, longed to be held by the boy, too. Yet there was a thin paper between the two, which neither knew how to pierce through.

Once, when the boy and girl were in the woods, they saw strings of grapes hanging from branches, black, ripe, mouthwatering grapes. The girl was not tall enough to reach them.

The boy said: "I know what to do."

The girl said: "What?"

The boy said: "I'll carry you so you can reach the grapes."

The girl was delighted: "Wonderful!" Then the girl realized something and said: "That means you'll hold me in your arms? How can you hold me in your arms now?"

What the girl meant was the boy couldn't hold her in his arms until they were married.

When it came down to it, the boy was a shy kid. What he didn't know was despite what she had said, the girl longed for him to gather her in his arms no matter what.

Fortunately the boy was not obtuse. When they were together again in the woods, the boy told the girl that nowadays in the cities outside the mountain women liked to talk about the "Three Measurements."

The boy said: "You have such a good figure. Must be the ideal 'Three Measurements'"

The girl's eyes shone with curiosity. What the boy had just told her was quite interesting.

After beating about the bush for a while, the boy said: "Want me to do your 'Three Measurements'?"

The girl said: "Alright. But, how can you measure? There is no ruler here."

The boy opened his arms and said: "My arms are the ruler. I guarantee you the ruler is one hundred percent accurate."

The girl couldn't help but smile shyly. She knew what was going on in the boy's mind. She said: "Won't that mean you'll hold me in your arms? How can you hold me in your arms now?"

Both the boy and the girl longed to hug each other, yet they couldn't find a way to do so. Nothing is as sweet as this tantalizing feeling one experiences during this time of pubescent love.

Later, the boy and girl were together again in the woods. As before they sat there and chitchatted some mundane nonsense. What they really wanted to say to each other was said through their eyes. When their passionate eyes met again, the boy cried out suddenly:

"Oh my, a caterpillar on your shoulder!"

Terrified, the girl screamed and threw herself into the boy's arms. It was probably an instinctive reaction on the part of the girl when she threw herself into the boy's arms. She wanted him to get rid of the scary caterpillar on her shoulder.

The boy held the girl tightly in his arms as if he were holding the beauty of the entire world.

The girl held the boy tightly as if she were holding the happiness of an entire lifetime.

The first hug between the boy and the girl was instigated by none other than a caterpillar. Yet, in reality, there was no caterpillar on her shoulder at all. None! That was a lie told by the boy. What is not clear is whether the boy had come up with the lie on the spur of the moment or as a result of long, careful planning. Either way, it is testimonial enough to the power of love.

Years later the girl left for the city where she worked first as a beauty salon girl, then an escort, and then the mistress of a fat cat. Once, the fat cat took the girl on a sightseeing trip. When they walked into the woods of the scenic place, the fat cat suddenly cried out to the girl:

"Oh my, a caterpillar on your shoulder!"

Terrified, the girl screamed. However, she didn't throw herself into the fat cat's arms. Instead, she took out a paper napkin and brushed off the caterpillar carefully.

The crisis was resolved, yet the girl squatted down, covering her face in her hands.

The same cry of "A caterpillar on your shoulder!" had pierced through so many years of time and hit hard the heart that had been numbed for so long. Who else in the world would be so sensitive to the tremors of the girl's heart as the boy had once?

The fat cat stood there and said: "Why, a mere caterpillar scared the wits out of you, and now you can't stand up!"

A sobbing sound leaked through the fingers of the girl.

(2004)

Big Buddy
Wang Kuishan

Dorm Room 6028 of the Chinese Department had eight residents. Chen Hao was the oldest. So everybody called him Big Buddy fondly.

By the time of their junior year, everyone in the class became involved in a romantic relationship, as if they had all been hit by a contagious disease at the same time. All the female students in the class had been "claimed" in the blink of an eye. That all had been claimed is not an accurate statement because there was still one damsel who was yet to be "claimed:" Liu Meiyan. When it came down to it, there wasn't anything visibly wrong with Liu Meiyan. If one had to be picky, then, she was a bit on the heavy side. 1.6 meters tall, yet 130 *jin* in weight. Liu Meiyan, for her part, though, was quite open about it. She would say in front of everybody "I gain weight even if I live on water alone. There's nothing I can do about it."

One day someone in the dorm room suggested they write an anonymous love letter to Liu Meiyan to invite her out for a date and see how she would respond. There was nothing else to do for fun anyway. The suggestion received warm, unanimous approval. Since everyone was bursting with Tang poetry and Song lyrics, writing up a sugar letter would be like a master chef preparing an appetizer. That evening they penned a draft. Having praised Liu Meiyan with all the beautiful words available, the letter invited her to meet in the plum tree woods north of the school's Big Sports Ground at 6 o'clock in the afternoon: "Stay till we meet." The letter further explained that the 6th hour (after noon) of the 6th day of the week was chosen for its auspicious ring: "Six Six Success!"

This letter was composed on Monday evening.

The next day the sealed letter was dropped into the mailbox.

The plum tree woods north of the Big Sports Ground was chosen as the site for the date because the window of Dorm Room 6028 commanded a very good view of everything inside the plum tree woods.

Over the next few days, Liu Meiyan's hearty singing could be heard in and outside the classrooms and on the way to the library. She might be a bit on the heavy side, but, honestly, she had a really good voice. When she sang Meng Tingwei's "Come and See Winter Rain in Taibei," one would feel as if it were Meng herself singing.

Six o'clock on Saturday afternoon arrived at last. In Dorm Room 6028, everyone squeezed together at the window and, eyes wide open, gazed toward the plum tree woods north of the Big sports ground.

Liu Meiyan appeared right on time. Once in the plum tree woods, Liu Meiyan lifted her hand to check her watch, probably wondering to herself: I'm on time. Now, you, the mysterious admirer, it's your turn to show your face.

Five past six. Liu Meiyan gazed left and right.

Ten past six. Liu Meiyan paced back and forth.

Fifteen past six. Liu Meiyan stopped pacing. She stood there and stood on her toes again and again to see better and further.

The spectators chattered and chuckled mirthfully.

Usually, Chen Hao would not partake in the things of his younger roommates and would stay far away from their practical jokes like this. He had a principle to follow: Big Buddy should behave like Big Buddy. Yet, this time round, the chattering and smirking of the younger roommates attracted him to the window despite himself. He took a look at the plum tree woods and was stunned: Liu Meiyan in a rosy down jacket and white jeans reminded him of someone. Last year when he went home for New Year's, his younger sister wore exactly the same clothes.

The sister, who had leukemia, had already died half a year ago. At this thought Chen Hao's heart beat wildly. He could feel something hot washing over his entire being. Without a word to anyone he pulled open the door and dashed downstairs.

That same night Chen Hao came back very late. His younger room-mates, already in bed, were in the midst of a heated conversation. When he pushed open the door and stepped in, a hushed silence fell on them suddenly. Without turning on the light, Chen Hao washed, got into bed, removed his clothes, and crawled into his quilt. The whole time Chen Hao didn't say anything, not a single word. He could hear his own heavy breathing.

Finally, Chen Hao opened his mouth. "I have an announcement for everyone: Tonight Liu Meiyan and I have decided to be boyfriend and girlfriend."

With that Chen Hao sighed deeply, a thousand-*jin* burden on his shoulder having been relieved. Chen Hao thought to himself: If anyone dares to say half a word against Liu Meiyan, I'll kill him.

Surprisingly, though, someone clapped his hands. Then, everyone in the room clapped their hands.

Tears flowed down Chen Hao's cheeks.

(2005)

Return Visit

Ai Ya

He wrote "twenty" on the check, signed his English name gracefully, and started to write a letter to his friend:

> Please, my friend, buy a hand-braided straw hat. Please, then, buy a ticket to my hometown, and at the corner of the station, buy a bunch of lychee from the elderly man who is often in his faded shirt. I know lychee is now in season. Afterwards, instead of getting on the train, please put the straw hat on, walk through the noisy, muddy farmers' market, turn at Old Wang's Beef Lo Mein stand, and you will be at my home. No need to knock on the door. Just call out: "Uncle Ah Lang's Son!" That's my Pop. Then, please place the lychee on the table and sit down to drink tea with Pop. Then, please stroll to the neighbor to see a young woman, an uncultured woman dressed in simple clothes. She was my first love. Please see if she still has the sweet smile on her healthy face. Has she given her husband another son? Please do all these on my behalf. Enclosed is US$20 to reimburse your expenses. Thanks.

He put the letter and check into the envelope, sealed it with tears and a lick, and put an airmail stamp on it. Then he picked up the pen and wrote the following in the record section of the checkbook:

> June 18, Return visit fare and misc. expenses, $20 exact.

(n.d.)

Butterfly Forever

Chen Qiyou

It is raining. The asphalt road looks cold and wet. It glitters with reflections of green, yellow, and red lights. We are taking shelter under the balcony. The green mailbox stands alone across the street. Inside the big pocket of my white windbreaker is a letter for my mother in the South.

Yingzi says she can mail the letter for me with the umbrella. I nod quietly and hand her the letter.

"Who told us to bring only one small umbrella?" She smiles, opens up the umbrella, and is ready to walk across the road to mail the letter for me. A few tiny raindrops from an umbrella rib fall onto my glasses.

With the piercing sound of a vehicle screeching to a halt, Yingzi's life flies in the air gently, and then slowly falls back on the cold and wet road, like a butterfly at night.

Although it is spring, it feels like deep autumn.

All she did was cross the road to mail a letter for me. A very simple act, yet I will never forget it as long as I live.

I open my eyes and remain standing under the balcony, blankly, my eyes filled with hot tears. All the cars in the entire world have stopped. People rush to the middle of the road. Nobody knows the one that lies on the road there is mine, my butterfly. At this moment she is only five meters away from me, yet it is so far away. Bigger raindrops fall onto my glasses, splashing into my life.

Why? Why did we bring only one umbrella?

Then I see Yingzi again, in her white windbreaker, the umbrella above her head, crossing the road quietly. She is mailing the letter for me. The letter I wrote to my mother in the South. I stand blankly under the balcony and see, once again, Yingzi walking toward the middle of the road.

The rain wasn't that big, yet it was the biggest rain in my entire life. Below is the content of the letter. Did Yingzi know?

"Ma, I am going to marry Yingzi next month."

(2006)

Cold Night
Yu Dafu[2]

Have to tell her to go back first; with a promise to join her in half an hour.

Have had more than enough to drink. The neighboring rooms are completely dark now, their guests long gone, the servants having turned off their yellowish lights. Coal in the stove, once glowing red, has crumbled into a smoldering mess, and the small door below the vent, once so red hot, almost translucent, has turned pale, too.

Feeling woozy all the time, what with sleepless nights and then drinking all day long. Have really gotten into talking to Yusheng, but with her hanging at my side all the time, I can't even stand up and to go take a pee.

Took me a while to talk her into leaving, on *her* condition of me joining her in half an hour. Shivered badly when, escorting her to the door, a gust of cold wind blew right in my face. With the door open, the reddish light from inside shone into the misty night, revealing snow-flakes drifting down.

"Snowing again! Snow may prevent me from coming, you know!"

Half joking; half out of a genuine desire to go home and see if any important mail had arrived the past week.

"How come! No deal then, and I won't leave!"

She opened her shawl, wrapped it around my body, and brushed her face, cool, smooth, and fragrant, and her soft, light breath and thin lips, against mine.

"Alcohol! Smells disgusting!"

She pretended to be angry and flashed me another stare. When she was about to brush her face against mine again, Yusheng cried out from inside the house:

"Stop it, Liuqing. Stop it! Having the audacity to do this in the court-yard! Ten dollars, fine!"

"I don't care, I don't. . . ."

She brought her face close to mine again, a laugh escaping her lips.

Wrapped in the same shawl with her, I cautiously treaded through the dark, slippery courtyard toward the gate, where the shopkeeper hollered "Cab!" Startled, I jumped out of the shawl and shivered again when another gust of cold wind blew into my face.

She turned her head and reminded:

"In half an hour. Don't forget!"

And left without looking back.

Through shivering cold I took a few steps along the wall to a dark corner and peed. Then, as I walked back to the house, my face was once again greeted with icy snowflakes. I looked up into the sky and couldn't make out anything except for a nebulous gloom; lowering my head somewhat, though, I saw a row of shingles on the rooftop: chilly, blurry, vaporous like beer.

Once inside the house, I noticed that Yusheng was already laying on the *kang*. A door behind me opened, and the shop clerk handed me a warm towel and a bill.

"Why the hurry? Want to go to bed, too? Go get me another pack o' cigarettes!"

The clerk was unhappy with the request, but since I was a regular, there was nothing he could do but go and run the errand with a big smile on his face.

I lay on the *kang* across from Yusheng's for who knows how long until the clerk shook me and woke me up, mumbling: "It's snowing real hard outside. Shall I call Flying Dragon and get you a cab, so you won't catch cold?"

"Fine!"

I woke Yusheng, wiped my face and hands with a towel, and had a smoke. We sat and waited for the cab, still very drowsy, neither in a mood to talk.

Upon hearing a sudden sputtering sound in the quiet air, I put on the coat and hurried outside with Yusheng. The courtyard was already too wet and slippery. More snowflakes hit my face.

"Snowing like this, I won't be able to leave again tomorrow, I'm afraid."

My voice sounded a bit odd to my own ears, like beating a drum wrapped with a layer of cloth.

The shops along both sides of the street had closed. All quiet, except for the cab's wheels grumbling through wet mud. It bumped along; the street looked all but deserted. Inside the cab was complete darkness, the dome light broken, it seemed. The snowflakes caught in the beams of the headlights looked so gossamer, so faraway, like in a dream.

The cab squeaked as it turned, its lights shining on a white wall. When it neared Yusheng's home, I became excited, suddenly, as if a pot of water was boiling inside me, something welling up in my eyes.

"Yusheng! Don't go home! Let's go back to Han's Lake. Let's go to Liuqing's place and chat all night!"

I broke the silence and thus begged Yusheng as I half stood up from the seat, pounded hard on the glass window, and ordered the cabbie to take us to Han's Lake.

(1926)

Sweetheart

Ku Ling

She didn't know how he had fallen in love with her.

What he liked the most was to nestle in her arms and put his face to her chest to listen to her heart beat.

"Put his ear to his heart/Listen to the sound of its beat" is a line from a poem she wrote her first year in college. She had felt her heart beat faster than normal ever since she was small. Sometimes, while doing any physically intense activity, she would feel her heart all but bursting out of her mouth. As she grew up, whenever she had to walk up to the second floor, she would hear her heart beat so hard. It hurt badly.

When it hurt badly, she would *feel* her chest inside which the heart was beating intensely, and ask her parents. Her father would lower his head and sigh and her mother would sob with tears all over her face.

When she knew she was afflicted with congenital heart disease, she cried, too; tears gushing down her face. Gradually, however, she became stronger and was not afraid of the hospital bed, intravenous bottle hanging high, and the nurses' white masks any more. Sometimes she could calmly gaze at the signals of her own heartbeat on the monitor dancing up and down and wonder when they would fall into a deadly horizontal line.

Perhaps God didn't mean to take her back yet. In the year she turned 30, a heart donor for her was finally available. The day before the surgery she cried the whole night, her tears soaking the white pillow and sheet. She cried for finally having another shot at life and she cried for the donor who lost her own to save hers.

All she knew was that it was a married woman her age who had died in a car accident. Since she had no way of expressing her gratitude to the donor, she kept the clipping of the newspaper story of her heart transplant, which carried their pictures side by side.

Then *he* appeared. The first time he paced into the patient's room hesitantly, she thought he was a reporter. Soon he became a regular visitor. Bored by long days of inactivity while recuperating from the surgery, she would often sit in her sickbed and comb and do her makeup with anxious expectancy. The joy of first love washed over her in waves. After all, thanks to her fragile heart, she hadn't even kissed once.

Now she could kiss to her heart's content. Another's heart beat in her chest with a healthy rhythm. Her heartbeat was not hurried, but very calm now. She could now put her heart at ease, hold tight in her arms the half-kneeling man, and say "yes" to his proposal.

Still, she didn't know why someone would come and love her, an imperfect, handicapped her, still fragile, with permanent scars on her chest. . . . Yet *he* didn't seem to mind at all. And he loved her with such passion. Every time she asked him, he would reply only with a smile. Perhaps he had been through a lot and had thus become reticent. She knew that he was married once but became single again.

She didn't know there was a small box hidden at the bottom of his dresser. One day, accidentally, she found the box, opened it out of curiosity, and saw his old wedding picture: The happy bride with a sweet smile on her face looked so familiar, like. . . . then she was stunned. She hurried to find the newspaper clipping. She didn't need to compare to know that his bride and her heart donor were the same woman.

That heart was beating hard in her chest. It hurt so.

(n.d.)

Feelings

Li Ang

She is a woman in her mid-thirties. Average looking. Her pale, smooth skin, though, gives her plain face a touch of attractiveness, especially when she fixes her hair into a nice roll high in the back of her head.

She has two kids. Both are boys. The older one is in grade school; the younger has just started kindergarten. She doesn't want to try again for a daughter. Instead she is thinking of going back to work.

When she got married years back she worked as an accountant. Later when she gave birth to the first son, she didn't feel comfortable letting someone else take care of him. Her husband would rather she take care of their son herself and didn't mind losing the extra income she was making. So she quit her job. During all these years her husband has done well with his business and has saved up some money. They have bought an entire floor of an apartment building as their home and lived a smooth, comfortable life. She is rather careful in managing finances, though, so they will not be caught short.

For example, she never leaves much cash at home. She always deposits extra money in the post office nearby and then withdraws a certain amount now and then for expenses. In addition to participating in investment pools with friends and relatives, she has a long-term deposit account with the post office with a monthly deposit of about 1,000 *yuan*. That way there will be money for the two boys' education.

She goes to the post office regularly. Although it is right around the corner once she comes out of the alley, she always makes sure she is properly groomed and dressed each time she goes there. It is a habit of hers. Even when she goes to the small grocery right next door to buy soy sauce and things, she doesn't want to appear unkempt.

Since she goes to the post office often and since she has to wait while her deposit or withdrawal is being processed, she begins to notice the employees working there. It's all so natural. Before she knows it, she begins to notice the director of this suburban post office more than anyone else.

He is a fortyish man, medium build, a bit on the heavy side, but looks fit. An honest face that shows signs of having been through things. Nothing striking. Yet there is an air of calmness, of confidence, of substance and depth that compels her eyes to linger on him a bit longer.

When her eyes meet his occasionally, she knows he is noticing her, too. Once, when a clerk hands him a bunch of deposit slips for signatures, he turns hers over to the front side and looks at her name and address carefully. She notices her own face reddening at the moment.

She continues to go to that post office regularly for the next two or three years. She is busy every day taking care of her husband and two kids and her big home. Only when she goes to the post office and sees the director of the post office there does she feel that there is someone in the world whom she wants to see. Most of the time when he is conscious of the look in her eyes, he will glance back.

Then, one winter afternoon, she went shopping with her sister-in-law. When she hurried back it was already past 6 pm. The relative babysitting the boys told her someone from the post office had called several times saying a check she had asked the post office to process on her behalf had been returned. The caller left a phone number and asked her to call back.

She looked at her watch: It was already past 6:30pm. She hesitated. Then the babysitter said: The caller said he would wait no matter how late.

She dialed the number. The man at the other end of the phone had been waiting and knew right away who she was. He explained the check had been returned because a clerk had put an erroneous amount on her deposit slip. He asked her to come back the next day with her seal to correct the error.

She recognized the voice as that of the post office director, inquired about the proper procedures, and then asked, politely, his name so she could take care of this smoothly the next day. The director said his last name was Zhang.

The next day when she went to the post office, she noticed a stranger sitting where the director used to sit, bent over things on the desk. She asked for Mr. Zhang to process the returned check. A female clerk took the seal from her without saying a word, went about correcting the error, and returned the seal to her a short while later when it was all taken care of.

She stepped out of the post office. The rare winter sun felt warm. As she walked slowly in the warm sunshine toward her home, she had this odd feeling: She would never see that post office director again for the rest of her life. He must have been transferred, or have been promoted to the general office, she thought. Yet before he left, he called her on account of that error on the check and waited for her return call after the post office had closed.

He said his last name is Zhang, she murmured.

(n.d.)

My Bride
Wu Nianzhen

The last night of our honeymoon vacation, my bride suddenly became worried about the new family life that would begin soon. After all, aside from me, she would have to live with my mother and my siblings. With me she had long since felt comfortable and at ease. With my family, well, it was far from being so.

I tried to comfort her about this. After a while her concern seemed somewhat eased. She looked up and asked: "How should I call Mother?"

"We all call her 'Ma.' However, you can use the same greeting you are accustomed to."

"You fool! Of course I will follow you in this." She hit me with her fist gently and said: "However, I'll have to practice first."

So between stepping into the bathroom and falling asleep, she was calling out "Ma!" "Ma!" the entire time, her face lit with joy and happiness.

On the way home the tourist bus broke down on the expressway and we were delayed for three or four hours. By the time we reached Taibei, it was well past time for dinner. I suggested we find a casual place to eat but she wouldn't' agree.

"'Ma' must be waiting for us." She said positively and murmured again, with a smile on her face: "Ma, Ma . . . "

As my bride had expected, Ma and my siblings were waiting quietly at the dinner table. It was already 10:00pm.

Ma grasped my bride's hand and made her sit in her own seat. Then she told me to sit in the chair left empty by my dead father. A long while passed before Ma found her voice and said with tears in her eyes: "From now on, you two will take care of this family. . . . "

My bride and Ma held each other's hand, smiling, their tears glinting under the warm light.

"I'll take good care of the family. . . . " My bride nodded, and called out suddenly, "Mommy!"

That night my bride sobbed long in my arms. Then she said: "I'm so sorry . . . I was too emotional. . . . I suddenly felt my heart being filled with the love of four people: you, Ma, my Dad . . . and . . . my Mommy. . . . "

She closed her eyes as tears flowed down her cheeks and whispered in my ear: "Ah, you fool, you don't understand. . . . "

But I do.

My bride lost her mother at five. For 23 years she has been a good surrogate mother to her two younger sisters. She never had a chance to say "Mommy" again. Once she told me: "At the time mother was already in a coma. Father carried me to the sickbed and said: 'Call Mommy, my child, call mommy. . . . ' I remember, vaguely, that I called as loud as I could: 'Mommy!'"

(n.d.)

The Love Story of A and B
Yindi

Time is a magician. When 30 years have passed, it is difficult to tell what is real and what is not real. Below is something strange that happened in my office this morning:

A and B were my high school classmates. A is female and B male. B was a roommate of mine in the dorm. We shared a bunk and were close like each other's shadow. When B and A started to date, I had the pleasure of being an occasional messenger between them, as well as a peacemaker now and then. However, the feelings they had for each other during high school were not mature yet. After graduation they parted ways; and each followed his or her own path; they each got married and started a family of their own. One thing they had in common, though: they both emigrated to America, A is a dentist on the East coast while B is a gynecologist on the West coast.

Yesterday afternoon, A called and said she wanted to come and see me. It turned out she was in Taibei and got my phone number from a classmate. She told me she was to return to the U.S. tomorrow. She sat in my office for about half an hour. Thirty years of time had lapsed. For a while we didn't know where to start and yet once we started we had so much to talk about. Before leaving she gave me a tin of tea leaves and asked if I was still in touch with B. I shook my head.

Then, a strange thing happened. This afternoon, B, whom I had all but lost touch with since graduation, called me, too. He said he had been back to Taibei for a conference and finally got hold of my phone number from a mutual friend. I said: "This call of yours is a bit late. If you had dialed this number yesterday, I would have told you A is in my office and is chatting with me over tea. You would certainly have dashed over to see A, whom you haven't seen for 30 years!" B said; "Really? Really?" He dashed to my office and asked, still gasping: "Perhaps A has changed her flight? Perhaps she is still in Taibei?" I told him to call up a few classmates who would know A's whereabouts. B was given this accurate information: A has boarded a 10:30 flight this morning to return to America.

B had such a lost look in his eyes. He then asked me for A's phone number and address in America and wanted to leave right away. I gave him the tin of tea leaves A had given me and said: "You both, without talking, brought me a tin of tea leaves. I'll keep yours, but hers, you can take back to America and enjoy. You didn't get a chance to shake her hand, but this tin of tea leaves, at least, still has a lingering warmth of her hand. Take it with you. Better than nothing, you know."

At that he took over the tin and hugged it to his chest, a smile appearing on his face. He said good bye and left me to linger a bit longer in the memory of this old-time love. I have always wondered: Which would be better, the two of them, after 30 years of no contact, missing each other again by as little as one day? Or, what if they had suddenly encountered each other again in my office that day? What kind of ramifications would such a reunion have?

(n.d.)

Nightclub-tique

Zhong Zimei

Monogamy has collapsed. The short, temporary relationships between men and women are now maintained through "open rendezvous" (no more "secret rendezvous"). Childbirth is handled by "Generational Reproduction" chain stores.

All "open rendezvous" happen at nightclubs. The nightclubs of the 20th century, though, are nowhere to be found. The nightclubs of the entire world are gathered in the vacuum 230,000 kilometers from the earth to the moon. They are made of colorful soft plastic, semi-transparent, big ones about one kilometer across, and small ones only 10 meters. These oblong things float in the atmosphere, rock slightly, and bump into each other softly, as spontaneous and romantic as can be. Hence a new expression is coined to describe this new nightclub phenomenon: "Nightclub-tique."

Tonight, John flew his spacecraft again to "Nightclub-tique." His partner was Gonzales—an impeccable beauty.

They had just finished the first round of French cognac when two tall and strong police officers appeared in front of them. One of them said to Gonzales coldly: "Give me your left hand!'

He gripped Gonzales's ring finger and lifted the nail easily, all the dark red parts glittering right before their eyes.

"A fake human indeed! Where is your product registration card? No? An illegal fake human! You'll have to come with us—"

"Wait a second!" John stood up and removed a golden card from his waist belt.

The coldness of the police melted away. One of the officers swiped the card against the magnetic buckle of his waist belt and gave John a salute:

"Mr. John, member of the Global Commission! You have two of your five amnesty rights left. All right, we will grant amnesty to this lady."

When the police left, the ashen-faced Gonzales threw herself into John's arms and cried gratefully:

"You won't despise me just because I'm a fake, John?"

John burst out laughing. He gently lifted the nail of his own ring finger.

"You're a fake, too? How can fake humans sit on the Global Commission?"

"Why can't commission members be fake?" It took John a while to stop laughing. "Let me tell you a secret. My card is fake, too."

John reached to wipe away the tears from Gonzales' cheeks. "The tears in your dacryocysts must be counterfeit. You should use Daiyu. That brand can't be faked. The world we live in today, there are too many fake things. Who knows, this French cognac may not be real. . . . "

Just then another group of police swarmed in. They were not coming for John, though. Instead, they dragged out the manager from his office. The manager was shaking from head to toe.

"The license for this nightclub is fake, damn it!' A police officer shouted.

John walked up and showed them his golden card.

An arrest was thus warded off. The manager bowed to John so many 90-degree bows and returned to his office.

"John! You are something! I'm so proud of having someone like you among us fake humans!" Gonzales snuggled in John's arms and said again softly, as if to herself; "How nice it'd be to return to monogamy. . . . "

Outside the window, the most splendid vista of nightclubs in the entire Milky Way still unfolds its endless story of "Open Rendezvous"—the story of Nightclub-tique, real and fake alike.

(2000)

family

Blowfish

Wang Renshu

He learnt about this from someone and decided to make the move.

Somehow he got a basket of blowfish and carried it home quietly.

Three successive years of disastrous harvest left him with barely enough grain to pay the landowner and little to feed his family of five. It had been excruciatingly difficult for him, all alone, to pull the family through from last winter to early spring. Now, all that was left was hunger.

But how could he let his family suffer hunger?

When his family saw him back with a full basket, they all jumped for joy, as if he were an angel.

The kids met him at the door, half dancing.

"Pop, Pop! What is it? Let's eat it!"

At this tears welled up in his eyes.

"Eat." he mumbled, terrified by his own voice, terrified for the lives of his kids; his heart nearly froze.

He told his wife to cook the fish and then left on the pretext of an errand. Not that he didn't want to die himself, but that he didn't want to watch with his own eyes how his family would die. So he wanted to stay away for the time being.

It was well past noon and he was still not back. The kids had been pleading with their mother for the fish

Now, his wife, who had been through a lot with him and loved him dearly, would never let the kids eat or taste anything before he had the first bite.

By the time the sun began to set in the west, the blowfish was still being cooked in the wok. It was then that he came back home, as if walking on air, dreading each step, his mind filled with pictures of his family, all dead, sprawled here and there.

Remembering his resolve to end the family's suffering, he quickened his steps. Even from a distance he could see the glistening eyes of his children waiting outside; then, he heard a chorus of their voices welcoming him home.

"Why, not dead yet?" he thought aloud softly.

"Pop! We've been waiting for you to eat together!"

"Oh!" He now knew.

The family scrambled to the table and ate with gusto. They hadn't had any fish for so long and every tiny bite tasted delicious. Afterwards, he lay in bed quietly and soon fell asleep, waiting for the Dark Angel of Death to descend.

The blowfish, however, had been cooked for so long its poison had all disappeared. So the family lived and would have to suffer hunger again, day by day.

He woke up and sighed: "Why is it so hard even to ask for death?" as tears welled in his eyes.

(1936)

Two Letters

Tang Xunhua

July 1, 1984

Dear Younger Brother:

Greetings!

I'm writing this letter to ask you to forgive me: I've lied to you for the last five years.

Each day of the last five years I was being tortured by the feeling of guilt and wanted to write and tell you the truth, but was forced to keep the lie alive again and again thanks to the hard life we led and to your sister-in-law being bedridden with paralysis. I am not a worthy brother! Remember the 10 *yuan* a month you have been sending to support our father out of filial love for him? The truth is: our father passed away five years ago!

Now, for reasons known to you, our life has turned around and your sister-in-law has been cured completely. It's high time to tell you the truth!

It is with heartfelt gratitude that I am sending you the 600 *yuan* you earned with your toil and sweat, which I took from you through lies and in the name of our dead father.

Could you forgive me? Could your wife, the sister-in-law I haven't had the pleasure of meeting, forgive me?

Best wishes!
Your elder brother

July 7, 1984

Dear Elder Brother:

Greetings!

I was saddened by the news that my father-in-law has long passed away and regret that as a daughter-in-law I have never had a chance to show him my filial love. How can I face my father-in-law when I meet him in my next life?

You were forced to lie by hard life, so I can fully understand. But could you forgive me for the lie I have told? In order not to devastate my father-in-law and to disturb your life, I did not tell you the news that your brother had laid down his life during the border war with Vietnam.

The money sent to you was taken from your brother's compensations. Since I am not hard-pressed financially, I am returning to you the 600 *yuan*. Please accept it.

I'd be so happy if Elder Brother could kindly forgive me, too. Please give my hearty congratulations to my sister-in-law on her complete recovery!

Best wishes!
Your younger sister-in-law

(1986)

Black Butterfly

Liu Guofang

His son nestled in his arms. A butterfly flew over, a big black butterfly. His son bolted from his arms and ambled after the butterfly. His son didn't catch the butterfly. Instead, he ran over and caught his son.

"Don't go after the butterfly," he said.

"Why?" his son looked up and asked.

"Butterflies are dead people."

"Do all dead people become butterflies?" his son asked.

"Yes, they do."

"Will Pa become a butterfly?"

"Don't talk nonsense."

His son still wanted to chase after butterflies, so he held his son's hands tightly in his own. So many butterflies were hovering and dancing overhead. His son lifted his head and chased them with his eyes, crying out: "See, so many people have become butterflies!"

He took his son back home.

From then on he didn't spend much time with his son. Soon he acquired a lover, a pretty girl. The girl liked him and stayed with him every day. Once the girl said, "Let's get married."

He said, "I'll miss my son."

The girl said, "Easy. I'll bear you a son."

For a long while he didn't say a word. Then he nodded.

So he divorced his wife. When he was packing his things up, his son grasped his hand and asked: "Where're you going, Pa?"

"A long business trip," he lied.

"Pa doesn't want me any more," his son said.

There was nothing he could say.

Just then a butterfly flew over, a very big black butterfly. He saw his son's eyes glued to the butterfly. It hovered around a few times and left.

So did he.

For a long time afterwards he didn't see his son. He missed him. When he missed his son badly, his new wife would pat her belly and say to him, "No need to worry. I'll bear you one."

There was nothing else he could do about it.

Except for waiting, waiting for his wife's belly to grow bigger. He waited and waited but his wife didn't bear him a son. He missed his son even more.

One day, he couldn't take it anymore, and he went to see his son without telling his new wife. Since he hadn't visited him for years, he didn't know where his son had moved. It took him a while to find the new address.

There he saw a child, much taller than he remembered, the innocent curiosity gone. He knew in his heart that the child in front of him must be his son but didn't dare to trust his eyes. He said to the child: "Do you know me?"

The child shook his head. He told the child to look harder.

The child looked again and said, "I don't know you."

"I'm your pa," he said.

"You are not my pa," the child said.

"*I am* your pa."

"You *aren't* my pa."

"I *am* your pa," he insisted.

The child stopped arguing with him. He ran into the inner room, came back with a small wooden box, and handed it to him: "My pa is in it."

He opened the box.

In the box lay a butterfly.
A big black butterfly.

(1988)

Façade

Shen Hong

Her husband will go on a business trip for a week.

She pretends to care a lot and asks him many questions: Where is he going? What's the weather like there? Shouldn't he pack some extra clothing just in case? She talks while packing for her husband, a can't-live-a-day-without-him look in her face. It is so touching. In reality, though, she can't wait for her husband to go on business trips so she can go and see her lover.

She used to be a proper woman. But eight years of married life has worn her out. After a full day of busy work at the company, she yearned to be comforted by her husband when she returned home. Yet he would be tied up with work and wouldn't be home until late in the evening. So her home was rarely brightened up with happy surprises such as her husband coming home with fresh flowers. Oh, she would be thrilled and hug him till she died. How many times had she dreamed of such a moment in her life and each time she would be disappointed. It looked like there was no way she and her husband could rekindle the kind of passion they had felt for each other while dating. At moments like this she would be hit by a nameless sadness and would feel lonely. It was around this time that a wealthy man began to pursue her. At first she was nervous and couldn't see herself saying yes to the man. Her curiosity prevailed eventually. In the thrilling adventure that ensued she tasted passions she had never thought possible her entire life. Now, she is awash with excitement whenever she thinks of the time she spends with her lover.

At this very moment while packing for her husband, she is planning in her head. First, she and her lover go to Arc de Triomphe to savor the French food there; then they go for a ride in the lover's shiny Nissan; afterwards, they go to the dance hall to dance cha-cha and sing karaoke. Yes, that "Meet at Midnight," which she has sung dozens of times. Usually it is after singing that song that she and her lover walk into the night, romantic, intoxicating. . . .

She finishes packing while planning, tiptoes into the bedroom, and picks up the phone. She hears her husband's voice from the other phone in the living room:

" . . . I've already told her the business trip will take about a week. She's still packing for me . . . don't worry, she won't suspect anything. Yes, we will have a fabulous time at the sea resort . . . Hey, all is clear at your end, too? Good. Okay, see you at the resort. . . . "

Her heart tightens suddenly, the phone slipping out of her hand. . . .

(1994)

Letters

Wang Peijing

In the heart is an invisible thread that links us to our dear ones no matter where we are in the world.

This story took place over 20 years ago. At the time I was 17 years old and had just graduated from high school. I joined a Tibet Volunteers team and was working on a highway project in Xixigeli. One of my roommates was a middle-aged rustic man called Big Mount Ma. Behind his back, though, everybody called him Big Monk Ma. Here in Xixigeli, sandstorms rage on almost year round, and here in Xixigeli women and green are rarely seen. It wasn't that bad during the day while we were busy laying stones and filling in earth. It became hard on us, however, when we lay in bed at night listening to the wind buzzing outside the Mongolian tents and wolves engaging in heart-piercing howls.

At that time communication technology was not as advanced. Even if it were, no telephone service could be established in such vast, wild desert.

Therefore, letters were the only way by which we could be linked with folks thousands of miles away. Although it would sometimes take more than two months for a letter to reach its destination, that sheet of paper carried with it the feelings between father and son, mother and son, husband and wife, and between brothers.

Big Monk Ma was illiterate. Every time he saw others' faces light up with joy upon receiving letters, he would sit aside and puff away on his pipe. About half a year later, Big Monk Ma had a rather thoughtful, worried look on his face for days. I wondered why. Moreover, he was especially kind to me. On the construction site he would always let me do light work and during mealtime he would generously give me a portion of his vegetables and meat.

One evening he told me what had been on his mind.

"Young man, could you do me a favor? I am illiterate, you know. I bought paper, pen, and envelope a long time ago but don't know how to use them. Could you write me a letter home? Just want to know how my kid is doing at school, and how are things at home."

"Certainly," I said. "Why didn't you ask me earlier? No trouble at all. Okay, let me do it now, so it'll catch the mail tomorrow. Homesick, wifesick, right?" Now I knew why he had been so kind to me recently.

Once the letter was on its way, Big Monk Ma became his old self again, working tirelessly, a smile appearing on his face now and then.

A month passed. Then another. Still no letters came for Big Monk Ma. So I offered to write another letter for him.

Days passed. More days passed. Finally Big Monk Ma received a letter from home. That afternoon we were busy working when the administrative assistant came to the construction site to pass out the mail. Thrilled beyond himself, Big Monk Ma gazed at the letter for a long time, caressed it with quivering fingers, and then folded it carefully and put it in his pocket. Someone called out: "Uncle Ma, what does your letter say? Can you read it aloud for us?" Big Monk Ma's face reddened, but he didn't take out the letter.

A short while later I went to the outhouse. Big Monk Ma followed. When we reached the outhouse, he said, "Young man, could you read it for me?" I took the envelope. I tore it open and pulled out a sheet. He took the envelope and felt inside to see if there was more. I read through the letter and said:

"Let's not read it."

A worried look appeared on his face. "What happened? What happened? What does the letter say? Read it for me. I beg you."

It was a rather short letter written with an unsteady hand:

Big Mount:

The kid is good. I want to sleep with you.

Kid's Mom

I finished but Big Monk Ma's eyes were still on my face. When I handed the letter back to him, he said: "That's it?"

"Yes," I said. "That's all. Your wife can write? The envelope and the letter were not written by the same hand."

"No, she can't. She never went to school."

I was young and foolish then, having not tasted the full range of human feelings, and leaked the content of Big Monk Ma's letter as if it were a joke. Many on the construction site would tease him endlessly: "I want to sleep with you! "

Not long after that I received a telegram that my grandpa was gravely ill. So I left Tibet. I haven't seen Big Monk Ma since.

Later I realized that his wife must have worked hard on that letter. It must have taken her a whole day, or perhaps several days, to learn one single word from her young son, and then copy the words, stroke by stroke, to complete that letter. That simple letter carried with it the deep feelings of a woman in the mountains, waiting for her man thousands of miles away.

Twenty years have passed since then. I hope it's not too late to say this to Big Monk Ma and his dear wife: I apologize for my youthful foolishness.

(2000)

Goldie

Ma Baoshang

Hai Chuan just got married. The bride's name was Goldie.

One day that year Japanese devils came to Little Village and massacred so many folks that its river turned bloody red. The Japs' atrocities lit the fire of hatred in the hearts of the villagers. That same evening, a group of young men, led by Yang, were ready to go into the mountains to join the guerrillas.

Hai Chuan, however, didn't want to leave his newly married bride behind. Disappointed, Goldie said: I thought I had married a real man, not a chicken-hearted sissy.

His face reddening, Hai Chuan said: All right, just you wait for the day I'm back with a few Japs' skulls for you to pee in.

A smile blossomed on Goldie's face: That's my man! You go and join the guerrillas and I'll wait for you, eight years, ten years, a lifetime, no matter.

So Hai Chuan went with Yang and the group of young men into the mountains.

Eight months later Goldie gave birth to a son and named him Little Chuan.

Goldie waited for eight years. Hai Chuan didn't return, saying he had to go on to fight Chiang Kai-shek now that the Japs were gone. So Goldie waited for another three years. Still Hai Chuan didn't return, saying he had to go to Korea to fight the Americans. So Goldie waited for a few more years. Then, she was told that Hai Chuan, now a general, didn't want her any more even though she had waited for him for so many years; he had married a modern city girl.

Goldie cried for three days and nights. On the fourth day she went to the village river to wash her tears and sorrow. She buried her anger and sadness deep down and placed all her hope on bringing up her son as best she could. As time flew by like water in the river, Goldie's world began to shine with hope and promise. Whenever folks praised Goldie, they would have a few unkind words about the heartless Hai Chuan. It was in such an environment that Little Chuan finally grew up, got married, and became a father himself. One day, his son asked him:

"Pa, everybody else has a grandma and grandpa, why me, only grandma, but no grandpa?"

Little Chuan muttered angrily: "Grandma is all we need. Who cares about Grandpa!"

Now, General Hai Chuan finally retired. Every day he walked with his birds and watered his flowers while reliving his past in his mind. All the fierce battles he had fought, big and small, became a blur gradually as the dust of time settled in his memory. In their place re-emerged the picture of a little village where he grew up, a little river that had nourished him, and a bride he had left behind many years ago. Sorrow would hit him and hit him hard. Goldie must be in her 70s now. And the son. Yes, the son must be about 50 years old, too. The old general missed his home village badly. One day he returned, with a deep sense of guilt, and stood in front of Goldie.

"Goldie, I've wronged you. . . . "

Goldie was calm as the cloudless autumn sky. She called in her son, and then her grandson, to meet the guest. "This is your grandpa," she said to her grandson. The old general burst into tears. He didn't dare to say anything tender to Little Chuan, but gathered his grandson in his arms and kissed him like mad.

The old general had been used to being treated like an important guest, but being treated like this in his own "home" made him feel awkward and heavy-hearted. He was especially saddened by the coldness his own son, Little Chuan, showed him. During dinner that evening wine was served. After a few cups, the old general didn't feel well and turned in early. When he woke up, the light was still on in the outer room. Someone was saying something. It was Goldie:

"Listen to me, Little Chuan, your pa stepped forward when our country was in grave danger. He fought in so many wars, going into battles with his head in his hand, not knowing whether he would live or die the next instant. He is a real man. If he owes anything to anyone, he owes it to me alone. Whatever he owed to you, I made it up on his behalf long ago. If you treat your pa like that again, I won't let you get away with it. . . . "

Tears gushed down his cheeks as the battle-hardened old general lay on the *kang* and listened. He thought, "Goldie is a piece of real, genuine gold! How in the world could I have abandoned her?"

(2001)

Straw Ring

Jinguang

Minzi and Erniu were high school classmates. They were good friends. Upon graduation, Minzi asked his family to go to Erniu's to propose. Soon afterwards the two good friends were engaged.

Minzi's family was poor. He had several brothers. The family of eight squeezed together in a simple shingle-roofed house which had only three rooms. But Erniu didn't mind. Poverty, she said, didn't mean

Minzi had no potential and prospect. As long as they loved each other and worked hard, they would be happy.

One thing Minzi's family had plenty of, though, was manpower. During harvest time his parents would tell him to go and help Erniu's family. One day, Minzi came to Erniu's to help harvest wheat. The two of them worked for hours on the Red Soil Slope under a scorching sun. Then Erniu urged Minzi to take a break under a big persimmon tree and drink some water. So Minzi sat down, drank some water, and the two of them chitchatted. Before long Minzi reached for the sickle and was ready to go back to work. Erniu grabbed his arm and said: "What's the hurry? Want to work yourself to death?" Minzi smiled and sat down again.

Erniu said: "So, Minzi, what will our life be like when we get married, with no house of our own and no money, either?"

Minzi picked up a stalk of wheat, removed the grain-bearing top, gestured with the remaining stem as he said: "We may not have money, but we have spirit and will. Remember I was good at writing in school. I'll continue to write and write my way into the city. Then, I'll bring you over to the city with me."

Erniu was surprised: "Really? Is that possible? Will you still want me when you are in a big city?"

Minzi said: "Hey, I am not worth a cent now and you still like me so much. I am not that kind of man, you know."

At this Erniu rested her head on Minzi's arm happily.

Minzi twisted the straw in his hands a couple of times and said: "Give me your hand."

Erniu looked up and saw a ring made of the straw. She gave him her hand. Solemnly Minzi put the ring on Erniu's finger. Erniu gazed at the ring for a long while as if it were the most precious thing in the world. Then she turned, put her arms around his neck, and kissed him on the cheek.

Minzi was indeed a goal-driven young man. During the next two years he read and wrote whenever he had time and published over 30 short stories and essays here and there in regional newspapers. Soon he became a well-known freelance writer in the county. When the County Writers Association needed another artist in residence to strengthen its program, Minzi was the one chosen. So he went to the city and became a full-time writer there.

Soon after he started at the County Writers Association, Minzi wrote two feature stories about the Tobacco Company. Its general manager was thrilled by the stories and promised to help if he needed anything. So Minzi asked the manager if he could arrange for Erniu to work in his company. The manager beat his chest and said: No problem. I've done it so many times before. One more time is nothing. So, within two months, Erniu started to work at the Tobacco Company as a full time employee.

The day Erniu moved to the city Minzi celebrated in a fancy restaurant called "Fortune Food." When the last drop of a big bottle of wine was gone, Minzi, somewhat tipsy, said: "Honey, we've made it into the city finally."

Erniu held his hand and said: "Yes, thanks to my man's can-do spirit and hard work."

Rubbing Erniu's hand in his own, Minzi said: "What a beautiful hand you've got here. I'll buy you a ring when I've made more money. Then you get to taste what it is like to live like city folks." With that he lifted her hand and kissed it like the romantic he was.

Minzi was a man of his word. If he promised something, he would deliver no matter what. Since that day the idea of buying Erniu a ring had been firmly lodged in his mind. However, given the low salary from the County Writers Association, Erniu giving birth to a baby daughter, which meant so much more to take care of at home, and his endless writing assignments and other work, the idea sank deeper in his mind, day by day, and year by year, until he had completely forgotten.

In the blink of an eye their tenth wedding anniversary had arrived. That day Erniu prepared ten delicious dishes at home and placed a bottle of good wine on the table. When Minzi came back from work, he was surprised. He patted his forehead and exclaimed: "Oh my, today's our tenth wedding anniversary! How could I have forgotten?"

With that he turned to go. Erniu grabbed his arm: "Where are you going?"

Minzi said: "I promised to buy you a ring, but haven't delivered yet. I have to go now before they close shop. . . . "

Erniu said, still holding his arm, "Oh, that won't be necessary. I've a ring already."

Minzi was surprised once again: "Already have one? When did you buy it?"

Erniu turned, opened a trunk, took out a red silky pouch, and handed to Minzi.

Confused, Minzi took over the pouch and gazed at Erniu. With a smile blossoming on her face, Erniu said: "Open it."

So Minzi opened it with careful fingers, layer after layer. When he reached the last layer, Minzi's hands quivered. So Erniu opened it for him. There on Minzi's palm was the same straw ring he had given her many years ago.

Minzi sighed with disappointment: "Ah, I thought it was a real one. Why are you still keeping this?"

Erniu said: "A ring is only a token. Straw ring or gold ring, it won't make any difference if you wear it in your heart. This ring from you I've always worn it in my heart. It's more precious than gold."

Minzi was touched beyond words. All he could do was to gather Erniu in his arms and hold her tight.

(2001)

Marriage Certificate
Mo Xiaomi

When their home caught fire, so many valuable things were burnt with it. Including their marriage certificate.

At the time the couple didn't think much of it. They continued to be husband and wife, and live their life together. If they could go on living like that until they were very old, perhaps that certificate would never be missed.

Yet the problem was they couldn't bear to live with each other any more and were getting ready to divorce.

The custody of the children and division of property and so on had all been talked about and agreed upon. So, one day, the two went to the Community Marriage Registrar's Office to finalize the paperwork. Yet when the registrar asked them to show their marriage certificate, they had nothing to show. They said their colleagues, neighbors, relatives, and friends could all vouch for them. Why did they need any certificate to prove it? The registrar, however, did not budge: "The certificate is a prerequisite. You have to prove that you *are* a couple first before you can be certified that you *aren't* a couple any more, don't you?"

So the two went about proving that they *were* a couple.

First, they found the "go-between" who introduced them to each other. The "go-between" confirmed by establishing the fact of how they had got to know each other, fallen in love, and gotten married.

They then found their mutual friends, a couple around the same age as they. That couple confirmed by establishing the fact of the two couples going on a honeymoon trip together.

They also found their former neighbors who confirmed by

establishing the fact of how the couple had become parents when their twins were born.

Finally they went back to their own employers. The personnel office of each side confirmed their marital status with a letter.

Then, with all these pieces of proof in hand they went back to the Marriage Registrar's Office. The registrar examined each document carefully and reissued them a marriage certificate.

It had taken them several months of single-minded, concerted efforts (they hadn't been of the same mind for so long) to prove they *were* a couple. Now, it seemed so easy to change *were* into *weren't*.

All of a sudden, though, the two began to hesitate. Since so many people had shown proof that they were a couple, why didn't they try again to prove that to themselves?

(2001)

Money Order

Bai Xuechu

When his father's funeral was over, Cheng Gang asked his mother to leave the village and come with him to Changsha. Mother wouldn't say yes no matter what. I'm used to the quiet in the countryside, she said, and won't feel comfortable in the hustle and bustle of the city. Cheng Gang knew only too well that mother didn't want to leave his buried father behind. When he was ready to leave, Chen Gang said to his mother: You never let me send you any money. From now on, however,

I'll send you 200 *yuan* support money a month. Mother said: It's not expensive living in the countryside. One hundred *yuan* is plenty if you really want to send.

Cheng Gang's home village is quite out of the way. The rural mailman comes only once or twice a month. Since in the recent years many young folks have left to be migrant workers elsewhere, their elderly parents are waiting for news from faraway places every day. That's why the day the mailman comes is as big a deal as a holiday. The moment he steps into the village he will be surrounded by a crowd of elderly aunties and old grannies, asking if there is any mail for them. Then, they will form groups of three or five to share their latest happy tidings and each other's joy.

On this particular day the mailman came again. Mother was cutting vegetables in the garden behind the house. Her neighbor Auntie Zhang had to call out several times before mother realized what was going on. She hurried to where the mailman was and was handed a slip of paper: a money order. Mother's face blossomed with joy right away: It's from my son Cheng Gang. Auntie Zhang took over the money order, stared at it over and again, and said, enviously: Oh my, 2,400 *yuan*! At this everyone swarmed over. The money order passed from one hand to another like some precious treasure until all the aunties and grannies had seen it, their faces lit with envious smile.

It was the first time Mother received money from her son and it was such a big sum! Mother was too thrilled to sleep that day. She got up in the middle of night and wrote her son a letter. Although mother didn't go to school, both father and the village school teacher had taught her a few words. Mother's letter had only a few lines asking Cheng Gang why he had sent so much money. Hadn't she said 100 *yuan* a month would be plenty? In his reply letter Cheng Gang said that since the mailman came to the village only once or twice a month, he was concerned that mother would not receive his support money in time. He said his salary was good and he had promised 200 *yuan* a month. Whatever money mother couldn't spend, she could put it aside for a rainy day.

Mother smiled happily when she read Cheng Gang's letter.

Months passed before Cheng Gang received another letter from Mother. It was short as before: Cheng Gang, you shouldn't send a whole year's support money in one sum. Beginning next year, be sure to send it once a month.

Before long another year had passed. Cheng Gang had wanted to go back to visit his mother but had got caught up working on a project against a deadline. He had wanted to send the support money once a month, as instructed, yet, out of concern that he might forget, he sent all 2,400 *yuan* in one big sum again. About 20 days later, Cheng Gang received a 2,400 *yuan* money order: It was sent by his mother. He was surprised and was just about to write his mother when he received another letter from her.

Mother said in this letter: Be sure to send money by the month. Otherwise, I don't want a cent from you!

One day Cheng Gang ran into a migrant worker from his home village and took him to a restaurant. In the course of the meal Cheng Gang inquired about his mother. The man said: Although your mother lives alone, she is quite happy. On the day the mailman comes, your mother is joyous beyond anything, as if it were a big holiday. And when she receives your money order, her joy will last for several days.

Cheng Gang's eyes were filled with tears. He knew now that mother had insisted he send her money once a month because she wanted to experience that kind of joy twelve times a year. It was not the money that she cared about, but the love of her son so far away.

(2002)

Soy Sauce

Zhao Wenhui

Xiu Juan and Xi Shun were college classmates. Upon graduation Xiu Juan was given a teaching position by the college, but for love she went with Xi Shun to this county town. The county education bureau had only one position in town for the two of them; the other had to go to a faraway place. So Xi Shun went to the Pointed Hill Valley grade school about 80 *li* from the county town. The living conditions there were bad and there was no transportation. Xi Shun could come back to visit only once a month. Everything at home fell on the shoulders of Xi Juan.

It wasn't too bad in the beginning. Once they had a baby, however, it proved to be tough on Xi Juan. Their salaries were not good. They needed to send support money to Xi Shun's parents, too. So they were tight all the time. Xiu Juan planned and economized on everything to make it work. For three years she didn't even buy one new dress. She was also very kind to Xi Shun's mother. One time the elderly woman came to visit. Xi Juan took her to the doctor for a physical, bought her medicine, prepared food for her, and carried warm water for her to wash with in the evening. With her thick, cotton-padded clothes on the elderly woman couldn't bend enough to wash her own feet. Seeing this, Xiu Juan squatted down, grasped her feet and began to wash. Afterwards, Xiu Juan clipped mother-in-law's toenails, too. The elderly woman said: "This is the first time I have clipped my nails the entire winter. . . . " That evening she sobbed for half of the night, her pillow wet with happy tears. Later, after hearing this from his mother, Xi Shun grasped Xiu Juan's hands and said: "What can I do to repay you for the rest of my life!"

During those days they were so in love with each other. While at school, Xi Shun would think of Xiu Juan all the time and often dream

of her taking their child to kindergarten. One time a mountain flood
cut through the road so Xi Shun couldn't go home for more than two
months. As soon as the road was fixed, he jumped on the first bus to the
county town.

When he saw Xiu Juan, his eyes glowed with a flame of desire. Yet neither
of them dared to do anything because their five-and-a-half year old son was
"in the way." Son asked father to tell him stories, so Xi Shun told him stories
while gripping Xiu Juan's hand and feeling it hungrily. Xiu Juan responded
likewise, her hand quivering. Both of them felt time was creeping too slowly.
Then, Xiu Juan gave their son a *yuan* and asked him to go to the small stand at
the alley entrance to buy a pack of noodles. Thrilled, the boy left half dancing
with the money in hand. Xiu Juan and Xi Shun had just snuggled together
when the son returned and banged on the door. This time Xi Shun came up
with a better idea. He went to the kitchen, came back with a plate, and told
his son to go and buy half a *jin of* soy sauce at the small grocery. "Son," he
encouraged, "I'm sure you can ace this challenging assignment!" The boy
puffed out his chest like a grown-up and marched away with the plate.

This time it worked. Xi Shun and Xiu Juan barely had enough time
to satisfy their hunger for each other when their son returned, crying:
"I walked slowly and carefully but the soy sauce still spilt. I didn't do a
good job with the assignment!" Xiu Juan gathered her son in her arms
and smiled, both shame and joy in her eyes.

Later, Xi Shun left his teaching job and started to work for the local
township government. From administrative assistant to deputy town
commissioner to commissioner to Party Chief to the Director of County
Petrochemical Fertilizer Factory, Xi Shun moved up step by step. Since
the fertilizer factory was the backbone of the county's industries, Xi
Shun's car was the best in the entire county. Dining and staying in
expensive hotels became a routine in his life, too. He changed gradually.
Before long he hooked up with a new college graduate. Xiu Juan refused

to believe what she had heard until one day Xi Shun asked for a divorce. Then she knew the same story she had seen on TV had happened to her.

When their son, now a college student, knew this, he came all the way home to talk to his father. But Xi Shun wouldn't listen. Desperate, the son said: "If you divorce mother, you won't be my dad any more." But Xi Shun had already made up his mind: "You will still be my son, no matter how you feel about me. However, I have to follow through on this." Hearing of this, Xiu Juan knew there was no hope.

Xi Shun was thrilled beyond himself when Xiu Juan said yes to his request. He took out the divorce agreement and asked Xiu Juan to sign. Xiu Juan held the pen between her quivering fingers. Her son said: "Ma, don't sign!" Biting her lip bitterly, Xiu Juan put her name on the agreement. While gathering the signed agreement, Xi Shun said: "You know where to find me when you run into difficulties."

Xiu Juan didn't say a word. Xi Shun wanted to leave right away but felt it would be too soon. So the three of them sat there, as if frozen. The room was deadly quiet.

A long while had passed when Xiu Juan stood up suddenly, went to the kitchen, came back with a plate, and thrust it into her son's hand: "Go and buy half a *jin* of soy sauce!" The son looked at his mother, confused, and didn't move. Xiu Juan cried out: "So, you don't listen to me, either!" Tears welled up in her eyes. Seeing this, the son took the plate and left for the small grocery.

Xi Shun was stunned. That plate pounded his soul like a hammer and opened up a floodgate of memories. His face reddened right away as if he had been slapped hard left and right, his head low. When the son returned with the soy sauce, he saw his father burning a sheet of paper with his cigarette lighter.

(2002)

The Secret

Liu Liying

An's wife likes to play poker.

Gan's wife also likes to play poker.

When they have leisure time, An takes his wife to Gan's to play poker. The four of them have fun playing poker. Yet, there is a problem: An and his wife lose all the time.

An's wife says An is slow and doesn't know how to play a hand.

An, on the other hand, thinks his wife doesn't know how to play cards.

Words have been exchanged between them several times. Once it got so bad both threw down the cards at the same time and left at once, fuming with anger.

After An and his wife leave, Gan's wife says to Gan, "This is not good, this is not good."

Gan says, "I'll go and invite them back. When they're here, let's swap. You and An play as a pair and me and An's wife as a pair."

Gan and An live in the same compound. So it doesn't take long to get An and his wife back.

Now that An and Gan's wife play as a pair, when An plays the wrong card sometimes, she doesn't feel comfortable scolding him. Sometimes Gan's wife plays the wrong card, too, and An doesn't feel comfortable saying anything, either. That evening the four of them play all the way till morning.

From then on whenever they have free time, they play poker. Once, as soon as An and his wife leave, Gan's wife makes a very long face.

Gan says, "Your face is like a long eggplant."

His wife says, "Of course my face is not as good-looking as An's wife's."

Gan says, "One hundred An's wives put together wouldn't be as good-looking as you."

His wife says, "Your mind was not on the game at all tonight. You were looking at An's wife all the time, 27 times altogether, to be exact."

Gan says, "Foolish woman! I was looking at the TV."

The next day An and his wife come again to play poker.

This time Gan's wife turns the TV off.

Gan tries to focus on the game. Gradually, though, Gan becomes somewhat less vigilant. He casts a quick glance at An's wife and then pretends as if nothing has happened. This time around, however, Gan has become wiser. Every time he looks at An's wife, he turns to look at his wife first. If his wife's eyes are on him, he tries his best to refrain from looking at An's wife.

When An and his wife have left, Gan's wife asks Gan: "You were looking at An's wife on the sly again tonight! Altogether 18 times. Is she that good-looking?"

Gan feels embarrassed.

Gan says: "Foolish woman!"

Gan's wife says: "I am the dumbest woman under the sky! Right in front of my eyes my man and someone else's wife exchange amorous glances!"

This time it is Gan's turn to be upset.

He pulls a long, long face.

His wife says, "Your face is like a pumpkin."

Gan says, "Let's not play poker any more."

His wife says, "Really?"

Gan says, "I won't play this stupid game anymore."

When An and his wife are home, he says to her, "The last time we played poker, you looked up at Gan 27 times. Today you looked 18 times."

An's wife stares at An and stares and stares.

An stares at his wife and stares and stares.

His wife says: "Whoever goes to the Gan's to play poker again is the turtle's son."

A few days later, Gan says to his wife, "At work today An came to my office and stayed for a long time. Perhaps An wants to come and play poker."

His wife says, "I ran into An's wife in the street yesterday. Oh, she was much warmer than usual. You and An are colleagues and we live in the same compound. Why don't you go and ask them over."

When An gets home, he says to his wife, "I spent quite a bit of time in Gan's office today. I was afraid that he was upset by us not going over to play poker."

An's wife says, "Faraway relatives are not as good as nearby neighbors. Whenever I run into Gan's wife, I feel bad. Why, all of a sudden, we don't go to play anymore. Every time we were there, they treated us to cigarettes and tea. Wouldn't they say things about us?"

An says, "Let's go then."

An and his wife run into Gan on their way.

Gan says, "Play poker."

An says, "Play poker."

This time around Gan and his wife are even more hospitable than before. The more they are so, the more An and his wife feel they are not worthy of such a warm reception.

That night when An returns home, he kicks his wife's slippers under the bed.

An's wife smashes An's favorite ashtray to pieces.

An's wife says, "Whoever goes to the Gan's to play poker again is the son of the turtle's son."

Gan and his wife also go through a bloodless battle. They don't speak to each for several days.

But before long, the four get together to play poker again.

Neither family wants to say "let's not play any more" first.

The last time they played poker was June perhaps, or August. The reason for discontinuing the poker game was Gan. He was hurt in a car accident which left him in a vegetative state. Around this time, An's wife came to see Gan's wife. An's wife wanted to tell the secret between her and Gan. Given the state Gan was in, it didn't look like they would ever play poker together again.

Gan's wife, however, didn't want An's wife to tell.

Gan's wife said, "No need to try and comfort me. I won't abandon Gan. I will take care of Gan for the rest of my life."

An's wife suddenly realized something: Given the state Gan is in, Gan's wife will never believe her even if she tells the secret between her and Gan.

Now An's wife regretted having had the secret with Gan: Looking at each other's face as a signal of what card to play.

(2004)

Happy Family
Wu Di

Like any other day he returns home from work. He is about to take out the key to open the door when the door opens. She stands by the door, a smile on her face. One, two, three kids peek from inside to greet him: "Welcome home, dad."

The three kids are beautiful. So is she. The kids busy themselves around him excitedly, getting him his slippers, his tea, his newspapers. He sits down in the cushioned chair, rests his head against its back, and takes a deep breath. It feels so different with a woman around at home. He notices she has cleaned the curtains and the cushions and tidied up things elsewhere. Somehow the entire room looks much brighter than before.

The kids are bright and thoughtful. They all come over to kiss him, the youngest one still smells like a baby. They "pester" him for a while, asking if he is exhausted from work, if he knows the latest news, and so on. They are sensitive to even his facial expressions so they know how far they can go and what questions they should not ask. They are experienced. Third Hair, the youngest, even recites a Tang poem for him. He is amazed. It's taught by the kindergarten teacher, he is told. He likes to call the kids this way: "Big Hair, Second Hair, Third Hair." They are like the kids he has seen on the television: bright, beautiful, and thoughtful. The boy keeps long hair, like a girl, his eyes big and deep. The girls have on puffy silky skirts and squat on the floor like little princesses.

He likes to call her "Mei." She comes out from the kitchen. She is beautiful, but not the in-your-face kind of beauty. It's the housewife kind of beauty, not quite like that of a young female secretary or a film star. She has on some light makeup, her thin lips fresh red. She tells him what kind of dishes she has prepared. They are all his favorite.

During dinner he sits at the head of the table where the head of a family is supposed to sit. The kids are enthusiastic and chatter with him nonstop. They are ready to answer any question he puts to them and are surprised by none. He asks: "How do you like Uncle Qin?" The kids reply without hesitation: "Dad, we like you better." She stops her chopsticks, smiles, and exchanges a knowing glance between them. Heavens, how can he not melt into this all? Third Hair goes on to say: "Uncle Qin likes to cry. He cries even when he dines with us." It feels so real, so like a warm, sweet, happy family. He is ready to cry, too.

A happy evening is finally over. She is ready to leave with the three kids. Third Hair prints on his face one last kiss with the same baby fragrant mouth. They are all neatly dressed as if they are going somewhere. They all say "goodbye" so sweetly. Just before they leave, he hands her an envelope with money in it. She hands him a card, the same promotion card of their company which he has seen so many times before. Yet he reads it one more time:

FIRST-RATE WARM FEELING OF FAMILY
Good news for single people in the world: Our company provides happy families of all stripes and types to meet the emotional needs of all kinds of single, lonely people. . . .

He breaks into a smile. Perhaps he should try a different flavor next time, a hot and spicy one that gives you no peace whatsoever. Old Qin said: You should try that kind of family life, too. It can be very exciting.

(2000)

portraits

Daigou

Shen Congwen

"Bastard! Won't get up until your Old Man spanks your ass?"

"Oh. . . . my sole still hurts so!" Daigou[3] screwed up his face to look as if ready to cry.

But he knew Pop's hands, which were good not only for pinching the earlobes, but also for picking pears, even hard and green ones, and bringing them to him. So, while wanting to whine more about his sole still hurting, he slowly let his hairy head peer out of the messy mosquito net of crude linen—and got out of bed.

"Hurry! Hurry up! Don't drag your feet!"

"Oh. . . ."

On a small, short-legged stool in the small, gloomy thatched hut sat Pop, Old Ou; he was braiding a straw string into an "ear" on a straw shoe. The hut, windowless, was dark and he had to work by the light leaking in from a crack in the fireplace.

"Don't you see Daigou of the fucking Shi's, that Hairy Duckling, already crawling up the Hill before daybreak?"

"My foot still—"

"Can't go for a little hurt like that?"

Daigo wiped his gummy eyes with the back of his hand, shook to loosen his shoulders, took a pair of straw shoes from the mud wall, and sat down to the left of Pop.

"I'll go and get a big load of straw—"

"Even ghosts wouldn't need your straw for the next few days. . . . What're you afraid of? Why can't you go and cut on the other side of the hill? If the Monk comes, run a bit faster is all. If you can't get to this side of the hollows, just throw it into the bushes, and climb up a tree. The poor old Monk, blurry-eyed, won't be able to overtake you. He will just peer around and then return to the Temple to sleep again—then you go back, carefully, all right?"

"Easy for you to say."

"Try not to cut with too much noise."

"What if he steals over and catches me? What if?"

"Stupid bastard! He hollers something like 'Stop thief! Stop thief! Anyone catches the little Miao devil, who dares to steal my firewood, please help me punch him to death!' He's really more bark than bite, trying to scare off little kids is all! You really think he'll dare to punch you to death if he ever catches you?"

Daigou trembled again at the thought of what had happened yesterday. Only he knew why he trembled; Pop didn't even notice.

. . . Cut! Cut! Cut! No sooner when his sickle had cut into the tree than its echo was already bounced back. Hairy Duckling, happy, was humming away—

Grand temple perches atop mountain high,
Multitudes gather here from far and wide.
Others ask blessings for their children,
Yours truly, for none but my lovely bride.

Suddenly, the old Monk, like a devil, appeared this side of the red wall. He rolled up the long sleeves of his robe and hollered, "Stop thief! Stop these fucking bastards!" and dashed toward where they were. Realizing the old Monk meant business, they gave up the unfinished tree and ran for it. They ran like mad, jumping through the woods and clamoring over two damn hollows, and ran, and ran, until they couldn't hear the old Monk hollering "Stop. . . ." They were out of danger now.

However, while running like mad, he stepped on a thorny twig, which seized the opportunity and bit into his sole. When Hairy Duckling managed to pull it out, so much blood had already been lost. And even this morning, the foot still hurt when touching the ground.

The foot thing was no big deal really, compared to the devilish face of the Monk. It still dangled in his mind and seemed to have the power to shrink Daigou into a tiny size, smaller even than the ants promenading on the kitchen stove.

Finally, in a faltering voice, he managed to give the reason why he didn't want to go.

"If I go again and am caught, even if he doesn't punch me to death, he can tie up my arms with some rope and haul me up high at the mountain gate for public display. That he can certainly do! Then, I'll be at the mercy of womenfolk on their way to the Temple, this one staring at me this way, and that one staring at me that way, cussing at the same time: 'Serves the little bandit right!' 'This little devil, already stealing at this fucking age, will have to be beheaded when he grows up!' and so on. How can I face the world after that?"

"Then, your Old Man will go to the Zhao's of Big Plains and ask Master Zhao to bail you out."

Upon hearing this from his old man, Daigo couldn't come up with any more excuse. If he were a city kid with some schooling, he might have found another way to reason with Pop. Poor illiterates, they were so dumb!

Bored and at the end of his wits, Daigo stood up, stretched with a yawn, and walked toward the kitchen stove, where he grabbed the sickle on the pole and fastened it behind his buttocks. Then, glancing at the ants on the kitchen stove, he said—

"Pop, get an extra piece of bean curd when you go to town today."

And left.

Between not being good at housekeeping and having a weakness for homemade wine for the sake of his joints, Old Ou was a little tight for cash. So he had to ask his ten-year-old to go to the other side of the Nanhua Temple on the hill and do something risky there. But he was a careful and confident man. He still remembered the fortune Blind Yang had told him three years ago: His life was caught in a swift current at the moment and would not change course until six years later. So he had decided to be patient and wait out the six years before he would quit drinking. In case Daigou was indeed seized by the Monk, he had figured, and tied up and hauled up the mountain gate for public display, he could take care of it like when Daigou's pop of the Shi's had done when caught stealing bamboo: He would carry a load of pine needles to Zhao Dafa's, knock his head at the feet of Dafa, and then his wife, and even the biggest trouble in the world would be gone. What Dafa had told him still rang in his ears: "Whenever you're in trouble with the Temple, big or small, come to me and it's as good as taken care of, 'cause the Monk would not dare to go against my will. I saw him cooking pig feet once. Once the word gets out, it'd be all over with him!"

However, Old Ou knew that he hadn't forced Daigou to go and be scared by the old Monk on account of Dafa's influence alone. In fact he had something else to fall back on. He knew that Daigou, young as he was, was smart and fast, and would never be caught by the blurry-eyed old Monk. Otherwise, on one side of the scale: a big load of dry pine needles, worth well over 200 units of money, traded for someone's influence; on the other side of the scale: a piece of firewood he didn't even get—he knew how to do the math.

(1926)

A Singer That Can Sing

Wang Meng

No one applauded when the singer finished her performance. So she said during a meeting afterwards: "What in the world does applause mean? Beauty? Art? Gold? How much is one *jin* of applause worth? Just some clapping of hands from the audience and she began to tread on the cloud, forgot who she really is, was elected a star, went to places by airplane, and recorded albums. What nonsense! What travesty of the soul! Believe it or not, if I were to swing my butt and sing some phony songs, I would receive much louder applause!"

She suggested a study be conducted to analyze audience responses to prove her point that applause had zero or negative value.

Not long after this, at the end of another performance of hers, the whole place thundered with applause. So she said during a meeting afterwards: "We sing songs to entertain the audience. If the audience doesn't like it, what good would a song do no matter how good its lyrics and melody? The masses have the sharpest eyes and they all have a scale in their heart. If the masses don't like to see and don't like to hear what we do, then we are not serving the broad masses of the people, but a small handful of the elite only, and that is a serious mistake, that is isolating ourselves from the broad masses, and that is narcissistic. What I heard was not just clapping of hands, but the beating of so many warm, passionate hearts!"

Sometime later, a meeting was held to discuss some unhealthy trends among singers and ways to guide the audience's tastes and raise their level of appreciation. She used the aforementioned applause-less performance as an example and proudly declared:

"I've stood my ground! I've stood my ground! I've stood my ground!"

Not long after this, another meeting was held to discuss the reasons why too few songs were well liked by the masses and ways to remedy the situation. She used the aforementioned thunderously applauded performance as an example and proudly declared:

"I've done it! I've done it! I've done it!"

(1985)

The Story Outside My Window
Yide'erfu

The window of my office faces a street. On this street is a farmer's market where no motor vehicles are allowed.

The first thing I do when I get to my office on hot summer days is to open the window for better air circulation.

One day, as soon as I opened the window, a middle-aged peasant came over and squatted down against the wall. In his hands was an old, dirty, torn white fur coat. What's the good of carrying such a lousy fur coat on such a hot day? I wondered.

Everyday for the next ten days this peasant would come and squat right outside my window, carrying in his hands the same lousy fur coat. Early in the morning when we had just come to work he would hurry over, sweaty, squat down, take a bite from the dry bun he had brought with him, and sip some water now and then. When we left for home at the end of the day, he would leave, too.

What's he really up to, coming to my window everyday like this? I began to be suspicious. One day, I peeked outside the window and asked him:

"Who are you?"

"I'm a peasant."

"Where are you from?"

"Elm Bay."

"Why are you coming here everyday?"

"Business."

"Business?"

He patted the ragged fur coat spread out on his knees: "To sell this thing here."

I laughed. "Who would want to buy your fur coat in this season? Besides, it is so hopelessly old and ragged. Even if someone wanted to buy it, he wouldn't pay you enough for even one meal. I'd go home, if I were you. It's a waste of time, not to mention the hot weather."

He listened, laughed "hee" twice, and shook his head.

My advice had fallen on deaf ears. Every day he would still come and every day he would squat right outside my window.

Elm Bay is about ten *li* outside the city. Every day he would journey for about twenty *li*, all on foot, coming in the morning and going home in the evening, for what? Selling that lousy fur coat? Is it worth it? I began to suspect there was something wrong with him.

One day he peeked inside my window and asked:

"Comrade, do foreigners come to this city at all?"

"This city is open to foreign visitors," I told him. "They come quite often."

His sun-baked face brightened up. He grinned and exclaimed, yellowed teeth visible through thick lips.

"Excellent! Excellent!" He said. "I won't be waiting for nothing then!"

I was rather perplexed and asked: "Why did you ask about the foreigners?"

He smiled mysteriously, "Oh, so I can sell them this fur coat of mine!"

"Foreigners buying that lousy fur coat of yours?"

"You don't know? Let me tell you something. These foreigners, they don't like our new things, but they really fancy our old things, the older, the more ragged, the better!"

"Who told you this?"

"Big Uncle of my nephew Ben."

"Where?"

"In this city of yours, too. About a month ago he went to my nephew's and said this. A lot of folks were present. He said he took a very old, broken armchair, a heirloom of some sort, to the farmer's market. A foreigner bought it from him for ten thousand *yuan*. Big Uncle became a rich ten-thousand-aire right there!"

"So, you found this old, dirty, ragged fur coat to trade for a foreigner's money and want to become a ten-thousand-aire too, is that it?!"

The peasant laughed "hee" again as he squatted down. He caught sight of a tall, blond-haired man passing by. As if having seen the God of Fortune himself, he bolted up, ran after the man, stopped him, thrust the fur coat in his face, and laughed "hee."

The tall man did not look amused at all. He was even more upset when the peasant, crazy-like, laughing, thrust the dirty fur coat in his face. The tall man hollered sternly: "What are you doing? Get lost!"

"You don't want to buy my fur coat? This fur coat of mine is old, dirty, a real heirloom!"

"You think I'm crazy? Buy this lousy fur coat of yours?!" The tall man exclaimed as he dodged and hurried away, as if fleeing a ghost.

The peasant watched the back of the tall man and cussed angrily: "Fuck! Fake foreigner!" Crestfallen, he returned to my window.

Although I found the whole thing ridiculous, I felt sorry for him, too. So I tried to talk him out of it again:

"Listen. I'm going to say this again: Forget about selling this lousy fur coat of yours. Even if a "real" foreigner comes, he wouldn't buy it from you, either. So, why don't you go back to Elm Bay and be happy with working in the fields."

"Working in the fields? How much money can I make working in the fields?"

"But it's better than squatting here every day and not making anything, not to mention this brutal weather."

"I want to try my luck. Someday I'll be lucky."

He is both ignorant and stubborn.

He comes here every day to wait for his luck, but his luck never shows up.

Right at this moment, he is still squatting right outside my window.

(1989)

Big Feet Zhuang

Hu Qiyong

Many years ago when she was being led off the bridal boat by the go-between, her head covered with a big red veil, the onlookers couldn't help but let their eyes wander downward, and then, someone cried out, as if having discovered something amazing:

"Big Feet!"

That's how the nickname "Big Feet Zhuang" became known in the Five Li Bridge area and beyond.

Big Feet Zhuang and her man had got together when they became "smitten with each other." At the time, her blind would-be mother-in-law did not approve of them getting married on account of this pair of "Big Feet." The blind would-be mother-in-law; the blind would-be mother-in-law's mother-in-law; the blind would-be mother-in-law's mother-in-law's mother-in-law, and the mothers-in-law of many generations back, had all had small, bound feet. All except for this generation, which had gotten itself a "Big Feet" daughter-in-law. So, the blind would-be mother-in-law felt her family's proud tradition would be spoiled. Only when the son whispered into his mother's ear that he had already gotten the girl "in the family way" did she relent, following a deep sigh. Luckily, unlike other mothers-in-law who had to "turn a blind eye" to things they didn't quite approve of, this blind mother-in-law actually couldn't see anything at all. Besides, less than half a year had passed before Big Feet Zhuang gave birth to a precious son, who was treasured by her man's family. It was not until then that true "peaceful coexistence" became possible between the mother-in-law and the daughter-in-law.

Good times didn't last long. Shortly after the son was born, Big Feet Zhuang's man caught a sudden illness and died before he knew what hit him. Big Feet Zhuang mourned in white from head to feet and cried until the sky had collapsed upon the dark earth. The blind mother-in-law all but cried herself dead. When the loud funeral was finally over, the relationship between the mother-in-law and daughter-in-law deteriorated fast. The blind mother-in-law kept mumbling of her daughter-in-law's big feet being bad luck, and her being the "ill star" that extinguished the light of life in her man. Everyday when Big Feet Zhuang carried food and water to her blind mother-in-law's bedside, there was the same complaint of it being either too hot or too cold, too salty or too tasteless. Several times the blind mother-in-law even threw the bowls onto the ground. Big Feet Zhuang felt disheartened and felt that life not worth living at all. If it hadn't been for her cute, precious little son, she would have hanged herself with a rope so she could go and join the ghost of her dead man.

Thus they jolted on together for several years until one day the blind mother-in-law embarked on her eternal journey to the afterlife. Once everything had been taken care of, Big Feet Zhuang took a look at herself in the mirror contained in the big red box used on her wedding day many years ago. She saw a gray-haired woman.

Her precious son had grown up and become manager of the village factory. He had been dating someone without letting her in on it. How could she not have gotten old? One day, the son brought home the would-be daughter-in-law. The girl was pretty enough and dressed tastefully from head to feet. Just when she was grinning with happiness, Big Feet Zhuang's eyes fell on a spot near the floor and remained glued there:

The girl's feet were big, at least three sizes larger than her own.

Trembling all over at the discovery, Big Feet Zhuang excused herself from the presence of the girl. When the girl finally left, she called her 1.8-meter tall precious son over and said, between tears, that him marrying the girl would be a no go no matter what and, if he insisted on marrying her, it would have to be over his Ma's dead body.

Naturally the precious son asked why. Big Feet Zhuang turned her eyes to the picture of her dead man and stared at it for a long time without being able to say one word.

(1990)

The Monument

Sun Yuwen

Winter was about to begin when Big Old Liu took his post at the River Mouth Traffic Control. At first his wife was thrilled. Now she didn't need to journey to the city once every week. One day when Big Old Liu was drinking and his tongue got loose, she was not so thrilled to know that he had been disciplined and relegated to this new post. Big Old Liu was not ready to give up drinking. When he went to buy liquor and came home, the cup was nowhere to be found. He had a stern look on his face: "What's the difference where I earn my food?" So the next day the cup was back on the table.

Big Old Liu was not really big. In the beginning when he left the army and became a police officer doing criminal investigation, everything seemed so mysterious. A few years later he got the hang of it. It was around this time that he started to drink. Others' faces wouldn't show when they drank, but he reddened with as little as one drop. Once, he and two partners were trying to catch an escaped criminal. It was freezing cold so he took a sip. The escaped criminal got away, but Big Old Liu had nowhere to run. He was reprimanded and sent down to River Mouth.

River Mouth is a small town. The other side of the river belongs to another county of another province. By the roadside is a small grocery store. The person behind the cigarette and liquor counter was none other than Big Old Liu's wife. Right across from the grocery store was a thatch-roofed shed, on its wall a few big words written in diluted lime:

River Mouth Traffic Control

This was where Big Old Liu worked. Alone. No one else. He stood by the roadside. She sat behind the counter. They could see each other all the time. In the old days she missed him a lot. He had a lot to say, too. Now, when she talked to him, he barely opened his mouth.

One of his daily routines was to bring his big white belt with him. Hers was to bring home a 4-oz bottle of liquor. He talked even less but drank more and more.

Although the road passing through River Mouth links two provinces, the traffic here is not that heavy. There were very few accidents for several years. As a result Big Old Liu was little known.

Big Old Liu journeyed to the city twice a year to attend study sessions or end-of-year evaluations organized by the superintendent. He always sat in the back so he didn't have to chitchat with others; others would rather leave him alone, too. When the meeting was over, others played poker, watched TV, and sang karaoke while he would go and see his son, who worked as a temporary worker in a co-op in the county town. When father and son got together, there was not much to say either. Liquor, peanuts, and pig ears were their language.

As the years passed, Big Old Liu all but remembered the vehicles that came and went; the drivers would recognize him, too. He would nod and they would honk in return and everything seemed harmonious.

The sun and the moon change constantly, but the road remained unchanged, and the traffic control remained unchanged. He was somewhat hunched now. His face wouldn't go red any more when he drank. Other than that, everything about him remained the same.

One day Big Old Liu quit drinking suddenly. For good. No one had tried to talk him out of drinking or to snatch the bottle from his hands. He had quit on his own. Some said he was not in good health because liquor had burnt his insides. Some said he had been reprimanded again by his superiors and didn't dare to drink again. Some said an accident had happened under his jurisdiction and his wife and son had given him no peace because of it. All kinds of theories. But no one really knew why.

Except for his son, who didn't want to tell anyone lest they should be laughed at. Eventually, though, the word got out from the son's co-op.

It was rather simple. A truck owned by the co-op had a collision with another truck while crossing the River Mouth bridge. Nobody got hurt. Only that the other truck suffered a dent in its rear. The co-op's management asked the son to talk to his dad hoping he would let the driver go with a slap on the wrist. Big Old Liu would not budge. He not only made the co-op pay for the 1,000 *yuan* in damages, but also tossed them a 50-*yuan* fine. Big Old Liu suffered no consequence for this, but his son lost the chance to be converted into a full-time employee.

So Big Old Liu didn't drink any more. He came to work all the same, but he looked worse and talked even less.

Then one day someone noticed that Big Old Liu didn't report to work. He was hospitalized for a grave illness with no clear diagnosis.

When the Bureau and Department heads came to see him, he only nodded. When the Political Commissioner told him that the reprimand he had received 15 years ago had been removed from his file, Big Old Liu's eyes brightened up. His lips moved, but no audible sound came out. They asked if there was anything else they could do for him, and his lips moved again. At this his wife wiped away her tears and left the room. A short while later she returned with a 4-oz bottle of liquor. Everyone else present was at a loss as to what was going on. Big Old Liu's eyes brightened up again as he reached for the bottle. He stopped breathing the next instant.

Not until after his death did it occur to some people that in his more than 20 years of service, Big Old Liu had been all but invisible. Other than being reprimanded once, he had never appeared on a podium, addressed an assembly, or received an award. Yet, when they looked into his army file, he had received so many commendations.

The Bureau and Department heads asked his wife what they could do for her, all she could do was cry.

From the same province and from far away came the drivers. She didn't know any of them. They tried to console her, but her grief seemed beyond consolation.

A driver suggested they raise funds to build a monument for Big Old Liu. Right where the old thatched shed was.

Within days they brought in sand, little rocks, and cement, as well as bricklayers and carpenters. She stopped them before they got started. She wanted them to build a pagoda-shaped traffic control shed.

So a new traffic control shed was built. It was empty inside, except for an urn and a 4-oz bottle.

And not a single accident has occurred at River Mouth since.

(1992)

Abandoned Baby

Ang Liang

These days Hare-lipped Ah Bao is quite a celebrity on Fragrant Flower Bridge Street.

It all happened early one morning when the sky had just begun to brighten up. Someone saw Hare-lipped Ah Bao, a dirty, raggy bundle in his arms, hurrying home through the street. A short while later the sound of a baby crying came from inside his home.

From that morning on, the Residents Association folks found, Hare-lipped Ah Bao became quite a different person. Ever so often, with the baby in his arms, he would stand against the door or stroll in the street, humming a lullaby of some sort, so out of tune, to get the baby to sleep. Now and then he would bend to kiss the baby with his cleft lip. The kind of loving care he was giving the baby could more than match that of many young fathers.

It was said that Hare-lipped Ah Bao found the baby in a bathroom. The rumor spread far and wide but nobody dared to confront Ah Bao with it. Ah Bao's thuggish reputation was well-known in the street. At the slightest provocation he would let you have it, cussing and punching, until you were completely down. Little Third-Born, one of his neighbors, had barely gathered enough courage to ask: "Ah Bao, are you the father of this illegitimate baby?" when Ah Bao glowered at him with such fury that he shook all over with fear.

When Ah Bao strolled in the street with the baby in his arms he was oblivious to the world around him.

One day, Ah Bao's fiancée Fatty came to visit. Before long she burst into sobs. How could she, a shy girl, face the world now that Ah Bao had gotten a baby from nowhere? She asked Ah Bao to give the baby away, but Ah Bao didn't want to hear about it, his eyes ablaze with fury.

People felt Ah Bao was being rather foolish to have ruined his own happiness for this abandoned baby. Not worth it.

Ah Bao, on his part, appeared as if nothing had happened.

A few days later a young couple came to see Ah Bao. Before long they erupted into a row. Ah Bao lost it again. He grabbed a broom and with it drove the couple to the street. They ran as fast as they could, rather embarrassed.

That same evening a residential police officer came to talk to Ah Bao. The couple were truly the biological parents of the baby, the officer said. They now realized their mistake and wanted their baby back. Ah Bao shouldn't have reacted like that. As to his expenses, lost pay, and bonuses, he would be reimbursed accordingly. As he listened, Ah Bao looked pale as death and didn't say a word. Finally, pressured by the police officer, he said, "I want to see something written down, that they will never abandon the baby again. Otherwise, don't even think about it!"

The police officer smiled: "That's easy. I'll get it to you in no time."

When the couple came to take the baby away, Ah Bao looked rather bad. They thanked him profusely, but he turned his back to them, his eyes shiny with mute anger.

People whispered: "Something is going to happen." But nothing happened. The more observant among people noticed tears trickling down his cheeks.

The elderly in the neighborhood said Ah Bao had been an abandoned baby, too; it was Crippled Uncle Liu who had brought him up as his own.

(1993)

False Teeth

He Liwei

In a traffic accident Old He was thrown against the bus door and dazed.

When he opened his eyes again and checked his ribcage slowly like fingering a piano's keys, he was relieved: everything was intact and still functioning in its post. However, when he opened his mouth to speak, he found that his front teeth had been damaged. His voice now sounded strange to himself.

So Old He went to the dentist and had two false teeth installed. The dentist said to him: Be careful what you eat, 'cause false teeth cannot bite or chew hard things.

Old He returned home and looked at himself in the mirror: Mmm, the false teeth look like real teeth. He sighed with relief: I have survived the accident unscathed.

Gradually, Old He forgot about not only the accident but also the false teeth in his mouth. One day his wife bought a salted duck from the market and steamed it right away. Soon his home was filled with a mouth-watering aroma. During dinner an eager Old He poured himself a cup of wine and started to attack the food with gusto. Delicious duck and fragrant wine in his mouth at the same time and going down together couldn't be any better! When Old He poured himself the third cup of wine, his wife looked upset. Old He announced, mumbling: "The last cup, the last cup, hahaha."

So it was the last cup. After he tossed the last drop from the last cup in his mouth, he picked up the last half of the duck's head and stuffed it in his mouth. Since skin and bone were stuck together, Old He held the half-head with his teeth and yanked with his fingers: Just then, a false tooth fell off!

Infuriated, Old He slapped his own face and cussed: "Damn it. Slept soundly all night yet wetted the bed at sunrise! What bad luck!"

His wife said: "What are you talking about? Mumbling and gabbling on like this. Are you so drunk?"

Old He opened his mouth wide: "Ahhhh—my tooth has fallen off!"

His wife said: "What? Your tooth?—Oh my, that false tooth of yours? Told you what's false can't be real and what's real can't be false!"

Old He sighed: "You know, I often take what's false as real. Can't help it."

(1994)

A Bridge Pillar
Yang Xiangsheng

The ribbon-cutting ceremony for the River Island Bridge was all but ready. Colorful flags flapped on the forty-four shiny light poles. Four large colorful balloons floated dreamily above the bridge. People in their best holiday outfits streamed in from all directions, buoyed up by the rapturous joy of having conquered the divide between the small island and mainland, which, though within sight, felt like an ocean away.

The ceremony was to begin at exactly two in the afternoon. The countdown had only three hours left, yet Director Qiao, the ribbon cutter, had yet to arrive. How nerve-racking! The invitation sent to him half a month ago had not been answered. The phone in his residence had been busy all the time. Even the urgent telegram did not generate more response than a pebble falling into the sea. At their wits' end, the village heads sent Grandpa Tian, who had once saved Qiao's life, to the provincial capital to invite the director in person. Grandpa Tian should have been back yesterday, but even his shadow was nowhere to be found at this moment. Village Chief Zhao was restless like an ant on a hot stove.

The honor of ribbon cutting belonged to no one but Director Qiao. This was the voice of all the folks on the River Island. Qiao was not only the highest-ranking official River Island folks had ever known, but deserved the most credit for building this bridge. During the war years, Qiao was seriously wounded in a battle. It was Grandpa Tian who, risking his own life, pushed him across the fierce river in a wooden tub. From then on River Island had been close to Qiao's heart. He had called for a bridge to be built left and right for many years so folks here could shake off poverty like a nagging illness. He had even donated thirty-thousand *yuan* to help make that happen. River Island folks were touched to tears because they knew that it must have taken Director Qiao, a straight shooter, years and years to have saved up such a big sum. Other than Director Qiao, who else in the world would deserve the distinguished honor of being the ribbon-cutter?

This question bouncing around Chief Zhao's head was as big as the river itself:

Perhaps the self-effacing Director Qiao is staying away from all this attention in order to safeguard his reputation? That can't be. Qiao once promised at a public meeting: "When the bridge is built, I'll come to congratulate you as long as I can still breathe. Even if it means I have to crawl!" Perhaps he is caught up with his work? That can't be either. Director Qiao has been retired for three years. "Building the River Island Bridge is the biggest thing in my old age!" He had said. Perhaps his good children are taking him on a sightseeing trip somewhere deep in the mountains? Only wish that were true. Director Qiao has no children of his own. He once said: "Giving all I have to building this bridge will be my biggest joy for the rest of my life!"

Then, why. Why? Chief Zhao was puzzled.

When Grandpa Tian finally returned from the provincial capital, Chief Zhao asked anxiously: "Why isn't Director Qiao with you?"

"I didn't see him," Grandpa Tian mumbled, gasping for air, as he pulled his snow-white beard.

"You didn't see anybody else?" Zhao's breath quickened.

"I saw his wife," Grandpa Tian said. "She said Director Qiao is not feeling well. So he won't attend the ceremony, but will come and take a look in the evening."

"Ah. . . . " Chief Zhao was disappointed. The Ceremony Committee held an urgent meeting and decided to ask the deputy-mayor to be the ribbon-cutter.

At nightfall, the bridge was brightly lit. People waited anxiously. "Here he comes!" They cried in unison when a black car appeared on the bridge, moving slowly.

When the car stopped, an old lady, in black, face ashen, stepped out and shut the door.

"Where's Director Qiao?" Chief Zhao asked.

"The old man is in the car." The old lady said calmly.

Chief Zhao walked up to the car: "Director Qiao, please come out. The folks here have been expecting you the whole day!"

The old lady rubbed her eyes and said in a quivering voice, "Okay, let me help the old man out."

When the old lady stepped out again, all eyes were on her, and on the black box in her hands: "The old man died five days ago. Here's his letter to you."

Trembling, Chief Zhao took the letter with both hands and began to read aloud: "Please accept my hearty congratulations as an old friend of River Island! Please allow my ashes to be buried underneath the bridge so I will have the honor of being one of its pillars, too. . . . "

Then folks lined up to bow and pay their final respects in front of the ash box.

(1994)

Higher Education

Si Yusheng

Having failed in the college entrance exams, Qiang, along with an elder cousin of his, went to a seaport city to find work.

Once there Qiang's eyes were dazzled by the beautiful sights. The elder cousin said: Not bad, right? Qiang said: Not bad, not bad. The cousin said: Not bad at all, but it has nothing to do with us. Everybody will look down upon us. Qiang said: Nobody will if we don't look down upon ourselves.

Qiang and the cousin found work at a warehouse repairing canvas covers. Qiang put his heart to his work and would even pick up loose rags on the ground in case they could be used.

One night a thunderstorm hit the seaport. Qiang rolled out of bed and rushed into the pouring rain outside. His cousin tried to stop him but couldn't. What an idiot! The cousin cussed.

Qiang checked one big pile of goods after another and tightened canvas covers that had been blown loose by gusts of wind. When the owner came in his car, Qiang was already drenched from head to toe. But all the goods on the storage ground remained intact. The owner wanted to give him a raise right there. Qiang said: It's no big deal, really. I was only checking to see if the canvas covers I repaired were sturdy enough.

The owner valued Qiang's honesty and wanted him to run another company of his as a manager. Qiang said: I am not up to the job. Why don't you hire someone with better education? The owner said: I think you're the man—you have something in you that's more valuable than any education!

So Qiang became the manager.

The company was still new and needed to hire a few college-educated young people as clerks. So it placed an ad in the paper. At the news Qiang's elder cousin rushed over right away and said: Give me a job, a good job. Qiang said: you are not good enough. The cousin said: Not even good enough to be the gatekeeper? Qiang said: Won't do. You wouldn't take care of the company as your own. The cousin's face reddened with anger: You have no conscience at all. Qiang said: My conscience lies in giving my best to whatever I do.

With the addition of the college-educated young men the business of the company flourished. As time passed, those young men got to know Qiang's level of education and began to complain: With our degrees and diplomas, how can we work for him? When Qiang heard this, he was not upset. He said to them: Since we're a team, let's give our very best to our work. As to this title of the company's manager, it doesn't really matter who wears it on his head. What really matters is not the title, but. . . .

Those college-educated clerks looked at each other and didn't complain any more.

A foreign company saw the potential of Qiang's company and wanted to talk about setting up a joint venture. Qiang's assistant said: I know they're a big fish. We should wine and dine them really well. Qiang said: Right.

The foreign company's CEO turned out to be an overseas Chinese accompanied by an interpreter and an assistant.

Qiang asked in English: Do you speak Chinese, sir?

Surprised, the CEO said: Oh yes.

Qiang said: Then, why don't we talk in our mother tongue?

The CEO said: Okay. At the end of the negotiation session, Qiang said: How about we have dinner together? The CEO hesitated but then nodded his head.

The dinner was quite simple, but each dish had a special flavor. All of the dishes had been finished, except for two steamed dumplings left on one platter. Qiang said to the waitress, offhandedly: Can you put these two in a bag for me? This request worried Qiang's assistant, who stole an uneasy glance at the CEO. The CEO stood up, grasped Qiang's hand, and said: Okay, we'll sign the deal tomorrow!

The following day, Qiang's boss treated the foreign CEO to dinner. Qiang and his assistant were at the table, too.

During dinner the CEO asked Qiang: I'm so impressed with your work. Which college did you go to, if I may ask?

Qiang said: I grew up in a poor family with illiterate parents. But they started my education rather early from simplest things, such as a grain of rice or a thread. After my father passed away, it was my mother who struggled alone to support me, food and schooling and all. She said: I don't care what you'll do when you grow up, but I'll be happy if you do a good job at it.

At this Qiang's boss became teary-eyed. He stood up and raised his glass: Let's drink to the health of your dear mother, who has given you the best education in the world! I wish she could join us today!

(1996)

Yellow Scarf

Xue Tao

The girl had to pass this small clothing shop on her way home from school.

She saw a yellow scarf which she liked very much.

She stopped and gazed at it long.

"You want it, child?" The middle-aged merchant asked. "This is the last one. You can have it for only ten *yuan*."

The girl shook her head. Money? She didn't have any.

"You can ask your parents for money. I'll save it for you. I can see you like it a lot."

Reluctantly the girl left.

The whole evening the girl tried to gather enough courage to ask for money.

In the end, though, she never said one word about the yellow scarf. She vowed she would never even bring it up.

Her family was not well-to-do. This the girl knew.

When the girl passed the small clothing shop again, she could see, from some distance, the yellow scarf flapping in the wind like a butterfly. She paused and gazed at it for a while before walking near it.

"Have you brought money with you?"

The girl shook her head.

The middle-aged merchant felt the yellow scarf in hand, looked at the girl again, pictured how perfect it would look on the girl, and felt sorry for her.

"You really like it, don't you?"

"Mmm," the girl nodded seriously.

The girl started to leave. Since she could not afford it, it wouldn't make sense for her to linger any longer.

Before she had gone far the middle-aged merchant took down the yellow scarf and ran and caught up with her.

"Child, you can have it free. Take it. It'll look good on you."

The girl was at a loss.

"No, I can't take things from people without paying." The girl said firmly.

"Take it. I want you to have it. I mean it."

"I can't! I would feel even worse than not having it at all."

The girl broke into a run.

As she ran, she turned her head and said, "I can see it from the school building. That's just as good. That's good enough for me."

The middle-aged merchant stood there, speechless.

From that day on the girl never passed the shop again. Since she couldn't buy the scarf, she might as well avoid the market altogether. Whenever she felt a bit tired doing her school work, she would look outside the window and gaze at the yellow scarf flapping in the wind.

Many days later that yellow scarf was still hanging from the merchant's stand. Why hadn't anyone bought the yellow scarf, the dream of the young girl?

For a simple reason: the merchant had a label next to the yellow scarf. On the label were written these words:

Not For Sale.

(1996)

Auntie Fei

Xu Huifeng

Auntie Fei is a neighbor of my maternal aunt, quite unique among women of her generation. The exceptional generosity, intelligence, and humor she showed at important moments in her life made her a legendary figure in my eyes.

The legend of Auntie Fei began with her marriage.

Auntie Fei is very charming although she is not considered pretty. Her pair of large eyes can speak and her nose is well-shaped. What's not pretty about her face is the half below the nose. She had a fall when she was a child and hurt her chin. It never completely healed. So her chin, along with her mouth, is somewhat pulled down on one side.

By the time of marrying age, her family, friends, and relatives were all worried. Auntie Fei said: I am not worried. So, why should you? She could write, paint, play the piano, and naturally, have high standards when choosing her mate. People dropped her hints that as an imperfect girl—her imperfection being quite noticeable—she should be realistic and settle for someone equally imperfect.

Auntie Fei didn't budge in her search for her Prince Charming. She liked a worker poet whose poems appeared in the newspapers quite often. So she sent him a letter with a picture of herself enclosed. The letter was passionate and serious. The picture was a beautiful one: a young woman holding a rose next to her mouth, her eyes glinting warmly at the viewer with a tint of shyness.

A few letters back and forth later, the poet couldn't wait to come and see Auntie Fei. He was so shocked by what he saw, however, that he invented a lie and left right away.

Auntie Fei knew the reason why the poet had left. She wrote him another letter saying he had forgotten something and should come and get it in person.

The poet came to visit again, skeptically. Auntie Fei got to the point right away: You were thrilled with me in the picture and disheartened with me in person. But you shouldn't look at a person's appearance only. Last time you looked at me with one pair of eyes. As a poet, you have to have another pair of eyes. Now what I want you to reclaim is that pair of eyes.

With that she took out her paintings, embroideries, and artwork she had made: little ornamental bells which rang musically, an earthen-ware pig biting into a watermelon greedily. The poet was delighted.

Then, Auntie Fei sat down at the piano and said, "Since you're leaving, let me sing you a song for memory's sake." As her fingers danced upon the keys, a beautiful song emerged from her lips. The song she sang was entitled "The Deep, Deep Blue Sea," a Yugoslavian love song popular in the 1950s. When the song ended, its last note still lingering in the air, the poet was so thrilled, his eyes shined with joy.

That's how Auntie Fei gave the poet another pair of eyes. They married happily, oblivious to the puzzled look from others.

And the poet did get a pair of good eyes. In 1957 the poet was condemned as a "Rightist" and was sent to the wild Northwest to be reformed. Concerned his wife would be implicated, the poet suggested they divorce. Auntie Fei held her husband's hand and sang the popular folk song "In That Faraway Place," with changed lyrics: "In that faraway place there is a Rightist man; I'd love to be his Rightist woman, following him to that faraway place. . . . " At this, her much-troubled husband smiled with tears in his eyes.

In 1966 her husband, long unemployed, got into trouble again, the biggest trouble ever. When he came home from the first denunciation rally, his face ashen, Auntie Fei didn't say much. She went and borrowed a pair of clippers and cut all of her husband's grayed hair. Then she spent the whole evening making him a tall hat with two buffalo horns growing out from either side. Then she painted a fiendish demon on the hat and wrote on it these words: Down With All Fiendish Ghosts and Gods!

At the denunciation rally the next day, her husband put the tall hat on himself. At this, the Red Guards couldn't help but laugh. The tall hat looked so funny. It meant this bad egg was *truly* repentant. Even her husband found the whole thing laughable. The hat was light and warm and shielded his head from the cold wind. Now that not a single hair was left on his head, there was nothing for the rebels to grasp.

So, from the 50s all the way to the 80s, when China opened its doors again, Auntie Fei sang those songs for her husband over and over. Together they had journeyed for over 30 years until he passed away. Then her two grown-up children left to live and study abroad. At age 66, Auntie Fei felt somewhat lonely.

She went to the park to exercise every day. Since she could sing, dance, and was talented in so many other ways, and had a good sense of humor, she drew a lot of attention among the retired folks. Perhaps looks are not that important when you are old, two widowers, one a retired engineer, and the other a retired teacher, soon began to compete with each other for her affection. Auntie Fei was equally warm and attentive to both, so both felt they were the chosen one.

That's why the two cultured men were even more than puzzled when they found out that the *real* chosen one was a crippled gardener.

Once when I ran into Auntie Fei, I told her about their puzzlement. Auntie Fei thought for a second and then said: "I thought those two were not cultured enough." The engineer and the teacher not cultured enough? I asked. How? She explained, lowering her voice to a whisper: During a retiree fishing trip organized by the park, she played a little trick and found out that the two more-educated men are actually less-cultured than the one who has received less-formal education. I couldn't help but laugh. Auntie Fei said: "I'll tell you more details later . . . something for your next novel.

I'm still puzzled. But I know that if Auntie Fei had made the conventional, reasonable choice, she wouldn't have been this charming. Auntie Fei is one of a kind.

(1998)

Time Travel

Cai Nan

A dead leaf arose from the ground and grew back on the bare twig; the twig turned green and the leaf alive with dewy hope; after a night of gentle spring rain a tender bud appeared on the twig. As you can see, this is a story of traveling back in time.

A life had just been pierced through by a bullet and withered on the execution ground. Then we see Du Jun's life, like that dead leaf, arise from the ground, his blood, already seeped into the earth and frozen there, come alive again and fly back into his body, and the hole in his body heal; Du Jun sits up, stands on his feet, and retraces his footsteps.

Du Jun breaks away from the two police officers holding him, leaves the public sentencing rally, and returns to his jail cell, which is lit by the faint light slanting through the tiny window high on the wall. Each day he has only two meals. For each meal he has only two dry buns which are hard to chew and swallow. As he chews, Du Jun thinks of the famous song by Chi Zhiqiang: "Holding the dry bun in my quivering hand, tears gushing down like flooded bank." And tears indeed begin to gush down his cheeks.

"What's the use of your tears now?" The County Party Chief has said during the trial, angrily: "You're still so young!"

Indeed, Du Jun *is* young. When he was appointed deputy director of the county's Agricultural Bank in charge of daily operations, he was only 31 years old, glowing with youthful energy. He *did* mean to do something with his life. Yet, there are too many temptations in this world. When you are still living a simple, spartan life while trying to do good things, it takes extraordinary self-control and discipline. Du Jun became disoriented when money, sex, extravagant cars and houses were dangled in front of his eyes.

It all started when the bank was building a new office complex. A construction company contractor came to visit and gave him a really nice wall calendar. Wrapped inside the roll of nice pictures was something even nicer: 50,000 *yuan*. Du Jun, who was supervising the construction of the office complex, couldn't sleep that night as two Du Juns fought till dawn. One wanted to return the money to the contractor whereas the other said: "Over my dead body!" In the end Du Jun found the middle way to resolve this: He deposited the money in another bank under his wife's name. Soon after, the construction work went to this particular contractor.

Whatever came after that was all easy. He didn't need to lose sleep over it any more. Once a company treated Du Jun to a fancy dinner first, then took him to a sauna house, and then, when the guest of honor had been massaged and made comfortable, stuffed two cartons of cigarettes into his hand. Once home, Du Jun found that each cigarette was actually a rolled up 100-*yuan* bill. The next day, without any hesitation Du Jun put his name on the company's application for a 3-million *yuan* loan.

After that, a Hong Kong businessman came to see him. The merchant wanted to strike a big steel deal with Bank Director Du. He took Du to Hong Kong. After five days of sightseeing, the businessman tossed the key to a nice villa into Du Jun's hand. To show his appreciation of the businessman's generosity, Du Jun embezzled 8 million *yuan* from the savings accounts of the bank's customers. No sooner had the new office complex been constructed, it collapsed and buried three of the bank's employees underneath it. The loan he had signed couldn't be recalled; the embezzled money had disappeared into thin air. Then? Word got out. The Disciplinary Commission investigated. The Prosecutorial Office took over the case. Dun Jun was sent to jail.

The first one to come and visit him in jail was the home room teacher from middle school. The gray-haired teacher didn't say a word. Quivering with emotion, he handed Du Jun a sheet of yellowed paper. Du Jun opened it. It was his application for the Youth League membership; still clear at the right-hand corner was his name in deep blood red.

Du Jun returns to his beautiful alma mater and becomes a middle school student again. He is a diligent student and sends in his application for the Youth League membership. When he doesn't see his name on the list of the first batch of students accepted by the league, he writes another application, bites his index finger, and signs the application with blood before handing it to the Youth League secretary. He is ecstatic when he finally puts the league badge on his chest. He wins a top honor during a Beautifying Our Society and Ourselves campaign. He returns the 100 *yuan* he found to its owner.

His old, simpleton parents come to visit from the countryside with a large canvas bag. They say to Du Jun, "Son, we've brought your favorite food when you were small: steamed corn and baked yams. They taste good!" Ashamed, Du Jun falls on his knees, his head almost knocking against the ground.

Du Jun walks in the fields of his home village. He goes to work in the fields with his parents. He sees a gang of kids digging yams and picking sweet corn and decides to follow them. As thick smoke arises from the sea of rich autumn colors, the gang of kids jump for joy. They set the corns and yams on the fire they have just made. Young Du Jun swallows the saliva in his mouth, runs back to where the adults are working, and reports what he saw.

Summer night is muggy and long. Little Du Jun sits in his father's lap and listens to him telling the stories of the 13 Brave Sisters while his mother fans the mosquitoes away. As he listens, Du Jun grows drowsy and falls asleep. In his dream, Du Jun becomes even smaller. Toddler Du starts to talk and walk around unsteadily. Baby Du Jun crawls on the ground and cries to be fed. Tiny Du Jun comes to this world after his mother moans one more time in convulsive pain.

Meanwhile, a spring rain falls on a leaf in the yard outside.

The leaf begins to bud.

(2000)

Black and White

Li Qixiang

County Magistrate Zhang has loved old operas ever since he was a child and looked up to characters such as the dark-faced Lord Bao and Magistrate Tang Cheng.[4] Clean officials are good officials and there are many good officials such as Jiao Yulu and Kong Fanseng.[5]

What saddens Magistrate Zhang the most is that some officials today are too *that*. In the last few years the news media has carried investigative stories of so many bad officials, Wang Baoseng, Hu Changqing, Li Chenglong, and so on, that in the eyes of some people there are no good officials in the entire Hong Dong County.

Magistrate Zhang wants to debunk this myth. He wants to be a good official to show to the world that there are still good officials in Hong Dong County.

In order to be a good official, Magistrate Zhang sets up a "monitoring post" for himself. He feels that as a leader it would be too passive of him to rely on outside monitoring by others. True, the county's people's congress, political consultative conference, disciplinary commission, and the masses—they all have the right to monitor. Yet, as the highest-ranking official of the entire county, if you want to be bad, all their monitoring cannot stop you. Therefore, the best monitoring is self-monitoring and the best discipline is self-discipline.

The "monitoring post" Magistrate Zhang has set up for himself is a board for the game of go. He decides that whenever he has done something good, something right, he will place a white stone on the board; conversely, a black stone will be placed. By the time there are more white stones than black stones, or the black stones have completely disappeared, it would mean that the East Wind has defeated the West Wind and he is truly a good official.

Magistrate Zhang has instructed the Department of Education to look into the cases of grade schools charging young pupils all kinds of ridiculous fees.

Magistrate Zhang has led a group of volunteers in planting trees along a country road.

Magistrate Zhang has approved funds for the environmental protection office to purchase two garbage trucks, which will alleviate the pressure of garbage collecting in the county town.

Whenever he has done something along that line, Magistrate Zhang places a newwhite stone on the board.

Then, the county decides to build a reservoir on South Mountain to better meet the irrigation needs of the surrounding fields. To smooth the fundraising process, some county departments and offices plan to give "expressions of appreciation" to provincial officials and offices in charge of allocating such funds. To do so they need Magistrate Zhang's approval. If he says yes, the reservoir will become a reality; if he says no, the reservoir will continue to slumber as blueprint. Magistrate Zhang has no choice. People have to eat. There will be no harvest without water. Without the reservoir people have to depend on Heaven, and if Heaven is not in a good mood to offer rain, people will have nothing but north-west wind to drink. Should he give himself a white stone or a black stone? The toughest part of all this for Magistrate Zhang is that some of these powerful officials from the province and beyond often come down to take a look at how things are going. Every time, the county's hosting offices will ask Magistrate Zhang to meet the visitors, wine and dine them, sing and dance at karaoke halls, and then go to the sauna and get them escorts. . . . Of course, you, Magistrate Zhang, won't do such things, yet that doesn't mean you can have a clear conscience. Red-headlined policy documents have been issued over and again to prohibit squandering public funds on extravagant wining and dining and enter-tainment. Why don't you take a public stand against such corruption?

For some time now Magistrate Zhang has been unsure while look-ing at his "monitoring post." Some of the "good" things he has done are actually part of his job descriptions. If he hasn't done them, it would be neglecting one's duty. There it won't matter much whether he gives himself white stones or not. Some of the things he has done he knew were not the right things to do but did them anyway, though unwill-ingly. Does doing "bad" things unwillingly make it less bad? On the other hand, these "bad" things, even if you don't do them, other people, when put in your position, would do them in a heartbeat. There is no way out of this.

Thus, gazing at the board in front of him, Magistrate Zhang finds the white stones and the black stones almost equal in number; no, the black ones seem to be gaining over the white ones. Magistrate Zhang is shocked: Am I a good official or a bad one?

(2000)

My University

Hou Deyun

The first time I failed the college entrance exams, I shed so many tears. Pa wiped away my tears with his big roughened hands and said: "Son, let's not cry. Let's review again and review well and test well next year, ah?"

The second time I failed the college entrance exams, I shed so many tears. Pa wiped away my tears with his big roughened hands and said: "Son, let's not cry. Let's review again and review well and test well next year, ah?"

The third time I failed the college entrance exams, I shed so many tears. I said to Pa: "Pa, I don't want to take the exams any more. I am stupid, so stupid. I will never pass the exams and go to college."

Pa wiped away the tears on my face with his big roughened hands and said: "Son, let's not cry. Let's review again and review well and test well next year, ah?"

With that Pa squatted down and sobbed. He said while sobbing: "Son, you aren't stupid. You are like your ma, not stupid at all. You *shall* go to college."

True, my mother was not stupid at all. When she was tired of the hard life in the mountains she left quietly, without saying goodbye. Pa had never blamed Ma for this. He said: "Son, it's all your pa's fault 'cause Pa had no money for your ma's illness. That's why she left us."

Life during those days was the hardest. To pay for me repeating school, Pa worked all kinds of odd jobs from sunrise to sunset and wouldn't spend a cent for himself, even for food or clothing. His hair grayed fast and his hands, like sandpaper, would produce a grinding noise when touching a stone, or rustling noise when touching a table.

When they touched my face, there was no rustling noise. My face would burn as if on fire.

My situation wasn't much better than Pa's. Like my grades, my mood went from bad to worse. I began to develop a phobia for college entrance exams. Sometimes I envied my mother lying there alone on the hillside, free from worldly worries. Wouldn't that be nice!

This year I had to succeed in the college entrance exams. I dared not fail. If I failed, it would be too much for Pa. He might not be able to get over it.

Yet, how could I succeed?

I hurried to school when I heard that the college entrance exam results were available. I took one glance and fainted. My teacher and classmates carried me to the hospital where I lay for a long time before I came to. I cried like heaven had fallen. I felt I had no face to go home and see Pa. I felt I must be the world's No. 1 stupid donkey. With each additional year at school my college entrance exam grades went lower. I felt I should die to end it all.

When I got home in the evening, Pa prepared a table of delicious food and bought a bottle of liquor. He must have slaughtered our big rooster, too. As to where he had got that brown carp I didn't know.

I didn't know why Pa wanted to prepare this table of food. It was neither the New Year's nor any holiday. What was going on?

Pa opened the bottle, poured two cups, and said: "Come, let's drink a few cups together. Pa and Son."

I took the cup without a word and drank.

Pa said, "So, son, how did you do this year?"

To my own surprise I blurted out: "Not bad. Should be enough to make it."

Pa grinned and chuckled happily. He said, "I sought out a fortune teller. He said you would make it. So I figured you would make it. Okay, let's drink another cup."

I gulped down another cup. Tears trickled down my cheeks and smeared against my face.

Pa chuckled happily again: "Son, what is it?"

I wiped my face with my hand left and right and said: "I'm too . . . too happy."

When the college admission cutoffs were available, I went to school and walked around it once, businesslike, without stepping inside its gate and then came straight home. I said to Pa, "My scores are quite a bit above the cutoffs. I might even get into a good university."

Pa nodded with a big smile on his face, "Good, good."

Time passed but my lie lived on. I didn't dare tell Pa the truth. I was afraid the truth might cost him his old life.

Some time later I received my university admission notice. Not bad indeed. I was accepted by Liaoning University. I had had the notice made by a typing service in the county town, the seal I had made myself with a potato. I had seen many university admission notices and thought I had done a decent job forging one for myself.

I decided that in a few days I would pretend to go to college while in reality I would try to find a job. I wouldn't ask Pa to send me money for tuition and expenses. I would tell him I made good money working while going to school in Shenyang. I might even send Pa money every month because I didn't want him to live that kind of hard life any more. Then, all I needed to do at the end of the four years was to buy a fake diploma and show it to Pa once. Everything would be fine.

When I showed the admission notice to Pa, he was thrilled. He went from neighbor to neighbor to tell the folks the good news. Pa used to be a man of few words, yet for the next few days he would chatter non-stop to anyone he ran into as if he wanted to spit out the words of a lifetime.

I even saw Pa talking to two small toddlers: "You should study hard.

That way you will grow up to be like my son: going to university in Shenyang!"

Pa had such a stern look on his face that the two kids stared at him, looking confused, and all of a sudden burst out crying.

I felt very bad. Really bad. I hated myself.

A few days ago I came to Shenyang and found Liaoning University. There, at the university's entrance, I had a picture taken. The photographer was a pro from a photography studio nearby, which cost me twice as much as would have otherwise.

After sending Pa the picture, I went to the job market to look for something to do.

My university life began.

(2003)

The Fat Cat's Woman

Lin Ruqiu

"Just you listen what kind of rascally scriptures he is singing: 'Only fooling around with them. Didn't mean to divorce you!' Fuck the son of a bitch! Want to grab one in your left arm and clutch another in your right, while tossing your old mama, me, aside like an old servant! I've had enough of such shenanigans!"

The woman took over the tea cup from her mother and sipped. It tasted flat. "Some women nowadays are so ridiculous and cheap. Skinny like a monkey, a piece of bony rib, what's there to bite into anyway? Yet they push themselves into his bony arms like crazy! Perhaps he is really like the nickname people have given them, Drunken Rib? Drunken Rib, Drunken Rib . . . "

Teeth chattering, the woman stuffed a spoonful of rice into her mouth. No, it tasted far worse than the "Three-Harmony Rice" at home. Although mother had prepared extra dishes for her sake, they were either too salty or too flat. Cheerlessly the woman managed to swallow half of the bowl of rice before she put the chopsticks down, no matter how earnestly her mother urged her to eat more.

The woman turned on the television. Still it had only two channels: one from the province capital and one from Central China TV. Worse, the screen would either "rain" or "snow," and be accompanied by lots of static. "This ghost-wouldn't-lay-eggs place, when will it have cable television?" The woman cursed and turned off the television.

Winter night in a mountainous village is black ink splashed on rice paper: it is dark everywhere, far and near. Gusty wind wails like ghosts and wolves. The woman didn't bother to say any more. Except for praying the "Scripture of Forbearance," what else was there her mother could do? The woman crawled into bed. The wooden bed felt cold and hard like she had been tossed into an ice hole. She tossed and turned and the more she slept the clearer her mind became. "This time at my home in the city, the heat is on, the room is warm, and everything is comfortable as can be. . . . " The woman closed her eyes to imagine what it felt like.

She thought of her husband again. No, he was not her husband in her eyes any more, since she left home around noon. At this very time, Drunken Rib must still be fooling around in the karaoke hall, holding the thin waist of some outrageous siren while screaming into the microphone. Perhaps he thought: I've tossed that cheap mountain girl onto the bouncy, dreamy mattress. That's extraordinarily generous and charitable of me! Is that so? The woman wondered. Is that so? She tucked the corners of the quilt. The room was leaky from all around. The quilt felt like dead skin. There was not an ounce of warmth in it.

The woman tossed and turned again in the cold bed, like making pot stickers with a listless fire: it can never bring the pot stickers to their proper sizzle. "Ah. . . . " the woman sighed, and sighed again. And another long sigh: "Ah—What else can I do, except for coming back to my mother's home? Ah, why didn't I see through this before? What else is there to live for if not for a good life? 'Men become bad when they have money; women have money when they become bad.' How true! What if I leave Drunken Rib and marry another fat cat? All fat cats in the world are rascally in their bones, aren't they? Replacing Drunken Rib with Braised Pork would be like using new water to simmer the same old medicine, what difference would it make? What if I find a good, but penniless man, a White Radish, and eat watery gruel with him every day, like here in my mother's home? No, no, I am not that stupid. Ah, this is looking for bitterness to eat myself. I was being stupefied. . . . " At this point, she felt so low and miserable.

The woman felt hungry and wanted to have a cup of hot tea, but her mother's place didn't have a hot pot and the water in the thermos bottle was only lukewarm. There were no milk, crackers, or coffee for a midnight snack either. The woman shook her head and checked her watch. It was not even four a.m. yet. "This ghosts-wouldn't-lay-eggs place, why did I come back to suffer all these indignities?"

When she crawled back into the quilt, she suddenly felt relieved. "I'm glad I didn't burn my bridges. I didn't bring up divorce to Drunken Rib, nor leave any paper saying something like that. All I did was to come back to my mother's for a visit. That is not allowed? Besides, I didn't say I would stay at my mother's for long."

The woman didn't hesitate. Early the next morning she got on the bus to return to the city. When she entered her home, Drunken Rib was rubbing his eyes and getting up. Upon seeing her, he growled: "Don't want milk. Make me a cup of Blue Spring Tea instead!"

The woman stared at him, swallowing the spit in her mouth, and swallowed again.

Drunken Rib coughed; his goldfish-like eyes growled again: "Where on earth did you go? Why did you stay out the whole night?"

Like a gas stove being lit suddenly, the fury in the woman's heart erupted in blazing fire: "I've had it! I've had it!" The woman stomped out, slamming the door behind her.

Outside the winter sun shone so brilliantly she couldn't open her eyes.

(2003)

Floral Shorts

Lu Jianhua

Ah, life was really tough for average folks during those days, especially poor peasants. If you tell this to the young people today they would never believe you. In my home village, for example, many peasants didn't even have a decent change of clothes. In the summer they had only one pair of shorts which they could wear to go anywhere. If they had to travel far, they would plan carefully so that they would not be away from home for two consecutive days. On hot summer days folks would sweat so much that shorts had to be washed everyday, yet they had only one pair.

Young peasant Zhang Xiang, for instance, ran into an embarrassing situation on account of this fact of life during those days.

One day he came back rather late in the evening from attending a relative's wedding. He had just taken a bath, changed, and started to cool off when someone from the Production Brigade came and told him to go in town and pick up a supply of chemical fertilizer. During those days, fertilizer was rationed and was very precious. If you didn't go and claim them in time, it would mean giving them up automatically.

Gazing at the newly-washed shorts on the bamboo pole, Zhang Xiang was at a loss what to do. If they had told him earlier, he wouldn't have washed this one and only pair of shorts of his. After agonizing over it for a while he decided to go to town no matter what. He would leave soon after midnight so he could travel naked under cover of darkness. As to the shorts, well, they would hang on his carrying pole and by the time he reached town, over ten *li* from the village, they should be all dry. Then, he would put them on.

Having thus made up his mind, Zhang Xiang went to bed. When he woke up, he stepped outside to check the weather. The sky was lit with stars and a crescent moon. From somewhere came a cool breeze, too. Delighted, Zhang put the shorts on the pole and got on his way. Naked.

All seemed quiet under the night sky. For a long while as Zhang Xiang hurried along, he didn't encounter a soul. Faint stars shining on the mountainous path, a gentle cool breeze in the air, he hummed jovially and quickened his pace. Before long the crescent moon sank in the west, the stars vanished, and the eastern sky showed a fish-belly paleness. Sensing that he was close to town, Zhang Xiang stopped to put on the shorts. It was then that he discovered, to his horror, that the shorts were gone.

Devastated, Zhang Xiang dropped down and sat his naked butt on the ground. He had to think fast. Going into town like this would never do. Retracing his steps along his ten-*li* trek to look for the shorts wouldn't do, either. Who knows where on earth he had lost them! He was ready to cry, but crying wouldn't do any good. He had to find a way out of this fix fast. Just then, through the haze of early morning he saw a few houses near the road. An idea flashed across his mind. He knew that in the summer, peasants usually hung their washing outside to dry. So he sneaked off the road, grabbed the first pair of shorts he saw from a clothes line outside a house, ran flying back to the road, and put them on with quivering hands.

As day broke, more pedestrians appeared on the road. At the sight of Zhang Xiang they all turned and burst out laughing. The young man was puzzled: What is going on? Then he lowered his head and looked at himself. His face reddened as if on fire. The shorts he had stolen were a woman's with floral patterns.

(2003)

Eunuch

Zhang Jishu

Eunuch is the nickname of our village chief Zheng Taijian.

Our village is a tiny, sesame seed-sized mountain village tucked in a corner of the deep and mighty Mount Tai Hang. You can cover the distance from the west end of the village to the east end before you finish smoking half a pipe. Its name is Summer Mugwort because the hill behind the village is covered with mugwort; during the summer the entire village basks in the fragrant aroma carried over by the southerly wind. People outside the village, however, give it a different nickname: Narrow Pass. True to this name, the village *is* narrow and small. Yet there could be another meaning. Although it is small and tucked in a corner deep in the mountain, someone did make a name for himself by passing, albeit narrowly, the imperial civil service examination near the end of the Qing Dynasty. That man lived till after the Liberation in 1949.

Our Village Chief's name was given by none other than our one-and-only celebrity. "Tai" means seal and "jian" means examine and decide. You see, the one who carries the seal and has the power to examine others and make decisions—he has to be an official! As it turns out, when Taijian grew up, he did become a village cadre, with the big village seal dangling on his hip from his waist belt. During the period of the People's Commune, the village became a Production Brigade, the head of the village the Brigade Commander; when the People's Commune was converted to township, the Brigade became a Village Commission, its head Village Chief. Regardless of the name, from a 20-something baby corn to a 60-something old corn flour, Zheng Taijian has been head of the village for 40 years. He has little to show for the 40 years of governance. Other than getting Summer Mugwort on the list of "Hardship Villages," he earned an interesting nickname for himself: Eunuch Zheng.

When he just started, Zheng wasn't like this at all. He was young, energetic, and resolute in everything he was doing: Fish is fish, fowl is fowl; no confusion whatsoever. Ever since the "Cultural Revolution," during which he went through the relentless County Revolutionary Committee Study Sessions for half a year, he has morphed into a different man. All the sap and backbone of his old self were gone, as if he had been afflicted with rickets. Whenever an official came down, he would be humble like a servant and start to stammer: "Com . . . missioner Zhang, make sure you eat . . . eat to your heart's . . . heart's content!"

"Party Chief Li, make sure you drink . . . drink to your heart's . . . heart's content!" "Director Wang, make sure you play . . . play to your heart's . . . heart's content!"

The villagers said the wine cups in Zheng Taijian's hands were as good as dusters in the hands of those notorious eunuchs.

One day, out of the blue, instructions came that the Village Chief had to be elected. The entire village erupted in excitement. Folks craned and asked each other: "We elect the Village Chief? How?" Those who had seen a bit of the world said: "Why not? Other countries even elect their presidents!" Soon two men made it known that they wanted to run for the Village Chief position. One was Little Three, a young man who had served in the Army. The other was Hothead Two. They came up with all kinds of ways to ingratiate themselves with the villagers: you brought eggs to the Zhangs in the morning; I sent sesame oil to the Wangs in the afternoon; you took the Lis to the restaurant; I dragged the Zhaos to the dance hall in the county town. On the day of the election after a month of busy campaigning, they cussed and became physical with each other. Someone almost died in the fiasco. In the end the town government had to declare the election results null and void and, once again, appoint Zheng Taijian the Village Chief.

The first thing Zheng Taijian did once he became Village Chief again was to ask for a sum of money from the township government, to buy a 29" color television set (made in Japan) to be placed in the office of the Village Commission. The day they set up the television, the Town Commissioner himself came to offer congratulations. He sat at the head of the grand table, eating, drinking, and watching television. The drama series *Yongzheng Emperor*[6] was on. In the drama series a eunuch was presenting some treasure to the Emperor. In real life the Village Chief was toasting the Town Commissioner with a cup in both hands. The Emperor cried out to the eunuch: "Get lost!" The Town Commissioner muttered angrily to the Village Chief: "Nonsense, you drink it for me." The same show was going on in real life as in the drama.

It was then that I thought of the word "eunuch" again. I remembered asking that old and one-and-only village celebrity when I was small: "What does eunuch mean?" The Old Man stroked his long silvery beard and said: "Well, it's a man whose testicles have been removed in order to serve the emperor." Then he added, sighing, "In fact, though, prior to the removal of the testicles, a eunuch has already removed his own heart and soul."

At the time I was too young to understand what the Old Man meant.

(2005)

The Female Visitor
Zeng Ping

I work at D Penitentiary. I have a good grasp of everything concerning the more than 30 inmates in my charge. I study them so I know how to help them reform with the right "medicine." It may sound like bragging, but I know everything about the inmates' families, relatives and friends, their cases, habits and hobbies, and so on.

One inmate is a former county magistrate. I've studied his case so thoroughly I can write a voluminous novel about it.

This former county magistrate-turned inmate has no family or relatives to come and visit him. It is not good for his reform. His wife has cut her ties with him by divorcing him and taking their son to shack up with some rich man. His old mother died of a hemorrhage right after her son got into trouble. Those erstwhile relatives and friends don't want to waste their time coming to visit an ex-county magistrate who has become useless for them now.

Yet there is this one woman who comes to see the ex-county magistrate now and then. At first I thought she was a relative of his. When I asked him, the ex-county magistrate said he didn't have such a relative, nor did he know her at all. I refused to have the wool pulled over my eyes by this sly ex-county magistrate. So I was determined to get to the bottom of it.

The woman doesn't come very often. Usually during the Near Year's and other important holidays. She would bring a few simple things: sausages, ham, instant noodles, tea, cigarettes, and so on. Nothing fancy. You could buy these things from any grocery store. I never saw the woman and the ex-country magistrate whispering secretively either. She would leave the things in the visitor's room and leave. So I had to bring him in and try to get him to talk, but he refused to confess anything. He said he didn't even know the woman's name. He had such a pitiable, look-how-I-have-been-wronged expression on his face. I became even more suspicious. So I began to search for other possible explanations. Perhaps the woman is the ex-county magistrate's mistress? I looked at the woman more carefully. Yes, she does look like a charming woman.

I felt obligated to dig deeper into this.

Whatever lame efforts the ex-county magistrate put up against me proved useless. I decided to approach the woman and talk to her directly. So, on the day of Mid-Autumn Festival when the woman came to visit, I "invited" her into my office. First I gave her a crash course in people's democratic dictatorship and asked her to cooperate; otherwise, I explained, she would have to face the consequences. So the woman surrendered quickly.

It turned out that the woman wasn't the ex-county magistrate's family or mistress or anything. Two years ago, when the ex-county magistrate was still in power, the woman was working in the county town while her husband was teaching in an out-of-the-way grade school. The couple had tried to get the husband transferred back to the county town for four or five years until they got so dog tired and dizzy from running around without making any headway. Desperate, the woman thought about the county's highest-ranking administrative official—the county magistrate. Somehow she plucked up the guts and walked directly into the magistrate's office. Tears gushed down her cheeks when she took out the transfer application and opened her mouth. As if driven by some mysterious ghost that day, the magistrate picked up the pen and signed the application without any fuss. He didn't take any bribe and didn't try to take advantage of her, either. Before long, the woman's husband was transferred back to the county town.

When I asked the ex-county magistrate, he said he had clean forgotten it. At the time, he said, the top municipal officials were coming to the county for an inspection tour and would arrive soon. He signed the form without even looking—just to get rid of the teary-eyed woman so that he could go and meet the visiting officials. That was all. He had forgotten all about it until now. As a county magistrate, he had had to deal with so many things on any given day.

That woman, however, still remembers it. The woman said: He is a savior of our family! When he was still the magistrate we didn't have a chance to thank him for his kindness. Now he is in jail, I can come and visit him now and then.

(2005)

Reckoning

Zheng Hongjie

My Big Aunt is a teacher.

Back then the rural classroom was simple at best. The paint on the cement blackboard had long faded with chipped patches here and there, revealing the rough surface underneath. Thus much of the contrast between white chalk and blackboard was lost although words were still legible enough. Big Aunt would stand in front of the class and point at each word emphatically while leading the young pupils in reading aloud: Long . . . Live . . . Chairman . . . Mao!

All the eyes of the young pupils would be on Big Aunt or the blackboard as they read aloud in chorus: Long . . . Live . . . Chairman . . . Mao!

Big Aunt was these kids' homeroom teacher at this rural grade school. Even today those "kids" still have vivid memories of being a young pupil of hers. Now, at the age of 54, Big Aunt teaches the third grade. Times have changed and both the "how" and the "what" of her teaching have changed. Last summer, for example, Big Aunt didn't let the kids go home to help with the harvest or the gleaning. Big Aunt said: On Children's Day, June 1, I'll take you all to the county town to see the changes there. What do you think?

Big Aunt continued: The visit will take a whole day. We leave in the morning and return in the afternoon. We'll take the shuttle bus. For the morning we will visit the county museum and tour the Century Square. For the afternoon we will see the movie *Little Radish*. Then we will come back. How does that sound?

Hurrah! The kids clapped their hands thunderously.

Then, Big Aunt said: We will bring our own lunch. Ask your parents to bake you a bun and boil you a couple of eggs, plus a bottle of water, and you will be fine. You can bring a cucumber or tomato or something from your family's vegetable garden if you want to. That will reduce your expenses. I have done the math: round trip bus fare, tickets for the museum and film, altogether about 12 *yuan* per person. So, please explain it clearly to your parents and then bring the money to me. All right?

Hurrah! The kids clapped their hands again.

By May 31, Big Aunt had collected money from all of the 47 young pupils except for three. These three said they didn't want to go. Big Aunt understood: The families of the three were among the poorest. She hesitated and then said to the class: We are a team. I think these three classmates won't go because they can't afford it. Shouldn't we all pitch in and lend them a hand? Okay, let me be the first to do so. Of course you don't have to give as much. Ten cents, one *yuan*, it doesn't matter. What's important is in our heart we want to help. With that, Big Aunt put down ten *yuan* from her purse.

The fundraising on May 31 was a success. It raised enough money for the three kids to go on the trip, too.

So, on June 1, Big Aunt took her class to the county town, where the kids had such a good time. On July 1 school would be dismissed for the summer break. On September 1 Big Aunt's young pupils would move on to the 4th grade. The grade reports had already been handed out.

Yet, on the afternoon of June 30, when all the other classes wouldn't come to school any more, Big Aunt called all her young pupils in. She wanted to have a meeting. Standing in front of the entire class, Big Aunt said, solemnly: There is some reckoning we need to do before the summer break. That is: I haven't had a chance to give you a report on the expenses of our trip to the county town.

The young pupils were stunned. None of them had expected the teacher to hold a special meeting about this. It had occurred to none that their teacher needed to give them a report on the field trip's expenses.

Scanning the puzzled eyes in front of her, Big Aunt said: In one's lifetime, one will run into or be in charge of accounts. Only once or many times, it is the same. Big sums of money or small sums, it is the same, too. They should all be as clear, accurate, and transparent as can be. Only when the accounts are clear and accurate can a person be clean. Only when the person is clean can he or she stand in the world holding the head high. Do you all agree?

Yes! The young pupils cried out in their quivering voices.

Big Aunt continued: I should have given you the report sooner but I have been held up by helping you review for finals, writing up the annual reports, grading the exams, and preparing the grade report and evaluation for each one of you. So I apologize. This report is long overdue, isn't it?

No! The young pupils shook their heads, some had tears in their eyes.

That afternoon, Big Aunt posted on the blackboard a large sheet of paper on which was a detailed report of the money collected and expenditures for each and every young pupil. The Grand Total: Income: 564.00 *yuan*; Expenditures: 561.80 *yuan*; Balance: 2.20 *yuan*.

Big Aunt asked every pupil to come to the board and take a look at the report. Then she asked: What shall we do with the 2.20 *yuan*? The young pupils looked at each other. No one wanted it. No one would suggest that their teacher keep it because they knew that would be an insult to her. Yet what should they do with the money? Big Aunt said: I've thought about this long and hard and have taken the liberty to use the money to buy a bag of M&M's, about three pieces a person. Now, I'll invite four of you to come to the front and hand out the candies to the entire class.

My Big Aunt stood there watching the 47 young pupils of hers sitting there and counting the candies in their hands seriously.

(2005)

The Outside World

Zhou Rencong

Qingqing's beauty is universally acknowledged.

She was attending a high school in the county town. In her class were so many city girls who were dressed in trendy clothes every day. Qingqing was from the countryside and didn't have the kind of money to spend on clothes. Yet all the teachers and male students agreed that Qingqing was the "school flower." Her beauty was natural and pure: her face, her slender figure, the long and rich braids cascading behind her back, and above all, her quiet and simple personality—nobody could top that.

At 19, Qingqing graduated from high school and returned to her home village. Right away match-makers came knocking. The most noticeable of the suitors was Zhishou, son of the local town commissioner. Zhishou asked the match-maker to deliver a passionate letter, saying he had been fond of her for a long time and had been waiting for her to graduate from high school. If Qingqing liked, Zhishou promised, he would arrange through his powerful father for her to work in the town's "Family Planning Office." Zhishou had been two grades above Qingqing and had been working at the town's Department of Land ever since high school graduation. Now he is officially a government civil service employee. His matchmaker added: So many girls in town fight to be the town commissioner's daughter-in-law, but Zhishou has his eyes on you only!

Qingqing's mother said: "You're 19 now. Old enough to start thinking about this."

Then a classmate of Qingqing came to see her. She was going to Guangzhou to look for work and asked if Qingqing would want to go with her. Qingqing wasn't sure. The classmate said: "You want to be stuck in the countryside for the rest of your life, with all that learning and knowledge bursting inside you? Let's go and see the world so we won't have any regrets. He who doesn't travel will never make a name for himself. Remember?" Qingqing bought the argument.

So she went to Guangzhou and found a job at a toy company. She worked a three-shift rotation and by the end of the month was paid 600 *yuan*. She was so thrilled when holding the money she made for the first time.

During the second month the boss, rich and smartly dressed, called Qingqing to his office and said to her: "Now I know for the first time what 'Lotus Flower Blossoming From Water' means." The look in his eyes as he said this made Qingqing afraid. Then the boss said: "I'll pay you 5,000 *yuan* a month."

Qingqing gathered enough courage to say: Not all girls would throw away anything just for money.

So Qinging left the toy company.

She was disappointed and felt keenly the lyrics she knew so well: "The outside world is so colorful and so helpless."

Qingqing used that month's wage to buy a train ticket home.

When she got off the train in the local town she ran into Zhishou. He looked so handsome. Qingqing felt something warm inside her and blushed.

Zhishou nodded to her slightly and went on his way.

Two months had passed since Qingqing came home, but not many match-makers came knocking on the door.

Qingqing thought about Zhishou all the time, and the promised job at the town's "Family Planning Office," yet she didn't know how to bring it up with her mother.

Her mother was quite worried, too. She even sought out the match-maker sent by Zhishou. The match-maker said: "Zhishou has a girlfriend already. They were engaged two days ago. The girl now works in the 'Family Planning Office.'" She went on to say: "Boys nowadays don't want to marry girls who have been outside the village. The outside world is so messy and girls who have been there, well. . . . "

Soon, through the busy work of matchmakers, even the homely girls in the village are engaged to be married. No one, however, has expressed serious interest in Qingqing yet.

(2005)

Shanshan

Danru

Not her. Let it not be her!

My eyes on the messy file on the desk, I sat zombie-like the whole afternoon. When I came to work this morning, I had felt tantalizingly hopeful for the day. Now my heart felt as heavy and as numb as lead.

The police department called this morning. They had found a young girl's body which seemed to fit the description I had given them. They wanted me to go and take a look. I prayed all the way there: Not her. Let it not be her! Yet, lying under the white sheet was the familiar pale face.

......

"What's your name?"

"Shanshan!" She had replied carelessly.

"How old are you?"

"Fifteen."

Pale, thin, she stood quietly in front of me. Half shielded amidst her long hair was a pair of stubborn eyes. Biting her lower lip all the time, she would give the shortest reply whenever asked a question. This was Shanshan, the first impression she gave me two years ago.

The year I was to graduate from high school, the topic for our writing exam was "After Graduation." Many of my classmates thought the teacher was trying to be humorous: Since "After Graduation" usually means "Unemployment," what's there to write about? In the end, though, everyone had to put down their wish for a future career. This was what I wrote: Social Worker.

"Mr. Guo Shen, I want to talk to you about Shanshan."

"Talk? Don't you see I'm playing poker here, miss? Nothing to talk about!"

"She was arrested at 'Fish Stalls.'[7] You don't care at all? Besides, she has picked up the habits of druggies. Do you know?"

"Damn the girl! Has money for drugs, but no money to bring home, you know? Each month she brings home some lousy money—not enough to buy me cigarettes! Now she wants to be a druggie girl. Tell her to go and die!"

"Mr. Guo Shen, she's your daughter after all. How can you. . . . "

"Nonsense! *My* last name is Guo. Hers is Ye. This old fool has worked hard to bring her up for her dead mother's sake. Hey, are you done? Three people are waiting for me inside. I don't have time to waste with you!"

"Mr. Guo Shen, Mr. Guo Shen. . . . "

That was the first time I had talked to Shanshan's stepfather. It was the last time he showed me any politeness at all. Afterwards, he would not want to say one word to me. Sometimes he would cuss and push me out the door.

After much effort I succeeded in finding Shanshan an apprentice position at a clothing factory, hoping she would gradually get back on track with her life. This girl had a good heart. Her attitude to me changed for the better day by day.

Then, Shanshan's stepfather would come to the factory to demand money. If Shanshan couldn't give him any, he would call her "Damn Druggie Girl" or "Damn Girl Whore" and give her no peace. At first Shanshan's coworkers were somewhat sympathetic. When this happened more often, however, their attitude changed. Some began to treat her coldly. Even those who used to talk to her wouldn't want to have anything to do with her any more. So, Shanshan stayed at this job for only five months.

"Sis, I haven't eaten anything for days." Shanshan appeared at the door of my office one day. This was the first time she came to see me on her own.

"Sis, why, except for you, does nobody else care about me or love me? Dad died so long ago. Then Ma didn't want me any more. That bad man beat Ma so often. He beat Ma to death! And coming to demand money all the time. I have no money. Really I have no money at all."

Shanshan stayed in my home that night. She sobbed in her sleep.

Then Shanshan disappeared. I looked for her in the "ports" she frequented and talked to the "contact" for the girls, but couldn't find her. I even went to the "fish stalls," the last place in the world I wanted to be. But she disappeared, leaving not a footprint behind, like a rock sinking to the bottom of the sea. She had been missing for three months.

"Little Yu, let go. We are not saviors of the world after all. The only thing we can say is we have done our best. Certain things are beyond us. Perhaps death is not a bad thing to her!"

"Director, how can you say that? She's so young. There's nothing that can't be resolved. Why she chose to end it this way, I don't understand. I don't understand at all!"

"I know you and Shanshan have become close during the last two years. But it's all over now. Go home and have a good rest. There's a lot to do tomorrow."

So it was all over when the case was closed. Yet tomorrow, how many more Shanshans would appear, and how little I could do for them? Perhaps Shanshan's death was a mute protest to this twisted society. How many people had given her another shot at life? Had she really gotten to where there was nowhere else to go?

I still remember once Shanshan asking me, innocently: "Can I call you sis? If you were really my sis. . . . "

(n.d.)

Applause

Haixin

1.

Thunderous applause. Mixed in it were cries of "Encore!" "Encore!" "Bravo!"

No sooner had that four-women family moved into the empty apartment next door than it began to rock with "sound and fury" right away. As their neighbors, we, a family of five, started to live a life filled with "sound and fury," too. It was especially bad every evening when waves of earth-shattering applause and hurrahs swept in through the window. It was like being, with my wife and our three daughters, in a concert hall where the crazed audience clapped and cheered frenziedly when a star was giving a fantastic performance. What was most annoying was the time from late afternoon toward the evening. Having worked for a whole day at school my wife and I needed to have some quiet time or do some leisure reading; our three kids needed to do their homework, too. I thought when our new neighbors' home was exploding with applause every evening, those living above and below must be having a terrible time, too. Indeed, they would complain to each other and even cuss when they met in the elevator. Mr. Zhu, an accountant living downstairs said angrily: "I've called the police, but the officer said between seven and eight p.m. every resident has the right to watch TV, listen to the radio, or play *majiang*!"

My wife said she visited our neighbors and tried to talk them into turning off the recorder playing the thunderous applause. But that six-tyish, gray-haired mistress of the house, Wang Lan Mu-Rong, a faded singer, still in her pajamas, would continue to drowse sprawled in the rocking chair, not even saying hello to her neighbor. The woman servant came with tea. The two pretty daughters told my wife they were still in college. They apologized for the disturbance their mother's "applause" had caused the neighbors. The elder daughter said: "I am really sorry. My mother would suffer from insomnia or get ill if she doesn't have her daily dose of applause and cheering in the evening!" The younger daughter said: "The applause is my mother's only entertainment. It's her life, too! She used to be a well-known singer."

2.

Every Sunday morning a tall, thin, gray-haired man would appear at the door of this family of four women. Dressed in a dark coat, a pipe in mouth, and a bunch of fresh flowers in hand, the man would press the doorbell again and again, but no one came to answer the door. He would stand there patiently, as if he had all the time in the world to wait, and press the button again until someone finally opened the door, the elder daughter, the younger daughter, or the woman servant. They all knew him well and were quite sympathetic. They would take the flowers but wouldn't let him in: "She still refuses to forgive." they said. "So you have to go." The Old Man sighed and turned to leave.

This Sunday morning, as he walked to the elevator still sighing, I approached him deliberately, like a snooping busybody. He said to me emotionally, "I am the owner of a record company. And I'm the head of this household. That faded singer who listens to the applause every evening is my wife. I love her so much! Ever since she retired from the stage, she has been living in that tape of her last, farewell performance which excited the most enthusiastic applause and cheering. Not only did the neighbors complain. Even me, the husband, couldn't take it any-more. So, I tried to erase the tape, and was more than half way through when she stumbled upon me. She pushed me to the ground and moved over here. It doesn't matter how hard I've begged her for forgiveness, she wouldn't listen! What crimes have I committed?"

(n.d.)

Mad About You

Sang Ni

Si Mana couldn't forget the applause!

The first time she performed on stage, when she finished the first song, the response from the audience was indifferent. Nobody applauded, which made it "illegitimate" for her to do an encore. Ah M, the master of ceremonies, had to come on the stage to smooth things over for her. He said to the swarming audience down there, frothily:

"Our Miss Si Mana has brought us Hong Kong fans several of her latest love songs that have been quite a hit among many young people. She likes Hong Kong very much. So, let's welcome Miss Si Mana to sing us another song with warm applause, her very best 'Mad About You!'"

Some sporadic, half-hearted applause aroses from the audience.

When the second song was over, the audience began to applaud more enthusiastically. It seemed their applause came from the heart. She was thrilled.

The applause for the third song was even warmer.

When she stepped out of the nightclub, it was already past midnight. Si Mana's boyfriend stopped a taxi to take her home.

In the car her boyfriend said bluntly: "Na, you sang badly tonight."

"What?" Si Mana said, "You meant my first song, right? I know I didn't do it well, but the audience in Hong Kong . . . they were so rude. No response at all. How do you suppose I could put myself into singing?"

"How can you blame the audience when you didn't sing well in the first place?"

"My second and third songs were better than the first. You know the secret?"

The boyfriend shook his head.

"I'm a moody singer. The audience's response means a lot to me and I need applause badly. It's stimulating!"

So the first time Si Mana performed on stage she heard applause from the audience. For this, she was so excited she couldn't fall asleep. She crawled out of bed at around midnight and sang a song in front of the floor-length mirror. She imagined that on the other side of the mirror a large audience of several hundred nightclub guests were listening. Then, as she imagined a thunderous applause arising from down there, she closed her eyes, excited, intoxicated, her soul soaring into the clouds in the sky.

However, the reviews by music critics were not only unflattering, they were sharp in their criticism. Since Si Mana didn't read the newspapers, she had no clue.

After performing on the stage a few more times, Si Mana fell ill. According to doctors' diagnoses, the cause of the illness was excessive excitement. Si Mana knew that the excitement was, in turn, caused by the audience's applause. Whenever the warm applause arose while she was performing on stage, her heart would beat so fiercely. The more frenziedly the audience applauded, the less she could control herself, and the more she let go of her emotions, so much so that she became hoarse and sounded like a different person.

The maddest was a recent evening. Si Mana had barely walked onto the stage and hadn't even opened her mouth when warm applause erupted thunderously, mixed with whistling and frenzied hurrahs. Si Mana was so excited she fainted! Her boyfriend jumped on stage and removed his jacket to cover her thin, semi-translucent dress, which revealed her bra-less chest.

(n.d.)

society

Bargain

Hu Yepin

Our quartermaster is tying the knot once again—or . . . why don't we call a spade a spade: he will be doing another woman once again. By "once again," it is meant that since he was promoted to quartermaster, less than two years ago, he has already done seven or eight women, every single time as sure a thing as could be. If things go on like this, who knows how many more women he will do. It seems that doing women forms half of his duties as quartermaster.

As to why he does so there is no need to look hard. The reason is simple: It doesn't really matter much to him how many women he does because, now that he has morphed into an officer and the place is secured by troops armed to the teeth, he can pull it off as easily as pulling the trigger of his rifle.

Of course people do this with different methods: swindling, false claims or charges, use of brutal force, what have you, but none could dispense with coercions. Our quartermaster, however, does it in a much more honorable way: money—not much money, though. The exact expenses for this purpose can be verified in the accounts he has kept, which he does out of his occupational habit. In the account book are listed the following entries:

No. 1: 40 *yuan*
No. 2: 35 *yuan*
No. 3: 44 *yuan*
No. 4: 20 *yuan*

No. 5: 50 *yuan*
No. 6: 30 *yuan*
No. 7: 55 *yuan*

Without such a detailed, item-by-item record of prices, I am afraid, he himself may forget, one day, exactly just how many he has done. This account book, he doesn't seem to treasure particularly, leaving it together with the "Accounts for Horse Feed" most of the time. Yet whenever a new friend comes to visit, he can't resist opening it for the visitor's benefit lest he wouldn't know, as if this account book brings him as much glory as the shoulder-strap for his colonel's rank.

Our clerk marvels thus about this account book:

"It's much better than a certificate of appointment!"

Which is not overstating the case. A certificate of appointment doesn't shine in the eyes of an officer any more, but such an account book does, with all of its novelty and out-of-the-ordinary mystique. For instance, even though what is entered in the accounts is nothing but the amount of *yuan*, yet each amount of that *yuan* has some kind of special meaning: 40 *yuan* equals one woman, 35 *yuan*, another woman; moreover, each *yuan* in the 40 *yuan* and 35 *yuan* equals a part of this or that woman. This fact alone would make the account book much better than a certificate of so and so being hereby appointed such and such a rank. Naturally, our quartermaster is more than flattered by the clerk's remark cited above.

And, indeed, no one would know with how much joy and pride he writes down No. X has cost him Y amount of *yuan*, hundreds of times more so than when he scrounges around with military supplies, to say the least.

And, indeed, tonight our quartermaster must be experiencing the same rapture as he adds a new entry in this account book of his. This new entry, "No. 8," apparently, is added right below "No. 7," and bears the amount of "70 *yuan*," bigger than all the other entries.

"This one is not a bargain!" Our quartermaster feels. In reality, though, 70 *yuan* is nothing to him: Barely an evening goes by that doesn't see a couple of hundred *yuan* pass through his fingers at the gambling table.

Yet women can't compare to the *majiang* game. Our quartermaster didn't mind losing two or three hundred *yuan* at the *majiang* table, but wouldn't want to spend a hundred *yuan* on a woman. So, this 70 *yuan* is not a bargain indeed.

Why does our quartermaster have such low regard for women? Naturally he is not without some reasoning of his own. He feels that there is no way women can compare to the *majiang* game: With *majiang*, you win some and lose some; money comes and money goes. You may have lost a hundred *yuan* yesterday but tonight you win two hundred *yuan*, who knows? Women, on the other hand, are quite a different thing: Forty *yuan* spent is forty *yuan* spent, a hundred *yuan* spent is a hundred *yuan* spent—you can't ever recover even half a dime! Therefore, an indelible truth presents itself in his soul, which becomes a sort of adage for him:

"Would rather lose it all in a single *majiang* game than do a single woman all my life!"

As could be expected, within less than two years, up to this very moment, our quartermaster has acquired eight women in a row. Each time a new woman is acquired, the old one would be discarded, like an old blanket, the quartermaster's erstwhile plaything becoming the playground for gangs of rowdy soldiers.

Really, how can anyone fail to see this? A woman, even at the price of 70 *yuan*, is indeed such a bargain!

(1929)

The Lottery

Lao She[8]

Lotteries have been in our village since time immemorial. Air Force Lottery? Great! We welcome it like our very own. The grand prize is 500,000 *yuan*? Holy smoke!

Second Sister started a lottery group by putting down 20 cents first. Having consulted my fortune, which was said to be most favorable, I put down 40 cents. For a whole day Sister and I calculated over and again and found that we were still 9 *yuan* and 40 cents short to buy one ticket. So, we went out to recruit prospective players: 50,000 *yuan*; 50,000 *yuan* divided among 50 players, each getting 10,000 *yuan*, 20 cents for 10,000 *yuan*! The whole village was crazed with excitement. Even dogs had heard so much of "50,000 *yuan*" that they would wag their tails at any mere stranger who could utter "50,000 *yuan*" instead of dashing over and sinking their fangs into his leg. The craze lasted for a week; we were able to scrape together 10 *yuan*, with me being the biggest stock-holder. Third Granny put down only 5 cents. Fourth Auntie and Fifth Auntie held joint ownership of one share; they even set up an account book for the purpose.

Where to go and purchase the lottery? Second Sister, not trusting my foresight in matters of money, paid five big coins to Blind Wang for an astrological reading, which turned out to favor the northeast direction. Of the four lottery vendors the city, Lucky You is in the northeast. So we decided to go and purchase at Lucky You. However, Lucky You is the smallest of the four and its merchandise is limited to things like cigarettes and kerosene. What if the 10 *yuan* were embezzled? Or the tickets they sell are counterfeit? So, we gave Blind Wang another five big coins to have another astrological reading. It turned out, he said, the northwest would be favorable, too. Not just favorable; in fact, based on careful calculation through his fingers, more favorable than northeast! Good Luck Forever, a much bigger vendor, is in the northwest. That's where Second Sister had purchased the silk and red quilt for her wedding.

A new question presented itself: who shall go and purchase the ticket? Ordinarily it should be me, being the biggest shareholder. However, I'm an Ox, and this being the Year of the Rooster, it should be someone who is a Rooster; a man, to be more exact, because a woman would bring bad luck. Only Third Born in the Li family is a Rooster. Somehow, all the other Roosters have suddenly disappeared into thin air. We wouldn't trust Third Born, being so little, to go all by himself. So we decided to send two men, both of the sturdiest Metal Life, to escort him. Then, on an auspicious day, the three traveled downtown to purchase the ticket.

Now that the ticket has been purchased, who should hold it? Whenever our village needs to do something collectively, we run into the same problem: Nobody trusts anybody else. After three whole days and nights of deliberations, the ticket was entrusted to the care of Third Granny, who has the virtue not of being trustworthy, but of being advanced in age, which would make it virtually impossible for her to flee with the ticket.

The night before the Lottery, nobody could sleep a wink. Take me for instance; once I receive my share of the grand prize—who else but us will win it—how should I spend the 20,000 *yuan*? Buy a small house? Sounds good, but what location, what style, and what decoration? I tossed and turned past midnight. No, not buying a house, but starting a business instead. Then, the store's location, style, kind, ways to make money, to expand with the money made, and so on . . . I tossed and turned the rest of the night. The stars in the sky, foamy bubbles by the river's edge, all looked like glittering coins. Insects cheeping during the night, birds chirping at dawn, all singing the same "500,000 *yuan*" song. Dozing off now and then, hands resting on my chest, I dreamed of glittering coins piled on top of me; I could hardly breathe! Then I bought a set of bone cards, at the ready for reading my fortune. If it was bad fortune, it wouldn't count; simply try again. As a result, it was all good fortune. I would hit the jackpot for sure.

The Lottery was drawn and the newspapers announced the top five winning numbers. The draw did hot have the numbers we had committed to memory. New house, new store, were all washed away with sweat. So we waited for the sixth and seventh prize-winning numbers: No luck with the top five prizes; a sixth prize, to say the least, should be a sure thing. I had my fortune read once again: most favorable. The sixth prize was 500 *yuan*, part of which could be spent on a new shirt for the summer, not bad. So, while waiting for the sixth and seventh prizes to be announced, I went through the top five winning numbers over and over, thinking of ways for the winners to spend the money, and couldn't help but feel jealous while thinking thus, and, one thought leading to another, I began to think about how the winners' blissful good fortune had a sudden, disastrous turn, such as being burnt to death in a fire of their own money, perhaps. So, it was really my good fortune *not* to have won the Lottery; however, if I *had* won, I might not have to die in a fire. No matter how I sliced it, it wasn't much of a warm feeling after all.

Then, the sixth and seventh prizes were announced. They still had nothing to do with us. It was then that we thought of the last digit prize. Even that played a joke on us: Ours was a 3, while the winning digit was a 2. No luck!

Woe was Second Sister and me, the organizers of the group! Third Granny wanted back from us her 5 cents. There was no way not to refund her. Once we returned her money, no one else would be willing to write off their 20 cents as a lost cause. Second Sister has been under the weather for the last two days. She has this amazing ability to feel under the weather whenever the woe hits her. So, I was left alone to take care of the 20 cents for everybody. Now that all is taken care of, Second Sister is not under the weather any more. As for me, well, I slept soundly last night.

(1933)

Comedy of the Power Poles
Su Shuyang

"Believe it or not, these days if you want to know what's going on in the world, just step out and take a look at the power poles!" Mr. Sun, my kind next-door neighbor, thus advised me one day.

Indeed, come to think of it, he was absolutely right. In my earliest memory, power poles were all wood, tall pines with white porcelain bottles on the tops. On these poles were posted theatre fliers, colorful ads, and jingles such as "Glory to mighty heaven, glory to mighty earth, our baby cries mightily in the middle of night. . . ." As if babies back then cried their eyes out so often that they had to be talked about ten thousand times by passers-by in order to live on. A few years ago, power poles were covered with

"Burn . . . !" "Cannon . . . !" "Deep Fry . . . .!" "A Thousand Cuts . . . !"

and such slogans, enough to show how resilient human life is: refusing to breathe its last until it can't take any more crushing blows. Nowadays it's quite a different story. Power poles have assumed the role of the powerful employment agencies, personnel offices, and housing exchange services. Yes, if you are being afflicted with chronic bronchitis and arthritis and whatever, you can go to the power poles and get helped: There they will give you, in a most generous manner, all kinds of ancient, secret remedies. This is progress! Mr. Sun, ever so kind and sharp-eyed, has thus pointed it out for us.

My wife and I, however, we are blockheads. Fifteen years into our marriage and we are still living this "Cowherd and the Weaver Girl"⁹ kind of life. We have always counted on the kindness of the Personnel Office Directors of our respective employers, but to no avail, and it has never occurred to us to resort to the power poles. A mere glance at so many employment exchange ads on the poles, all so earnest and touching, and you'd be convinced of their efficacy. Otherwise, why bother wasting so much paper? Having been doing surveying work in deep mountains for six years without returning to Beijing even once, I had no clue that this is how it is done. Now, I wanted to try posting ads on the power poles, too, begging the kind-hearted to go and take my job in the deep mountains so that I could return and take theirs in Beijing.

Before posting, I went on a little scouting tour starting from our own Peace Alley southward, checking the "literature" on each and every power pole along the way.

What luck! On the 13th power pole from North New Bridge toward South Route West, I found a print ad: Looking for someone with a noble soul who will volunteer to exchange his job in Beijing for a job in the deep mountains. Anyone interested please call a certain Comrade Wang at this number or talk to Wang in person at this address, and so on.

I almost choked with feverish excitement. I read the godsend ad for the fifth time, gesturing wildly. An elderly popsicle lady thought I wanted to buy one and shuffled over. I ran over as quickly as I could to the address, looking for Comrade Wang.

Once there, I felt strange, as if I had been there before. But it didn't matter. I came to look for a Comrade Wang. And out came a full-figured woman. Oh, my, I know her! Sis Wang, my wife's best friend. Even better!

Sis Wang invited me in and treated me to tea, sunflower seeds, and pleasantries. Then, I couldn't hold it any longer: I said, "So, tell me who has asked you to put up that ad? If you help me exchange jobs with him, I'll owe you, him, and yes, the power poles, a thousand thanks!" Sis Wang burst out laughing. "Why, it's she, your own wife!"

What? Dammit! Ah, the power poles!

(1980)

Street Corner

Shen Shanzeng

A high school classmate of mine once told me this story:

He is quite a smart fellow, but was unemployed at the time. All he did everyday was eat and sit around at home doing nothing. One day, he got hold of two of his friends and together they went out looking for excitement.

They stopped at the sewage ditch near a busy street corner, squatted, and looked down intently. In less than a minute, they were surrounded by five or six people looking over their heads. "What is it?" someone asked.

"Oh, a big rat . . . white as snow . . . this big!" The classmate of mine indicated with his hands.

"Look, its head has just come out!" His co-conspirators cheered on. Seven or eight heads craned to see.

"It's drawn back, but will come out again."

In less than ten minutes, the ditch was surrounded by several layers of people, those from the outside layers asking those of the inside layers:

"What is it?"

"What is it?"

"A white-haired rat . . . green-eyed . . . its tail two feet long."

"Oh, my!"

At this point the classmate of mine and his co-conspirators withdrew from the scene quietly.

When they came back after wandering around for a while, the street corner next to the ditch was besieged with a thick, large crowd. The traffic jam was so bad that the whole place became a parking lot of long lines of busses and trucks, all honking like ravens.

"What's going on?" the classmate of mine grabbed the hand of a man, who was craning hard to see, and asked.

"A huge rat." The man broke free of his hand and squeezed into the thick crowd. Someone hollered from beside the sewage ditch: "Its head is coming out!"

Oh, what splendid stupidity!

(1981)

Spring Night

Wu Jinliang

"Have got to ask if I see another man," Chen Jing thought as she glanced into the dim street lights in the alley. A sigh arose deep inside her: "Ah, this darned bicycle!"

From behind came a bicycle bell ringing. Before an "Ah" escaped her lips the young man on the bicycle had already flitted past her.

What! The young man returned. Chen Jing was seized with fear. "It's so late and he. . . ."

"Did you just call me?" the young man was already off the bicycle.

"Oh . . . no." Her sense of self-preservation kicked in and she was at loss for words.

"Your bicycle broke down?" A pair of eyes, half laughing, gazed at her.

Chen Jing tried to compose herself. "The chain has got stuck in the shield," she mumbled, her head low, a ray of hope glimmering in her heart.

"Then, Miss, I won't be able to help. Without tools nobody can take off the chain shield."

Chen Jing's heart was filled with darkness again.

"Is your home far from here?"

"My home?" She was at a loss again and began to push her bicycle forward.

"All right, on the left of this alley's entrance there's a bicycle shop. Someone may still be there. Why don't you go and try there!" With that the young man flew away on his bicycle.

"Thanks but no thanks!" Chen Jing almost cried. It was already 11 o'clock in the evening. What bicycle shop would still be open! "Liar!" she cussed in her heart. "May you have a bad dream tonight."

When she came out of the alley, though, she couldn't help glancing toward the left side. The light in a small house along the sidewalk was still on.

She was still hesitating when a young woman in her twenties stepped out and hollered: "Hey, Miss, come on in!"

Why, it was a bicycle shop all right! Chen Jing felt the world around her suddenly brightening up; all her fear and frustration was gone.

It was a simple, barrel-straight house facing the street. The door to the interior room was closed. The outer room had only a desk, a bed, and a bicycle. A young man was bent over the desk turning over the pages of something.

"Come on in," the young man said, standing up, a screwdriver in hand. "This place is a bit small."

"It's you?" Chen Jing was taken aback.

"It's me," the young man smiled. "Told you the shop would still be open, didn't I?" He winked knowingly.

"My brother went escorting my sis-in-law to work. Upon coming back, he woke me up as if the house were on fire. It turned out. . . . " The young woman in her twenties followed behind, chattering.

"That's why we need privately-owned shops," Chen Jing thought. She smiled at the young woman gratefully: "Sorry to have bothered you."

"Oh, don't mention it. My brother was worried that you wouldn't dare to come in, so he woke me up to holler to you. Really, you're a bit too timid. I wouldn't have been afraid at all."

Chen Jing turned red with embarrassment.

Soon the bicycle was fixed by capable hands.

"How much?" Chen Jing was hoping that the young man would charge her a bit more than his usual fee.

"How much?" the young man looked surprised. He smiled the next instant: "Five *yuan* will do." A big hand, covered with grease, reached over to Chen Jing.

"Five *yuan*?! That's plain robbery!" Shocked as she was, Chen Jing took out her purse.

"Brother!" the young woman broke in. "You're in the mood to joke at this late hour!" She slapped the greasy hand away and turned to Chen Jing:

"Miss, don't you mind him. He likes to joke regardless of time and place. We are not a bicycle shop, so how can we take your money for a simple thing like that?"

Her face flushed.

"Okay, no more jokes!" Her brother stood there, wringing his hands, and grinned happily. His teeth looked white and clean.

Once on her way again, Chen Jing felt a gentle breeze breathing into her face and her long hair, ticklish, yet pleasant. The street lights felt brighter tonight; they were shining brilliantly. The air had a hint of intoxicating fragrance in it, too.

Oh, spring night!

(1982)

Request for the Purchase of a Kettle
Xu Shijie

"Little Wei? Please come to the Office of Logistics. Your request has been granted."

"What request?" Little Wei was taken aback.

"That, that—" From the other end of the phone came the sound of sheets of paper being turned. Manager Wu read slowly in a solemn voice, "that request for the purchase of a kettle."

"Oh, Good Heavens! This is what season now—the request has been granted! Last winter we had a heating stove in the office and the air was so dry that we needed a kettle badly. But now . . . " Little Wei glanced at the fan shaking its head left and right and couldn't help but laugh. "Ah, a crappy kettle took as long as half a year! Hey, Old Wu, did you send the request all the way to Beijing?"

Little Wei had never expected that the request for a kettle would require such long and convoluted procedures. The first time he made the request to the Office of Logistics, it was mid-November of last year. At the time, a certain Manager Zheng granted the request right away. However, after he had waited anxiously for half a month, not even a shadow of the requested kettle presented itself. So, he went to the Office of Logistics again. Manager Zheng wasn't there. Another manager, Wang, closed the magazine *Beyond the Eight-Hour Shift* in his hands, took a drag on his cigarette, and said, rather businesslike:

"Comrade Wei, a kettle seems no big deal, but what if the other offices know about this and come and make the same request? Things could get out of hand."

Little Wei almost lost it. "Why would they want kettles! They are all working in the new building with central heat. We are the only ones left behind in the old wooden house, and we are the only ones who need to have a heating stove."

"This 'us' and 'them' mentality of yours . . . is . . . not conducive to unity!"

Little Wei was shaking all over with anger. He went to talk to Manager Wu, the Number One boss of the Office of Logistics, and got this as an answer: "Since the other two managers don't seem to agree, you should send in a written request to the higher-ups for consideration." This "consideration" lasted for more than five months! Yet the request had been granted, after all. Last winter was now long gone, but there would be winter this year for sure. Just in case something might happen at the last minute, Little Wei hurried to the Office of Logistics and filled out a receipt form in triplicate.

Manager Wu, holding his thermos cup, was studying the written request, filled to the brim with comments, when Little Wei stepped in. Wu raised his hand to smooth his thin, silvery hair, his dull eyes looking hard over the reading glasses on his nose, and said, reluctantly: "Nothing can be done about it. Bureau Director Zhao didn't give specific instructions."

"What kind of game is this? A crappy kettle has to be approved by Bureau Director Zhao?" Little Wei couldn't believe his ears. He bent over Manager Wu's shoulder and took a glimpse at the written request.

"Oh, my, it's Director Zhao indeed. Hey, didn't Director Zhao approve?"

"The word 'approve' is exactly the source of our trouble here!"

"How?"

Manager Wu took a sip from the cup and said, slowly, "Manager Zheng 'approved' the request; Manager Wang 'disapproved;' Chiefs Li and Zhou only checked their names on the written request; Deputy

Director Sun 'approved' with a comment on the importance of 'paying attention to working conditions of the masses;' Deputy Director Qian had this to say: 'Even a crappy kettle has to go through so much red tape. Ludicrous! How can we go on without streamlining government functions and rectifying our working style? I suggest using this case to start an education campaign among the cadres.' Which of these did Director Zhao 'approve'?"

"This. . . ."

(1982)

The Two Patients

Jiang Zilong

Professor Zhuang, forever proud, can't take it anymore. As an eminent professor of a prestigious university, he's never received such treatment, even when he became ill during a lecture tour outside China. Theoretically, high-level intellectuals are entitled to the same treatment as high-ranking cadres, yet how can this "high-level intellectual" compare to that "high-ranking cadre," Manager Wang, occupying the bed opposite his? Wang's bed is always being visited by a division director or a section chief or a cadre of some sort and by a pretty young woman or two now and then. The nightstand by Wang's bed is piled with expensively-packaged nutritious food. And he is being attended to by a crew of six young men, in three shifts, twenty-four hours a day. Even the doctors and the nurses check the powerful Manager Wang first before coming to see

Professor Zhuang, a Chemistry Professor of no inconsequential stature. If they spend half an hour examining Wang, they finish with Zhuang in less than ten minutes. His bedside is all but deserted; his son is engrossed in missile technology research thousands of kilometers away; his daughter is studying abroad, and his wife has to take the crowded bus every day to bring him food and a thermos of hot water. His department cannot be counted on, either. He will be thrilled if the department sends someone down once or twice a month. When a man has fallen so low, his scholarship, his fame, and his self-image prove to be the most useless. Professor Zhuang, however, is unwilling to come off his high horse. Every day he lies in bed facing the wall, indifferent to the comings and goings of those in Manager Wang's bed. Who knows what kind of manager Wang is? Nowadays "company, inc." is everywhere; a big business with thousands of employees is a "company, inc." while anyone and his brother or cousin can hang out their own "company, inc." sign, too.

One day, Manager Wang's illness suddenly deteriorated. The doctor sent word that they should expect the worst. Wang's bedside was surrounded by even more people. Even the high and mighty Deputy Manager Liu came. Liu didn't want to comfort the dying with insincere and empty words. He was quiet for a moment and then spoke simply, asking Manager Wang if there was anything he would like to request and if there was anything on his mind, and promised everything Wang asked for. Having said all there was to say, Liu stood up to leave and make the necessary arrangements. Up stood all the people who had been attending to Wang, too; they all scrambled to help Deputy Manager Liu, some rushing to open the door for him, some hustling by his side and humoring him with their laugh; the patient was left to himself on the bed. It was quite a sight. Deputy Manager Liu flew into a rage:

"I am not the one dying! Why are you all helping me?"

It was then that Professor Zhuang turned his head and saw Manager

Wang, alone on his bed, breathe for the last time. Zhuang, tears streaming down his face, knew he was luckier being a "high-level" intellectual than a "high-level" cadre.

(1985)

Bright Yellow

Liu Xinwu

When she woke up one day, it was already too late.

Shan ransacked several markets until she finally bought a golden yellow one-piece dress. Dazzlingly yellow.

She wore the dress on her date.

"I almost didn't recognize you!" her boyfriend said, looking her up and down, his eyes lit up in surprise.

"You never thought I could get a dress like this, right? I stayed at home for no more than half a month—I was a bit under the weather, you know—and when I came out again, guess what, this shiny yellow is so hot now! What do you think, do I look good!"

She wore the dress to work at the accounting office and was surrounded by several female co-workers as soon as she stepped in.

"Hey, you didn't get it right. What's hot now is bright yellow, not this apricot yellow!" exclaimed the almond-eyed Wu Shuli.

"In the old days only the emperor could wear bright yellow. Girls nowadays, every one of them wants to be the empress." sighed Big Sis Han.

Shan was not troubled by Big Sis Han's comment, but broke into a sweat by what Shuli had said.

When she returned home, mother reprimanded, "This new dress of yours, you've worn it for only two days, and you toss it around like dirt!"

"What do you know? It's not the right yellow!"

Mother shrugged. Girls nowadays, they dare to strut around in yellow. In her day as a girl she didn't even dare to say the word "yellow." "You're so yellow!" That would mean, "You're a bad egg!" Almost.

The next time she went out with her boyfriend, she turned around to let him see more clearly: "It's bright yellow, fair and square, the right color!" When she stopped turning, she pointed at the girls in yellow far and near and declared: "See, that's wrong, that's wrong, too. They didn't get the real thing. Apricot yellow, how timid! Light yellow, how immature! Earthy yellow, how boring. . . . "

The boyfriend wanted to show off his ability to think independently, "I thought lemon yellow is not bad!"

"Lemon yellow? Why not orange yellow!"

Shan wore the bright yellow dress to work at the accounting office. Wu Shuli was the first to scream, "Cool! Really cool this time! A two-piece dress, much more lively than the one-piece dress, so boring!"

Shan was still blooming when Shuli stepped closer and felt the material of the dress between her fingers, her almond-eyes wide with astonishment: "Oh! This material is not right! What's hot today is shiny satin; yours is—"

Shan withered.

The next time she went to see her boyfriend, she saw him craning his neck and looking around up and down the street. She patted him on the back: "Who are you looking for?"

The boyfriend turned and said: "I—I thought you would still be wearing bright yellow. It's bright yellow everywhere and so hard to look for you!"

Shan had on a light purple one-piece dress instead.

(1985)

Comedy of Birds
Zhong Jieying

I used to go to the Little Park every day for my morning exercises. There I met an old man who became my chatting buddy. Then they broke ground here to build the Grand View Garden to shoot the TV drama series *Dream of the Red Chamber*. Since construction was going on everywhere, I hadn't been to the park for quite some time.

One day, in the farmer's market, waiting in a long queue, I saw the old man coming over with a long face, his bird cage in hand. I don't know why but every time I saw him I would be reminded of Second Uncle Song in *Teahouse*.[10] Everything about him, his face, his gait, his mannerisms, and his affections for his bird were almost an exact copy. Rather than find out his real name, I simply called him "Third Uncle Song."

"My Brother, you see this thing is really. . . . " Third Uncle Song began. It turned out the "Old Men Bird Club" had made a big decision recently. To show their true affection for the birds, each charter member of the club was to set free one of his most favorite birds. A grand ceremony would be held in the park on the afternoon of a certain day to mark the occasion.

"Fantastic, Third Uncle! It shows such infinite virtue on your part! I'll have to write up a feature story about this."

"But it hurts my heart so to let it go!" The old man lifted the cage to show the beautiful skylark inside, tears welling up in his eyes.

"Look at it this way: How would you feel if you had been locked up in the cage your whole life?"

"Far from it! It's really happy living in the cage. This bird of mine, you see, is quite extraordinary. I got the egg from an old neighbor and hatched it myself on my warm chest. Since it was still a little thing, I've been feeding it really good stuff, a mix of rice, egg yolk, and minocin. It is so healthy. It has never even sneezed once. Oh, its voice, so soft and sweet. Even the radio station came and taped it once for a sound effect! You see, if I let it go, where would it get its food? Would it find egg yolk and monocin mix in the forest?"

Then I realized that times have changed, and Third Uncle Song is much more enlightened than Second Uncle Song.

It was a fine and sunny day when I went with the bird club for the grand ceremony to write the feature story. The old men were all dressed up for the occasion, new clothes, new shoes, new everything. They lined up, standing arrow-straight like well-disciplined soldiers, and raised their cages high. At the word "Free!" from the Club President, all the cages opened at once. All the birds, big and small, flapped their wings and soared into the sky to their freedom.

Only Third Uncle Song. . . . "Ah, My Brother, look . . . look what's wrong . . . " he sounded ready to cry. Somehow his little precious bird didn't want to come out. No matter how you patted, prodded, cheered, and hollered, the bird refused to budge. At the end of my wits, I thrust my hand in, took it out, and tossed it into the air. It did fly, cheered on by the applause of excited club members, before crashing to the ground.

No, it didn't want the freedom that was handed to it.

I took the dead bird to an ornithologist to be studied. Here is his diagnosis: Lack of exercise and abuse of medicine damaged its nervous system and caused Ataxia; high dosages of egg yolk and high cholesterol concentration caused coronary artery disease, death caused by rupture of heart.

Poor thing—end of my feature story.

(1989)

Chief Staff Member
Sheng Xiaoqing

They sighed with relief when they finally moved into this office after endless rounds of lobbying and pleading. Once inside this spacious, relaxing environment, a strange new feeling emerged. Old You said: The days of having five sets of in-laws looking over your shoulder is over. Now the poor little daughter-in-law is liberated. She is the true mistress of the household! Young Qiu said: Now the seven pairs of big feet trampling the poor little earthworm are lifted. It can plow the earth as freely as it wishes.

Theirs is a newly-formed section in the bureau.

Since they know how hard they have fought to win new freedom and dignity, they both looked stunned when told that one of them would be selected to be the Section Chief. Old You said to the Bureau Chief: Why bother? Why bother! Young Qiu said to the Bureau Chief: What for? What for! The Bureau Chief and other higher-ups were touched: Let it be, let it be. This section, this Government Reform Section, is a temporary thing in the first place. It is set up to deal with the Municipal Government Reform Commission when it comes down to inspect. Therefore, the conventional wisdom that "A section without a chief cannot function for one day" should really be re-examined.

It was in the spirit of camaraderie without any old trappings of rank and power that they arranged their desks. Young Qiu offered to let Old You have the best spot in the office—right next to the south-facing window. Old You, on the other hand, placed the heater and telephone on Young Qiu's desk. In order not to disturb Old You in this spacious office, Young Qiu moved two big file cabinets to the middle as a sort of screen. Now the office has a certain depth of feeling, as it should. Old You, for his part, brought a pot of precious clivia from home and placed it on Young Qiu's desk. Everything here seems warm and harmonious.

The two of them can say whatever is on their minds and do whatever they want to. If Old You cannot come to work, he doesn't need to request leave from the Bureau Chief. A word to Young Qiu is good enough. Young Qiu will take care of all of his work quietly. If Young Qiu is out of the office to run a personal errand, and some higher-up happens to come down to inspect their work, Old You would say: Young Qiu was here only a moment ago. See, his briefcase is still on the desk; he can't be far. If by the end of the day Young Qiu has not found his way back, Old You would quietly put his briefcase in a cabinet and take it out the next day.

This kind of precious freedom and peace would last forever if no outsiders come to ruin it all. They both feel so.

But there is no avoiding outsiders; petty, snobbish outsiders.

One day a half-known face came in. He walked straight to Old You's desk, handed him a "Health" cigarette, and said:

"Chief You, I'm here to ask a favor of you."

Old You, stunned like a little deer, looked up and hastened to correct:

"No, no, no, I am not the Section Chief . . . " and passed the "Health" cigarette to Young Qiu.

Refusing to budge, the man handed Old You another "Health" cigarette: "Come on, the Section Chief's desk is always the furthest from the door. If you are not the Chief, why are you sitting at the Chief's desk? Don't try to fool me. I have something really urgent to ask you."

Old You couldn't take it any more. He cussed at the man and kicked him out. Concerned that Young Qiu might have wrong ideas about this episode, he didn't stop cussing for a long while.

Young Qiu said: "Outsiders don't know. So no need to worry. It's all the same, calling one Section Chief or not."

"That's a no-no, an absolute no-no. . . . "

The bureau has a business meeting every Saturday attended by the Bureau Chief, Party Secretary, and Chiefs of all the sections and offices. Bureau Office Assistant Liu would always put Old You's name, You Qizhong, in brackets whenever he sends out notices. He has to do so because Old You is not a section chief. Yet Old You has to be included not only because of his seniority, but also because the Government Reform Section has to be represented at the meeting. After attending the meeting a few times, Old You felt a bit uncomfortable, especially after he heard whisperings that, with his name in brackets, his rank is now as good as that of Deputy Section Chief. So he would plead sick from then on. Since one of the two has to be present at the meeting, Assistant Liu began to send the notice to Young Qiu with his name in brackets. Worried that Old You might get wrong ideas about this, Young Qiu pleaded sick after attending only two meetings. He urged Old You to go to the next meeting. Hence, through their mutual efforts a balance of some sort was maintained.

Yet within and outside the bureau there is always an army of "Part-time Directors of the Department of Personnel" who indulge in crowning people with titles. They would always greet Old You as Section Chief You and inquire about his health; they would always greet Young Qiu as Director Qiu and marvel how far he could go, and so on. Sometimes, something deep inside them, some kind of vague desire, would be aroused by such warm greetings and accolades. Yet they both know what the other has had to put up with being trampled by seven section chiefs and being trashed by five directors for so long. Neither of them wants to be the boss of the other. All they want is a quiet and peaceful life. So they feel ashamed of the vague desire that rears its head now and then, as if they have betrayed the pact between them. As a result they both are caught in a feeling of shame and guilt, churning deep down.

Worried that outsiders greeting him as Section Chief might hurt the feelings of Young Qiu, Old You put up a sign above his desk which read: "Desk of Section Staff."

The sight of this sign cut Young Qiu to the quick. Old You is so old now and has dedicated his talent and life to his job for so many years and hence more than deserves to be a Section Chief! So Young Qiu also put up a sign above his own desk to show the difference:

"Desk of Deputy Section Staff."

The sight of this new sign cut Old You to the quick. Although Young Qiu is young, he is exceptionally talented and hence more than deserves to be a Section Chief. Yet by calling himself "Deputy Section Staff," hasn't the young man, by implication, acknowledged me as "Chief Section Staff?" Since this section has no section chief, wouldn't "Chief Section Staff" be as good as "Deputy Section Chief?" That can't be!

Thus, Old You is worried all day long lest his carelessness hurt the heart of a young man while Young Qiu is worried lest his arrogance wound the pride of respectful veteran Old You. Gradually their worry wears them down and they both become much less open. In such a cheerless, repressive environment they drag through each day, heavy-hearted, as if it were a long year. Ah, when can they see the light at the end of the tunnel?

(1990)

Carpet

Hang Ying

Professor Chi's book was published finally, which brought him a decent amount of royalties.

A dedicated scholar, Professor Chi is not very attentive to the details of his everyday life. Ever since the death of his wife, it has been up to us, his graduate students, to take care of this thin elderly man. To help him choose the best way to spend the hard-earned money, we held several serious "seminars."

Professor Chi's home was in dire need of furniture. The repeated lootings during the Cultural Revolution had left his home all but bare walls. Professor Chi insisted, however: "The money has to be spent on something most urgently needed, something that will facilitate the writing of my next book."

We suggested one thing after another and every one of them was vetoed by Professor Chi.

We racked our brains and were soon at the end of our wits. Professor Chi, for his part, sat in the willow chair, gazed at the ceiling, and sighed: "I don't have a lot of time left. . . . "

"Then what *do* you want to buy?"

"I've been thinking about this for a long time. . . . Okay, you'll know when we get there. Come with me. Oh, yes, ask the University's Logistics Office to send a cargo van. Expenses to be deducted from my salary."

We were puzzled, but what was the use in asking? So we got the cargo van and went downtown with him.

He told the driver to stop and park the van outside the Department Store, got out, and marched in the store and right to the elevator. "The top floor!" he said.

The top floor is for fur products, jewelry, fine arts, and carpet. He walked straight to the carpet section, bent to check the labels carefully, and then pointed at a brand and declared: "That's it!"

"What?" We cried in chorus and tried to talk him out of it: "What you really need is some new furniture, not this expensive carpet!"

"Oh, I need this badly. Here's the money. Take it to the cashier's."

I took over the money and said, as a last attempt to change his mind, "Even if. . . . why spend so much money on this thick carpet?"

"Well, it has to be this thick; thin carpet wouldn't be any good."

Seeing that there was nothing else for us to do but to carry out his wish, we took care of the payment, rolled up the carpet, and carried it to the van.

Once back in the University residential compound, we carried the carpet right up to the second floor where his apartment is and waited for him to come up and open the door. He thanked the driver and turned and waved to us:

"Go on. Carry it to the third floor!"

"Third floor? Why?"

"Just do it. You'll find out."

So we carried the carpet to the third floor.

Then he came up to the apartment on the third floor right above his own and knocked on the door. It was so noisy inside he had to knock again, much more assertively.

The door opened to reveal the smiling face of Big Dai, a young man working in the university's cafeteria. Boisterous bursts of laughter from inside the apartment filled the narrow hallway.

"Oh, it's Professor Chi. Your apartment and mine are separated only by a thin board, but we rarely see each other! Come in—"

Professor Chi hesitated and then said: "Eh . . . it's like this. I've brought you a gift, nothing much, something I've been wanting to give you for a long time."

Big Dai tap danced a beat and clapped: "Ah, I've heard of your good fortune. So now your neighbor gets a slice, too! Lizhu, come over and thank our. . . . "

His mouth froze instantly when he saw us carrying the carpet into his home.

Inside were six or seven young people, each glowing with loud pleasure and sweat. Lizhu, the hostess, hurried to the door and froze before her words of gratitude gushed out. Silence fell on everyone else inside, too, as if the Monkey King had just played a trick on them. They all stared at the carpet, speechless.

"We appreciate your generosity and will be more careful," the hostess found her voice, "but this gift of yours—"

"You'll have to accept. You'll have to!" exclaimed Professor Chi, "Let's spread it out and see how it fits!"

So we started to unroll the carpet. When the host and hostess wanted to intervene, Professor Chi said with a serious look in his face: "No big deal, really. This carpet would be as good as being installed in my home!"

Once back to Professor Chi's home on the second floor, we all complained that he shouldn't have bought the carpet, let alone give it away.

Professor Chi didn't try to defend himself. He sat down in his old chair, gazed at the ceiling, listened attentively, and smiled: "It's worth it, no matter how expensive!" Then, he pointed upward and asked: "That's not giving it away. See, the carpet is installed on the ceiling of my home, isn't it?"

(1993)

A Bird

Lu Fuhong

Every morning when he strolled in the park, he would linger in front of the blind old man, who had a cane in one hand, a cute bird cage in the other. It was such a beautiful bird although he didn't know what kind it was. Its feathers were smooth and lustrous, its eyes shiny and lively, its singing so pleasant to the ear. More than anything else, the bird had an extraordinary name, Ah Jie. Every time the blind old man talked to the bird in his fatherly voice, "Ah Jie, Ah Jie," he would feel something welling up deep inside.

He is an old man, too, sort of an oddball. Ever since he retired, he has come to the park every morning. There is nothing much other than that. He doesn't know how to play chess or poker. He has no interest at all in gardening or raising a puppy or a bird or any other pet. Yet the moment he saw the blind old man's bird Ah Jie, a desire arose from deep down— he had to have the bird no matter what!

Once he had this intense desire, he tried to approach the blind old man whenever he could. The blind old man was kind and amicable. Soon, without much trouble, they became good friends.

He was thrilled.

The blind old man lived all by himself. Every morning he hurried to the park to walk with the old man and his bird. The old man and his bird—they were the most precious thing in his eyes. Every few days he went and bought a lot of bird food and brought it to the old man's home. He would sit there and chat with him while watching the bird pecking away at the food. Sometimes he gazed at the bird until he forgot himself. Luckily, the old man couldn't see.

One day he couldn't help it any more and asked the blind old man to name a price and sell the bird to him. The blind man was shocked by the request, shook his head, and said, "This bird is not for sale. Period!"

"I'll pay you well," he said desperately, "whatever price you name, hundreds or thousands of *yuan*, I'll pay, no question asked."

"If you really like this kind of bird," the blind old man murmured, "I can ask someone to get one for you."

"But I want none other than this one!"

The blind old man would not budge no matter what he said. Unwilling to give it up just yet, he went and talked to the blind old man several more times. The answer remained the same: "Not for sale!"

He felt extremely disappointed and despondent. As if there were a heavy lump in his heart. He fell ill. He knew exactly what caused it. When his children and grandchildren asked him to go and see the doctor, he barely nodded in acknowledgement.

A few days later, knowing he was ill on account of the bird, the blind old man came with his precious bird, the bird he had vowed never to give away.

"Younger Brother, if you really like this bird, I'll give it to you. It's yours now."

Tears welled up in his eyes and dropped onto the sickbed. Strangely, he felt much better right away. He grasped the blind old man's quivering hand and would not let go.

"Younger Brother, really, this bird is not anything rare or extraordinary. In fact, it cost me just a bit over ten *yuan* when I bought it. Yet, all these years—"

"Elder Brother, no need to say any more. I wanted this bird not because it is rare or extraordinary or anything of the sort."

A few days afterwards, the blind old man came. Hearing no bird singing when he entered, the blind old man asked: "Where's the bird? Ah Jie?"

He didn't reply at first. Then he said, "I let it go."

He didn't dare to look in the face of the blind old man, but could imagine how surprised he must be.

"What? You let it go? How could you have let Ah Jie go?" The blind old man's voice quivered.

"Yes, Elder Brother, I did let the bird go. You know, I've been a judge all my life. I've tried my best to treat every case, average citizen or the rich and the powerful, the same, so I thought I had a clear conscience. Until recently, when I took another look at each case more carefully. I knew I did misjudge in one case. At the time when I realized the mistake it was too late. The man died of illness while in jail. Now I've retired and nobody else knows, yet, ever since I saw the bird in your cage, Ah Jie, I have had no piece of mind. Elder Brother, the young man whose case I misjudged was also named Ah Jie! I still remember his face!"

He erupted in tears. He saw the blind old man standing there as if frozen, but the old man didn't say a word.

A few years later the blind old man passed away. As a good friend of the departed, he took care of the funeral and everything else. While sorting out the things left behind by the blind old man, he found a picture inside a notebook. In the picture was a handsome young man. It was a picture of Ah Jie.

(1993)

I Had a Dream

Chen Rong

"Chubbie, let's hurry and get up!"

"It's still dark!"

"You promised last night to get up early and complete the work!"

"Mmmm—mmm, I just had a dream. . . . "

"Don't talk nonsense. Let's hurry and put on our clothes. Or your dad will beat you!"

"Really, Ma, I did have a dream!"

"Fine, fine, be a good kid and listen to ma. Come on, raise your arms!"

"In my dream I became the President."

"You failed your math. How can you be the President? Step into the pants!"

"But I did. Yes, the first order I issued was . . . "

"Put on your shoes!"

"I was sitting in a grand chair. The Minister of Education knelt in front of me. And I ordered: Assign ten times more homework to the children of school teachers!"

(1995)

American Apple

Li Jingwen

You have to admit that the moon in foreign countries is bigger than the moon in China. I don't even need to bring up the moon landing, spacecraft, UFO studies, and such. Just this apple, no big deal, really, but damn! How can the Americans grow such apples? The red ones are so red, green ones so green, shiny, wax like, as if painted on. They are real, but look so artificially made.

Not to brag about it, but as a small local newspaper reporter, the first time I saw an American apple was in an illustrated foreign magazine in our internal reference room. It looked like a supermarket with piles of apples neatly arranged, a pile of red apples, then a pile of green apples, then a pile of red apples again, and then another pile of green apples, and so on, stretched out like a dragon. Especially the red apples, they looked so red, so surprisingly red, that there wasn't even a hint of green on them.

In this city of ours where people like to chase whatever is fashionable, many kinds of foreign apples flood in like mad, the most attention-catching of which are American apples. The arrival of American apples added to the sorrow in my heart. I felt like a young lad suffering from unrequited love, who, despite his burning desire, does not dare to do anything bolder than casting furtive glances at my beloved girl from distance. For a thousand times I had let my reporter's imagination run wild and savored in my mind how sweet and fragrant American apples would taste, but I would not walk close to them. Damn, one American apple for 50 *yuan*, more than the price for a whole case of our native "Red Fushi!" Not that my wallet cannot afford a few such American apples.

It's just that in my heart I didn't want to waste my money on such hot foreign things. Get lost, expensive "American girls!"

On a weekend I took my daughter shopping. Damn, of the tens of thousands of merchandise on display in the grand shopping mall her eyes were attracted to American apples alone. And she wouldn't give me peace until I said yes. I tried all the tricks I knew to divert her attention elsewhere and even bought her her favorite Haha fruit milk, Wang Wang crispy egg rolls, and fruit jelly, but failed in the end. She pouted unhappily the whole day and evening and didn't want to say one word to me. When she woke up the next morning, she still had not forgotten. I had never seen such stubbornness for so long in my daughter, even at her young age. I was shocked. These red American apples had such scary appeal to the young children.

As I tossed and turned in bed I thought of Aesop's fable about a fox who dismisses the grapes he cannot reach as sour. Although I didn't dare to criticize American apples publicly, the kind of resentment that had crept into my mind was not too different from that of the notorious fox.

Besides, I figured, no matter how I sliced it, I shouldn't have denied my daughter and dampened her fledging curiosity about the unknown in the world. That is to say, I should have let my daughter experience what the American apple tasted like. So I burned the midnight oil for a few days, sold a few more stories, made a bit more money, and dashed to the grand mall. There I took out a one-hundred-*yuan* bill and bought two American apples from a young, all-smiling sales girl. When I got home with the two apples, my daughter jumped for joy, but she didn't want to eat them! Instead, she placed the apples right next to the white rabbit, her favorite toy. Every night before going to bed, she would take one last look and feel the apples in her hand gently. I said: Why don't you eat them. I'll buy you more if you like them so much. She would shake her head, her eyes still fixed on the mouth-watering apples. She didn't have the heart to bite into the apples that looked so perfect in her mind.

Not long afterwards, at the end of an important business press conference, the sponsors gave each of us veteran reporters an exquisitely-packaged gift box, each containing four American apples. I was so thrilled with the gift, which felt so heavy in my hands. At my insistence, my daughter finally gave in and agreed to eat an apple. Watched by my daughter's eager eyes I peeled off the beautiful skin of the apple with a knife carefully, almost religiously, but still felt as though I was committing a crime.

I had expected my daughter to jump for joy again, yet at the very first bite, she froze, a puzzled look in her vivid eyes. She licked her mouth a few times as if not sure of her own taste. Then, with apparent disappointment, she placed the apple in my hand: Why does it taste like this?

I took a bite and my eyebrows furrowed right away, too. Indeed it tasted far worse than "Red Fushi."

So we left the exquisite box of American apples untouched and forgot about them for a long time. When we thought about them again, the apples inside were already rotten beyond recognition.

(1998)

Expectations

Liang Haichao

Old Man Tian had been a simple, honest peasant. He thought Principal
Zhang of the village grade school was the most respectable because he
was educated, cultivated, and soft-spoken, unlike the ordinary village
folks who were so shamefully unrefined. Old Man Tian had only one
son, whom he took to Principal Zhang and said, "I put my son under
your care. If this child amounts to anything when he grows up, my
family will be indebted to you forever." Since they resided in the same
village, Old Man Tian was only too eager to help out with all kinds of
household chores: carrying water, buying coal, grinding wheat, watering
vegetables, and shouldering home village-issued grain. When Principal
Zhang thanked him profusely, Old Man Tian said, "No big deal. There's
nothing else I can do for you anyway. Besides, you're teaching my son."
Old Man Tian was poor, but he was strong. Principal Zhang took care of
Old Man Tian's only son all the way through high school. Then he had
a word with the village Party Chief, and Old Man Tian's son became a
teacher at the village school. Old Man Tian glowed with glory.

Old Man Tian's son taught at the village school for many years. For a
long time, his monthly stipend was only six *yuan*; then it was increased
to 30 *yuan*, 60 *yuan*, 80 *yuan*, and 150 *yuan*, where it stuck. Old Man
Tian's son lived a simple, frugal life. Now, seeing new buildings going
up like spring bamboo, Old Man Tian's son sighed often. Like his pop
he had only one son. So he let his son learn about doing business. To
ensure his son's future, he got him a godfather: his high school classmate, now manager of the town's department store. Upon graduation
from junior high, the manager-godfather arranged for him to work in

the department store as a sales clerk. Before long, the son opened a grocery of his own and was doing quite well. The son wasn't content, though. He expanded to the county town and was doing splendidly there. However, the son would not let his own son get into the business.

The son said: Doing business is hard. More than half of the hard-earned money goes to officials from all sides. If you don't do so, they will throw this fee and that fee in your face until you either close shop or cry uncle. He felt doing business was not as good as being an official. Being an official you don't have to run around through rain and snow and suffer sleepless nights. People will knock your door with money. That's easy money indeed.

So the son would often take his son to go and "play" at the homes of several county officials. The play wasn't easy or fun and within years he had all but "played" away his department store. The son's son did get a job in the county government, though. The son's son was quite capable and worked all the way from a mere administrative assistant to Deputy County Magistrate to Deputy County Party Chief, coming and going in an expensive car everyday. Even his little precious son rode in a Santana or Audi between their home and the kindergarten, to the hopeless envy of everyone. He had a fancy villa, too.

When village folks were not busy, they liked to gather and chitchat about Old Man Tian. They said Old Man Tian's vision was not as good as that of his son, his son's not as good as his grandson's, the grandson's not as good as the great grandson's, and so on. It was rumored that the great grandson's son was an up-and-coming young man, already a deputy township commissioner somewhere at the tender age of 20! This family has had it all mapped out. If you still have any doubts, just count it on your own fingers: Which official doesn't live in a nice building of his own? Which doesn't have a concubine or two on the side? Which has paid for the expensive home appliances at home with his own money?

No wonder nowadays anyone and his brother who know anyone at all would squeeze their way into officialdom, bloody nose or broken head no matter. Those who don't know anyone would try to know someone by hook or crook.

However, when Old Man Tian's grandson, great grandson, and great-great grandson came back to the village to visit in their expensive cars, village folks would shy away from them. Old Man Tian has long moved on. His son and daughter-in-law are frosty-haired now. Having lived in the county town for a few years, they suddenly decided to return to the village for good. The old couple lived in a big empty house built by their son and grandson years ago. They watch a lot of TV, especially the popular talk show "Focus." They are glued to the screen when the show is on. Old Man Tian's daughter-in-law says to his son: Why do you worry? How many more days can our old bones last? Old Man Tian's son says: You don't know a fart!

(2002)

Concerned Departments

Liu Dianxue

Early in the morning Third Uncle Harelip came again.

The young gatekeeper wouldn't let him in. The Office had left instructions: If the old harelip comes again keep him outside and stop him from coming in and chattering non stop.

Third Uncle Harelip flew into a rage at the young man: "Not letting

Grandpa in? How did you all come and sit on the throne in the first place? If Grandpa didn't fight the Japs for eight years, Chiang Kai-shek for four, and let a mortar blow up my mouth like this, could you be sitting on the throne now? Today, your Grandpa is looking for Concerned Departments to solve some problems. I am not Bin Laden, so why don't you motherfuckers let me in?"

Ducking from the barrage, the young man walked back into the gate room and did not dare to come out again. He called the Office Chief. The Chief said let him in. The young gatekeeper laid down the phone, craned through the window, and cried out, angrily: "Come in!"

"Come in? This building has more than a dozen floors up and down, where should your Grandpa go? On which floor is Concerned Departments? Why can't you say one more sentence? That mouth of yours knows only how to eat but not how to talk to the masses?" Third Uncle Harelip shook the slip of paper in hand and howled.

The young gatekeeper had to come out again. He took the wrinkled paper and looked at it. It was a veteran's heath report with penned-in instructions from former mayor Qian Youxiang: "Concerned Departments should work together to take care of this old comrade's problem."

The Concerned Departments referred to, of course, were the Civil Affairs Department and Association of the Handicapped. These two departments have long moved out of the Municipal Government Building. This damned old man, near blind, yet so damn cocky, as if any pauper who once fought the Japs is automatically made a prince. Who gives a crap! Eager to dismiss him, the young gatekeeper pointed at the building vaguely: "8th Floor. Have to climb up. Power outage for the elevator."

Power or no power for the elevator, Third Uncle Harelip didn't even know what kind of donkey the elevator was. He started to climb up the stairs, flight after flight, sweating profusely, until he reached the 8th floor, gasping for air. Holding onto the handrail for support, he asked a young cadre sitting inside the office across: "Miss, which room is the Con. . . . Concerned Departments?"

The young girl cadre didn't understand his Sichuan accent. Her hazel-brown eyes glowering, she asked: "What did you say? Which room?"

"Concerned Departments?"

"What's Concerned Departments? Which department are you looking for? This building has more than 200 departments!"

"No, I'm only looking for Concerned Departments to take care of my problem. You're working in this building, but don't know Concerned Departments? That's how you work?"

The girl cadre shook her head and didn't want to speak to the old man any more. As she shut the door, she grunted: "I don't know. Go down and ask."

Third Uncle Harelip followed the flight of stairs down. When he reached the 6th floor he noticed a piece of paper affixed to the door; on the paper were written these words:

Close The Door Behind You.

He didn't know all the words. But the "C" in the first word and "D" in the third looked like something "Concerned Departments" on his slip of paper. Perhaps he was at the right door and this was the Concerned Departments he had been looking for? So he went in. The office felt warm. Inside sat four people, two men and two women, talking, sipping tea, reading newspapers. At the sight of a harelipped old man, everybody stopped and looked in his direction.

Third Uncle Harelip asked: "Is this Concerned Departments?"

None of the four people replied. After a while, the oldest of them, a male cadre, said: "Old man, who are you looking for?"

"Concerned Departments."

"Which concerned departments? We're all concerned departments, and none of us are concerned departments. You are not going about it the right way."

Third Uncle Harelip thought this man sounded like a human being talking. He looked a few years older and more in charge than the others, for sure. Third Uncle Harelip showed the man the report in his quivering hand and said: "Please take a look, comrade, the mayor told me to look for Concerned Departments to take care of my problem. I've looked for two years and here I've found you at last!"

The male cadre took the paper, glanced at it, and said, positively: "Oh, this mayor has been promoted to the provincial government. Since this mayor left instructions on this, why don't you go to the Department of Civil Affairs? This falls within their purview. They're the department you should look for. So why are you here? We're in charge of Spiritual Civilization here. Who has time for your problem?"

"Civil Affairs? Which floor?" Third Uncle Harelip seemed to have understood.

"They're not in this building. They're outside."

"Outside?"

Third Uncle Harelip descended flight by flight until he reached the ground floor.

As he passed the gate room, the young man smirked and asked: "Did you find Concerned Departments?"

"Yes, I've found it. It's Outside." Without even a glance at the young gatekeeper, Third Uncle Harelip walked out of the entrance hall confidently to look for Concerned Departments to solve his problem.

(2003)

"Oh, Isn't This General Manager Gao?"

Liu Jianchao

"Oh, isn't this General Manager Gao? Why are you eating soup at this small stand?" Everyone squatting around with a bowl of soup in hand and slurping noisily turned to look.

"My stomach is not feeling well," Gao Feng said, patting his beer belly as he sat on a small wooden stool. "A bowl of hot soup will warm it up."

"Hey, boss, hurry and get Manager Gao a bowl of hot soup. Hurry, 'cause Manager Gao is a busy man. Manager Gao, I'm told that you've just landed the All Power Garden project. Oh my, that's a huge investment, over 100 million *yuan*, right? You yourself will make 20 million *yuan* and perhaps more. Nowadays, making big money isn't all that easy. Hey, boss, hurry up with the soup! You should take it as a huge compliment that Manager Gao wants to eat soup from your stand. I know for a fact that Manager Gao always takes his morning tea in a five-star hotel or something like that."

A group of migrant workers came to the soup stand and cried out for more soup and chili sauce.

"Hey, hey, step aside and don't try to push to this side. Don't you see Manager Gao is eating soup here? These people, they are so uncultured. There are only two things in their lives: food and money. They'll do anything for money. Manager Gao, once you've secured that 20 million *yuan* in hand, the migrant workers of the entire city would be stunned out of their wits!"

As the migrant workers broke their baked buns into pieces and stuffed them into their soup bowls.

Manager Gao looked up. "You're not eating soup?" He said.

"No. I'm just strolling around, you know. I'm not busy these days anyway. I saw your Toyota Crown from a distance, your license plate number is: one six eight eight eight. Wow! How lucky! Good fortune all the way, as they say, right? Although you parked around the street corner, I spotted it right away."

General Manager Gao stood up to leave without finishing the soup.

"General Manager Gao, see you later! Hey, boss, you probably don't know him. He is General Manager of Hong Fa Real Estate Development, Ltd. Oh, we are thick buddies, you know."

General Manager Gao Feng's car vanished without leaving behind a shadow.

✳   ✳   ✳

"Hey, isn't this General Manager Gao? Why, you're here to take a bath?
Gao Feng looked annoyed. So did his client.

"What a client! It's a convenient excuse for your dear wife, right? Ha! Ha! Ha! It isn't easy to be a man these days. I've seen General Manager Gao come in three times a week, but never with a client."

"You've been following me?"

"Oh, no! I don't have the guts. The boss here and I are thick buddies, so I'm here often to lend a hand: 'General Manager Gao still wants No. 18, Miss Lili!' Oh, what a wench, dewy fresh, lovely, and the way she does her work! Miss Lili likes to tease, too, and calls you 'Boss Ma'".

Gao Feng was really irritated now.

"Hey! Here comes Boss Ma, hurry and take good care of him! Okay, get Miss Lili. General Manager Gao, you don't really need to use an alias. The girls here are all very professional and will never betray their clients. Unlike that Lewinsky who sent the evidence Clinton left behind for DNA test. I've read in a newspaper that there is a reporter in the South who specializes in collecting used condoms from girls and saving them in the fridge so he can use them for blackmail. I told Lili she should never do that, no matter how much money people will give her. Lili! Hurry! Boss Ma has been waiting here!

Without a word, General Manager Gao turned and left.

* * *

"Oh! Isn't this General Manager Gao? Why, you have time to come and pick up the kid yourself. Your dear wife used to do that every day."

"I am not busy today."

"Must be once in a blue moon, 'cause you're juggling ten thousand things every day."

"Why are you here? Your kid goes to school here, too?"

"Me? No, I'm here only strolling around, having nothing important to do anyway. I've heard that the crime rate has gone up recently. Several neighboring cities have had children kidnapped. Did you read about the real estate tycoon whose son was abducted and the kidnappers demanded a ransom of 500,000 *yuan*!? They got the money, but killed the kid anyway. How sad. The kid was only 12 years old. General Manager Gao, how old is your precious son now?"

General Manager Gao turned his face away. More and more people came to the school's entrance to pick up their kids. Small peddlers cried out loudly in the crowd to push whatever cheap little commodities they were carrying.

"General Manager Gao, you gave your son a really good name: 'Gao Hao'. Hao, meaning mid day sun in the sky, right? The little fellow is quite handsome, like you. He sits in the middle of the third row of 7th Grade, Class 5, doesn't he? Good grades. Member of the Student Council, too. At the school's sports meet last week, I saw the little fellow winning second prize. Isn't that something?"

"Why don't you go and pick up your kid?"

"My kid doesn't need to be picked up. Lives close to school. Just a few steps away. Not a very good school. The kid doesn't study hard, either. A few days ago the kid whined about transferring to a better school. I said 'transferring to a better school? I can't even pay for the tuition of this school!'"

The bell rang. School was dismissed. The crowd began to push toward the school's entrance.

"Hey, General Manager Gao, I see your son. Gao Hao! Your dad is over there! Your dad is here to get you home in his car. See that? 16888! General Manager Gao, the little fellow has heard us. Your precious son is easy to recognize. With that birth mark right between the eyebrows. A sign of being blessed!"

Without a word General Mangaer Gao pushed his son into the car and crawled in himself. Before leaving, he lowered the window and said to me: "Come to my office tomorrow."

"Okay, see you tomorrow, and I'll be there on time."

The next morning I received the wages General Manager Gao had owed me for two long years.

(2004)

Cat and Mouse Play

Ling Dingnian

"Look!" The scout reported excitedly.

The Field Marshal couldn't help being excited, too, and said to his

Second-in-Command, "The supplies and commendations from the Imperial Court have arrived."

The Field Marshal was right. The Imperial Court had dispatched the Assistant Minister of Finance with the commendations and urgently-needed supplies of food, clothing, and weapons. The most thrilling of all to the rank and file, and to the Field Marshal himself, was that the Emperor had gifted him a yellow mandarin jacket.

When the grand celebration banquet was over, the Second-in-Command said to the Field Marshal: "The Emperor has shown his heavenly, infinite kindness by gifting you a yellow mandarin jacket. I swear I will serve the Imperial Court to my last breath so I will be worthy of His Majesty's kindness!"

"Certainly, certainly. As long as you follow me, the Field Marshal, single-mindedly, I will make sure you will all get something in return."

The wine had probably gone into the Second-in-Command's head and his tongue loosened up. He said, glowing with excitement: "Field Marshal, I propose we strike while the iron is hot. Right now the morale of the rank and file is at its peak and we have just been provided with fresh supplies. If we launch a surprise attack tomorrow night and take the enemy completely off guard, we can drive them into the desert where they will stay forever. That will take care of our border troubles for good!"

The Field Marshal chuckled: "You must have had a drop too much. Annihilating the enemy is of paramount importance and has to be considered from a long-term perspective. Why don't we talk about it tomorrow?"

The Second-in-Command thought it made good sense. He continued to drink to his heart's content and didn't bring up the surprise attack business again.

Days had passed, yet the Field Marshal still hadn't said a word about the strategy session. The Second-in-Command found it strange and couldn't help but approach the Field Marshal about it.

The Field Marshal told everyone else to leave the room and then showed the Second-in-Command his calligraphic writing entitled "Cat and Mouse Play." The Second-in-Command studied it for a while but only half understood. He could understand "playing with the mouse" for a while. But for how long? Forever? Noticing the puzzlement in his face, the Field Marshal indicated for him to sit down and said, solemnly:

"Look at the generals who have risked their lives fighting for their monarchs in all dynasties. Once the victory is secured and the war is over, how many of them have had a good ending?"

Although not a well-read man, the Second-in-Command had heard sad stories of brave generals before. He nodded thoughtfully.

Then the Field Marshal said: "The Story of King Gou Jian of Yue from *Records of the Historian*[11] says: 'When the birds are downed, bow and arrow will be put away; when the rabbits are killed, the dog will be slaughtered, too.' This is an axiom from time immemorial and you and I should never forget."

The Second-in-Command, not an obtuse man really, understood most of what the Field Marshal meant. He recalled a battle they had fought about half a year ago. It was on a dark night near the end of winter. The cold wind whistled throughout the night and all through the next day. Scouts came back to report that troops of Prince Yelu of the Xiong Nu[12] were all stationed in the Peacock Valley for shelter from the vicious wind. From a strategic point of view, once they had secured the high points surrounding the valley, the Field Marshal's army could go in for the kill. It would be easy. Yet, when the Field Marshal positioned his troops, he left a section of the noose in the north not as tightly secured as elsewhere. At the time some generals raised their concerns. The Field Marshal thus explained: When cornered, the beast will fight desperately. This way we can minimalize casualties among our rank and file. Understand?

Thanks to this loose end in the north, whatever was left of Prince Yelu's army broke through the ambush and escaped.

That, the Second-in-Command thought, seemed to be the essence of the "Cat and Mouse Play." True, if we had annihilated the enemy in that battle, the border might have had a few years of peace, yet with a peaceful border what would we generals and soldiers do? Would the Imperial Court still support us, let us have our own way, and send endless supplies in our direction? He suddenly understood everything and said, with both hands in front of his chest: "This general will follow the Field Marshal in this 'Cat and Mouse Play' to the end!"

In the midst of fierce laugh, the two raised their wine cups again.

(2004)

Red Envelope

Guo Xuerong

When kids his age hadn't even heard of it, She Jian had already understood it only too well and had it indelibly etched in his heart. He was a high school senior at the time. He had good grades, good extracurricular activities, and was good-looking. She Jian was favored by all his teachers and well liked by his classmates. While he was making the last-minute preparation for the college entrance exams, his mother was diagnosed with esophageal cancer and was hospitalized. The costly surgical operation would drive this low-income working class family to near bankruptcy. When She Jian's father had put together the money needed for the operation, he still sighed profusely, his eyebrows tightly knit. It was in the midst of mysterious, heated arguments among his family and relatives that She Jian heard the term "Red Envelope" for the first time.

She Jian's paternal uncle was vehemently opposed to giving red envelopes on moral grounds: Saving the ill and the wounded is the sacred responsibility of the doctors. Giving them red envelopes would be totally unnecessary. It may be counterproductive because doctors may feel insulted. His maternal uncle, however, advocated giving red envelopes and had this to say to his paternal uncle: Are you an extraterrestrial? Have you been eating human food? Look around. Giving red envelopes has been an open secret among society for so long, and is the common practice of families of the ill everywhere. Nowadays, even for simple operations for appendicitis and hernia, people would give red envelopes. We have such a big operation coming. The patient can't do anything herself. Yet if we the family, fit and healthy, don't take care of it, won't the doctors think we are crazy? The paternal uncle rebutted passionately, "The root cause of bribery is people who bribe. For whatever personal reasons, they bribe and hence disrupt the normal operation of society. The givers are more criminal than the takers!" Thus, it was with a heavy, guilty heart that She Jian's father scraped up the money for several red envelopes of various sizes.

She Jian didn't have to be a genius to understand what a red envelope contained and what it meant. He hated the red envelope with all his heart. It was in this frame of mind that She Jian took the college entrance exams, applied for medical school with his high scores, and was accepted by a clinical medicine program.

He worked double hard in college. When he graduated a few years later, with high recommendations from his professors, and to the envy of all of his classmates, She Jian was assigned to the municipal hospital.

The first time She Jian received an envelope was two years after he started at the municipal hospital. His face reddening, She Jian said to the patient's family, "To have a successful operation is my job. The operation involves risks so you have to sign here. But that's only a procedure." The patient's family pleaded earnestly, pathetically, like beggars in the street. The only difference was that a beggar would be begging for She Jian to give while the patient's family was begging for him to take. As they pushed the envelope back and forth between them, She Jian felt the thick stack of money inside and couldn't help but feel itchy. The She Jian that had accepted the red envelope was sharp in mind and quick in movement. The operation was completed in one breath and every detail and stitch was near perfect.

Gradually, She Jian came to feel that there should be no red envelopes, morally speaking; yet they were indispensable psychologically. With or without red envelopes, whether they were physically in his pocket could have a big impact on his mindset in the operation room. Occasionally, when he didn't get red envelopes, he would be listless no matter how much strong coffee he would drink prior to the operation. On the other hand, the thicker the red envelopes, the more focused and functional he would be. He would be able to rise up to any unforeseen difficulty, danger, or change of conditions and bring the operation to a successful conclusion. Thus, boosted by the ever bigger, thicker red envelopes, She Jian became a better doctor day by day, his fame traveling far and wide.

Soon he became the municipal hospital's best and a veritable poster boy for its services. Titles such as "Young Expert of the City" and "Leader of the City's Medical Profession" were bestowed on his head. The Municipal Department of Public Health and heads of the hospital cherished him as a treasure. Operations on all big shots, big wheels, and big fat cats were his privilege exclusively.

What he had never expected, though, was that even the big shots in the municipal government and in the Department of Public Health would give him red envelopes when they came for operations. They were so firm and persistent on this. Several times, She Jian would return the envelopes after the operations, but those big shots explained to him: "Living by the mountain, you eat from the mountain; living by the water, you eat from the water. Every profession and trade has its own rules, but the logic is the same. Don't break the rules no matter what."

Just when it looked as if his career and fame had nowhere to go but higher, She Jian stumbled and crashed. It was a simple, minor operation which even an intern could have managed. Yet he failed. He failed to follow common sense, not anything especially complicated or challenging. As a result of his error, the patient became paralyzed and would remain bedridden for the rest of his life. Luckily, though, the patient and his family would not sue for malpractice: The patient was none other than She Jian's maternal uncle. Only She Jian knew he had not been focused and fully functional during the operation. The reason? He had not received a red envelope.

(2005)

Homeless

He Peng

Old He has been a police officer for more than 30 years. This is the first time he has encountered a difficult situation like this: Minutes before the victim's body was to be cremated, her family changed their mind.

He feels sick in his heart as he listens to the sobbing voice of Zhao Yanhong's mother at the other end of the telephone while glancing at the girl's body lying in the visitation room at the cremation plant, a young budding life cut short by violence.

Old He tightens his fist and bites his lips as he continues to listen to the sobbing, broken voice at the other end of the line.

While investigating this case, he has been to Zhao Yanhong's home several times.

Her family is from a small county in the Northeast. Before Yanhong was even born her parents came all the way to Beijing to start a trading company. Soon they made enough money to buy a home and a car and begin to live a comfortable life. Their problem started when their daughter Yanhong had grown to school age. Schools don't care where you live. They only recognize your residential registration. Yanhong's parents had to donate a big sum of money to the school in exchange for the permission for her to attend school there. Even at the time of registration, the school didn't forget to treat her as a visiting student and charge her the proper fee. Every year when the school gave awards to outstanding students, she was not eligible because of her visiting student status. Every year she would watch, teary-eyed, classmates with lower grades going up to the podium to receive awards.

From grade school to middle school, from middle school to high school, each time her parents had to bring a big bundle of money to the school in exchange for the permission for her to register, year after year. By the time of the college entrance exams, her parents gave out several bigger bundles of money but didn't come home with the permit for her to sign up for the exams. She had no choice but to return to her hometown in the Northwest and sign up as a "non-school youth." In that small county town Yanhong's family has nothing left but their residential registration. So Yanhong stayed at a hotel for a week, took the exams and fled back to Beijing where her family has no registered residence either. True, they own their home, but legally it is still their temporary shelter.

Since then she had been in a rather sad mood. She couldn't understand why as far as she could remember the sky over her head had not been as blue as that over her classmates. The day before it all happened, she had been mad for the whole day for no obvious reason at all. The next morning her mother told her to go to the scenic area of the western suburbs for a change. Nobody had expected her not to return alive. She was raped and then strangled to death.

Old He is brought back to the present by the choking voice at the other end of the phone. He feels warm tears trickling down his cheeks. The veteran police officer takes out a tissue to wipe away the tears and then checks his watch: It's already ten o'clock. What should he do? Sweat oozes from under his big felt hat.

When Yanhong's mother seems to have calmed down a bit, Old He says, "Didn't we talk about this yesterday? Since this is a murder case, the body has to be taken care of in a timely fashion. Now the visitation hour is over and the family is still not here yet.

After a long silence, he hears the broken voice of Yanhong's father come on the line, "Old He, after thinking this through, we've decided not to have her body cremated in Beijing. Instead we will take her to our home in the Northeast for burial."

"What? Burial?"

"Yes. Our baby doesn't have Beijing residence. For this she suffered so much while alive. We are afraid our baby will be a homeless ghost, too, and will be treated as second class. It would be better to take her back to our hometown where she has legal residence. That way she and her legal residence will be united at the same place and she can lie in peace."

Old He hangs up the phone and walks out of the visitation room with a heavy heart. Although all this sounds a bit laughable and ridiculous, it is perhaps the only way the parents can console the spirit of their dead daughter.

An unspeakable sadness washes over him.

Suddenly a strange thought occurs to him: Yanhong grew up in Beijing and had almost no Northeastern accent in her speech. True, a burial there would mean body and residence are united at the same place, yet with no indigenous accent, her ghost would probably be treated as second class, too.

(2005)

Creativity

He Kaiwen

On his way home from work, Chen Qiang passed a real estate office building. Even from some distance away he could see a big crowd gathered at the building's entrance. Following the eyes of the crowd, he saw a man about 9 floors up, hanging from the side of the building. The man looked like he was struggling in mid air; his right hand holding onto the rail of the 9th floor balcony, his left hand stretching outward, his feet braced against nothing at all.

"Someone wants to jump off the building!" Alarmed, Chen Qiang took out his cell phone and dialed 110 and 120.

A short while later, a 110 police car arrived. A police officer stepped out and began to shout to the crowd through a megaphone:

"Please step back and make room for the rescue." Then he shouted to the man hanging in midair; "Listen, don't let go! The fire truck is on its way with a long ladder to save you!"

Before long the fire truck arrived. The firefighters, all clad in red, extended the long ladder into the sky and ever closer to the man.

Unfortunately, the ladder couldn't reach that high up. The firefighters began to place an air cushion directly below where they believed the man would fall.

Soon, top municipal government officials arrived too. They formed a rescue command team right away.

Chen Qiang is a warm-hearted young man. He is always ready to help his neighbors whenever they are in need and intervene whenever he sees injustice even at the risk of his own life. Since "110" and "120" personnel couldn't make any headway in their rescue efforts, he ran into the building and up the stairs to the 9th floor.

As he ran around and looked for a way to get to the balcony, he came to an office with this sign at the door: "Eastern Real Estate."

There a young saleswoman stopped him from entering.

"Miss, a man is going to jump off your balcony! Please let me in so I can rescue him!"

"Rescue? No one here needs to be rescued. Mind your own business!"

"'110' and '120' vehicles are all here, too. You haven't heard a thing?"

A short while later, police and firefighters also came up to the real estate office. The young saleswoman greeted them with a big smile on her face: "Officer, it's a misunderstanding." She said.

"Misunderstanding? There is a man clinging to the balcony of this floor. Why aren't you doing anything to save him?"

The saleswoman explained: "Oh, that is a creative marketing strategy: using a suicide dummy to attract prospective clients' attention. That you are all here proves the success of the strategy."

(2005)

Roses

Yang Kui

When school started again after the Lunar New Year, pressure for the 8th-graders was mounting even higher. In addition to scheduled exams, we were being grilled with mock tests every two or three days until we were almost browned. Not until the graduation exams were over and vacation started did we sigh with relief. The teacher said: "This time we will pass Taichung to visit Mist World and Sun Moon Lake."

We said while in Taichung we'd want to climb the mountain to see the "Roses That Can't Be Crushed." The teacher smiled and nodded.

That day we got off the buses at Tunghai University and followed a path along the small river for four or five minutes. Then we saw roses everywhere covering hills and vales as far as the eye could see. An old gardener was watering the flowers with buckets on a carrying pole.

The teacher said to him: "We are middle school students from Kaohsiung, three classes, over 100 people. Sorry for bothering you. We've just finished a lesson on 'Roses That Can't Be Crushed.' So, here we are to see you in person!"

The old gardener smiled: "Oh, no bother, no bother at all. However, roses have thorns. So just see with your eyes. Don't touch. The other day a gentleman came and reached to pick the moment he stepped in. He was pricked so, oh, you should have heard him cry out in pain."

"Hahaha, didn't even know roses have thorns. What a stupid bull!" Over 100 middle school students burst out laughing, which shook the entire garden.

Ten years later several of us female students came to the United States to study biology.

Last year on the anniversary of "9/18," the University of Chicago held a big rally against the Japanese government twisting facts in their history textbooks. A newspaper story said one of the speakers would be the old gardener who had been invited to attend the University of Iowa's International Writing Program. The topic of his speech was "Children Under the Japanese Rule." This news opened the floodgate to our memory. So we went to the rally.

When the rally was over, many eager people swarmed around him to chat. We had to act decisively. Two grabbing his arms left and right, one pushing from behind, we got him into our vehicle and got under way.

"Do you recognize us?" We asked.

The old gardener shook his head: "I've heard Chicago used to be haven for the Mafia don, who was as powerful as Shanghai's Du Yuesheng.[13] Even the President of the U.S.A. couldn't do anything about him."

"Aiya! You used to call us 'little girls'. Now that you're in the States we've suddenly become kidnappers!"

"'Little girls?' You've been to Tunghai Garden?"

"Yes! You gave each of us a rose twig and told us how to cut and plant . . . "

A classmate gave me a look not to say any more.

The old gardener seemed puzzled. I could barely hold the laugh bursting inside me.

Finally our vehicle arrived at a residence in the suburbs. We helped the gardener out of the car and led him toward the house. Before entering, he paused by the front yard covered with roses, amazed. Once inside the living room, I guided him to the floor-length window with my arm around his waist. There he saw even more roses in the back yard. He seemed even more amazed.

My classmates patted him on the back and said: "Surprise! This is a new generation of Tunghai Garden!"

"Ah!" He exclaimed, joy blossoming on his face.

(2006)

The Pearl Jacket

Dong Rui

In the hallway outside the operating room a big crowd was waiting. All was quiet even though excitement and anxiety were visible in the air. In this atmosphere of nervous waiting it was so quiet you could hear a pin drop. So many people were so concerned about one person's surgery. This was the first time anything like this had happened in this hospital.

A little before nine this morning a badly hurt woman had been rushed in by an ambulance. It was a hit and run.

The driver had vanished. Whether this was an accident or attempted murder was a question no one could answer. When the emergency room doctors had their first look at the face of the injured woman, they cried out in shock.

She had been hit so badly that the doctors could not save her life. Since the fatal injuries she suffered looked both suspicious and puzzling, the forensic pathologist recommended an autopsy be performed immediately.

The coroner, a Doctor Da, broke into a sweat as he made the first cut. All the assistants and nurses around him looked at each other.

"Rare . . . " Doctor Da said. "The kidney and heart are artificial. And the lungs and intestines are . . . "

"Artificial?" Several doctors asked in chorus.

"No. The intestines are soft rubber. . . . But the kidneys are purchased. Only half of the lungs are left, and these are not original, either. It's hard to tell, though, if they are artificial or . . . somebody else's."

An assistant drew a blood sample and was about to take it to the lab when Doctor Da took a look and said, shaking his head, "She lost her hematopoietic function. So her blood . . . was all transfusion!"

"What about her skin and muscles?"

"About ninety percent of her skin has been changed. Otherwise it wouldn't be this pale. Look at this." Doctor Da pointed at an area close to her right armpit. It showed dark color and therefore was real. But it was only a tiny area. "The most vital is the heart. See, it's transplanted, too."

Everyone craned to see as Doctor Da wiped away the blood covering the heart he now held in his hand. On its side could still be seen the tiny print: Made in XXX Country.

"Now, let's take a look at her head. False hair, false eyes, false eyebrows, false nose, false teeth, false chin—and look at these! Inserts in the breasts, as well as in the buttocks, too. Well, we can simply say there is nothing in her that is real. If word gets out, it would be a sensational scandal; her entire family would be humiliated. So, let's keep her secret to ourselves."

Then it was time to examine that most female of parts.

Doctor Da looked long and hard and then sighed. "Clear trail of male sexual traits. The tract was completely man-made!"

The assistants all looked at each other, dumbfounded.

Doctor Da walked out of the coroner's office, picked up a jacket, and waved it a few times in the air. "This jacket, dotted with real pearls, is worth 100,000 *yuan* at least. Any one of you a relative? Please come claim this and the body, too."

Then he added: "This pearl jacket is genuine. The only one for which an exchange is guaranteed if found false."

(2004)

One Drizzly Afternoon
Tao Ran

The autumn rain fell on the street. He walked on cheerlessly when he looked up. One quick glance and he knew, through experience, that the pretty young woman could be a stowaway. Ordinarily he could have waved his hand to stop her and ask to see her identification. Yet, he didn't.

This pretty young woman is too hot.

If . . . if what? He was shocked and didn't continue the thought.

The young woman, an open umbrella in one hand, a basket of meat and vegetables in another, walked ahead of him. That posture, that willowy gait. Oh!

He followed.

Suddenly they were inside the same elevator. He noticed the nervousness in the young woman's face and felt even more sure of his suspicion.

This woman is like a little frightened deer and I am the hunter. He thought to himself gleefully. This woman is alone by herself, and me, Chen Shanlin, I'm all alone, too.

The elevator door opened. The young woman bolted. Stunned, he nevertheless responded fast. He bounded forward and slipped out just behind her.

The young woman turned her head to look at him, she was like a lamb waiting for the slaughter.

A tender feeling of pity arose inside him. Yet, he had already advanced so far there was no way he could retreat voluntarily.

He cleared his throat and said as clearly as possible: "Miss, your ID."

The young woman was so stunned it took her a while to find her voice again, stammering: "I don't have it with me. I've left it at home."

"I'll go with you then."

At that, his heart quivered. A lone man and a woman alone. . . .

Two people in a small home. The rain brought in by them fell on the floor.

He stood in the living room, feeling somewhat awkward. "Your ID?" He asked again.

The young woman said. "Wait here. I'll go look for it in the bed-room."

Yet after a long while she didn't come out.

This he had expected. She is a stowaway. How can she have an ID? She is only playing a game! Okay, let me just sit on the sofa and wait for you. See if you can produce an ID from thin air!

At long last the young woman came out and handed him an ID, tim-idly. He was taken aback.

He looked it over and said: "I'm sorry. I need to check. . . . "

As he was about to press the walkie-talkie, the young woman came closer, nestled up to him, and said in a quivering voice: "Ah Sir, please give me a chance!"

It turned out to be a fake ID.

In the physical entanglement that followed, he suddenly lost control. The police officer and the stowaway suddenly morphed into a man and a woman.

When the storm was over he would pretend not to have seen. The young woman said: "Don't turn me in."

At any rate, one more stowaway in Hong Kong wouldn't mean any-thing. It wouldn't sink the land. Just pretend I didn't see anything.

When he returned to the street, his partner had been looking for him anxiously. "Hey, where the heck have you been? A whole hour. You could have done anything. How can I report this to the boss? What if there was a robbery?"

He nodded and bowed to apologize. In his heart though he contin-ued to savor this drizzly autumn afternoon and the maddening young woman.

(n.d.)

truth and art

He

Guo Moruo[14]

Lately the short story has become quite in vogue among artists in the West. The shortest has no more than a dozen lines. Would the piece I've come up with below be worthy of the name at all?

It was getting late. So he went downtown to purchase firewood.

On his way home, he looked up and saw the crescent Moon in the sky. Wrapped in a pure, flimsy robe, as if having just stepped out of a fragrant bath, she flashed him a smile. Around her were many bright-eyed fairies, all smiling at him. He gazed up at them silently, in awe: Oh, Light! Love! How should I live my life to earn your favor! How lucky are those who *have* earned your favor!

Hello, Mr. K! Where're you going?

It was Mr. N, one of his former classmates. K pulled his mantle to reveal a piece of firewood and said,

"Hey, you always run into me purchasing firewood."

N smiled. He smiled, too. Then he asked N,

"Where are *you* going?"

"Visiting Mr. Y. Why don't you come and join us for fun?"

"No. Visiting with firewood in my arms?"

"Don't want to come and have fun?"

"No, I've got to go home."

They went separate ways at H Shrine. He went on home murmuring his own poems.

(1920)

Theme

Lu Xun[15]

I dreamed of myself in a grammar school classroom learning to write: I was asking the schoolmaster how to establish a theme.

"Impossible!" the schoolmaster said, staring at me over the top of his spectacles. "Let me tell you something. . . . "

"A male child was born to a family. The family was so thrilled. During the one-month birthday celebration, the family showed the baby to their guests, probably to invite some auspicious comments.

"One man said, 'This child will be wealthy.' He was duly thanked.

"One man said, 'This child will be powerful.' He received auspicious comments in return.

"One man said, 'This child will die one day.' He was rewarded with blows from everyone present.

"To say the child will die is telling the truth. To say the child will be wealthy or powerful is telling a lie. But the one lying was richly rewarded, while the one telling the truth was beaten.

"I don't want to tell lies, and I don't want to be beaten, either. So, master, what should I say?"

"Okay, then, you'll have to say, 'This child! Oh my! How. . . . indeed! Ha ha ha! Hee hee hee! Hee hee hee!'"

(1925)

Two Unforgettable Impressions
Xia Yan[16]

I forgot what exactly the editor had asked me to write about, but thought that it was something about impressions of war-torn Shanghai. There are so many such impressions that I will have to choose two that I experienced firsthand to write about; two that I will never forget.

Impression One
On February 15, at Sun Yat-sen Boulevard, I got on a cargo truck loaded with military supplies and food donated by some organizations for the 19th Route Army troops in Zhenru. Once past the Da Yang Bridge, we didn't encounter any continuous barricades except for sporadic earth mounds and low-lying farmland here and there. Since it is now a busy route with lots of traffic, the old, rather bumpy road has been resurfaced and the ride is now quite smooth. When the truck reached a speed of about 40 miles an hour, the driver started to chat, rather frothily, with the cargo clerk sitting next to him.

All of a sudden, a Red Cross vehicle, less than a hundred yards ahead of us, stopped, as if it had run into an earthen wall; its five or six uniformed occupants, like beans being poured out of a plate, were scurrying into the fields on both sides of the road. No doubt the cause of all this were the Japanese Imperialist airplanes. So our truck stopped too and we ran and hid behind an earthen mound or inside a ditch.

There was only one airplane; it flew very low, hovered around our two vehicles, dropped a bundle of white and blue leaflets, and turned and dragged its tail to the east.

With a sigh of relief, we all came out. The driver said it would have been all over for him if the leaflets had been a bomb, which had fallen less than two or three yards away from where he was. He said there were two pilots; the one dropping the leaflets seemed to have waved with a smile on his face. The leaflets, so many of them, were scattered here and there, but the real bombshell was this: mixed in among the leaflets which denounced the defiant 19th Route Army were declarations in Japanese signed by the Committee of Japanese Revolutionary Soldiers. They were rather long, at least seven or eight hundred words, which ended with these slogans:

"Turn your bayonet around to kill your *real* enemy!"

"Have the courage to shake hands with Chinese revolutionary soldiers!"

Many of us were stunned.

"Strange, there are such people among the Japanese?"

"And pilots, too."

But the truck driver, apparently not so impressed, said, wiping away the dust on his face, "What's the use dropping the leaflets on us? We aren't Japanese soldiers after all."

"Just so that you'd know: There are such people among the Japanese!" someone snapped.

Impression Two

The date is blurry now, and the place is a hospital for war wounded near Ai Wenyi Road and Mei Baike Street. The soft afternoon sun slants in through the window facing the street. At the low, small desk is a female volunteer: a medical school student, writing a letter for a wounded soldier of the 88th Division, who speaks with a Zhuji accent.

"So, no money to send at this time, no date for return, either. . . what else?" the girl presses on.

His eyes on the pale slender hand scribbling on the paper, the soldier with a broken ankle grins, a dazed look on his face.

"What? Wounded as you're, you're smiling? . . . Have you lost your mind?" the girl flares up, reddening under his stare.

"Never seen such pale, soft hands! See, our hands are covered with calluses big as broad beans. Hey, Old Kong!" He hollers. "Remember what happened at Quanjia?"

Old Kong, his face wrapped in bandages revealing only eyes, also from the 88th Division, looks up slowly, and lies down again.

"A few days before Old Kong was wounded, he and I were grabbling with a Japanese soldier at Quanjia to get his rifle. That soldier, he was so fierce, and no matter how we hit him, would not let go. Finally, with Old Kong grabbing the rifle, I forced open his hands. Oh, yes, his hands looked just like ours."

A pause. Silence. The girl student's eyes were riveted on his hands.

"The Japanese grip the spades and axes the way we do, too, I figure," another wounded soldier mumbles.

(1932)

The Ferry

Gao Xiaosheng

Four men came to the ferry.

Of the four, one was rich; one burly; one powerful; and one, a writer. They all wanted to be transported to the other bank of the river.

The ferryman said, "To get you across the river, you'll have to share your most valuable thing with me first. Whoever doesn't do so will not get on my boat."

The rich man gave him some money and stepped onto the boat.

The burly man waved his fist in the ferryman's face and snarled: "Can you handle *this*?" and got on the boat.

The powerful man said: "Once you get me across the river, you can quit this hard work and I'll find you some clean and easy money." Delighted, the ferryman helped him onto the boat.

Finally, it was the writer's turn. He said, "My most valuable thing is writing, but I can't come up with anything good for the moment. I'll sing you a song instead."

The ferryman said: "I can hum a tune, too. Who wants to listen to you sing? Okay, if you really don't have anything else to offer, a song will do. But it has to be good. Otherwise. . . . "

So the writer sang a song.

The ferryman shook his head. "What kind of singing is that? Not even as good as him (gesturing to the powerful man) speaking!" With that, he pushed the boat away from the shore with his long pole, leaving the poor writer behind.

Dusk having thickened, the writer felt cold, hungry, and miserable. His wife and kids were waiting for him to come home and find money to buy things and cook supper, yet he was still stuck on this side of the river. "Oh, Heaven!" he cried aloud, "I have never done anything horrible my entire life, why leave me nowhere to go!"

Upon hearing this, the ferryman turned his boat around and came back. "This cry of yours, it sounded better than your singing. Since you've shared with me your most valuable thing—your genuine feelings—please get on the boat!"

So the writer crossed the river, his heart filled with happiness. The ferryman was right, he thought: without expressing genuine feelings, a writer would have nowhere to go.

The next day, remembering that the ferryman had gone with the powerful man, the writer decided to take his place. From that day on, a new ferryman worked on the river from dawn to dusk.

The writer treated all his passengers fairly and with genuine feelings, regardless of wealth and power, and would expect no more and no less from his passengers.

It dawned on the writer, about a year later, that he had never changed his livelihood because writing and ferrying were not that different after all:

Both were about carrying people, forward, to the other shore.

(1980)

Explosion in the Living Room

Bai Xiaoyi

Having made tea, the host placed teacups on the table in front of the guests and covered them with the lids, which clinked pleasantly. Something occurring to him, the host placed the thermos on the floor and hurried into the inner room. Out came the sound of drawers being opened and searched.

The guests, father and daughter, were left alone in the living room. The ten-year-old daughter was appreciating the flowers by the window. The father reached for the teacup. His fingers had barely touched its thin handle—Crash! And there was the sound of something breaking into pieces.

The thermos on the floor had fallen over. Startled, the girl turned to see what happened. Nothing extraordinary, yet a near-miracle: Neither father nor daughter had touched the thermos. Heaven knows! When the host had placed the thermos on the floor, it did wobble somewhat, but didn't threaten to fall.

The sound of the crash brought the host from the inner room, a box of sugar in hand. Seeing the steamy mess on the floor, he said, offhandedly, "No big deal. No big deal."

The father had an urge to say something, but held it back.

"I'm terribly sorry," he finally said, "I touched it accidentally."

"No big deal," the host said again.

When they had left the host, the daughter asked, "Dad, did you touch it?"

"I . . . was the closest to it," the father said.

"But you didn't touch it. You didn't touch it at all."

The father smiled. "What would you have done then?"

"The thermos fell by itself. The floor is uneven. When Uncle Li placed it on the floor, it wobbled back and forth and then fell. Dad, why did you say you. . . . "

"Your Uncle Li couldn't have seen all this, could he?"

"But you could have told him."

"No," the father said. "It's better to say I touched it. It sounds better to the ear. Sometimes you don't really know what's going on, the more truthfully you describe it, the more false-like it sounds, and the less people believe you."

The girl was silent for a while, then said: "So we have to leave it like that?"

"Yes, leave it like that."

(1985)

White Gem

Ru Rongxing

White gem? I know there are red, green, and blue gems . . . yes, even black gems, but have never heard of white ones. Are you kidding?

X paused as if annoyed by my interruption: Looks like you are not interested in the story. Fine, I won't tell it.

Skeptical as I was about his story, I became even more interested, yes, even fascinated. What kind of story, really, is X's story about the white gem? How will it end?

So I tossed X a cigarette and urged him: C'mon, go on with the story. I am very interested.

X smiled nonchalantly, lit the cigarette, and started to tell his white gem story—

Once upon a time there lived a boy, 8 years old, perhaps. One day he ran into a man in the street who, somehow, looked familiar, but at the moment he couldn't recall the man's name. Who was he? The boy racked his brains for three days. Anyway, the boy finally succeeded in recalling who the man was. It turned out he had been the boy's neighbor and had moved away about two years ago. That was why the boy couldn't recall his name for a while.

At this X stopped, the same nonchalant smile in his face. Then he took out his own pack of cigarettes, slipped one into his mouth, and tossed one to me.

I took out my lighter right away and lit X's cigarette for him. Naturally I lit my own, too. However, my interest was not in the cigarette. I thought X wanted to take a drag on the cigarette so he could tell the story more vividly. Then, I thought, up to this point no white gem had appeared yet. We had not even gone beyond the prologue. And I thought, the real story was yet to come—I was dying to know what happened between the boy and the white gem. Or, what happened between the white gem and the boy's neighbor?

I couldn't wait for X to open his mouth again.

Yet X seemed not ready to do so anytime soon. With a rather content smile on his face, he dragged on the cigarette slowly, appreciatively, and even went so far as to blow me a big, perfect smoke ring.

I couldn't take it anymore and urged X again: Buddy, why are you torturing me like this? Tell the rest of the story!

"Finished! I've finished the story." X said, blowing me another big, perfect smoke ring.

Finished? The way I stared at him my eyeballs must have looked bigger than chicken eggs. How? How could you have finished the white gem story? What happened to the white gem? And where the heck is the white gem in the story anyway?

X, however, appeared to be unaffected by these questions. With the same content smile on his face, he said slowly, "The important thing is not whether there is a white gem in the story or not, not whether what I've just told you is a story at all, but that you've been a loyal, captive audience of mine despite the doubts you have about it all—yes, you didn't believe the story, but fell into its trap with your eyes open anyway!"

"What? You've been fooling me?

"You can put it that way. But the real question should be: Why were you fooled? Why have so many people believed the stories being fed them despite their doubts?"

With these two big questions, my friend X gave me a long, meaningful look, and laughed.

(1997)

To Kill the Sister-in-Law

Jia Pingao

The way I would tell the story, this would be how Wu Song[17] killed his sister-in-law.

Golden Lotus, you slutty woman! How could you have the heart to betray your marriage vows and conspire with your lecherous lover to kill my brother? True, Wu One was worthless, but there is me, Wu Two. How could you think you could get away with the vicious crime against my brother? So, open your despicable eyes wide and see how this steely sword will go in white and come out red. Then I'll cut off your head to appease his ghost, and cut out your heart to find out just how a woman's heart could be so dark!

Why didn't she cry or beg for her life or fall down with fright? Instead, the slut had changed into a silk, pink dress; put a fresh rose in her hair, and lay down on the soft-quilted bed. Oh my, what a beauty: her eyes glistening like two stars, her rich hair a cloud of shiny black, the collar of her silk dress unbuttoned, revealing the curves and her bouncy breasts. She used to be his sister-in-law, so he had never looked at her long. Now, under his sword, she indeed looked stunningly beautiful. How could there be such beauty in the world? It had to be a pact between God and the Devil! Oh, Heaven, was she trying to display all her beauty one last time before she died?

Oh, such a rare beauty, how can I kill her? True, she did help murder my elder brother, but my elder brother truly didn't deserve her. A beautiful flower dumped on a heap of cow manure. She didn't deserve that. If Wu Song hadn't been Wu Two, if Wu Two hadn't had a dwarf for an elder brother, I would have felt sorry for this woman and felt that this marriage wasn't right. Yet Wu One was my elder brother and we suckled the same breasts when we were babies. How can I not honor my elder brother by carrying out this revenge? Yes, those who kill must pay with their own lives. Even if you were the precious daughter of a divine being; even if you were Guan Yin, the Goddess of Mercy herself, I would still have to kill you. Otherwise, Wu Song would not be Wu Song the Heroic any more.

She smiled. It was not a cold or bitter smile, but a warm, intoxicating smile. This woman! I'm about to kill her and she flashes me this smile, just as she did that snowy day when she treated me to wine and delicacies to welcome me back home. This woman, she does have feelings for me, and, truth be told, I have loved her, too. Do I really want to kill her? If I had responded to her amorous advances that day and had acted impulsively, what would have happened to me? I would be killing not only her, but also myself. It's exactly because I am Wu Song the Heroic that I have avoided the sin that would be condemned for a thousand years. Yet, isn't it because I am Wu Song the Heroic, that pushed her into the lecherous arms of Xi Menqing?

Wu Song, why are you thinking such wayward thoughts right in front of your elder brother's altar? The memorial hall is filled with the yin aura; the ghost of your murdered elder brother is crying out for justice. How can you let someone go who is so brutally vicious? True, you, Golden Lotus, had no love for my elder brother. You could always marry someone else. Anybody would do. Of all people in the world, why did you choose that lecherous Xi Menqing? Okay, even that would have been okay if you had not conspired with him to murder my elder brother. If I let you go today, what would people say about me! As if having my elder brother cuckolded is not enough, now the Sunny Hill Hero has to be cuckolded, too! Some may even say Wu Song didn't kill his sister-in-law because she had once loved him. What kind of image I, a hero, would have in the eyes of the world?

So, I'll have to kill you, Golden Lotus. Wu Song has no choice but to kill you!

Why can't I lift the sword? Why is it so heavy? Once it falls, the most stunningly beautiful woman will be gone. There will be no Golden Lotus in the world any more. How many people will regret and complain that I, Wu Song, is too stone-hearted. Elder brother, elder brother, what should I do? I've already killed Xi Menqing. Why don't we let this rare beauty go?

Ah, ah, how I wish it were the Sunny Hill tiger we are talking about here.

Fine, let her be. Yet, if I don't kill her, would she stay with the Wu family and be a good woman for the rest of her life? No doubt she would marry again, or hook up with this or that amorous rascal. Such a beautiful little thing. I would rather kill her than let others carry her away. Yes, when I kill her, and watch her warm red blood flushing down her creamy white chest, her almond eyes quiver spastically before she breathes her last, wouldn't that be even more exciting? Since I can't return her love, I might as well let her die under the sword of the one she loved. Wouldn't that be a perfect, win-win solution of it all? That is it, Golden Lotus, hence I'll kill you.

That, in a nutshell, is how Wu Song killed Golden Lotus.

(1998)

Tiger, Tiger
Liu Gong

When he was young, Sheep Lin was rather short and weak. During

grade school he was often beaten black and blue in the face by the bul-
lies. His father wondered if this might have anything to do with his poor
son's name, which didn't sound strong by any stretch.

So "Sheep Lin" was replaced by a new name: "Tiger Lin." Well,
strangely enough, Tiger Lin turned out to be much more potent. No one
dared to bully him anymore.

Tiger Lin liked to paint tigers, too. He painted so many of them yet
none was good enough for any show or exhibition. By the time he graduated from high school and joined the army, he had not produced any
tiger painting that would be worth anything.

But Tiger Lin, stubborn, remained undiscouraged. While in the army
whenever he had leisure time, he would pick up the brushes and paint.

One Sunday evening while aglow with the joy of having just finished another of his tiger paintings, he heard a string of short, urgent
notes from the company commander's whistle and bolted out of the
study room. A nearby village was on fire! Following the order of the
commander, Tiger Lin and his comrades dashed toward the village with
buckets and washbasins in hand.

Fanned by a gusty wind the fire raged on and turned the sky red. The
soldiers fought hard but failed to bring the fierce fire under control. The
commander ordered Tiger Lin and several other soldiers to get on the
roof and remove the shingles in order to stop the fire from spreading.
Tiger Lin was the first to get on the roof. Others followed close behind.
Soon a two-meter wide buffer was established. Just when he was ready
to get off the roof, Tiger Lin fell to the ground and lost consciousness.

He remained in critical condition for three days in the hospital. On
the fourth day he woke up. A week later he could get off the bed and
walk a few halting steps. A month later his life returned to normal. All
except that he could not speak.

And for a while Tiger Lin was frustrated by his inability to speak and express himself through his vocal cords. He felt so alone in the world.

Still struggling with loneliness, Tiger Lin picked up the paint brushes again. To capture the spirit of the tiger, Lin would go to the zoo to observe the tigers there. He would stay for an entire day, having nothing but the water and slices of bread he had brought along, and would not leave until sunset, when the zoo staff started to clean up for the day.

So the cycle went: observing tigers and painting them and observing them again, rain or shine, every day, for over half a year. Then, encouraged by the company commander, Tiger Lin sent his paintings to be shown at an art gallery at the provincial capital. It turned out to be quite a success. A five-tiger painting of his drew a large crowd. An American art merchant, captivated by Lin's paintings, wanted to sign a deal to purchase them all. The Provincial Art College wanted to invite him to be a visiting professor, too. Although he couldn't speak, Lin could communicate through written words, or through a "spokesperson."

Tiger Lin became a hot celebrity instantly. Radio and television stations and newspapers fought each other for a chance to interview him and carry his story. Meanwhile, around this time a government agency was organizing a cultural delegation to visit Germany, and Tiger Lin was on the list. They told him to be ready to go at any time. When the army top brass knew this, they decided to do everything possible to restore his speech so he would project a positive image of the Chinese army abroad.

A team of well-known specialists was put together quickly. They came up with a surefire surgical plan, which, once approved by the top brass, was performed right away. As expected, the carefully planned surgery was a success. Tiger Lin's ability to speak was restored. For the successful surgery the team of specialists was commended by the top brass and won awards in Scientific and Technological Advancement.

Nothing could be better.

As soon as Tiger Lin was discharged from the hospital, a cultural officer from the regiment took him to a studio prepared for him exclusively. On the table were spread the finest rice paper and painting brushes, waiting for Lin, and for his inspiration to strike. But Tiger Lin stood there as if numb. Nothing happened.

"Tiger, why don't you paint?" the cultural officer urged.

"Paint what?" Tiger Lin stared at the officer, puzzled.

"Tigers, of course! Aren't they your passion?" With that, the cultural officer placed a painting brush in Lin's hand.

"I . . . I really don't know how. . . . " As Tiger Lin stammered, sweat oozed from his forehead.

What the hell was going on? No sooner had he been . . . than. . . .

(2000)

Autumn

Xia Xueqin

Ma Chao loves to paint. He has loved to "fool around" with paint and brushes since he was a small child. During the fifth grade, his teacher took the class to an art gallery. There young Ma Chao was mesmerized by a classic Chinese painting entitled "Autumn." He stood there gazing at it for so long without blinking. Trees in deep forests melting into the autumn colors, soft, dream-like fusion of water and ink, and the joy of the woman at the time of harvest. All of this reminded young Ma Chao of his dead mother. And a motherless child is always exceptionally sensitive. He didn't wake up from the trance and tear himself away from that painting until the teacher called for his class to leave. As he turned to leave, Ma Chao caught the name of the artist: Shi Bangqiao (Stone Board Bridge)

From then on Ma Chao began to dream of becoming an artist when he grew up. Later he learnt about the grand master artist Zheng Bangqiao.[18] Young Ma Chao figured Shi Bangqiao must have learned painting from Zheng Bangqiao because their names were the same but for one character. Shi Bangqiao's name began to take root in young Ma Chao's mind like a seed. Whenever he saw a painting by Shi Bangqiao reproduced in the newspaper, he would cut it, paste it carefully in a notebook, and look at it again and again with such admiration. Ma Chao didn't know what had happened to him. Perhaps it was because of his dead mother, or the strange name of Shi Bangqiao.

Dreams do not always translate into reality, however. Ma Chao applied to an art college when he graduated from high school but failed to get in. He was devastated. Yet Shi Bangqiao remained in his mind despite his failure. He began to work in a factory but his admiration for Shi Bangqiao didn't change and he still liked to "fool around" with his paint and brushes. Before long he began to have this idea: that he should own a Shi Bangqiao painting.

One day in a casual conversation Ma Chao mentioned this idea of his. A friend from the Municipal Artists Association liked the idea. "Easy," the friend said. "I have his address and phone number. All you need to do is to go and ask. Ah, why do you want to have a Shi Bangqiao painting? His art is . . . so-so, you know?"

"In his painting there is a woman, very much like my mother," Ma Chao said and hurried out the door.

All his friends laughed and thought him odd. That friend from the Municipal Artists Association did keep his promise to help establish the contact.

So with two big gift boxes of expensive, fresh and preserved fruit that had cost him a full month's wages, Ma Chao went to Shi Bangqiao's home like a young man meeting his would-be father-in-law for the first time. Shaking nervously, he stammered through the purpose of his visit.

Shi Bangqiao took a casual glance at him and said: "Why don't I know you?"

"True, you don't know me, but I've known you for almost 20 years."

"Who are you, anyway?"

"Nobody, nothing but an admirer of yours."

"I have so many admirers. How can I give each and every one of them a painting?"

"But . . . I. . . . "

"You know a painting of mine can sell for ten thousand *yuan*."

His head low, Ma Chao didn't say another word. A short while later, he put the gift boxes on the table and left.

Three years later Ma Chao came to Shi Bangqiao's home again. This time he brought with him a lot of money. Shi Bangqiao glanced at Ma Chao and said: "You're looking for me?"

"Yes, to buy a painting!"

A smile blossomed on Shi Bangqiao's face. He led Ma Chao into his studio. "See? These are all new paintings. Pick any one you like." Ma Chao grabbed one, threw the money on the table, and turned to leave.

Shi Bangqiao saw Ma Chao to the door politely, mumbling repeatedly: "Please come again. Please come again."

Ma Chao then began to tear the painting into pieces right there.

Shi Bangqiao's face went red with anger. "You. . . . how dare you tear up my painting!"

"This is not your painting. It's actually my money! So I can do whatever I want with it." With that Ma Chao walked down the stairs and left the building.

Not long after, Ma Chao quit his factory job and opened an art gallery on his own street. Ma Liang Gallery was a huge success and soon became the best-known and most successful in the entire city. Many artist friends would come there to sit and talk about art and life, and life and art. Once someone asked Ma Chao, "What's your secret? You've just opened this gallery, and it's a wild success!"

"Secret?" Ma Chao smiled. "The only secret I have is don't take these paintings too seriously. Yes, just sell them like so many green vegetables and carrots at the farmers' market."

All his friends were stunned. "That's blatant sacrilege of art!"

"It's true," said Ma Chao. "Real art is priceless. Whatever can be priced, sold, and bought is merchandise, and nothing else. Right?"

The friends were stunned once again and whispered nervously among themselves.

(2002)

Wrong Number

Liu Yichang

1.

When the phone rings, Chen Xi is sprawled in bed gazing at the ceiling. It is Wu Lichang. She invites him to go to the Lee Theatre to see the film playing at 5:50pm. He springs to life right away. With nimble movements he shaves, combs his hair, and changes clothes, whistling joyously "The Brave Chinese." Finally, he stands in front of the dresser's mirror to take a look at himself. He feels he should buy a name-brand sports shirt. He loves Lichang and Lichang loves him. Once he finds a job they can register to get married. He's just returned from the United States. Even though he has a college degree from an American university, he still needs some luck to find a job here. If he is lucky, he can find a job soon; if he is not so lucky, he may have to wait for a while. He has sent out seven or eight application letters and has been expecting to hear from them for the last few days. That's why he has been staying at home: waiting for the clerks of the agencies where he has applied to call. Unless it's absolutely necessary, he will not go out. However, when Lichang calls to invite him to a movie, he wants to go. It's already 4:50 pm. If he is late, Lichang would be upset. So he strides to the door, pulls it open, pushes open the metal security door, turns and closes the door, closes the metal security door, gets into the elevator to go downstairs, steps outside the tall apartment building, walks to the bus stop cheerfully, and has barely reached the stop when an out of control bus jumps the curb, knocks down Chen Xi, an elderly woman, and a young girl, and crushes them beneath the wheels.

2.

When the phone rings, Chen Xi is sprawled in bed gazing at the ceiling. It is Wu Lichang. She invites him to go to the Lee Theatre to see the film playing at 5:50pm. He springs to life right away. With nimble movements he shaves, combs his hair, and changes clothes, whistling joyously "The Brave Chinese." Finally, he stands in front of the dresser's mirror to take a look at himself. He feels he should buy a name-brand sports shirt. He loves Lichang and Lichang loves him. Once he finds a job they can register to get married. He's just returned from the United States. Even though he has a college degree from an American university, he still needs some luck to find a job here. If he is lucky, he can find a job soon;

if he is not so lucky, he may have to wait for a while. He has sent out seven or eight application letters and has been expecting to hear from them for the last few days. That's why he has been staying at home: waiting for the clerks of the agencies where he has applied to call. Unless it's absolutely necessary, he will not go out. However, when Lichang calls to invite him to a movie, he wants to go. It's already 4:50 pm. If he is late, Lichang would be upset.

The telephone rings again.

Thinking it must be the clerk of some agency, he turns and hurries to answer the call.

It's a woman's voice at the other end.

"Can I talk to Big Uncle?"

"Who?"

"Big Uncle."

"We don't have such a person here."

"Big Aunt is not home either?"

"Wrong Number." He grunts and puts the phone back in its cradle, strides to the door, pushes open the metal security door, steps out, turns and closes the metal security door, gets into the elevator to go downstairs, steps outside the tall apartment building, walks to the bus stop cheerfully. When he is less than 50 yards away from the bus stop, an out-of-control bus jumps the curb, knocks down Chen Xi, an elderly woman, and a young girl, and crushes them beneath the wheels.

April 22, 1983:

A fatal accident at a bus stop in Taikoo Shing was reported in the newspaper that day.

(n.d.)

existential moments

Light

Wang Luyan

I lay in Mother's arms, filled with anger. Mother held me tight, sobbing, her tears dripping onto my neck. I lay there, motionless, filled with anger.

"Why did you have to bring me into this world, Mother?" I asked angrily.

Mother didn't reply; she looked ghastly pale.

Suddenly I thrust out my right hand and tore at my chest furiously.

"For Mother's sake, my child. . . ." Mother seized my hand.

I began to cry.

Wind whistled through the loquats outside the window. Raindrops, large and cold, fell onto my heart. I gazed at Mother—her face so ghastly pale—and reached to put my arms around her neck, which felt so thin and bony.

"Let me die, Mother!" I wailed, hanging on to her neck.

"Can't, can't child, my child. . . ." Her tears continued to fall onto my face.

Dim light shone on her hair, her messy, frosty hair.

Silence. Silence. Not a soul in the world, except for Mother and me; not a sound between heaven and earth, except for the wailing wind and rain.

"Let go, let go, Mother. I return to you this heart, I return to you this heart! You shouldn't have given me this heart when giving birth to me. What's its use in this world of ours!" With that, I

tore at my chest again with desperate fingers, bursting with anger and
sorrow.

"Oh, child!" Mother wailed with abandon. She seized my hand,
which I struggled to break free.

Wind whistled through the loquats outside the window. Raindrops,
large and cold, fell onto my heart. Dim light shone on her hair, her
messy, frosty hair, her tears gushing forth. I held tight her neck, her thin,
bony neck, wailing with abandon, too.

A teardrop from Mother's eyes fell into mine, mixed with my tears,
which gathered into a river.

Wading upstream in the river I entered Mother's eyes, landed in
Mother's heart, and noticed that it had withered.

"Mother, you've given so much of your heart to your child, yet the
heart you've given your child has received no blessings, only curses; no
joy, only sorrow. So, here, Mother, I'll take it out and return it to you!"

I unbuttoned the clothes, cut open the chest with fingernails, dug up
my bleeding heart, and placed it atop that of Mother's. The two hearts
blended into one, our blood coursing with warmth again.

Hastily I sealed the chest, buttoned the clothes, stole away from
Mother's heart, came out from Mother's eyes, and retraced my steps
back to Mother's knees.

Mother didn't know.

"Mother," I said to her, wiping away my tears, "I won't be
despondent any more. I don't mind being 'human' from now on."

Mother smiled, her heart filled with joy, her eyes glinting with hope.

Only Light, only the light on the wall, that knew what I had done
inside Mother's heart, couldn't bear to see the smile and dimmed sadly
thereafter.

(1924)

That Ball of Cloud

Pu Benlin

Have I seen a ghost? He tried to comfort himself again. His mind remained wrapped in thick melancholy, which refused to be pried away, like the ball of cloud surrounding the tip of the Heavenly Summit.

He came to enjoy the scenery but had lost all interest. All those vivid rocks, elegant green pines, and translucent creeks trickling down, were nothing in his eyes but a blur.

Early this morning when descending from the North Sea, he was so captivated by Nature's wonders, as if drunk, half dancing all the way, lingering at each sight to take it all in. Impatient with him "dragging his feet" all the time, his buddies went down the mountain first, promising to wait for him at Jade Screen House.

He sighed deeply.

He felt sad about himself: How can a man, a proud man, be so stuck with such a trifle and lose all peace over it!

It was a trifle indeed. At the top of the Glory Summit he had bought a bag of Cloud and Fog Tea from an old woman for the price of one *yuan*. He knew he had gotten a bad deal even before he reached the Lotus Summit. There the same kind of Cloud and Fog Tea was sold for only 80 cents.

"Worthless jerk!" He cursed himself. What's 20 or 30 cents nowa-days? Working overtime just once, not eating popsicles a few times, or . . . he tried hard to break out of the cloud of melancholy, only to find himself hopelessly buried in it. As he continued down the mountain, he felt giddy, each step heavy as lead.

Finally he reached Jade Screen House and dropped down under a pine lazily. Right across was a peddler's stand. He became even more infuriated with himself by what he saw: there was the exact same kind of tea selling for only 50 cents.

He sighed again and closed his eyes.

"We thought you'd never come down!" Several of his buddies suddenly appeared in front of him.

He sat there silently, his hand stroking the bag of tea instinctively.

"What, you've bought the Cloud and Fog Tea, too?" exclaimed a buddy.

He nodded and murmured, "A short while ago . . . here." He felt his face blushing.

"Then you've got a very good deal. See, we each bought four bags, all at the top of the Glory Summit. Each bag cost 50 cents more."

"Really?" His eyes shone suddenly; his heart beat with an unknown joy. Strangely, the world around him became fascinating again; every summit and every green pine came alive like before.

The lost interest returned. His whole being trembled with a wild joy. He turned to gaze at the tall Heavenly Summit again, fierce, grand, thrusting high into the sky. He noticed something strange about it: Where's that ball of cloud?

(1985)

Mullet and Mackerel

Lin Jinlan

The Great River roars to the east, its waves washing down the sand.

A Mullet comes surfing the crest of a wave. With a fierce stroke of its front and back gills it jumps more than a foot into the air. Then it relaxes the gills and floats down into the wave. It repeats the feat and marvels in English: "Try again!" Yes, when it is in a good mood, English words—though only a few—bound out of its heart. This sport of "Wave Surfing" is indeed the joy of life.

Nicknamed Stick Fish, the Mullet is long and slim with tight muscles, like a smooth stick, yet agile as water snake and much more graceful. Indeed, its grace is something no other fish can ever cultivate.

Just then, a Mackerel casually flits by, its eyes glinting with alertness. Instead of rushing to meet the Mackerel, the Mullet straightens itself and puts on an indifferent air. The Mackerel, to its credit, goes straight to join a crowd of smaller fish without stopping. It wouldn't have mattered much if they were strangers, but they have been through thick and thin together. What is this all about!

The Mackerel is also called the Hemp Mackerel in the south and Imperial Fish in the north; Imp Fish for short. There is nothing imperial about its appearance, though: dark grey back, deep blue belly, marked with half-visible dots, much like a clown's costume. Looking down at its tail, however, you will see its tail resemble the rudder of a ship. Looking at its entire length from the side, you will see how it looks like a helmsman, and then, feel its imperial air. With a tiny movement of its tail it can wave small fish over and wave them away.

Feeling slighted, the Mullet says:

"As the saying goes, the same tidal wave washes the same fish. Once upon a time a wave washed ashore two fish. They were stuck in the same sand hole and were baked by the same wind and sun. Although they never knew if they would live or die, they each tried to moisten the other with their saliva. That was truly 'going through thick and thin together'! Finally, as luck would have it, another wave came and swept them back to the Great River. Then what? Once they were back in their elements, they had their nose in the air and pretended not to see even family! No wonder the Great Master Zhuang once said: 'Hang together through thick and thin; fall apart once back in smooth sea.'"

The Mackerel waves its "steering gear" and says with a straight face:

"What are you hollering about? This Great River is not big enough for you to feel comfortable? Having the audacity to cite the Great Master! Is that what Zhuang Zi said? Did he say 'fall apart once back in smooth sea' or 'would rather fall apart once back in smooth sea'? Did he say 'would rather' or not? With or without 'would rather,' would it make any difference?"

The Mullet has a hard time following as the Mackerel fires away because in this old acquaintance's face it has discovered so many new teeth, tightly aligned together, each so sharp, glittering, each quivering nimbly. The Mullet, dizzied, retreats as fast it can. Although the Mackerel has no intention of biting its friend, it does look ominous enough. It then grins and says, half-jokingly:

"When we hung on through thick and thin together, you said all you wanted was a mouthful of water; nothing else mattered. Now even a river-full of water is not enough. You want everything: fame, money, power, the color in vogue, all except for the two words: 'would rather.' Why don't you quit showing off your knowledge of Zhuang Zi to me and go back to your sand hole!"

Not until then did the Mullet feel the muddy sand right underneath its belly. "Have I really returned to the sand hole?" It wonders. "Who would ever stay together with anyone else through thick and thin?" It turns to gaze around the big roaring river. Imperial or not, the crowd of small fish gathering around the helm of the Mackerel seem proud and happy. The Mullet sighs: "This is really an eye-opening experience for me. Even the proudest fish in the world has to bend its head, let alone me."

With that, it goes from underneath the Mackerel and passes through the crowd of small fish to return to the bottom of the river. Even at this time, though, it will not forget its graceful manners: "Please . . . Excuse me . . . " English words that bounce out of its heart only when it is happy escape its lips now.

(1988)

Beautiful Ears

Sha Miannong

One quiet night he jumped into the river behind the village to take a swim. Just when he started to enjoy it, a flying saucer landed noiselessly by the riverside. An extraterrestrial, donning a helmet, walked out. Scared out of his wits by the sight, he crawled ashore and broke into a run without even putting on his clothes. The extraterrestrial overtook him in two to three big steps, stopped him, looked him up and down, and burst out laughing:

"No wonder your earthlings proclaim that the most beautiful clothing in the world is human skin."

He lowered his head to see his naked body under the moonlight and instinctively reached to cover the part below the belly. The extraterrestrial laughed even more loudly:

"Truth be told, the ugliest part of the human body is not down there. It is in your head, instead—your ears!"

With that, the extraterrestrial returned to his ship and took off.

The ugliest part of the human body are the ears? The walls of his home are covered with pictures, one of them being the Four Greatest Beauties of Ancient China. Oh, look at them, look at their ears. Their old beauty is all gone. Yes, the harder he stared at their ears, the bigger they grew, and the uglier the Four Beauties became. Indeed, they all became cats!

It suddenly dawned on him why so many poets in the world had poured their hearts into describing the beauty of human eyes, mouths, noses—almond eyes, peachy lips, classic, well-sculpted nose—and into celebrating human hair, chin, teeth. . . . yet no one had ever bothered with describing how beautiful ears were!

He heard a laugh escaping his lips. We humans are probably making fun of ourselves. The ears are already ugly enough yet we want them to grow bigger; the bigger the better, the bigger the more fortunate, the bigger the longer we live. Pooh! Pigs have really big ears! No wonder nowadays so many women wear earrings. It is to divert our attention? Divert it downward? What's more, people say double eyelids are prettier than single eyelids, yet although everybody's ears are "double lids," why hasn't anybody said ears are pretty?

Once home, he looked at himself in the mirror and gazed hard at his ears. What do they look like? Two question marks hanging from both sides of his head, handles of an earthen pot, two holes in a mountain, pickled radish. . . .

How could he bear the sight of himself with a pair of ugly ears!

It occurred to him that some young women, unhappy with their thick eyebrows, would shave them completely and paint slender ones instead; some obese people would even go under the knife to remove the extra fat in their bodies; one Swedish soccer star, Pea Sundhage, even had her breasts removed in order to run like fierce wind in the field.

So he cut his ears!

Nowadays, even though his hearing has weakened dramatically, he believes he is much more beautiful than all the people between heaven and earth. Everyone else, however, has discovered, from the sight of his ear-less head, that the ears of every one of us are so beautiful!

(1990)

A Hawk in the Sky

Xiu Xiangming

A sunny spring day. The sky is high and dreamy blue. The spring breeze feels warm and gentle, like the breath from the lips of a young woman asleep.

At the foot of a small hill outside the village sit two old men, Old Man Zhu, and Old Zhong. Both have celebrated their eightieth year and are highly respected by the entire village as wise elders.

Once it has climbed overhead, the sun begins to grow lazy. Time slows to a crawl. Having exchanged pleasantries Old Man Zhu and Old Zhong settle down like two heavy sandbags without another word. They keep taking long drags on their pipes, basking in the sun as if they want to suck the juice out of life.

A hawk appears in the sky. No one knows when it came. No one knows where it came from. Oh, it soars high in the sky.

The hawk looks quite experienced and capable. With its wings spread out arrow-straight, it stays in the air, motionless, as if it would crash down at any moment, yet it seems fastened to the sky, like the stars fixed in the galaxies. What a feat!

Old Man Zhu sees the hawk first. He turns and shoots a glance at Old Zhong. He is filled with pride for his discovery. He has never expected himself at this advanced age to be able to see a hawk so high in the sky. A man's eyes are directly linked to his heart and good eyesight means he is not old yet. Although Old Man Zhu is thrilled beyond himself, he appears calm as calm can be. There is little he has not done or seen.

"Hawk!"

Old Zhong is refilling his pipe; the jade bowl twists and turns hard in the pouch as if it can never be filled.

"A hawk in the sky!"

Old Zhong takes the pipe bowl out of the pouch, presses it with his thumb, and succeeds in lighting it by drawing hard on it like a bellows. White smoke puffs, calmly and gently, out of his nose.

"Are you deaf?" Old Man Zhu cannot take it any more and exclaims through his clenched teeth.

"You are blind!" Old Zhong roars all of a sudden. He gives Old Man Zhu an angry stare but pays no attention to the hawk, as if he has already seen it, long before Old Man Zhu did, even though he has just caught a glimpse of that thing flying in the sky.

"That's a hawk?"

Old Man Zhu's proud head suddenly feels like a heavy block. He looks up into the sky and still feels stupefied.

"What is it then, if it's not a hawk?"

Old Zhong grunts.

"If it's not a hawk, how can it fly so high?"

Old Zhong grins contemptuously.

"If it's not a hawk, what do you call it?"

When Old Zhong pulls the pipe out of his mouth, words come out popping like bullets:

"That's an eagle!"

Now it is Old Zhu's turn to growl at Old Zhong. His lips, quivering with anger, a pout so pronounced one could fasten a donkey onto it.

"Why! A whole forest of birds, you are the loudest. Hawk or eagle, aren't they one and the same?"

"One and the same? Say mama gives birth to two daughters. They look almost the same. A man marries the elder sister, but the younger sister sleeps in his bed instead. Will that do?" Old Zhong sways and swings as he speaks, his head held high.

Old Zhu trembles from head to toe, his quivering lips drawing in each breath laboriously.

So Old Zhong lowers his voice and explains:

"An eagle's voice is hoarse while a hawk's is smooth; an eagle howls while a hawk sings; an eagle snatches chickens while a hawk takes rabbits; an eagle is big while a hawk is small."

"Even a small eagle is bigger than a big hawk!" snaps Old Zhu, each word like the teakettle stop being popped out by steam, his saliva sprinkling across Old Zhong's face.

Old Zhong bolts up. He knocks the pipe bowl clean against the bottom of his shoe, thrusts it into the sash tied around his waist, walks threateningly close to Old Man Zhu, his face blue with anger.

"Old rascal, you've got a ready tongue!"

"Old shameless, you've got a sharp tongue!"

"Why don't you look again, eagle or hawk?"

"Why don't you open your eyes, hawk or eagle?"

"It's an eagle!"

"It's a hawk!"

"If you lose, then you're an eagle?"

"If you lose, then you're a hawk?"

"Eagle, eagle, eagle, eagle!"

"Hawk, hawk, hawk, hawk!"

The two of them keep lashing at each other without either side gaining the upper hand, their faces red with passion.

Just then the bird falls down and lands right at their feet. It is a hawk-shaped kite.

Like ducks being choked by long vegetable leaves, the two old men stretch their necks as long as they can to see better, their eyeballs rolling in disbelief, not a sound coming out of their wide-open mouths. They look like blocks of rotten wood.

A kid comes running over to pick up the kite.

The two men spit loudly and then start to leave, each waddling like a broken kite.

(1992)

A Serious Speech to Promote
Mark Twain's Humorous Speeches
Sha Weixing

Ladies and Gentlemen:

I am here to solemnly recommend to you a book entitled *Mark Twain's Humorous Speeches.*

This is a fantastic and sure-fire guide to wealth and good fortune. Bao Yugang, Li Jiacheng, Greek shipping tycoons, and top CEOs of American Big Three Auto, you name it, they all read this book when they were young and are still benefiting from it today. That's how they became billionaires. Remember the saying: *In books are embedded gold houses*? It is this book they are talking about. Truth be told, before I was halfway through the book I was already making 240,000 *yuan* playing the stock market, and 1.6 million *yuan* buying and selling foreign currencies. The most amazing thing about this book is that it also teaches how to evade taxes so that your success in the business world is guaranteed left and right and whichever way.

What? I beg your pardon? Mark Twain is an American author? This book has nothing to do with business and economy? Says who? Please stand up! Who? Please stand up!

I am shocked! Someone among you has the audacity to say Mark Twain is an American author? That's the most ridiculous joke I've ever heard! What is Mark? You don't even know this? Mark is German currency! I repeat: It is German currency! American currency is U.S. Dollars, French currency is Francs, British currency is Pounds, German currency is Marks! Don't you know this?

So, Mark is German currency. What about Twain? What? You don't even know what Twain is? Are you serious? "Tw" means "two" and "ain" means "one." So "Mark Twain" means "21 Marks," which, going by the current official exchange rate, is equal to over 100 *yuan*. This book is a collection of speeches authored by 21 German Marks.

How could the Mark speak? I assume that everybody here knows that Mark is currency; currency means money. In the old days we listened to whoever had power. Nowadays we listen to whoever has money. If money can't talk, how can it make people listen to it? Money is quite a gifted speaker. It speaks not only Chinese, but also English, French, German, Japanese, even Esperanto. In the world we live in today, money is the most gifted speaker, and the most authoritative speaker. Since money is the most gifted and most authoritative speaker, naturally it delivers the best speeches. It not only delivers speeches, but issues orders as well. Indeed the magic power of money is boundless: It can reach heaven; it can talk to spirits; it can buy power; it can take you to your lover's bed.

Yes, those who have money can make ghosts talk; those who have money, even if they are sons of turtles, can sit on the throne; those who have money can say the dead are still alive; those who have money are *always* right even when they are dead wrong. Store owners sell counterfeit goods to make money. Officials sell official seals to make money. Professors sell steamed buns to make money. Girls take their clothes off to make money. In the presence of the national money-making campaign I can't help but sing at the top of my lungs: "Arise! All who refuse to be slaves! Let our flesh and blood become our new Great Mall! As the Chinese nation faces its greatest greed. The thundering roar of our people will be heard! Hand over! Hand over! Hand over! . . . "[19]

Hand over what? Money, of course! Other people hand over the money in their wallet so it becomes money in our wallet.

Alright, I apologize for getting carried away. However, how can I help but sing joyfully when we are talking about money, the most exciting, most thrilling topic in the entire universe?

Now, let me get back to the main topic today. To sum up, this book is a collection of speeches by 21 Marks. It's a precious book that will teach you how to use 21 Marks as the seed money to make profit instantaneously, to strike it rich right away, to become a fat cat soon, and to finally sit atop a mountain of glowing wealth. No, this is not the Little Red Book of the Cultural Revolution, but the Little Golden Book of the market economy. Right now bookstores all over the country are pitching books on how to get rich fast: *Money-Making Magic in Three Minutes; World's Ten Greatest Tycoons and Their Secrets to Wealth; Smart Businessmen's Smarts; How to Become Rich Overnight,* and so on. These books are hot and have brought truckloads of money for the bookstores. But I have to warn everyone that their potential is limited because they are all patchwork books and hence not well respected at all. Indeed they pale miserably when compared to the book I am solemnly promoting to you today. What I am solemnly promoting to you today, *Mark Twain's Humorous Speeches,* is a classic among books of this kind. Its author is a great master, a great great-master, a great great-great-master, a great great-great-great-master . . . he is Mark . . . Marks, the very same Marks who authored that great classic *Das Kapital*!

The listed price for this book is extraordinary, too. Since it is a collection of speeches by 21 Marks, its price is, naturally, 21 Marks, which, according to today's exchange rate, is 114 *yuan* and 23 cents. This price of 21 Marks will never change so it is immune to economic crises and inflation. It is 21 Marks no matter when and no matter which country. So, all of you here today, if you are interested, please get your money ready. We'll award prizes for every thousand copies sold. The top prize is the title of Chairman of Board of Trustees of a Sino-German joint venture with assets of 2 million *yuan*; the second prize is an extravagant one-month vacation in Germany; the third prize is 2,100 Marks. The award ceremony will be attended by the mayor and German Ambassador!

If anyone is curious how I could have given such a hilarious speech, as I just did, my reply would be: "My source of inspiration is my favorite author Mark Twain and this collection of his famous speeches."

(1993)

Precious Stone

Xu Guojiang

Hai came back from the beach and called out right away: Cui, come and take a look!

Cui, Hai's wife, was busy tidying up the bedroom. She said: "What is it you're so excited about?" She came out and saw a rapturous Hai with a stone in hand. She said: "Oh, a stone. What's all the fuss about?"

Hai's enthusiasm, however, remained undampened. He said: "Take a closer look. What kind of stone is it?"

Cui took a look at the stone: round at one end and pointed at the other, much like a spinning top. She measured it with her eyes: less than 20cm long, its bottom the size of a small rice bowl, its surface smooth and orange in color. She said: "What's so special about this stone? You can find stones like this easily on the beach."

Hai said: "Oh, don't be deceived by its appearance. This is no ordinary stone, I can assure you. See, feel how light it is."

Cui took the stone, felt it a couple of times. Indeed it is felt much lighter than an ordinary stone.

Hai said: "This stone floated on the sea and was washed ashore."

Cui laughed: "Liar! This thing is not wood or sea foam. How can it float?"

Hai said: "Why don't we give it a try?"

In the courtyard was a big vat more than half filled with water. Hai dropped the stone into the water. It went under but then floated to the top with its pointed end up, above the water. Cui was surprised. She said: "No wonder you are thrilled like this. It's a precious stone indeed!"

The next morning when Cui was getting ready to cook breakfast, she noticed that the water in the vat looked so clear, like a mirror. She called Hai. Hai came and tasted the water: So fresh and sweet. Hai was delighted: "Try it yourself. Tastes better than the mineral water they sell in stores."

The young couple was so happy they had found this precious stone.

Around noon the sky became cloudy and soon it began to rain. Cui went out to the vat and noticed that the stone had sunk to the bottom. What happened? Cui asked Hai. Hai said: I don't know. Something to do with the rain, perhaps?

Hai turned out to be right. By evening the sky had cleared up. The sun was setting in the west. And the stone, well, it resurfaced from the bottom of the vat, bobbing on the surface as before.

Hai jumped for joy: "Precious stone! Precious stone! It can foretell the weather. We can issue weather forecasts from now on!"

Word got out quickly and folks in the village swarmed over to see the stone with their own eyes. Before long the word spread so far it attracted the attention of an evening newspaper at the provincial capital. One day the paper sent a reporter down to take pictures and interview Hai. A few days later, the story about the stone appeared in a prominent place in that paper. Instantaneously the precious stone became the topic of the day and aroused the interest of many people. Rare stone collectors, meteorologists, and everyone else descended on the small village to see the stone with their own eyes. A fierce bidding war ensued among people who wanted the stone, and its value rose astronomically. In the end a fat cat walked away with it for the price of 20,000 *yuan*!

Holding the big bundle of brand new money in hand, Hai could barely contain himself. That night he had a dream. He went to the beach again and saw so many precious stones dancing on the crest of each wave. The next instant the stones transformed into colorful money: Renminbi, Hong Kong dollars, American dollars; all came cascading down in waves, carrying him away. He laughed himself awake and told Cui about the dream. Cui, soundly asleep, turned her face away. Hai, however, couldn't sleep any more. He thought: Who knows, I may find another stone like this on the beach. If only I can find one more, no, two more, three more. . . . I will become as rich as that fat cat, too. As Hai dreamed on, the new day dawned. He got up, hurried through breakfast, and left for the beach.

The sea was such a deep blue under the early morning sunshine, the vast sky, and a few white clouds. On the sea in the far distance were a few ships. Seagulls wove their own dreams up and down in the air. Oh, how lovely!

Hai came to the old place, his eyes scanned where the waves washed the sand. Time drifted away with the gentle sea breeze, but Hai remained empty-handed. There were no other stones. Then, the wind became gusty. The tide rose again. Hai decided he couldn't go home like this. He wanted to give Cui a joyous surprise again. His eyes brightened up suddenly: On the crest of a huge wave floated a stone! Thrilled beyond words, he jumped toward it. The mountainous wave crashed ashore. Poor Hai. He had barely reached out his hand when he was swallowed by the sea.

(1999)

Immortality

Huang Keting

Mr. Shishu went fishing in Hongchen Pond. In less than five minutes he caught a big greenish brown carp.

The fish in the water became worried when they found the greenish brown carp missing. They all knew that the carp was swimming to the surface of water when it disappeared. Where did it go? Everybody had a different theory.

The boldest theory, though, came from a black carp, a learned fish who had jumped above the water once. "Perhaps the greenish brown carp has become an immortal and is on its way to Heaven!" It said.

At this many fish began to recall all the remarkable things about this greenish brown carp. Some said it was only natural this carp had achieved immortality because it was most favored by its solid, illustrious genealogy thanks to a 27th-generation ancestor who had once jumped over the Dragon Gate. Some said the greenish brown carp had a most auspicious name: Don't you see? The "gre" in "greenish" is the same as "gre" in "great?" Even if it hadn't become an immortal in Heaven, it would, by destiny, become a king here on earth. Some said this carp's looks were out of the ordinary, too: it had not only two whiskers around the mouth, but also a rainbow hue on its tail!

The Crucian carp, meanwhile, had remained quiet the entire time. It tried to recall every little detail about the greenish brown carp before its disappearance. It found that the greenish brown carp had swallowed some kind of hook-shaped elixir right before it was elevated to heavenly immortality. So, seeing Mr. Shishu's bait coming down to the bottom of the pond again, it swam over quietly and took the "elixir" into its mouth, too.

Shishu pulled when he felt the line tightening. But he pulled too hard. The Crucian carp's lips were torn just when it was pulled out of water, the hook slipped, and the carp got away. Horrified, it returned to the bottom of the pond and warned its friends: Never be tempted to bite anything in the shape of a hook.

A silver carp, not impressed, said, "You, with your pitiable tiny mouth and chin, and without even a hint of red in your tail, want to become an immortal, too?"

An eel came by and said, "Yeah, born with such a lousy body, it won't work no matter how much elixir you swallow!"

The silver carp touched the Crucian carp's broken lips roughly and said: "Luck itself is not enough. You had the elixir in your mouth but had to watch it slip away. Blame it on your lot!"

Once home, the Crucian carp said to its children, "Never be tempted to bite anything in the shape of a hook. Once in the mouth the thing hurts all the way to the heart!"

Its son said, "How can I become the best fish of all if I don't swallow the bitterest of all bitter things? The real reason the rare opportunity, when it came, slipped away was that you were afraid of pain, of hardship, and of sacrifice. Didn't the old sages teach us: 'Prior to assigning me great tasks, Heaven would temper my will, harden my bones, and starve my body?'"

When Shishu dropped the bait into the water again, neither the silver carp nor eel dared to go and take a bite. They knew that they had not been virtuous enough to be eligible for immortality because they had mocked the Crucian carp. They didn't want to embarrass themselves. At the sight of the "elixir," a perch, excited, made a dash for it, but it was one second too late. The Crucian carp had returned, in one bite swallowed the "elixir," and had been elevated to Heaven.

This bold move by the Crucian carp left the other fish in an unsettled state. Both the silver carp and eel were full of regrets. They were worried that the Crucian carp, now an immortal in Heaven, may seek revenge; they blamed themselves for having let a golden opportunity slip away right in front of their eyes thanks to their indecisiveness. They vowed that at the first sight of the "elixir" again they would move as resolutely as the Monkey King.[20]

When Shishu noticed that he had caught a Crucian carp with broken lips, he couldn't help but laugh.

Seeing all this, a sagacious old man said: So long as there is Heaven above there will be fish to catch on earth.

(2000)

Two Pines

Li Yongkang

On a mountain in a scenic area grow two special pine trees. While they were still nestling in their mother's bosom—and playing inside the pine seeds—a young scholar came to visit the scenic area. Tired from walking, the traveler took a rest and began to read aloud from a book as thick as a brick. The two pine seeds listened attentively and realized that the young man was reading Chapter 4 of the Book of Mark from the *Holy Bible*:

> Hearken; Behold, there went out a sower to sow: and it came
> to pass, as he sowed, some fell by the wayside, and the fowls of
> the air came and devoured it up. And some fell on stony ground,
> where it had not much earth; and immediately it sprang up,
> because it had no depth of earth: but when the sun was up, it was
> scorched; and because it had no root, it withered away. And some
> fell among thorns, and the thorns grew up, and choked it, and
> it yielded no fruit. And others fell on good ground, and did yield
> fruit that sprang up. . . .

The young scholar closed the book and went on his way. The two seeds, however, could not remain calm any more.

One said: I will fall on good ground.

The other said: I will fall on good ground.

One said: I will make sure to grow up well if I fall on good ground.

The other said: I will make sure to grow up well if I fall on good ground.

......

A gust of wind blew. The pine seeds shook like bells. Soon, without feeling anything, they left their mother and floated in the air until they fell. One seed, as it had wished, fell on good ground. The other seed, however, fell into a stony crack atop a tall crag. Indeed the one that had fallen onto good ground germinated soon and grew happily. The one that had fallen on the crag sighed but soon cheered up. It germinated slowly and developed roots. Atop the crag the wind was gusty all day and the soil thin. So, to establish itself, it gave almost all of its nourishment to the growth of a few but firm roots.

For a while its siblings nearby laughed at it, saying it would never grow into a tall pine. A hundred years later, the pine on the crag grew only to the thickness of a rice bowl. Yet its finger-shaped roots, sinewy, sturdy, hanging onto the stony crack, represents the resilience of life and makes it a highlight of the entire scenic area. Tourists swarm over here to take pictures with the proud pine in the background. Many artists have been inspired by it in their paintings, pictures, and poems.

The seed that had fallen on good ground grew into a pine as thick as that of a water bucket. Since it lived in a low valley where soft, drizzly rain is plentiful, its roots, thick and thin, soon developed into a messy, beard-like entanglement. One year, a gusty wind blew over and knocked it down. Uprooted, it withered and died soonafter.

One night the pine on the crag said to the pine on good ground: "I still haven't grown into a real pine!"

The one on the good ground said: "I thought I was living for myself while I was living for the wind the whole time."

"So we both live to make others' dreams look better."

With that, the pine on the crag opened its arms to hug the pine on the good ground to have a good cry, but caught nothing. The pine woke up. It had been a dream.

Quiet night. Windless. A full moon over the mountains.

(2003)

The Same River Twice?

Han Lei

Every summer or winter break he travels to famed mountains and rivers to sketch and paint.

This time he came to Mount Cha'er, a scenic wonder. In the presence of precipitous crags, sky-high ancient trees, cascading falls crashing down, and creeks murmuring through rocky paths, he was thrilled and set up his tent right away. From sunrise to sunset he sketched and painted in a dazed frame of mind.

Then he noticed the majestic west peak of Mount Cha'er was the first to receive sunshine in the morning. That would be an ideal place to paint the sunrise.

At daybreak the following day, the morning fog still heavy, he left the tent with his bag full of supplies and hurried to the west peak.

A short while later he heard the sound of running water ahead of him. It turned out to be a creek which cut across his way. The creek was only a few feet wide. He could jump over if he gave an all-out effort. He could step into the water and wade across, too. Yet, through the morning fog, he could see the blurry shapes of rocks and trees ahead, which looked spectral enough. He didn't want to try anything risky. As he hesitated, he noticed several small felled pines nearby. Yes, they could be used to build a small bridge. He dragged and placed four or five of them side by side across the creek. A bridge a few feet wide was made. He crossed the creek safe and sound as if he were on dry land.

From then on the way was smooth and clear and he reached the west peak right before sunrise. Before long, a watercolor of Sunrise at Mount Cha'er was born.

When the fog melted away under the morning sun, he retraced his steps down the west peak, half dancing, humming joyously.

As he neared the creek, he couldn't help but laugh.

He laughed at himself for having been a coward earlier. This little creek bubbling in front of him: It's nothing indeed.

It's no more than one big step wide and can be crossed easily. Yet this morning he had labored to build a bridge across it. What a waste of time!

As he got to the little bridge and was about to cross it, he couldn't laugh any more.

He was stunned, his mouth wide open in shock: Oh my, what kind of creek is this? It's actually the thread of sky separating east and west peaks of Mount Cha'er!

He retreated a step, then another.

His terrified feet knocked a rock down. Several moments later he heard the sound of it hitting the bottom.

He retreated two more steps.

He stared at the tree trunks spread across the "little creek," at the footprints he had left this morning while crossing them in big strides; yet this time around he couldn't bring himself to cross it again. In fact, he didn't even have the guts to stand there any longer and take another look.

His legs were so weak and shaking badly.

(2004)

Hands

Ma Xinting

It's so quiet in the spacious office. The door is slightly ajar. Everyone else has left for the day except for Meimei, the secretary. With her back to the door she is busy typing on the keyboard with her long and nimble fingers. Then she pauses and gazes outside the window thoughtfully. The bright sky begins to darken like a drop of black ink falling into a basin of clear water. The inky drop expands slowly like a dream until the entire basin of water turns black.

As she is lost in the trance, a pair of hands cover her eyes from nowhere without making the slightest noise. She grasps the hands and pulls them downward, hard, but the hands hold her head against the back of the chair firmly, like a lock.

Whose hands are these? She tries to think.

"Let go!" she cries.

The pair of hands doesn't move.

"You're hurting me!"

The hands still don't move.

"If you don't let go, I'm going to pinch you!" She breathes hard, her well-shaped chest bouncing uneasily.

Yet, the pair of hands remains locked on her face as if she hadn't made the demand.

"I'm going to scream!'

Nothing happens. It seems she has to guess who it is before the hands will let go.

"Wang Guo?"

Apparently she is wrong. The hands refuse to let go.

"Li Xing?"

No. The hands are still there.

"General Manager Zhang?"

"CEO Feng?"

"President Gao!"

She makes a few more guesses; each time she is wrong.

She feels a soft kiss on the side of her cheek.

"Now I know who you are," she says.

The hands that have been covering her eyes let go suddenly.

The lights in the office are so bright she cannot open her eyes to see for a while. "You've hurt my eyes," she says, rubbing them slowly.

No answer. She forces open her eyes despite the dazzling light.

All is empty in front of her. She turns her head. All is empty behind her. Surprised, she scans and searches the entire office. There is no one there.

She hurries out of the office. The long hallway is empty. She runs downstairs, flight after flight. All the hallways. They are all so empty. . . .

(2005)

Gift of a Bright Moon

Ling Qingquan

The Daoist master lives in a thatched-roof hut deep in the mountains in order to cultivate his mind. One moonlit evening, he took a long stroll in the forest and experienced a sudden enlightenment about the meaning of his existence in this world.

Returning to his abode with joy, the Daoist master noticed his hut being visited by a thief. He stood outside the door and waited. Before long the thief emerged from inside the hut, empty-handed, and was met by the master at the door. Knowing the thief wouldn't be able to find anything valuable, the master had already removed his jacket and was holding it in his hand.

The thief was stunned. Before he could do or say anything, the master said: "Ah, since you traveled such a long distance through the mountain to see me, I cannot let you leave empty-handed. Besides, the night is getting colder. Here, why don't you take this jacket of mine?"

With that, he put the jacket on the thief's shoulders. At a loss for words, the thief left with his head low.

As the Daoist master watched the thief walking through bright moonlight and disappearing into the woods, he couldn't help but sigh: "Poor man. If only I could give him a bright moon."

With the thief gone, the Daoist master stepped inside his hut, stripped to the waist, and sat down to meditate. He gazed at the bright moon outside the window. Soon his entire being merged into the world around him.

The next day, being caressed by warm sunshine, the Daoist master opened his eyes from a deep meditative state. Then he saw the jacket he had given to the thief lying at the door, neatly folded. The master murmured with joy: "I have indeed given him a bright moon!"

(1980)

Red Light

Luo Yanru

All the passengers had got off the plane at the small airport. Good, someone waved for my car.

I stole a glance at this young woman. Not pretty, but she had clear
features. The two long eyebrows looked like thin woods skirting a translucent lake. Well-curved lips were closed firmly, which gave an air of
unique personality.

"People's hospital." With that she closed her eyes and rested her head
against the back seat as if she were completely worn out.

I pulled down the meter and got under way, driving more attentively
than usual. I don't know why but somehow I couldn't help glancing at
her a few more times in the rear view mirror. I didn't glance too often
though, lest she thought I had bad intentions.

About half way to the destination I saw tears trickling down her eyes,
like pear flowers with raindrops. An unspeakable tender feeling arose
deep inside me.

"Visiting someone sick, miss?" I knew I shouldn't be talkative with
customers.

She wiped away the tears and nodded.

"How bad is it?" Damn! Why did I ask this? One thing I have hated
the most as a cabbie for the last few years is passengers who can't shut
up the moment they get into the car. What ghost has got possession of
me? What do I care?"

"Dying." The moment she breathed out this word, she broke into
a convulsive sob; the dike had burst. She cried so hard that my heart
ached in tender sympathy.

I had seen dying patients before. The only difference between them and dead people was one last breath. She must be so anxious to see this dear one of hers. A delay of one second could mean they would never see each other again in this world!

I stepped on the gas and ran through one red light after another: even at the risk of being caught by police and being fined. I wanted to help her.

As I stepped on the brake when we reached the destination and the car came to a screeching halt, a heroic feeling welled up inside me. I felt so proud. All right! Just wait to see gratitude in her eyes. . . .

Pah! Someone's open palm landed on my left cheek with such force. Her face, her good-looking face, now twisted into a greenish ball. She muttered through clenched teeth: "It's all because of reckless drivers like you, who run red lights all the time! Otherwise my husband wouldn't be lying in the hospital breathing his last at this very moment!" With that she tossed 200 *yuan* into my face like trash. . . .

(2006)

Time

Xiu Shi

"I'll be done in a moment," Tianna says to Yunxun, who has just arrived.

"No problem." Yunxun replies softly.

Tianna removes the bath robe. She sees herself in the mirror as the soft silky piece slips off her shoulders slowly, pauses when it passes her bosom, and continues to fall, gliding along the curve of her buttocks, until it reaches the floor. Like a spring silkworm emerging from its own cocoon, a mature woman's body is revealed.

She closes the door and turns on the bath tap: Warm water gushes down like a waterfall. Her naked body stands next to the door with dewy green myrrh patterns etched in it, enveloping the room in an involuntary, dream-like state. Warm pearly bubbles permeate every inch of her soft skin; her creamy neck and arms glint with crystal, wet light. Tianna picks up the shower lotion she bought on her way back from vacation in Iceland, pours a tiny scoop of it on her palm, and applies it to her body gently.

The shower lotion is made of 21 kinds of fragrant grass and plants gathered from atop mountains 7,000 feet and higher above sea-level and mixed with Iceland's lahar and Greenland's ice. Its bubbly foam, yellowish, has a hint of amber to it. Immediately a quiet fragrant aroma expands throughout the bathroom and penetrates the louvered door into the bedroom. On the ruffled quilt in the bedroom, *The Best Love Poems of the American People*, is still open to page eighteen. Those lines seem to be basking in the quiet fragrant aroma:

My life is a hummingbird that flies
Through the starry dusk and dew
Home to the heaven of your true eyes
Home, dear heart
To you

In the living room Yunxun waits joyously. Yunxun is the owner of Sunrise Bookstore. The last Friday of last month, the busiest evening of all evenings, Tianna was seeking shelter from the rain under the small canopy in front of the store. Raindrops wetted her pear-brown hair and trickled from the tips of her hair down to her sensual shoulders.

The tight-fitting T- shirt that is so hot this summer looked like the gossamer wings of a tropical apricot butterfly caught in the rain. Tianna stood there motionless in quiet despair, her hands crossed on her chest. Yunxun opened the door slightly and handed her an umbrella. She took it and, without turning her head, without saying thank you, and without promising when to return the umbrella, stepped into the restless tide of pedestrians in the street and disappeared. Last Tuesday Tianna finally came. It was a sunny spring afternoon. Clutching a purple handbag, Tianna floated into the small bookstore like a spring breeze and returned the umbrella to Yunxun. They got to know each other and a romantic relationship began.

"You're this city's colored Butterfly Forever!" Yunxun was fond of saying.

At this moment Yunxun's hand is holding a rose he has just bought from a flower shop. It's an genetically processed rose, the fresh red of its petals showing a golden edge, feeling more real than a silk rose anyway. As Tianna hums lightheartedly in the bathroom, Yunxun smiles gently. Three weeks have passed and Tianna finally agrees to go with him to see the stage show, *Swan,* which boasts a cast of over one hundred performers, yet draws an audience of less than twenty people. The theater is small and is located just down the street. Every time they go out, Tianna will prepare herself to grandly. It gives him endless pleasure.

A few petals fall on Yunxun's shiny black leather shoes. The clock chimes resonantly. The muffled siren of a passing ambulance comes through the window. Yunxun feels somewhat tired. His body slips slightly against the back of the sofa, his elbow resting on a cushion. Having nothing else to do, he gazes at the rose: on its foot-long stem are thorns sparsely spread. The three dark green leaves are still soft. Yunxun breaks into a smile. Crow's-feet slowly creep to the corners of his eyes.

Tianna is so absorbed in the bath. Two thirds of her body is covered in the snow-white foam from the shower lotion. She bends to wash her lower legs and ankles, as if she is indulging herself in a deep-valley hot spring, oblivious to the passage of time and change from day to night beyond the valley. The snow-white foam is ruined and formed again. Tianna's body reveals itself with the same rhythm Mother Earth does as darkness and light flow into each other. The foam floats amongst her hair and in the air as Tianna hums the little song she learned when she received the entomology award at Flemingson Institute.

Yunxun sits waiting patiently. Then he lets himself sink into the sofa. He spots a pair of red-spotted beetles stuck to the book hanging above the fireplace and smiles. His hair scatters loose on the cushion, revealing the gray hair like the autumnal reed in the countryside. A few more rose petals fall. Yunsun feels even more tired. He thinks he might as well take a short nap.

Bubbly water falls from the sky and rinses off the foam on Tianna's body. Her skin, having absorbed enough moist fragrance, feels tender and creamy like a baby. Her soft body feels lazy, listless, yet her eyes glisten with joy. The water flows away from her feet. The quiet air now throbs with the sound of water coursing. Tianna steps out of the bathroom naked, the bright red bath towel failing to cover her body entirely.

She has barely stepped into the living room when she is stunned; the bath towel slips off her body. Yunsun sits before her, and old man; his hair completely grayed, his tired face lined with deep wrinkles; his dry, bony hand dangling by the sofa like an onion peeled half way through. On the carpet a throng of ants quietly bite and chew at a withered rose.

Then, Yunxun wakes up. He struggles to straighten up, looks at Tianna, and stammers:

"My dear Butterfly Forever, if you had come a moment later I would not have been able to wait for you!"

(n.d.)

the strange and the extraordinary

Little-Hand Chen

Wang Cengqi

Where I come from, we had very few obstetricians. Most people would simply ask an old mama to assist during childbirth. Which old mama to ask was rarely left to the uncertainty of the moment. A big, wealthy household would almost always have the same old mama for its First Daughter-in-Law, Second Daughter-in-Law, Third Daughter-in-Law, and so on, to ensure the safe birth of their precious grandchildren. The old mama would need to come in and pass through interior rooms and so on—a stranger just wouldn't do! The old mama would be quite familiar with such households; she knew which maidservant had long hands and would be good for holding the mother from behind. Moreover, most people had this superstitious belief that using an old mama was "auspicious," and would ensure a smooth birth. And all old mamas had an altar for the Goddess of Male Offspring set up at home, and burnt incense sticks there everyday.

Who would ever ask a male doctor to assist during childbirth? Where I'm from, all the doctors were men, with the exception of Flower Face Li, who had followed her father's footsteps and become the only female doctor for the entire city. But she was an internist, and, well, an old maid, not an obstetrician. When a man goes to medical school, he would *never* think of becoming an obstetrician. It would be *so* beneath him and he would feel so ashamed. There was an exception to this rule, though: Little-Hand Chen, a well-known male obstetrician.

Little-Hand Chen was thus nicknamed thanks to his hands, smaller than those of even most women, and softer. His specialty was difficult births. Transverse births, breech births, you name it, he could handle them all. People said his small hands were light and nimble, and actually reduced pain for the mothers in labor. Big and wealthy households, however, would not use his services unless they had no other choice. Most average households were much more liberal on this. Whenever they ran into a difficult birth and the old mama was at a loss for what to do, someone would say, "Go get Little-Hand Chen, then."

Timing is everything when it comes to childbirth because two lives are at stake here. So Little-Hand Chen had a horse, shiny, snow-white from head to toe. Knowledgeable folks say this horse walked like a pheasant: light, quick, and smooth. Where I'm from, it's mostly rivers and lakes and few people keep horses. Every time a detachment of mounted troops passed by, big crowds would swarm along the tall banks of the canal to see. It was quite a spectacle. Since Little-Hand Chen often rode on this white horse on his house calls, people soon thought of him and his white horse as one and the same and referred to them as "White Horse Little-Hand Chen."

Other doctors, internists and surgeons alike, looked down upon Little-Hand Chen and dismissed him as nothing more than a male old mama. Little-Hand Chen, however, didn't mind this at all. Whenever he was called for, he would jump on the white horse and fly to wherever he was needed. Mothers moaning in labor would immediately feel calm upon hearing the bells around the white horse's neck jingle. Once off the horse, he would rush to the mother's side and, sometimes soon, sometimes not so soon, would come the first cry of a newborn baby. Little-Hand Chen would emerge from the room, sweat still on his forehead, and say to the man of the household: "Congratulations! Congratulations! Both mother and baby are safe!" The man would grin with happiness and hand him a sealed red envelope with payment for the service. Little-Hand Chen would put the envelope in his pocket, without even opening it, wash his hands, drink a cup of warm tea, mumble a "Much indebted," and jump on his horse. Soon the jingling of the horse-bells receded in the distance.

Little-Hand Chen saved numerous lives.

One year, Joint Army troops came to our place. During those years a war had been dragging on between two armies, the Nationalist Revolutionary Army, locally known as "Party Army," and "Joint Army" of warlord Sun Chunanfang, thus dubbed because Sun claimed to be the "Commander-in-Chief of the Five-Province Joint Army." The Joint Army troops, about the size of a regiment, were stationed in Heavenly King Temple. The regiment commander's wife (or concubine, nobody really knew) was having a difficult labor. Several old mamas were called in, but none could help. The woman howled in pain like a swine being slaughtered. So the regiment commander sent for Little-Hand Chen.

When he walked into Heavenly King Temple, the commander was pacing back and forth outside the delivery room. Upon seeing Chen, he said:

"Both mother and child you'll have to save for me, or your head will roll! Now go in!"

Well, the woman in labor was a bit larger than usual. It took Little-Hand Chen the strength of "Nine Buffalos and Two Tigers" to finally succeed in pulling the baby out. Dog tired from "wrestling" with the fat woman for most of the day, he emerged from the delivery room with unsteady steps and said to the commander:

"Congratulations, commander! It's a boy, a young master!"

The commander grinned toothily: "Much obliged!—this way please!"

A small banquet was already set up, waiting. The deputy commander was the host. Little-Hand Chen drank two small cups of wine. Then, the commander took out twenty big silver coins and handed them to Chen:

"These are for you! Hope you won't feel underpaid!"

"Overwhelmed! Overwhelmed!" Replied Little-Hand Chen.

With wine in the belly and 20 pieces of silver in his pocket, Little-Hand Chen got up to take his leave: "Much indebted! Much indebted!" He said.

"Have a safe trip!" The commander said.

Well, Little-Hand Chen stepped out of Heavenly King Temple and climbed onto his horse. The commander then drew out his revolver and shot him from behind.

"My woman," the commander said, "how dare he touch her for so long with his hands! Except for me, no man is allowed to touch her body, ever! This insolent rascal! Fuck his granny!"

The commander had never felt this wronged.

(1983)

Gold Washer

Xing Ke

He washed gold his entire life and remained poor his entire life. Of course he was an "amateur" gold washer at best, his real "profession" being cultivating farmland. He was already 70 years old, bony, visibly hunchbacked, but kept on washing gold and cultivating farmland.

Every spring, as soon as he had planted rice and corn seeds into the good earth, he would follow the warm sunshine to the riverside where he stripped off his tattered shirt; his sun-scorched back would be scorched even more until it oozed with dark oily sweat.

He chose a place close to the road to set up his gold mining site. The tools were simple: a spade, a pickaxe, a metal rake about a foot long, and a gourd dipper. The most important of these was a boat-like winnowing fan. At the bottom of the U-shaped fan was a thumb-sized niche called a gold trough. With the winnowing fan popped up by the river, one end touching the water, he would bend so low and dig and spade the rocks into the fan while gasping for air. Then he would pour gourdfuls of water into the fan while raking out rocks bigger than nuts; smaller rocks and sand would be washed away by water. What remained was a small amount of fine sand, which he would "wash" again in the water—shaking the boat-shaped winnowing fan in the water long and hard until all the sand was washed away and gold—if there was any—fell into the thumb-sized trough. Each day he could wash four or five winnowing fans of rocks and sand, each yielding very little gold; one or two pieces the size of one-quarter to one-half a grain of rice would be a good harvest. Often, though, he would get nothing.

Whatever gold he found he put inside a small buffalo horn and then stuffed the horn with a stop, rags wrapped inside a piece of silk tied into the shape of clove of garlic. Once he finished washing and spotted a few pieces of sand gold in the trough, he would grin happily and tremble with joy and reach to pick them up with quivering fingers. He would hold the gold in one palm, fish out the buffalo horn case from a pocket, unplug the silk stop, and let the newcomers join those which had already gathered there.

Day after day, year after year, he followed the same routine and repeated the same moves. At that time gold was cheap. One ounce of sand gold was worth 70 to 80 *yuan* at the most. Unlike now, a gram of pink gold is worth more than 50 *yuan*. Even through several years of washing, the yield was not even an ounce of gold, so he lived in poverty. Yet he would not give up and he refused to be disheartened. He would wash quietly day after day, year after year, using the same tools, the same method, the same moves.

Curious passers-by would stop and watch him work, but nobody would say anything, lest the gold would be scared away. He would keep doing what he was doing, oblivious to whoever was watching, an alchemist absorbed in a world of his own.

Only once did he have a chance of striking it rich, but luck passed him by. Narrowly. One day—no one remembered the exact day or month or year—a bridegroom was accompanying his bride to visit her home. The young bride was riding a donkey while the bridegroom walked behind. Just when they passed the gold washer, the bride fell from the donkey and landed on the pile of rocks and sand the old man had just dug up. Stunned, the bridegroom hurried to her side. The bride blushed, smiled mysteriously, and hastened away once she was on her feet again.

The gold washer thought the bride had fallen because she had been so taken by the sight of him gold mining.

They hadn't gone far before the bridegroom asked his bride: "Why did you fall?"

The bride smiled like a flower. She bent closer, gave him a meaningful look, and whispered, "I've found a piece of gold." She unclenched her right fist. In it was a piece of gold the size of a nut; it glittered under the sun. Obviously, the gold had been unearthed by the gold washer.

The bridegroom couldn't help but turn his head. The old, hunchbacked gold washer was still digging away with his pickaxe; its echo could still be heard. The young man took another look at the gold in his hand and looked again at the old gold washer, not knowing if he should feel joy for his own luck or sorrow for the old man.

(1985)

Hunchback Tan

Liu Renqian

Hunchback Tan was a fish snatcher. His hunched back made him a perfect match for the trade of fish snatching. Once the off-season for farming began, he would put on his old fishing shirt, throw the bamboo fishing basket on his back, pick up a short stick, and get on his way. He wandered from village to village, pausing only to peer in pond after pond. He was born with osprey eyes, knew how to gauge the wind and the water, and knew the habits of fish. If he saw a pond and said he would go in and snatch a carp flower (a kind of fish), what he did snatch would not be a "knife" (a nickname for another fish); it had to be a carp flower.

A most amazing trick about Hunchback Tan snatching fish was called "Catching the Idiot under the Willow." If you were taken off guard by an unexpected guest and were clueless as to where to get any food at short notice, your neighbors would say: "Why not go and grab two fish at Hunchback Tan's? Easy!"

So you hurried to Hunchback Tan's, took a peek in his fish vat, but saw no fish in it. "All gone?"

Hunchback Tan would say, without actually replying to your question: "Having a guest?"

"My kids' Second Maternal Uncle . . . nothing to offer him."

"Aiya," Hunchback Tan replied. "If upset, the uncle might throw the dishes on the ground! Alright, let me see what I can do."

With that, Hunchback Tan smiled, stepped out, and came to a big willow by the edge of the Fragrant River. He found a spot near its roots, waded in, squatted, and snatched. When his hand re-emerged from underneath the water, it held a "Tiger-Head Idiot" which thrashed and splashed furiously. Before a cigarette was finished, there was be enough for dinner. Hunchback Tan patted the fishing basket and beamed with pride, "This is called 'catch and sell.' Can't get any more fresh than this."

Hunchback Tan was quite flexible with his customers. If you were a bit tight at the moment, it didn't matter. You could leave with a fish and promise to pay later. Hunchback Tan would smile and say, wiping the hand that had just snatched the fish, "No big deal, no big deal. Folks are all neighbors and friends around here . . . bumping into each other a few times a day. Who'd run away just for that?"

Even when the village had to treat visiting officials, they would send someone to Hunchback Tan, too: "Do you have two "knives," about half a *jin* apiece? Must be alive, for making soup."

"I do, half a *jin* apiece." Hunchback Tan replied and reached into the vat for the fish. Fresh out of the water, the fish splashed furiously and bounced hard when dropped into the basket.

The village man grabbed the basket and said: "Pay later?"

"Okay, pay later." Hunchback Tan saw the man out of his door.

Hunchback Tan was nice to everyone, rich or poor. So everyone in the village knew him to be a kind man.

In addition to snatching fish, Hunchback Tan used a large fishing net to catch fish, too. During the day he went around looking at ponds and rivers. In the evening he rowed a small boat in the river he had chosen and cast the net. The following day, before daybreak, he rowed the small boat as far as 20 *li* to the county town to sell the fish in the market.

Hunchback Tan had a knack for the net, too. A magic hand. No one in the village had ever seen him pulling up an empty net.

One night the neighboring village caught someone stealing fish. The thief had cast his net in the neighboring village's fish pond. When the thief was caught, there was already a big pile of silvery fish in his boat. Fuming with anger, the neighboring villagers gave the thief a good beating. The thief, crushed, confessed: It was the cadres in his own village who had asked him to come and cast the net with a promise of him getting 40% of the proceeds of the catch.

The fish thief was none other than Hunchback Tan. His entire village was scandalized: Hunchback Tan, stealing fish?

No one knew that the neighboring village's fish ponds had been frequented by Hunchback Tan for a long time. The deal, though, was 50/50 between him and the village cadres, not 60/40, because if he cast his net in his own village's ponds he ran a greater risk of being caught.

(1986)

Perfect Robbery

Feng Jicai

The area right between Old Town and Concessions was among the wildest in Fort Tianjin. Here were gathered beings of all stripes and colors; the setting for the strangest things one could imagine.

One day in the 1920s, a young couple came and rented a small house to get married. Soon the house was filled with brand new things: new bed, new dresser, red pot and green basin. On both sides of the front door appeared a pair of red Double-Happiness. The next morning after the wedding, the couple left their new home to go to work. Their neighbors didn't even have a chance to get introduced.

Three days later, soon after the couple left for work, there came flying down the street a cargo tricycle pedaled by an old man, wiry, sun-baked, the muscles in his legs bulging like iron balls. Squatting on the tricycle were two young men, late teens, sticks, axes, ropes in hand. It looked like the fierce trio was here to reckon with some archenemy.

The old man brought the flying tricycle to a screechy halt outside the newlyweds' home. The two young men jumped off, dashed to the door, and turned and snapped: "Pop, nobody's home. The door's locked. See this big foreign lock?"

The old man flew into a rage. His eyes almost popped out of their sockets. The veins in his neck wriggled with passion. He jumped off the tricycle and cussed: "This unfilial beast! Having the balls to desert his parents and set up his own palace here. Second Born, Third Born, smash the door open for me!"

And down came the axes on the lock, which gave way in no time. The door was open. Everything inside the newlyweds' home was right before their eyes. The old man was more infuriated. He jumped up and down and cussed frothily:

"You heartless beast! We nursed you, fed you, picked up after your shit, brought you up. And now you become this ungrateful dog! Your ma is bedridden with illness and we are dirt broke. What kind of son are you? Can't cough up a penny to save your dying ma, but have the money to enjoy yourself with your nymph in this love-nest! Your ma is dying! Hear that? Enjoying yourself! Let me see how you can enjoy yourself again! Second Born, Third Born, why are you still standing there? Move everything here back home for me! If you two dare to fart one word for your elder brother, I'll break your legs!"

The two young men began to drag heavy trunks, carry armfuls of bedspreads and clothing, and throw them on the cargo tricycle.

The neighbors came out to see what was going on. After listening to the old man carrying on for a while, they picked up some cues about the newlyweds. Such an ungrateful dog! If he wouldn't even do anything to save his own dying mother, then who would give a damn if this was happening to him? Besides, the old man was exploding like an endless string of New Year's fireworks; who wanted to get hurt trying to intervene?

A short while later the house was all but empty. The two young men reported, "Pop, all that's left are big things. We can't lift them."

The old man howled thunderously, "Smash!"

And smashed indeed was whatever that was left. Only then did they stop. The old man was still very angry, though: "Wait till I see you tomorrow!"

And they left with the loaded tricycle.

For a whole day the door remained wide open, unattended. The neighbors kept a respectful distance. Nobody ventured one step closer. Nobody left. They all wanted to see what would happen when the newlyweds came home.

Late afternoon the young couple came back, chitchatting, happy smile on their faces. At the door they stopped, shocked by what they saw. They turned to ask the neighbors, who began to disperse right away. An old granny stayed to chastise the ungrateful, unfilial young groom:

"This morning your pop and brothers came. This is their doing. Why don't you go back and see your pop and ma!"

The groom was more than perplexed and couldn't help blurting out: "My pop and ma? Pop died a long time ago, ma died last year, too. I have no brothers in this whole world, except for a sister married to as far as Manchuria!"

"What?" the old granny was surprised. It didn't make sense at all because what had happened this morning was so real. "The man is your pop for sure!"

The couple hurried to the police station to report the crime. The investigation lasted for ten long years but they didn't find one trace of the groom's "pop."

Strange cases of robbery had happened in Fort Tianjin, but this one was the strangest of all. The old man had not only robbed the newly-weds of their possessions, but also of their dignity by being their "pop" for one day. Moreover, they had to swallow both the injury and the insult because there was nothing they could say about it. If they couldn't bear it any more and breathed one word about it to others, they would only have the misfortune of being laughed at. Talking about rubbing salt into an already bad wound!

(1988)

One Move Game

Xu Xing

The sky was blue and high. A gentle breeze was in the air. Under a tall tree Hao and an old man were playing chess. Spectators thick as wall, all quiet as if their lips had been zipped. A young lad passed by from nowhere. He stopped, took one causal glance, and declared:

"One more move and the game is over!"

Surprised, both Hao and the old man looked up and saw a handsome young lad: soft-skinned, cherry-lipped, with an unworldly air about him. Instead of being annoyed by the uninvited comment, Hao was quite pleased:

"May I ask if the young master indulges himself in this pastime, too?"

"Only occasionally."

"Then, please explain how this game is over with just one more move?"

"The old man is already in a fix. You can win the game with just one more move, if so desired."

Now Hao was one of the best chess players in this area. Smart, bold, he thrived for his most daring moves. So many times had he made one unexpected move, which finished off his opponent, that he became known as: "One Move Game." The young lad sounded like he had read Hao's mind. Thrilled, Hao reached out both hands and invited him to play.

The young lad's name was Jie, and he came from a family of masterful players. His game, cunning, unpredictable, full of surprises, had also earned *him* the nickname: "One Move Game."

A game between two well-matched players began, surprising moves upon surprising moves, one mini-climax topped by another mini-climax, to the joy of eager, ecstatic spectators. Jie looked as if he had exhausted his tricks but still could not withstand Hao's assaults. He was defeated when Hao made one sudden-death move. Elated, Hao laughed heartily; words of praise poured out of his mouth: "Jie, you're a marvelous player! A marvelous player!" And everybody knew that the praise was meant more for himself than for anybody else.

Young as he was, Jie remained calm and said: "I'm quite ashamed. Ashamed!" He then asked, "May I have the pleasure of another game to learn from the true master?"

"The pleasure is mine!" Hao said without hesitation.

Before the game began, Jie suggested, nonchalantly, almost meekly: "Can we make a bet on the game, to make it more interesting?"

Hao laughed off the proposition: "How could you, a mere traveler, bring any real money with you?"

Jie was incensed. He sighed and then removed from his arm a gold-ornamented jade bracelet. It looked precious: rich emerald and shiny gold. It glittered dazzlingly when placed on the chess board. Hao was amazed. So were all the spectators. They murmured and whispered among themselves in admiration.

"Real money I have none," Jie said, "but I'm willing to bet this instead."

Hao was thrilled by the jade bracelet and thought it was a god-send. He turned and pointed at the grand mansion not far behind and declared:

"I'm betting this mansion along with all the fortunes inside plus my wife and my concubine."

Jie looked rather surprised. He hesitated and then said, "Now that you have gone this far, let me raise my stake up a notch."

"What is it?" Hao asked.

"Since I am not worth a penny other than the bracelet, I'd have the pleasure of serving you and your family for the rest of my life if I lose the game."

Now the bets from the two sides were well matched, there would be no grounds to complain or regret later.

The game began. Hao, elated by his earlier victory, and anxious for a repeat, tried to finish off Jie with one of his sudden-death moves again. However, this game wasn't the same old game any more. Facing the waves of fierce assaults from Hao, Jie looked somewhat tense yet was able to wriggle himself free over and again at the exact moment when he seemed hopelessly cornered. He played defense by way of offense and patiently lay in wait for his opponent to make a big mistake. Occasionally he let himself make an erroneous move, leaving his Cannon in a vulnerable position, but Hao, ever suspicious, didn't take the bait. Then Jie did the same with a Horse, but once again Hao stayed put. Not knowing what was really going on, the spectators sighed and tensed up in unison as the fortunes for both sides rose and fell. When his Wagon slipped into a trap, Jie looked rather woeful, but there was nothing he could do about it. By then a contemptuous look had already appeared on Hao's face. Having weighed the situation back and forth, left and right, Hao felt he had to take this Wagon, which would bring him only one move away from victory. Little did he expect that once he gulped down the Wagon, the situation changed dramatically. With one quick move Jie had Hao's palace tightly clamped with two Horses and the King trampled to death. Hao was one step too slow to victory. His face ashen, sweat trickling down his forehead, Hao looked up into the sky and hollered in a heart-piercing voice,

"One move and I'm finished!"

Hao's grand mansion and all of his fortunes, with the only exception of his wife and concubine, were taken by Jie.

When Hao was about to leave, Jie took out the jade bracelet and presented it to him with both hands:

"As the saying goes, as we are foes while on the chess board, so are we friends while off the chess board. Since you are really fond of this, why don't you have it as a souvenir?"

The spectators were all amazed by the young lad's show of generosity and gallantry.

Hao took the bracelet hesitantly and gazed at it long and hard. All of a sudden he smashed the bracelet on the stone table on which they had just played and screamed:

"What a swindler! Want me to use this to swindle others?"

The "jade" bracelet was worthless paste.

(1994)

Bee Bandits

Wang Qian

This time around Honeybee raiser Ah Kui limped into Unicorn Village
with a large gang, sharp daggers dangling at his waist, his head covered
in hat and veil, ready to kick ass and kill. By now he was already head
of the notorious Lake Bandits. At the mere mention of the gang's name
wealthy people around Gold Rooster Lake would be scared out of their
wits. There was something different about Ah Kui and his gang, though.
They used their bees, which sailed along with the boats on the lake,
more than their guns and knives. The bees could go and attack and then
return as fast as the wind; they were not armed with guns and knives,
but they were just as lethal.

Everyone knew that this time Ah Kui came to Unicorn Village for
no other purpose than to get Three-Treasure Xu, the wealthiest in the
entire village. They had had a long-standing love and hate relationship
and the time for reckoning had come.

The story goes back several years when at the time of each spring Ah
Kui would sail to Unicorn Village with his bees and release them into
Xu's vast fields of blossoming rape flowers. Ah Kui, tall and handsome,
speaking with a different accent, was friendly with everyone. Young
women and girls were all very fond of him. Three-Treasure Xu had an
18-year-old daughter by the name of Evening Fragrance. This girl was as
pretty as she was sensible: slender, cherry-lipped, walking like a beautiful dream. Ah Kui and Evening Fragrance fell for each other right away
and before long their passions prevailed in the fields of yellow rape flowers. They vowed to love each other in this world and forever beyond.
Three-Treasure Xu, however, refused to give his blessings to his precious

daughter's union with a nobody coming from nowhere. Besides, he had already promised his daughter to someone else through a match-maker. So, desperate, the young couple decided to elope in the middle of the night. Their movement somehow woke Three-Treasure Xu, who, along with a gang of family servants, gave chase in the darkness. The young lovers were caught before long, and Xu dragged back Evening Fragrance. In the maddening commotion, Xu knocked Ah Kui off the boat with a carrying pole. Fortunately, Ah Kui was saved by the Lake Bandits but was crippled for the rest of his life. Afterwards, Ah Kui drifted around with his bees but barely made enough to get by. At the end of his rope, Ah Kui joined the Lake Bandits to rob the rich and nothing else. Since bee-raising had been his trade, Ah Kui trained his bees to assist in the robberies. They turned out to be quite effective every time. By and by he ascended to the head of the gang. Apparently Ah Kui came back this time to get even with Xu on account of that incident with the carrying pole.

Ah Kui, flanked by his gang and a large cloud of bees, sailed into Xu's compound. Soon everyone in the Xu family, young and old, was caught and bound to the stone poles of the buffalo shed. When Three-Treasure Xu saw that the bandits were led by none other than Ah Kui, he kicked and cussed like mad. Without saying a word Ah Kui let loose his bees on Xu. Under the furious bee attack, Xu's head became swollen like a watermelon in no time and he could barely breathe.

Ah Kui grunted contemptuously. The bees were soon waved while Ah Kui's gang pulled a big sack over Xu, covering him from head to toe. Hearing Xu moaning inside the bag, Ah Kui felt so revenged.

Two bandits carried a radiant beauty from inside the residence. Just a quick glance and Ah Kui knew it was Evening Fragrance. She still looked pretty despite the smeared makeup on her face and her messy hair. Her eyes, though, were blank. She struggled and cried wildly, "Hee

Hee . . . Ha Ha . . . Married . . . Married!" Ah Kui's heart tightened at the sight but he did not move. He had been told that when Three-Treasure Xu dragged his daughter home that night years ago, he forced her to marry into the wealthiest family in town. Yet, no matter what, Evening Fragrance would not obey the order and eventually went mad. Now what he saw right in front of him proved the story to be true.

Ah Kui gave the two bandits a look and they tied Evening Fragrance up onto a stone pole, too. Everyone in the Xu family sobbed and howled and Evening Fragrance continued to heehaw like she didn't give a damn. Ah Kui gestured with his index finger and a bandit presented him with three small boxes. They each contained a most venomous and brave hornet which he had put his heart into raising. Ah Kui always brought them along when he went out to rob the rich.

He took one of the boxes and, oblivious to the hoarse and desperate begging from Three-Treasure Xu, walked slowly toward Evening Fragrance, his face expressionless.

"Who am I?" he asked suddenly.

"Married! Married . . . " Evening Fragrance carried on.

With one quick move Ah Kui brought the hornet to Evening Fragrance's face and let it lodge a sting right below her lips. With the sharp venomous needle buried in her soft flesh, her once-cheery lips swelled up grotesquely. Ah Kui took out the hornet from another box and let it lodge a sting at the end of her left eyebrow, and then did the same with her right eyebrow. Instantly her pretty face assumed a twisted, hilarious look.

"Beast . . . " Three-Treasure Xu cussed weakly.

Ah Kui stared at Evening Fragrance hard and long. Disappointed, he gestured for the bandits to leave. As he turned, he heard a sweet, soft voice from behind:

"Ah Kui—"

He turned back and saw what had happened: The two eyes in that red, swollen face shone beautifully with light of intelligence.

"Ah Kui, don't go. . . . " Evening Fragrance was not her mad self any more. She called shyly, "Take me with you, Ah Kui. . . . "

Ah Kui hesitated for a second; then, he limped hard straight out of Xu's compound and returned to his boat.

From that day on, not even the shadow of Bee Bandit Ah Kui was seen on Gold Rooster Lake.

It was said that ever since he was told the story of what had happened to Evening Fragrance after their failed elopement, Ah Kui had searched up and down the Yangtze River valley for the surefire folk remedy for her condition. He didn't return to Unicorn Village until he had found it.

(1995)

Deadly Game
Yi Nong

In the small town of Yu there once lived a family named Fang. The Fangs had practiced medicine for generations. Their reputation reached far and wide. The patriarch of the family, Fang Xuzhu, was a master of two crafts: Chinese medicine and the game of go.

Fang Xuzhu began to practice medicine at the tender age of ten. He diagnosed by looking, smelling, asking, and feeling the pulse, much in the manner of a grown-up. That was how his reputation as "Child

Prodigy Doctor" began. His father, Fang Xingzhi, loved the game of go. Growing up in such an environment Fang Xuzhu picked up many tricks and strategies. Once, when he was 11 years old, his father was playing with a grand master and was caught in a predicament. Watching all this happening, young Xuzhu couldn't help but get in the game on his father's behalf. A few moves later the situation for the black and the white changed dramatically and victory changed hands in a wink of eye. That grand master, impressed, was full of praise for the young player and said he had a great future ahead of him.

Fang Xingzhi died at the age of 70. On his death bed he gave his son two things: a copy of *Chinese Pharmacopoeia* and a copy of *Twenty-Four Game of Go Strategies*. From then on, Fang Xuzhu would have the pharmacopoeia in one hand and the book of strategies in the other and study them at the same time. As he traveled long and deep between medicine and the game of go, he drew nourishment from both crafts and soon grew to be a true master of both.

In the year 1939 the Japanese invaders had advanced to the town of Yu. Within 24 hours the streets were strewn with dead bodies and blood was flowing in rivulets. The Japanese commander Yuji Kabayashi showed appreciation for Chinese culture and had a passion for the game of go. When he heard of Fang Xuzhu's reputation as a go player, he came to the Fang compound right away. Fang, however, remained calm in the presence of Japanese swords and bayoneted rifles. When he knew the reason of Yuji Kabayashi's visit, Fang smiled and said: "Judging by your look, you are afflicted with grave illness and shall die within two days if left untreated."

Yuji Kabayashi was shocked. It turned out that the night before, while attempting to rape an abducted woman, who fought fiercely, he had been kicked between the legs. A dull pain still bothered him at this very moment.

Yuji Kabayashi thought for a second and then said: "Could the Prodigy Doctor treat my illness, then?"

Fang Xuzhu turned, went into a nearby room, and soon re-emerged with a bag of herbal medicine.

His eyebrows knit, Yuji Kabayashi asked: "How can I trust that this is not a bag of poison, since I've killed so many people of the town of Yu?"

Fang Xuzhu said calmly: "In the eyes of this doctor you are just a patient, no more and no less. Why on earth would a doctor want to kill his patient?"

Yuji Kabayashi laughed: "You are indeed one of a kind. As a token of appreciation for treating this commander, I don't want the *Chinese Pharmacopoeia* any more. However, you'll have to give me the *Twenty-Four Game of Go Strategies*."

Fang Xuzhu said: "The *Twenty-Four Game of Go Strategies* is a precious gift from my father on his deathbed. It's not something I'll part with lightly. However, I'll present it to you with both hands if you can win this little game I'll lay out."

Yuji Kabayashi had a very high opinion of his own game of go, so he nodded. Fang Xuzhu laid out the game board and asked Yuji Kabayashi to go back and ponder over how to win it, and to come back the next day.

Fang Xuzhu didn't bother to show Yuji Kabayashi to the door. A smile played around his lips as he watched Yuji Kabayashi and his troops leave. His wife came and said: "If Yuji Kabayashi wins the game, will you give him the book, the precious gift from your late father?"

A serious look appeared in Fang's eyes. He said, "The Japanese invaders have slaughtered our people and raped our women. As a doctor I cannot kill Yuji Kabayashi, but I can avenge my country with a game of go, can't I?"

Mrs. Fang didn't understand what her husband meant. Fang Xuzhu explained: "Yuji Kabayashi's illness is from a fierce kick to his lower body, which has caused a swelling there. The medication I have pre-scribed requires the patient maintain a calm equilibrium and frame of mind after taking it. Then the patient will be cured in two days. This game board I've set up looks simple, but is in reality quite difficult. After taking the medication, Yuji Kabayashi may start to work on the game. If he fails to determine the moves needed to win, Yuji Kabayashi will fly into a rage. Rage will wound his spirit, which will lead to the loss of *qi*, which will lead to his death."

The following day Yuji Kabayashi didn't come back to the Fang's as had been agreed. Instead, a gang of fully armed Japanese troops came to "arrest" Fang. The Fang's door, however, was locked with a big note on it written in forceful brushstrokes:

Deadly Game for Yuji Kabayashi

Signed: Fang Xuzhu

(2000)

Qu Yuan's Wisdom
Cao Dequan

Two thousand three hundred and fifty years ago Qu Yuan[21] was the prime minister of the Kingdom of Chu in charge of all governmental affairs. One spring day he traveled to the state of Gui to select the best and brightest for civil service. As word spread, all the learned young men from far and wide came to take the exam The exam was closely monitored, yet when it was over, something strange happened: Of the 100 best answers, 99 of them were exactly the same. Only one was different. Qu Yuan thought the exam questions must have been leaked. Otherwise, how could so many people have given the same answer?

He recalled that one day prior to the exam, while he was drafting the questions, someone came to visit. That could be how the questions had been leaked. What to do now? Nullifying the exam results would mean losing the confidence of the people. Not a good solution. Recruiting them all? That would be detrimental to the interest of the Kingdom. Not good either. He pondered on this long and hard.

By dawn the following morning, after a sleepless night, Qu Yuan hit upon an idea to tell which among the 100 applicants were truly talented. He called in all the applicants, gave them each 100 rice grains, and told them to go home and plant them. They were to return after the autumn harvest. The one with the best harvest would be the winner. The date set for their return was the Mid-autumn Festival.

Ninety-nine of the applicants left with their seeds. Except for one. Qu Yuan asked him: "What's your name?"

The applicant said his name was Zhaohan.

"Zhaohan, it's true that your answers are different from all the others, but I've put your name at the bottom of the list. You feel it's unfair?"

"Excellency, " Zhaohan said, "I am a tiller of the soil. I feel most fortunate that I can read during the off-season and can take part in the exams. No, I don't feel any unfairness."

"All right," Qu Yuan said, "take these 100 rice grains home and come back and see me in autumn."

"Thank you, Excellency."

On the day of the Mid-autumn Festival, Qu Yuan came to the state of Gui again as he had promised. All the applicants submitted their harvests to be counted carefully. One had harvested 8,000 grains of rice, another

10,000, still another 20,000, and another 40,000, and so on. The highest was a stunning 100,000! Qu Yuan had his assistant record them all, one by one. Soon little mountains of grain were spread out on the grand table. Yet there was not a hint of smile on Qu Yuan's face. Not a single word from him either. He was waiting for one man who was yet to show up. It was not until night had fallen that Zhaohan arrived, all sweaty. He held out a small pouch in both hands and opened it gently. Qu Yuan counted the grains contained in it himself: three hundred!

The Prime Minister announced in a loud voice: "Zhaohan has submitted three hundred grains."

All the others present burst out laughing at Zhaohan. "What a lousy farmer and clueless applicant. One hundred rice grains harvesting no more than three hundred grains? Hahaha!" Qu Yuan gestured for everyone to stop laughing and said:

"Zhaohan, tell us what happened and why the harvest is so meager."

"Excellency, " Zhaohan said, "I sifted through the one hundred grains you gave me one by one and found that most of them could not be used. In fact, only three were good, which I sowed in a piece of fertile soil. I did have a decent harvest, which I sifted through once again to toss away the unpresentable grains. That's why I have only 300 grains, but they are all good grains. This I can assure His Excellency. My pop and ma said: Don't go. With only 300 grains your harvest must be the poorest; don't bother the Prime Minister. However, I promised His Excellency in the Spring that I'd come and I have to keep my promise. So, here I am, with a trepid heart. Please forgive me, Excellency."

With the 300 grains in hand, Qu Yuan said to Zhaohan and the other 99 applicants:

"Zhaohan, you may be young, but your heart is pure as a lily, your soul simple and honest as seeds of rice. I hereby solemnly declare: Zhaohan is the only one who is truly the best and brightest."

Stunned, all the other applicants asked Qu Yuan why he had chosen Zhaohan.

Qu Yuan said: "You should all know the answer yourselves! Did the grains you took back home actually burgeon and grow? All of the grains I gave each of you, all but three, had been cooked. So, this question not only tested your skills, but more importantly, your honesty."

The 99 applicants stood there speechless, their heads hanging low in shame.

(2000)

Bird Cypress

Sun Fangyou

Near the end of the Qing Dynasty in the state capital of Chen there occurred a big, strange case of crime: The thousand-year-old bird cypress in the Mausoleum of Tai Wu was stolen.

The Mausoleum of Tai Wu in the State of Chen had undergone significant expansion during the Dynasties of Tang and Song. Upon establishing the Song Dynasty, the First Emperor Zhao Kuangyin issued an imperial decree to expand the mausoleum, a massive project which took many years to complete. The newly-expanded Mausoleum of Tai Wu shone magnificently in the midst of tall pines and ancient cypresses. Among the trees was a thousand-year-old bird cypress, the rarest and most precious tree in the world. It is said that furniture made of bird cypress boards would show vivid bird-like patterns, so vivid as if the birds were ready to fly into the sky. Therefore, furniture and artifacts made of bird cypress are priceless.

This particular bird cypress stood right behind the Mausoleum of Fuxi. It was so thick that even two men could not encircle it. The theft happened during a holiday celebration at the Mausoleum of Taiwu when countless pilgrims came to seek blessings. One day there came a shipping magnate from the South. To show gratitude for his good fortune, the man said, he had brought with him 100 tall, arrow-straight cedar trees. All of these trees he set up around the thousand-year bird cypress. Since it was a unique way of a pilgrim showing his gratitude for his blessings, the Chief Monk didn't suspect anything. About a month later someone noticed, accidentally, that the bird cypress had withered. When the cedars were removed, it became apparent that the cypress' top had been supported by the cedars, its precious, priceless trunk had been stolen.

When the crime was reported to the county court, County Magistrate Song Shiyuan was shocked. He led a team to work on the case day and night and soon took the thieves into custody. There were five of them, their leader being known as He Seven. The bird cypress, evidence of their crime, had already been cut into two halves and sawed into boards. Each board, when looked at closely, had a bird-like pattern, and breathed such a fragrant aroma. It was rare, precious treasure indeed.

Song Shiyuan had the thieves escorted to the county court and interrogated one by one. All of them confessed. They had had their eye on the bird cypress for a long time. During the holiday they disguised themselves as pilgrims and used the cedars they had bought as a cover story. To make it easier to transport the bird cypress, they sawed it into sections and then into boards.

With both confession and evidence, there was nothing else left to do but to throw the thieves into jail. In the middle of night, however, the five men were killed by guards when they attempted to escape. Now, with the suspects dead, the case went dead with them, too. Fortunately, all the suspects had sworn their confessions in blood. So, Song Shiyuan submitted the case file to the state government and had the bodies of the thieves buried.

The following day Song Shiyuan had the bird cypress boards appraised and paid to make them into furniture as dowry for his daughter.

The bird cypress furniture had already been made before the final word on the case came. Then, to everyone's surprise, the State Governor himself came.

Having taken a look at the bird cypress furniture Song Shiyuan had made for his daughter, the State Governor called Song Shiyuan into a well-guarded room. He shot a glance at Song Shiyuan and said, with a smile on his face: "Much painstaking planning must have gone into it for the County Magistrate to obtain the bird cypress, right?"

Song Shiyuan was stunned and at a loss for what to say.

The State Governor took out a letter from one of his long sleeves and said: "He Seven was anything but a fool. The day they succeeded in stealing the tree, he sent me a sealed, secret letter. It was only on account of our friendship that I didn't make it public!"

Song Shiyuan, his face ashen, fell on his knees right away to thank the State Governor.

The following day, Song Shiyuan sent the dowry furniture to the State Government.

Not long after that, Song Shiyuan was arrested and thrown into jail. Since the evidence against him was rock solid, he was beheaded three days later.

(2001)

The Horse Whisperer

Jiang Xinjie

In the Year 26 of Jian'an (AD 221), Guan Yu was defeated and caught by Sun Quan but refused to surrender. Soon he was put to death; his legendary horse Red Hare was presented to Ma Zhong by Sun Quan.[22]

One day Ma Zhong submitted this report to Sun Quan: Red Hare has not eaten for days and will die soon. Shocked, Sun Quan sought out a nobleman named Bo Xi from the river valley. Bo Xi, a descendent of the famed Bo Le, was known to have a knack for equine language.

Bo Xi came with Ma Zhong to the stable next to his residence. There, next to the manger, lay the once grand Red Hare. Nobody knew what was wrong with the horse. Except for Bo Xi. He told everybody to leave and then put his hand on the horse's back gently and sighed:

"In the old days Cao Cao in 'Ode to the Old Horse' sang these memorable lines: 'As the old, retired horse still dreams of pulling off another 1000-li run, so does the great man, though in old age, still cherish the ambition for greater things.' I know you miss the noble General Guan Yu so much that you'd rather follow him to the netherland. However, when Lü Bu lost his life at White Gate, you were not so saddened as wanting to follow him. Why this time? You don't want to give up your 1000-li ambition, do you?"[23]

Red Hare sighed: "This I've heard: 'When a bird is dying, even its singing is sad; When a man is dying, his last words will be from his heart.' I feel so fortunate to have met you and will tell you what is in my heart. I was born and grew up in Xi Liang. Then I was taken by Dong Zhuo, that arrogant jerk, who killed the young Emperor and slept in his imperial dragon bed. I hated this traitor of the Han Dynasty deeply."[24]

Bo Xi nodded: "Then I heard that at the advice of Li Ru, Dong Zhuo gifted you to Lü Bu. Lü Bu was then the bravest general in the world, as the saying goes: 'As Lü Bu is the best of men, so Red Hare is the best of horses.' So you two were well matched, weren't you?"

Red Hare sighed again: "Oh, you don't understand. Lü Bu was the least honorable man in the world. For wealth he killed Ding Yuan; for beauty he assassinated Dong Zhuo. He joined Liu Bei yet took Liu's Xu Zhou; he formed alliance with Yuan Shu yet put to death Yuan's envoy.[25] 'Man without honor can not be trusted.' To be mentioned together with a man without honor has been the biggest shame in my entire life. Then I went to Cao Cao. Cao had numerous brave generals under his banner but none could be called a true hero. I was worried that I was destined to serve despicable masters and die a worthless death. Later Cao Cao gifted me to General Guan Yu. I had seen his extraordinary bravery at Tiger Pass and his exceptional honor at White Gate and admired him ever since. General Guan Yu was thrilled at the sight of me, too, and bowed to thank Cao Cao for the gift. Cao Cao was puzzled by such a show of gratitude. So General Guan Yu said: 'I've heard that this horse can run a thousand *li* a day and feel so fortunate to have it at last. From now on, it doesn't matter how far you and I travel apart from each other, I can still get to see you within the day.' What an honorable man! As the saying goes, 'As a simple bird will fly far and high when following a phoenix, so will an average man achieve honor when in the company of a paragon of virtue.' How could I help but serve him till my death?"

At this Bo Xi sighed: "Everybody has said General Guan Yu was a noble man of honor. Hearing it from you has convinced me of the truth even more."

Red Hare sobbed: "I have always admired the extraordinary honor of Bo Yi and Shu Qi who would rather die than eat Zhou's grains.[26] Genuine jade would rather be smashed to pieces than be smeared with impurities. Good bamboo can be broken but its joints can never be destroyed. A noble man would die for his bosom friend. An honorable man lives for his honor. How can I be at peace if I eat Wu's grain just so that I breathe in this world for another day?"

With that, Red Hare fell back and died.

Bo Xi burst out crying: "A horse can be this noble, what about us humans?" Afterwards he reported back to Sun Quan. Sun Quan cried, too: "I didn't know Guan Yu was such an honorable man and had him put to death. How can I face the world under Heaven?"

So Sun Quan issued a decree to give a grand burial to Guan Yu, his son, and his horse Red Hare.

(2001)

Style

Xiang Yuting

The Old Master was in the salt business. The Old Master wasn't into the salt business.

His ten-li salt farm and over a hundred acres of snow-white salt beach were run by his general manager Chen Three and Third Wife.

The Old Master was into gambling and would frequently travel dozens of li to town to gamble.

In town were gambling houses and theatres. There the Old Master had bought a grand three-room river-front home on a busy street. When it rained or snowed or when the Old Master felt like it, he would stay at the vacation home.

Usually when he returned home, he would spend the night in Third Wife's suite and wouldn't get up until the sun had already climbed high in the sky. By then all the farmhands had already gone to work. Third Wife would have breakfast with him and brief him on a few things she deemed important. It was never clear whether the Old Master was listening or letting the words into his ears at all. Usually, when the breakfast was over, he simply lay down the bowl and chopsticks, worked on his teeth with a toothpick, and then took a stroll in the courtyard. When he was in a good mood, he would tell the servants which flower or plant needed to be watered; when he was not in a good mood, he would have a stern look on his face and stride to the horse-drawn wagon waiting outside.

The wagon then carried the Old Master to town.

Thus, everyday, in the midst of jingling bells, sprawled on the bench in a half-awake state, the Old Master would be drawn out of the salt farm and beach on his way to town.

At the end of the day, well past midnight at the earliest, and sometimes around daybreak, the jingling bells of the horse-drawn wagon would be heard again. Sometimes, though, the Old Master's wagon wasn't seen for three or five days in a row.

That was why many new farmhands, who would start right after the Spring Festival, work till the fields were covered by green wheat, till late autumn when it was time to harvest the salt, never had as much as a glimpse of the Old Master.

If the Old Master had any concern, he would tell Third Wife while in bed, who, in turn, would tell Chen Three.

As to Chen Three, well, he would try to see the Old Master once every ten days or half a month to update him about things he'd like to hear, such as new income figures. When the Old Master was delighted, he would ask Third Wife to prepare a few dishes and they would drink a few cups together.

This year during the salt harvest season Chen Three had been so busy dealing with salt merchants from all over the country that he hadn't come to see the Old Master for over half a month. One night when the Old Master returned home from town, he asked Third Wife, "Haven't seen Chen Three for a while. Where has he been?"

Third Wife said: "Oh! This year's salt harvest is very good. Haven't had a chance to tell you."

Third Wife added: "It rained much less this spring and summer. So the salt harvest is extraordinary! Salt merchants from Heaven-knows-where swarm over here. Chen Three's been running around like a head-less dog trying to handle them."

Then Third Wife said: "The line of salt wagons coming and going would stretch as far as two or three *li*!"

The Old Master didn't say a word. The following day on the way to town, as if hit by something, the Old Master told his "chauffer" to take him to the salt farm.

At first his "chauffer" thought he hadn't heard it right. He asked again to make sure: "Master, did you say you wanted to go and take a look at the salt farm?"

The Old Master didn't say another word. The "chauffer" knew the Old Master really wanted to go. The Old Master was a man of few words. Whatever he said he had said it and he would never repeat it.

So the "chauffeur" turned the wagon and urged the horse in the direction of the salt farm.

Well before reaching the salt farm, they were stopped by merchants' wagons crowding the road.

The Old Master stepped off the wagon, squinted to see the long line of wagons, stroked his chin a few times, and hurried toward the retail station with his fine walking cane.

No salt farmhands greeted him as the Old Master hurried along. Nobody knew who he was anyway.

Even before reaching the retail station he could hear a loud commotion there. . . .

"Your Honorable Mr. Chen. . . . "

"Your Honorable General Manager. . . . "

The Old Master knew this Honorable Personage was none other than Chen Three.

When he got nearer, the Old Master saw Chen Three being surrounded by a throng of salt merchants, all dressed in fancy long gowns and felt hats, this one handing him a cigarette and that one lighting it up for him. Even the two servants who were holding Chen's teapot and cooling him with a large fan benefited from such show of attention, each having a cigarette in the mouth and blowing smoke rings like they were something.

The Old Master got even nearer. Still no one paid him any attention.

Feeling every bit of the slight, the Old Master found a bench behind the loud crowd and sat down. Still Chen Three had not noticed him. Vexed, the Old Master jabbed his cane through the crowd and prodded him in the back.

Chen Three was startled. Before he could ascertain who the little old man behind him was, the Old Master called with a stern face: "Chen Three!"

Chen Three knew right away: "Old Master, why are you here?"

The Old Master turned his face away, pointed at his boots with the cane, and said, nonchalantly, "See what's in my boots. It bothers my feet."

Chen Three knelt down at the Old Master's feet right away to work on his boots.

Everyone present was puzzled. What happened to the proud and powerful Master Chen? Manager Chen? Why was he now on his knees checking the boots of this little skinny old man?

Chen Three removed the boots ever carefully, held them close to his face, bent to check inside this way and that way, and shook them several times as if his life depended on it. Nothing fell out. He reached in and felt with his fingers . . . still he couldn't find anything. So he said to the Old Master: "Old Master, there's nothing inside!"

"Well—" the Old Master groaned, a displeased look on his face. "That can't be. Look again more carefully."

At this, the Old Master plucked a gray hair from his head, snapped it into his boot, and pointed at it: "See, what is this?"

Chen Three picked up the gray hair between his fingers. For quite a while he didn't even dare to lift his head to look the Old Master in the face. As to the Old Master, well, he kicked into the boots and stood up to leave without giving Chen Three even a glance.

(2001)

Tragicomedy
Gao Kuan

The funeral for Deputy Mayor Zhou wasn't solemn at all. By the way, he had died in a car accident on an inspection tour to the villages.

Inside the grand funeral home in the Southern Suburbs gathered a large throng of the late Deputy Mayor Zhou's family, relatives, and subordinates. Some tried in vain to wipe away their tears; some cried with abandon; some did their best to put on a sad face. The only genuine tears, though, were those shed by the late deputy mayor's own family. Several young kids, not appreciating the meaning of the occasion, giggled and chased each other through the cracks between grownups, who gave them a dirty look and told them to get lost.

The late Deputy Mayor Zhou himself, however, was lying quietly in the crystal casket, a healthy glow on his face, as if he had just finished delivering an important speech and was taking a noon nap, as had been his habit. There was not a single sign of pain. Around him were placed flowers with elegiac strips. Inside the big picture, framed with black cloth, he smiled solemnly.

Somehow the Master of Ceremonies today was Director Teng of the Propaganda Department, who was near retirement and stuttered badly. A black band on his right arm, a little white flower, already flattened, on his chest, Director Teng rubbed his eyes hard. No tears came out, but the eyes were reddened for sure. He scanned the throng enthralled in sadness and craned so that his mouth reached the mike about half a head taller than he was, and announced solemnly, and slowly:

"La . . . ladies . . . and . . . gen . . . gentle . . . men; dis . . . disting . . . . guished gue . . . guests . . . dig . . . digni . . . taries. I . . . here . . . by announce . . . that . . . the . . . fu . . . funeral for Deputy May . . . Mayor Zhou be . . . gins."

He paused and by force of habit clapped his hands.

"On be . . . half of . . . Deputy May . . . or Zhou, I ex . . . tend my hearty gra . . . titude to all the dis . . . disting . . . guished gue . . . guests . . . . and fri . . . friends."

He clapped his hands again.

Some in the audience whispered to each other; some covered their mouths with handkerchiefs; some couldn't help laughing aloud.

Director Teng himself didn't laugh. He looked even graver and dragged on:

"Now, I . . . I give you Dir . . . rector Zhang of the Per . . . sonnel Depart . . . ment to deli . . . ver the eulogy."

Director Zhang strode to the podium, a small handkerchief in hand. He tilted the mike skyward because he was half a head taller than it, and began to speak in a low, slow cadence, which was quite tear-inducing.

"Comrades, our dear Deputy Mayor Zhou has left us forever. We . . . we will never see him again. Ah . . . !" He trembled and couldn't help but break into a loud sob. He had been a protégé of the late deputy mayor and climbed up the ladder on account of that. Therefore his feelings for the late deputy mayor were quite genuine.

Led by the late Deputy Mayor Zhou's family, everyone in the audience cried with wild abandon.

"Comrades!" Director Zhang shouted into the mike this time, which frightened some in the audience. "Let's turn our sorrow into strength. Comrades. . . . Deputy Mayor Zhou has worked like a horse for our industrial and agricultural developments, how can we ever forget him? He has been a good Party member in our heart, a good cadre, a good public servant. . . . Do you all still remember, it was he who led us in building up our nation's first green food base, Asia's greatest Globe Wood Products, Ltd, and importing an entire production line of artificial diamonds. . . . He led us in trying to tame and clean up the Huai River. . . ."

Just then someone screamed: "Oh! The dead body has exploded!" It woke everyone from their grief. They all looked up. Nobody knew when Deputy Mayor Zhou had crawled out of the casket. He walked toward the podium with a smile on his face, grabbed the mike from Director Zhang, and bowed to the audience down there.

"Dear citizens, this is the last time I give a speech to you. I can't lie in death with my eyes closed because I have a guilty conscience. I have to confess everything: For the green food base, I took a kickback of 6 million *yuan*; for Globe Wood Products, Ltd., I took more than 4 million *yuan*; for the Huai River project, I took another 2 million *yuan*. So before I go, I beg for forgiveness from every one of you, old and young, and I beg for mercy from our country's law. Farewell!"

Before anyone realized what had happened, Deputy Mayor Zhou was back in the crystal casket, lying quietly. On his face was the same healthy glow, like he was taking a nap after an important speech.

It turned out that Deputy Mayor Zhou had taken a new resurrection pill invented by Professor Lamb of a top-notch University. The odd thing about this new magic pill is that those who have taken it, without exception, will have the same making-a-clean-break experience.

(2002)

Merchant of Wills

Teng Gang

One evening in June 1875 a merchant specializing in collecting wills appeared in a small town in the southern valley of the Yangtze River. He decided to lodge in a small inn by the river surrounding the town. At midnight he went through the town's streets and alleys and put on the walls a poster, which read:

> Good are the words of a dying man, his will more precious than gold. Indeed the last words of a dying man are the most precious

treasure he leaves behind to humanity. This merchant specializes in collecting wills at ten silver coins apiece. All wills are welcome. On-site service is provided. Contact: West Wing, New North Gate Inn.

The word spread fast and caused quite a stir in this small, quiet town. First people wanted to know if this was for real because, well, it sounded so ridiculous: someone wanted to buy wills! And at this high price; about 100 times higher than scrap copper or iron. Yet those who had visited New North Gate Inn would testify that it *was* for real. The merchant, who wore a red band around his forehead, not only told them he wasn't joking, but also explained the rules of his trade: Not all wills are marketable. He buys only wills dictated to him directly by the dying men. That's why he's paying such a high price. Then, the merchant showed them the small rattle-drum in hand. It was quite a mysterious device. Once the will-bearing slip of paper was inserted in through a crevice and the drum rattled a few times, the will would stay in it forever. The drum could not be opened again, the merchant said.

Once the authenticity of the story was ascertained, the kind-hearted townspeople had many new doubts and suspected that it was some kind of hoax. First, why would anyone buy wills, of all things in the world? For that question, the merchant repeated what he said in the advertisement: There is nothing more precious in the world than a dying man's last words. Then he asked: Can you name anything more precious than the last words of a dying man? What will he do with these wills? As a merchant he has to make money. But how? To whom will he resell the wills? Who will buy the wills at an even higher price? For all these questions the merchant dodged as much as he could. He did finally say, however: "Since it is I who pays you, not the other way round, what's there to hoax you about?

Despite all the doubts and uneasiness townspeople had about the merchant, the one thing they were all absolutely positive about was: No one would sell his will to the merchant. No one would do so just because the merchant will pay him ten silver coins. Besides, a man's will is private and may involve things a family would never want to share with outsiders. How can anyone tell such private matters to a merchant stranger?

The clockmaker living by the town's gate turned out to be the first dying man since the merchant came. Like everyone else the clockmaker had felt what the merchant was doing was both ridiculous and suspicious and that no one would ever sell his will to him. However, as he was breathing his last, he suddenly asked his family to bring in the merchant: He wanted to sell his will. His family was vehemently opposed to it. With tears in his eyes, the clockmaker said: "This is my only wish before I die. Please don't disappoint me." So, his family brought in the merchant. The merchant spread a red cloth on his knee, jotted down the clockmaker's last words on a slip of paper, watched him breathe his last, rolled the will up and inserted it into the drum, tossed ten silver coins on the table, and left.

Then, the most incredible thing happened: Every dying man would invite the merchant over to dictate his last words. Soon it became an indispensable ritual for any dying man in this small town. The merchant was thus established and his business became ever more in demand. People remained as puzzled as ever though: What does the merchant do with the wills he has bought? How can he make money? Why have all the dying men brought in the merchant and sold their wills to him?

One evening, the merchant left the town on a horse-drawn wagon. Shaking the rattle-drum in hand he would cry out: "Wills wanted, ten silver coins apiece!" As the townspeople watched the merchant leaving, watched him shaking that rattle-drum filled with wills, they wondered why they felt so uneasy in their hearts.

(2003)

Dance of the Pearls

Xie Zhiqiang

The King accepted the tribute from the Old Man, who said he had come to present His Majesty the two pearls on behalf of all the subjects in his hometown to express their reverent affections for him.

Ever since the King came to the throne there had been many assassination attempts. He felt in this kingdom there were enemies hidden in every corner. This was the first time his subjects had expressed their loyalty to him directly.

The Old Man said: "Your Majesty, this pair of pearls have been ancestral treasures in my family. At the mere touch of poison, they will dance as if enraptured."

The King was delighted. He had been jumpy about his food because several of his servants had already died from poison. Before every meal he would have a servant test the food first to make sure. So, the King ordered his servants to bring up poisoned food for the test.

As expected, once the two pearls were soaked wet in the delicacy, they would jump up and dance rapturously on the table like well-trained court dancers. They danced gracefully and when they "bounced" into each other now and then, there was such a pleasant ring in the air.

Pleased, the King awarded the Old Man with many precious things in return. He gazed at the pearls again: They look like agate yet they aren't agate; they feel like jade yet they aren't jade either; they are such rare, precious treasures in the world. With them in hand the daily cankerous worry about his food vaporized. He knew, of course, that to conquer the heart and soul of the entire kingdom was a different matter altogether.

The two pearls became loyal servants of the King, a secret known to

the King alone. However, attempts on his life still came in his direction
like moths flying to the lamp. Every few days the pearls would dance on
account of the delicacies brought in for the King. The King would issue
decrees to search for the conspirators among his chefs, cooks, helpers,
and the courtiers behind them—catch a whole string of them, and have
them executed or replaced with another bunch.

Before long everyone in the royal palace knew about the two pearls.
And the King cherished them even more. He instructed his servants to
take care of the pearls the same way they took care of his family and
relatives. Pearls were inanimate things and could not be bestowed any
royal titles, but in reality, in all aspects of their life, they were being
treated well above many of the favorite courtiers. Even when the King
presided over courtly proceedings, he would be accompanied by the
pearls left and right.

All the courtiers couldn't help but be awed by the pearls as if the pearls
could penetrate their minds at its deepest, darkest recesses. For a while everything in the royal palace was calm and orderly. Every time the King dined the
two pearls would be with him. They would stay soaked in the delicacies while
the King was eating. He didn't want to take them out.

During the meal the King would use his wooden spoon to touch the
pearls in the plates with such tenderness as if they were his bright and
mischievous princes and say: Why don't you dine with His Majesty?

By the time the King laid down his bowl and spoon, the pearls
would be covered in grease and bits of food all over. So the servants
would give the pearls a bath in the presence of the King. They would
prepare a special liquid: sheep or camel milk mixed with petals of fresh
flowers, especially budding oleander blossoms, which were so fine and
fragrant. Once cleansed, the King would hold the pearls in his hands
and kiss them again and again. He felt the pearls were his ever-depend-
able lifeline. During his bath, if the servants handled the pearls with the

slightest carelessness, the King would fly into a rage. In reality, the pearls wouldn't suffer even the slightest injury while dancing as intensely as they did every time.

Gradually even the dances of beautiful court girls would not appeal to the King. Then, he was bothered by a new worry: The pearls haven't danced for a long while. The King loved the dance of the pearls, yet when they danced it would mean danger had got threateningly close. Bored to death, the King told his servants to put poison in the food. He wanted to see the pearls dance no matter what. Having not touched poison for a while, the pearls danced so frenziedly that they bounced off the table and landed hard on the stone floor. The King cringed, afraid they would get hurt, though he was pleased by their seemingly unflappable loyalty.

The King would indulge in recalling the dances of the pearls as a way of satisfying himself. He remembered a sense of deathlike aura in the last frenzied dance of the pearls. He began to use even more care to hold them. The pearls used to take a bath both before and after the meal. Now the King decreed that there should be an additional bath both in the morning and in the evening. The blossoms used for preparing the bath were collected fresh from hills and vales, but that wasn't good enough. The King had a greenhouse built specially for this purpose so flowers would be blooming all year round.

Soon the pearls themselves got used to bathing. During the summer when the weather got really hot, the pearls would shake restlessly. That was not dancing, though, but their way of expressing their wishes. The King, however, thought the pearls wanted to dance. Once immersed in the bath liquid, the pearls would be thrilled and then calm again. The King ordered the servants to give the pearls more baths on days when it was either very hot or very cold. The pearls gave out such a dreamy fragrance all the time as if they had absorbed the essence of all the nectars from the most fragrant flowers between heaven and earth.

Now the King didn't want to watch the pearls taking bath anymore because that was a time-consuming process. Instead he would wear them wherever he went. He found that the pearls could even augment his virility and sexual appetite. He could dance frenziedly like the pearls, too. Only that his bed would be his stage and he would mimic the moves of the pearls in his nightly forays. He was amazed by how potent he was at his age. It must be a gift from the pearls.

Then, the unfortunate thing happened at last. The thing that had been cooking for so long. The King was poisoned. As usual the pearls had been immersed in the food but gave no reaction. They didn't dance as they were supposed to.

The King had a convulsive pain in the stomach. He knew what he had dreaded for so long had befallen him at last. Why didn't you dance? He mumbled to the pearls.

The Old Man who had given him the pearls came—Per the King's decree he had been working as a gardener taking care of the greenhouse. Biting his lips in pain, the King stammered to the Old Man: "You've murdered the King!"

The Old Man said, with a smile on his face: "Majesty, you've spoiled the pearls. Ever since my earliest ancestors, the pearls have always bathed in poisonous water. That's why they are so sensitive to poison that, as I said, at the mere touch they would be excited and dance."

The King said: "But they didn't dance this time. . . . "

The Old Man said, calmly: "Majesty, it's because you have changed their nature. They've become used to the kind of life you've given them. Now, at the mere touch of fragrant bath water they would dance. But you don't see all this."

Dark blood oozing from his mouth, his life flickering one last time, the King saw flashing across his mind a pair of pearls dancing frenziedly.

(2004)

Mr. Purple Gold

Yang Xiaofang

Mr. Purple Gold was a star of the Chinese Opera. Legend has it that she had drifted over here with a Yangzhou river gang when she was a small child, or had been kidnapped and brought over from Yangzhou. Even today nobody knows for sure. Whenever her name comes up in the city known as the Capital of Folk Medicine, people would sigh profusely with mixed feelings. Why? Because its crown jewel, the Crystal Voice Opera, thrived with her and eventually died thanks to her, too.

People in the Capital of Folk Medicine had taken enormous pride in its Crystal Voice Opera. Originally from the Qing Dynasty and enriched by "Nan Yang Airs," it had developed a unique style: elegant, graceful, and ethereal, all in one. If one really wants to trace its origin, then the opera goes back to one of the Imperial Court's entertainments called "Octagon Drum" brought back by members of the city's wealthy Eight Big Families: Jiang, Jiang, Liu, Li, Geng, Ma, Rao, and Tang. To trace it back even further, one has to mention a man well-known in the Capital of Folk Medicine: Jiang Guiti. Jiang started as a foot soldier and, thanks to his extraordinary valor in battle, was promoted to be a senior general, commander-in-chief, and governor of the Rehei region. The Empress Dowager Cixi herself was so fond of him that she adopted him as a godson and pampered him with the title of Forbidden City Son-in-Law. Gradually his entourage from the hometown evolved into the Eight Big Families. When it first came to the Capital of Folk Medicine, Crystal Voice opera was sung among the elite circles only. Gradually it spread beyond those circles and was adopted openly by opera singers.

Since Crystal Voice had its origin in the Imperial Court, naturally it was highly regarded and its practitioners were not treated as the other lowly opera singers; rather, they were all respected as gentleman, regardless of gender. They took pride in being virtuous and would reject any monetary reward as beneath their dignity. Their livelihood depended on donations only. Crystal Voice Opera organized into various clubs: Noble Joy Club, Purple Gold Club, and so on. Its performances followed certain rituals and protocols. If a family wanted a club to perform at one of its big celebrations, the host had to come with a red-colored invitation at least three days in advance. If the invitation was accepted, the host had to arrange to transport all the music instruments and lamps to his home on the morning of the celebration. Before the performance, the host had to set up three tables in the main-room, cover them with red blanket, put a red-candled lamp at both ends, place in the middle 12 plates of simple desserts—which would be removed once the performance was over—and line up a number of armchairs in front of the tables for the singers and accompanists to sit. At exactly the appointed time the group of "gentlemen," all in appropriate long robes, arrived at the front door and the host, waiting inside the door, raised both hands and cried out: "Welcome, gentlemen! Please come in!" At this the group would proceed to the tables without fluster, sit down, and sip tea. Then the host said "Please!" a second time and the performance began. When Mr. Purple Gold was as young as ten years old, she was already an actor in one of these Crystal Voice clubs.

One spring Mr. Purple Gold started to perform in the Crystal Phoenix House on Good Virtue Street in West River Beach. She was the beautiful age of sixteen then. This playhouse's specialty was Crystal Voice Opera. When the poster for Mr. Purple Gold's performance appeared on the wall, it created quite a lot of excitement. Night after night the Crystal Phoenix House would be packed to full capacity.

On her debut night, Mr. Purple Gold sang "Daiyu Burying the Flowers."[27]

Once the overture of spring, summer, autumn, winter, wind, flowers, snow, and moon was over there from behind the screen came Purple Gold in small, pin-toed steps, lovely but not ravishing, light but not airy, fresh but not puckery, modest yet not bashful, lively yet not overly gay, blithe yet graceful, having makeup yet not over-rouged. When she cast her first glance down the stage, everyone in the audience thought that pair of eyes, as beautiful as spring water, autumn moon, and inky jade nursed inside white jade, were looking directly at him and no one else. The entire audience was hushed. Everyone was still lost in his own colorful trance when Purple Gold opened her red-lipped, white-toothed mouth slowly. Out oozed a spring swallow like sound, which drifted and flew into the hundreds of ears down the stage and conjured up tens of thousands of wonderlands: cloudless sky and deep valley, maze like twists and turns, precipitous falls and leisurely ramble, soulful lament and unfathomable sorrow, sudden pauses and change of tempo, hovering in the clouds and weaving in and out. . . . The very first line "Daiyu comes to the back garden with tears in my eyes" alone took nine keys, eighteen tones, and seventy-two long notes, more than ten minutes, to finish. Everyone in the audience was so enthralled that when the last note ended, a heavenly silence fell over all. The next instant, the entire house roared with thunderous applause and cries of joy! From nowhere came flying a golden arc onto the stage: someone had tossed a ring, followed by several dozens of such golden arcs flying toward the stage. . . .

From that day on Crystal Phoenix House had an exclusive contract with Mr. Purple Gold, who would perform once every ten days. Ten days are not long yet the rich and powerful of the Capital of Folk Medicine waited so anxiously that they lost their appetite entirely. At the end of each performance, there on the stage would be a full plate of pearls and gold or diamond rings. On the tenth of the month of October, the audience once again waited at the Crystal Phoenix House from morning till evening, but Mr. Purple Gold was nowhere to be seen. On the stage were only a few accompanists. It turned out the night before Mr. Purple Gold had packed up all her gold, silver, and pearl treasures and fled with a merchant.

Not another sound of the Crystal Voice Opera has been heard in the Capital of Folk Medicine ever since. For one thing, listening to any other singer would be like tasting wax; it would be cruel. For another, one theory goes that the first man to toss Mr. Purple Gold a gold ring on her first night of performance was actually an accomplice of hers so that people of the Capital of Folk Medicine would follow suit; they were too sickened by it all to have any interest left. No audience, no performers, as simple as that. That's how Crystal Voice Opera is a dead song today. Virtually no one knows how to sing it.

(2002)

The Death of Li Damin

Chen Yonglin

The death of Li Damin, chief of South Hill Village, had something to do with a dog.

It had happened on a typical morning. Dogs were barking and chickens were cooing around, but there was no birds chirping. Li Damin hadn't heard birds chirping for years. They had all died out from eating seeds mixed with pesticide. He wasn't surprised by the absence of birds in the countryside any more. When he opened the door of his courtyard, however, he was surprised by the sight of a dog lying on a step, its hair shiny black. When the dog saw Li Damin, it stood up and sniffed around his legs, wagging its tail, whimpering sadly.

Whose dog is this? Li Damin went through all the dogs in the village and couldn't think of whose this one could be.

Li Damin's woman said: Let's keep it. The woman came out with a bowl of tasty spare ribs. The black dog wouldn't eat; its eyes were fixed on Li Damin all the time. Li Damin said: "Eat!" The black dog started to eat. Li Damin said: "A smart dog."

If Li Damin had foreseen what would happen, he would never have kept the dog.

A few days later the black dog dragged Li Damin out by the corner of his pants. So he followed the dog.

Quite some distance later they came to the graveyard. The dog stopped.

Li Damin kicked at the dog angrily. When he kicked again, the dog bounced away.

He didn't think much of this, though.

A few days later the black dog once again dragged Li Damin out by the corner of his pants. When they came to the graveyard, it stopped again.

This time around it got Li Damin thinking: Can the black dog be a messenger from Death? Otherwise why has the dog dragged me to the graveyard twice? Perhaps the dog wants me to select a spot before it is too late?

Li Damin wanted to kill the black dog now. He put rat poison in a steamed dumpling and threw it to the dog. The dog sniffed it once but wouldn't eat it. Li found a rope, made a noose, and wanted to put it around the dog's neck to kill it, yet the dog bounced away and kept a respectful distance.

"This dog is a devil! It's here to take my life!"

Lying in bed at night, Li Damin couldn't fall asleep. "I'm only 40 years old. How can I die at this young age? Because of the sins I have committed?" Li Damin went through the litany of all the things he had done, from stealing watermelons when still a young boy to taking 3,000 *yuan* from Li Mugen last month. He was terrified by what he had come up with. He had done so many bad things that even he himself couldn't bring himself to believe it.

He broke into a cold sweat. Yes, he deserved to die ten times and more.

The next morning Li Damin went to Li Mugen's with 3,000 *yuan* in his pocket. Li Mugen had given him 3,000 *yuan* so the lot for building his new home would be approved and so he could get into the village bamboo product factory. When Li Damin handed the money back to Li Mugen, Mugen refused to take it no matter what. He begged, tears in his face and in his voice: "Chief, what did I do wrong? Did I say anything wrong?" Li Damin shook his head. Mugen said: "Is it because the village wants to take back the lot? Or doesn't want me to work in the factory any more?" Li Damin said, "Neither. It's only that I don't feel I should have accepted this money from you." Mugen fell on his knees: "Chief, I beg you not to return this money to me. Otherwise I can't eat or sleep!" Li Damin wanted to help Mugen on his feet again, but Mugen refused: "I'll be on my knees until you take back the money." There was nothing Li Damin could do other than pick up the money on the table and put it in his pocket again.

Then Li Damin went to Li Changhe's. Changhe was not home. His woman, however, Yumei, was feeding their chickens in the courtyard. When she saw Li Damin, her face blossomed with a smile: "Come in, come inside." Li Damin went inside and said: "Sis, I'm here to apologize. I was out of my mind when I did that and I am so sorry." Yumei knew what Li Damin meant by that. She and her husband used to be working in the town's petrochemical factory. When it went bankrupt, Yumei wanted to transfer their residence back to the village so they could be assigned a few *mu* of farmland and making a living that way. When Yumei came to Li Damin's with a big bag of gifts, it happened his woman wasn't home. Li Damin grabbed Yumei into his arms. Yumei said: "If you don't let go, I'll shout!" However, a few days later, Yumei came again. She said: "You can have your wish." So, Yumei and her family's residence was transferred back to the village and was assigned four *mu* of good farmland.

Li Damin took out the 3,000 *yuan* and said: Yumei, this little money is my compensation to you. . . . Yumei's face went ashen right away: "Chief Li, is it because you don't want to contract the fish pond to us? Must be someone seeing the little money we made last year and wanting to get the fish pond himself? Chief Li, take it back no matter what. . . . I have 1,000 *yuan* cash at home. Let me go and get it for you so you can buy cigarettes and things. If you want me now, you can have me." Yumei began to unbutton her clothes. Li Damin said: "No, a thousand times no." Yumei had already stripped from the waist up. Li Damin wanted to run, but was blocked by Yumei: "If you leave, I'll cry rape!" It was Li Damin's turn to beg tearfully: "My good sis, don't do that. I beg you to let me go. What I did was wrong, and can't undo it. What do you want from me?" Yumei said: "I only want you to take me. I beg you to take me. I won't rest until you have taken me. Only then I'll know you won't contract the fish pond to someone else."

Afterwards, Li Damin went to two more families. The result was the same.

Li Damin went home and fell ill. He went to the hospital but the doctors couldn't find what was wrong. A month later, Li Damin died.

Li Damin's deathbed wish was to use the illicit 100,000 *yuan* he had received to build a bridge across the river right outside the village.

The black dog was adopted by Li Mugen. Now and then it would drag him to the graveyard by the corner of his pants. Mugen thought: "I haven't done anything really bad, why has the dog tried to bring me to the graveyard?" When the black dog did so for the fifth time, Mugen thought he understood. When they came to the graveyard, the black dog once again stopped in front of a grave covered with wild weeds and began whimpering sadly. Mugen walked closer and saw two holes, thick as a rice bowl, atop the grave. It must have been the work of weasels. It used to be that once they got to this spot, Mugen would turn and run as fast as he could. Now, Mugen understood why the black dog had dragged him to the graveyard: He set to work right away. It didn't take him long to pull all the weeds on the grave and fill up the holes firm with a spade.

The black dog wouldn't drag Li Mugen to the graveyard any more.

Later Mugen found out what was behind all this: In that grave was buried Old Man He, the original owner of the black dog.

Mugen sighed deeply: "Ah, Li Damin died a wrongful death."

(2004)

Parrot

Tao Li

I had a parrot. Its cage hung from the south-facing window. Except for mimicking the way I read poems aloud, it wasn't into learning human speech. One evening 13 days ago, it said to me suddenly: "Tomorrow all families in town will have their doors locked from inside. And you, the poet, will write your poems with white paint on black paper."

"Nonsense!" I cussed at the parrot. The following day, however, I *was* ordered to say at home, the door having been locked from inside, the windows sealed up. Only the south-facing window was open.

A cobra attempted to crawl in through the south-facing window. The parrot, furious, told the cobra to back off. So the cobra turned and left.

During those 13 days I received food and other things from the south-facing window. I didn't know where they came from. Everytime I asked, the parrot would say, mimicking the way I read poems aloud: "Charitable giving comes from the charitable heart!"

So my life continued almost as peacefully as before. What puzzled me the most, though, was those poems I wrote with white paint on black paper: No matter where I had hidden them, if I ever slept a little, they would be gone; vanished without a trace.

I thought the parrot would know something about the mysterious disappearance of those poems. Yet it denied it. It said there was nothing mysterious about the disappearance: Writing poetry is only an illusion in my befuddled mind.

"Illusion? It's absolute reality!" I said.

"You understand reality?" The parrot said in a teasing tone, "Now, including yourself, there are only 13 people left in this town. That's reality, you understand?"

"Only 13 people? Where are the others?"

"Three of the 13 will die on the central square. You have to go there!"

"Why?"

"To witness their heroic death and to write an epic about it."

Through the south-facing window I went to the street. All the doors were locked from inside. All the windows sealed up. Not even a wild dog in the street. Not a bird flying in the sky.

The morning sun shone on the central square. At the southeast corner of the square lay three dead bodies, forming the shape of a triangle. In the middle of the triangle was a dead cobra, the same one, I thought, that had wanted to crawl into my home.

"Serves it right!" I thought to myself gleefully. Although the cobra didn't hurt me, I would shiver every time I thought of it. As to the three people, whether they had died heroically, and whether I should write about their deaths in an epic, I didn't give it a thought.

I did think of what the parrot had said. And I did the math: Nine people should still be alive in town. Where are they? Perhaps it's high time to look for them. So I went to knock on a door nearby. A cobra fell dead from the eaves, but nobody came to answer the door.

Some of the doors had bloody smears on them, blood oozing through cracks.

I turned to hurry home. I wanted to see the parrot and receive its prophecy. Yet, the parrot was gone: Its hooked mouth hung from the cage; its shiny green feathers scattered all over my desk.

The parrot mouth hanging from the cage started to talk suddenly: "The other nine people have died, too. Now, you are the only one alive in the entire town. Hey, poet, a cobra is coming!"

I heard the sound of the cobra slithering.

Now, the only choice I had was to stand on the south-facing window and be a parrot.

Notes

[1] A writer of fiction and literary criticism, president of the Writers Association of Hunan Province.

[2] (1896–1945) One of the most gifted short-story writers of the early 20th century, known for the psychological depth in his work.

[3] "Substitute Doggie," meaning "child" in the parlance of the Miao people.

[4] Lord Bao: real name Bao Zheng (999–1062), a much-praised judge from Song China, known for his uncompromising uprightness and fairness. Tang Cheng: hero of a popular classic opera.

[5] Jiao Yulu (1922–65): Party Chief of a backward county, who died of liver cancer while leading his people to fight poverty. Kong Fanseng (1944–94): an official who volunteered to go and work in poverty-stricken areas in Tibet and died on the job.

[6] (1678–1735) The fourth emperor of the Qing (Manchu) Dynasty and the third Qing emperor to rule over China, from 1722 to 1735.

[7] Slang expression in Hong Kong, referring to places where young underage prostitutes "work."

[8] (1899–1966) One of the greatest writers in modern China, known for his novel *Camel Xiangzi* (1939) and play *Teahouse* (1958); died at the outset of the Cultural Revolution (1966–76) under suspicious circumstances.

[9] A popular Chinese love story about a couple separated by earth and sky who get to see each other only once a year.

[10] One of Lao She's best-known plays.

[11] One of the greatest works comprising of, among other things, annals, historical figures, and realistic narratives, in 130 volumes, authored by Sima Qian (ca. 145–90 BC), which serves as the template for all Chinese historical records. King Gou Jian of Yue (reigned 496–465 BC): the king of the Kingdom of Yue (present-day Shanghai, northern Zhejiang, and southern Jiangsu) near the end of the Spring and Autumn period (722–481 BC).

[12] Also called the Huns, the nomadic people of Central Asia, and active in the areas of southern Siberia, western Manchuria, and the modern Chinese provinces of Inner Mongolia, Gansu, and Xinjiang.

[13] (1887–1951) Ringleader of the notorious Green Gang, the most powerful secret society in old Shanghai, also known as "Big-eared Du."

[14] (1892–1978) One of the most erudite scholars and prolific writers in modern China: translator, poet, fiction writer, playwright, memoirist, philosopher, historian, and the first president of the Chinese Academy of Sciences (1949–78).

[15] (1881–1936) Also called Lu Hsun. One of the greatest modern Chinese writers, known for his short story "Diary of a Madman" (1918), the first Western-style story written in vernacular Chinese; "The True Story of Ah Q" (1921–22); and many other highly influential stories and satirical essays.

[16] (1900–1995) An important playwright, screenwriter, and man of letters of modern China.

[17] A hero in the *Water Margin* by Shi Naian (ca. 1296–1370), one of the great classical novels of Chinese literature, famous for slaying a tiger with his bare hands and avenging the murder of his older brother.

[18] (1693–1765) A famed artist of extraordinary talent.

[19] A play on the Chinese national anthem.

[20] A hero in the classical Chinese Novel *Journey to the West* by Wu Chen'en (1500–1582).

[21] (332–296 BC) Considered by many as the Father of Chinese Poetry; his death is commemorated by the Dragon Boat Festival.

[22] Guan Yu (died 219): military hero of the Three Kingdoms period (3rd century AD) who was later canonized as Guan Di, god of war and protector of China. Sun Quan (182–252): founder of Wu, one of the Three Kingdoms. Ma Zhong: a general of Sun Quan, who captured Guan Yu.

[23] Cao Cao (155–220): founder of the kingdom Wei of the Three Kingdom era, known for his unscrupulous cunningness. Lü Bu (156–98): a fierce warrior and general during the Eastern Han Dynasty and Three Kingdoms periods.

[24] Dong Zhuo (139–92): a warlord who deposed the rightful heir to the throne of the Eastern Hang Dynasty and was later assassinated by his adoptive son Lü Bu.

[25] Liu Bei (161–223): a powerful warlord and founder of the kingdom of Shu of the Three Kingdoms period. Yuan Shu (159–99): a major warlord of the late Eastern Han Dynasty.

[26] Two prince brothers during the Spring and Autumn Period (770–476 BC), who would rather starve to death than serve a Zhou king they despised.

[27] Lin Daiyu: one of the principal characters of the classic Chinese novel *Dream of the Red Chamber*, known for her delicate beauty and poetic sensibilities.

About the Translator

A native of Nanjing, China, Shouhua Qi came to the United States in 1989. He earned his Ph.D. in English Literature from Illinois State University, Normal. He is currently Associate Professor of English at Western Connecticut State University, Danbury. He is the author of numerous books including *China Complex: From the Sublime to the Absurd on the U.S.-China Scene* (2008); *Red Guard Fantasies and Other Stories* (2006); and *When the Purple Mountain Burns: A Novel* (2005). He is also one of the foremost translators of the novels of Thomas Hardy into Chinese. He lives in Connecticut.

STONE
BRIDGE
PRESS

Other Titles of Interest from Stone Bridge Press

China Survival Guide: How to Avoid Travel Troubles and Mortifying Mishaps
by Larry and Qin Herzberg

China Fever: Fascination, Fear, and the World's Next Superpower
by Frank S. Fang

Chinese 24/7: Everyday Strategies for Speaking and Understanding Mandarin
by Albert Wolfe

Tokyo Fragments: Short Stories of Modern Tokyo by Five of Japan's Leading Contemporary Writers
Ryuji Morita and others; translated by Giles Murray

A Wild Haruki Chase: Reading Murakami Around the World
edited and compiled by The Japan Foundation

The Broken Bridge: Fiction from Expatriates in Literary Japan
edited by Suzanne Kamata

Pop Goes Korea: Behind the Revolution in Movies, Music, and Internet Culture
by Mark James Russell

All titles available online and at booksellers worldwide.
sbp@stonebridge.com • www.stonebridge.com